I0634554

JOHN BROWN'S BODY

JOHN BROWN'S BODY

AN ALPHONSO CLAY MYSTERY
OF THE CIVIL WAR

BOOK ONE

Jack Martin

OPEN ROAD
INTEGRATED MEDIA
NEW YORK

All rights reserved, including without limitation the right to reproduce this book or any portion thereof in any form or by any means, whether electronic or mechanical, now known or hereafter invented, without the express written permission of the publisher.

This is a work of fiction. Names, characters, places, events, and incidents either are the product of the author's imagination or are used fictitiously. Any resemblance to actual persons, living or dead, businesses, companies, events, or locales is entirely coincidental.

Copyright © 2010 by Jack Martin

ISBN: 978-1-5040-7816-0

This edition published in 2022 by Open Road Integrated Media, Inc.
180 Maiden Lane
New York, NY 10038
www.openroadmedia.com

To the memory of my late wife Sonia, who placed most of what is good in me. She loved me despite my flaws; she will be in my heart until the end of time.

JOHN BROWN'S BODY

PROLOGUE

DECEMBER 27, 1862

Cororal Hezekiah Whately was cold, wet, and afraid, yet oddly optimistic. For days, he and his blue-uniformed comrades had been crammed into a stinking, uncomfortable space of the river steamer, an area designed for a quarter of their numbers.

The trip from Union-occupied Memphis down the foreboding Mississippi seemed to take an eternity. The scores of transports finally pulled into a large, stagnant bayou; his captain said it had the outlandish name of Chickasaw. His appointed superior officer, a beardless college boy, was excited, and communicated this to his troops. Whately, like so many of his comrades, was beginning to catch a glimmer of an end to the war here in the West. When his regiment had been herded like cattle onto the ship back in Memphis, no one but Uncle Billy Sherman, U. S. Grant himself, and possibly some of the headquarters staff had been certain of their destination. Of course, many had speculated—some had even dared to utter the name Vicksburg—but few dreamed Grant and Sherman had the nerve to try for it so soon without securing an overland line of supply.

Whately thought about Vicksburg as he and his jostling

companions shuffled down planks into the frigid mud at the edge of the bayou. He had acquired some education back at the Miskatonic Academy in Massachusetts before he got that girl in a family way, refused to marry her, and had to leave for the West. He knew the significance of that small Mississippi River town, brooding on two-hundred-foot bluffs above the river. The Confederate government had crammed it with cannon. No Union vessel, not even the famed ironclads, dared come within range of its great guns. So long as Vicksburg defied the Union, the Confederacy controlled this stretch of Old Man River. Grant's mighty army was separated from the Union forces of General Butler (which had taken much of southern Louisiana in a smart amphibious operation). The grain, meat, and hard-core fighting men of Texas could flow into the Confederacy, and the Confederacy had a better-than-fair chance of establishing its independence.

And if Vicksburg fell, it would be the beginning of the end for the Confederacy, thought Whately as he slogged through the sucking mud to relatively drier ground, peering upwards, trying to catch a glimpse of the town itself at the top of the bluffs. But with the river mist thick as pea soup, all he could see were skeletal trees dotting a gentle upward slope, disappearing into the shifting tendrils of fog, from which Whately took great solace.

Undoubtedly, the Confederates knew by now something was happening, but they could not know exactly what or where the blow would fall. They had shipped in scores of heavy cannons and their crews, but lacked infantry. Those poor souls must have believed, just as Whately had until hours ago, that Grant was not ready to thrust directly down river. Richmond did not have fighting men to spare and would not shift them to Vicksburg until the need was pressing. The mighty cannon, so deadly to ships, could not, by themselves, stop a determined infantry assault. Infantry had to be stopped by infantry. Whately knew this from experience.

What Confederate infantry there was in Vicksburg should have been evenly spread along a miles-long perimeter, but there hadn't been days for them to prepare, as there would have been if Grant had sent his ponderous army overland from Memphis.

Whately was proud of the corporal stripes his literacy, taught far from the Mississippi Valley, had gained him, although he felt he really deserved officer straps on his shoulders. He was now smugly certain he could see the simple brilliance of Grant's plan: load twenty thousand troops under Uncle Billy onto every transport you could find, run them down the river ahead of word they were coming, and throw them straight at the unprepared Rebs. The relatively few defenders would have time for one, maybe two, volleys, and then the blue horde would overwhelm them. He knew there was a chance he could be killed in battle, but if he were out front, a colonel, or, better yet, a general, might notice him, and those officer straps could be his by nightfall.

Whately's pulse quickened from that prospect *and* the effort of going up the moderate slope, as he glanced at his blue-clad companions to his left and right, frowning. The mist blurred their outlines, making them oddly unsubstantial, almost ghost-like. In an instant, wariness overcame him, and he took his Springfield musket off his shoulder, carefully checking that the percussion cap that would ignite the powder charge was firmly in place under the hammer. He now felt very lonely, even though he was surrounded by twenty thousand companions, and wished he could see more of them than his nearest neighbors.

He chided himself for a nervous fool. *That's what comes of growing up in Central Massachusetts.* The stories he'd grown up with; the things he'd believed as a child. *Like the whippoorwills*, he thought, smiling ruefully at the memory, eyes scanning the shrouded landscape. His father had told him tales of whippoorwills that would sit outside the window of a dying person, timing their plaintive, spectral cries to the last gasps of the doomed man. His father had muttered that whippoorwills fed on souls and would try to catch them as they fled the bodies. If they caught the soul, they would titter gleefully until dawn. But if it evaded them, they would fly off immediately, silent and sullen.

Suddenly, he became conscious of something he'd half-heard for some time—the unmistakable cries of whippoorwills. He peered hard into the bare branches of the trees he was passing and noticed the familiar New England bird. As he mechanically kept marching forward, he frowned. *What's this? Whippoorwills would have long gone south.* Then he laughed at his own foolishness. *This* is *the South.* A bit of the home he had left and would never see again. *Strange how their cries rise and fall, almost as if . . .*

Whately started. He could hear his own labored breathing; the slope was becoming quite a chore. *Those damn birds are keeping time with my breathing! But it cannot be! My old man had just been throwing a scare into a gullible child. But what if . . . ? I should at least let the rest of his regiment know . . .*

Hezekiah Whately opened his mouth to shout a warning that something was up—that something was wrong. But in that instant, from the mist in front of him, the inhuman, blood-chilling scream that would become known as the 'rebel yell' issued simultaneously from thousands of throats, followed by a solid sheet of fire, as thousands of rifles and dozens of cannons discharged their leaden burdens simultaneously.

Then, a .58 caliber ball entered through Whately's open mouth, blowing out the back of his head.

Major General William Tecumseh Sherman ("Cump" to the very few who counted him as a friend) sat stonily on a large black horse at the muddy shore of the bayou. He had expected some resistance, was prepared for some losses. The war had hardened him. He now thought of a thousand bleeding bodies as a small thing, something to get out of the way before breakfast. But this was starting to look like more than a thousand—a great deal more. The morning mist was beginning to clear, and he could now see up the wintry slope to the attractive little city on the bluffs . . . and his boys, the men of which he had become so proud. The blue lines had stopped, far short of the top of the bluffs. They wavered under the intense, continuous Confederate fire. But although they were not going forward any longer, they were not breaking and running, despite the increasing number of little blue figures falling, writhing with agony, or ominously still. Sherman ignored a flock of whippoorwills flying past him, silently and sullenly, and considered what he must do.

The assault was clearly a failure. His boys were brave, but they would not charge against impossible odds. Sherman was proud of his army being American, but that could be a drawback. American soldiers were not Prussians who would blindly follow a fatal order. Americans fought as they worked their farms or businesses, wanting to see some prospect of it making a profit.

Sherman clawed unconsciously at his scrubby, reddish beard, and then decided. "General Logan!" he shouted.

A tall, handsome brigadier with a drooping moustache rode up and saluted.

"General Logan, pass the order to withdraw. This assault has failed. More death is pure waste."

Logan, an ambitious former Congressman who was proving to be a surprisingly able officer, saluted smartly and galloped off.

Sherman resumed evaluating the wreckage of his grand assault, destroyed in a quarter of an hour, and thought glumly about what it meant. *At least it wasn't like Bull Run.*

He had been at Bull Run, the first real battle of the war, commanding a brigade under the ponderous General McDowell, confident of an easy victory over the Rebels. The war was going to be over before properly started, he was certain. Then the unexpected counterattack by the determined Confederates, a few unexpected troops materializing on the army's flank, and, boom, it all fell to pieces. Sherman supposed that was where the rumors of his craziness began. His memories of the day were of his screaming at his troops as they began to run away, cursing them, threatening to shoot them with his Colt, and half meaning it, yelling, "Hold, you yellow bastards! Hold! The battle is ours if we hold!" But nothing could stop the blue torrent from sweeping backward, a wave of dejected, whipped soldiers washing up on the outskirts of Washington. Even Sherman had joined the wave, after finding himself alone, watching a gray line advance, thinking of the possible fate awaiting the brother of a Republican senator in Richmond.

It had shaken him more than he wanted to admit at the time. He'd been promoted and given an important command in Kentucky. But in him now was the seed of doubt. He began telling everyone that this war would last for years and hundreds of thousands would die. For that, the newspapers—*Damn them to hell!*—had dubbed him crazy, and his superiors had relieved him. Then a slouching failure from the pre-war army, Sam Grant, who had somehow gained two stars on his shoulders, gave him command of a new division in *his* army, assembling at a place called Shiloh. And at Shiloh, once again, the rebels had come at him screaming their inhuman yell.

Sherman did well with his division, in fact feeling arrogantly proud of it, but he also knew at the end of the day, the army was mauled and on the ropes. He went to the slouching little man that evening, expecting to hear orders for retreat from a beaten failure that drank too much. Instead, he saw a quiet, confident man, sober as a judge, puffing on a cigar, and heard the soft words, "They whipped us today, but we'll lick 'em tomorrow." Which was what happened. From that day forward, Sherman would die for Grant.

And now, drawing his thoughts to the present, focusing on his men making their way back to the transports as best they could, Sherman wished he could die. Grant's enemies, always with him, were again whispering that he was a lucky drunkard who had no business commanding a regiment, much less an army. The brilliant thrust at Vicksburg would be presented as evidence of drunken incompetence. Sherman knew his career was at stake, too. Not even Senator John Sherman could screen forever a brother who had, with the lonely exception of Shiloh, an unbroken record of military failures. Most importantly was what this would mean for Grant. He adored the man, and he'd conducted the very operation that had let him down. He knew Grant would not reproach him, which made it all the worse.

But the plan was good! Sherman screamed in his mind, his face contorting, as he gripped his saddle horn as if to break it. *There was no way it could have failed. Unless . . . the rebels had been warned long in advance they were coming. Soldiers talk, of course; they talk to everyone in sight. But the soldiers had not known. Only a handful of generals and staff members were informed before they got on the steamers in Memphis. And those people would have never accidentally let a word—*

Sherman stilled, while his mind, always a nervous mechanism, whirled frantically. In a few moments, he had examined the possibilities and dismissed all but one. *Ridiculous, but undeniable. There's a traitor in the highest levels of Grant's army. A traitor? Impossible! A traitor!* Sherman's wild eyes became even wilder. *I must root out the traitor. But who could it be?*

He couldn't start throwing around accusations without a name to go with it. Suspicions fester in the army and sap its strength, and newspapers would start up the chant of his craziness again. He had to be sure who it was before he contacted the War Department. But the traitor would not be easy to find. He had to be among a group of people whose loyalty was considered absolute. He needed someone good, someone experienced at ferreting out secrets. "Lieutenant Brown!" he shouted in a grating voice.

From the group of staffers on horseback, waiting at a respectful distance, a slight, nervous figure detached himself and rode up to the commanding general.

Despite his building rage, Sherman had to smile at Lieutenant John Brown, whose position on his staff was loosely defined as "intelligence." The small man always acted like he was terrified of Sherman, never dreaming the stern general rather liked him, and certainly respected him. Unlike others, Sherman never had the heart to mock Brown for the coincidence of his name being identical to that of the mad abolitionist who helped to trigger this war. After all, a man named Tecumseh cannot easily mock the name of another.

Despite his unimpressive physique, Brown had been a solidly successful detective on the Providence Police Department before the war, and he had procured the evidence that sent the abominable Professor Slaughter and his key followers to the gallows for crimes none had suspected until the nervous little man nosed around.

"Sir," squeaked Brown in a cracked, involuntary falsetto.

"Lieutenant Brown, what do you see out there?" asked Sherman, gesturing vaguely at the men straggling to the steamers.

"Defeat, General," muttered Brown.

Sherman nodded. This ability to instantly define a problem was why he liked Brown. "And to what do you attribute our defeat?"

"Treason," said Brown in a low voice.

The general had to catch a gasp. "The Rebs, you mean?"

Brown paused a long moment, and then said in a whisper "In our own ranks, sir." Sherman grimaced savagely. "Is it that obvious?"

"No," came the apologetic voice. "Most people will not easily see it. As I assume you know, the treason must come from the highest levels, from the most trusted. It was like that with the monstrous Slaughter, a respected and honored man with a kindly manner. I was nearly fired for persecuting a public benefactor until I was able to trace what had come in on that ship from Constantinople, and that the money for the ship was Slaughter's. No one will believe treason like this until there is incontrovertible proof."

"Can you get the proof?"

"Perhaps—if I have your permission to pursue this inquiry everywhere in the army—with no restrictions."

"You have complete authority," said Sherman without blinking. "Look everywhere; spare no one's feelings. Report only to me; tell me of anyone who impedes. I want who did this."

"Yes, sir," said the little man nervously. Brown saluted and cantered off, not waiting to be dismissed.

Good, he's not wasting an instant. It might take some time. After all, Slaughter had thought himself safe for the better part of a year. But if anyone can find the bastard who caused this, the man who the papers call "The Wizard of Providence" will. And when Brown finds him . . .

A cavalryman originally from County Cork, Ireland, stood nearby and happened to be watching Sherman when he smiled. The Irishman, a hard trooper who'd killed his first man at fifteen, shivered and crossed himself at the sight.

CHAPTER ONE

THE BEAST OF NEW ORLEANS

Major General Benjamin Franklin Butler, United States Volunteers, military governor of Louisiana, stepped out of the luxury hotel on Bourbon Street and breathed deeply, contentedly of the cool, moist air. Most of the inhabitants of New Orleans regarded this morning's weather as unpleasantly frigid, but Butler was from New England, and the air felt near tropical for a winter day to him. Proudly, he sauntered down the street toward his military headquarters, also known as the old customs house near the docks.

Someone unfamiliar with Butler would have found the general a hilarious, even clownish, sight. His prominent stomach was emphasized by the tight cut he favored in his uniforms. His flabby, mustached face and badly crossed eyes gave him an unfortunate resemblance to a toad. The effect of his full-dress uniform, rarely worn by most generals, was spoiled by the carpet slippers he wore in place of boots; General Butler was a martyr to corns. A casual observer would have been forgiven for considering General Butler a dimwitted buffoon.

That would be a very bad mistake.

Benjamin Butler was a shrewd lawyer, a power in the

Massachusetts Democratic Party, without principles or compassion, utterly ruthless in achieving his goals, which were usually things benefiting Benjamin Butler. Two years ago, he had done everything in his power to gain Jefferson Davis the Democratic Presidential nomination, but when the Civil War broke out, he leaped into bed with the Republicans so quickly, it took the collective breath away from all political Washington. At the outset of hostilities, Confederate sympathizers in Maryland had rioted, cutting telegraph wires and burning railway bridges, trying to isolate Washington from the North: giving the impression that America's capital would fall to the Rebels and the war be over before it started. This is when Butler pulled some strings, gained command of some of the regiments of Massachusetts's volunteers, and moved them south with commendable speed and efficiency. He led his troops into Baltimore, shot a number of rioters, hanged a few of the less fleet of foot, and announced he would hang as many more as it would take to restore the authority of the United States government. Maryland settled into a sullen peace, and Washington had secure communications with the rest of the North. A grateful Lincoln appointed Butler one of the most senior generals in the service of the United States.

The Administration had determined the mouth of the Mississippi must not remain in rebel hands and gave Butler the plum assignment of commanding an amphibious expedition to take New Orleans. Butler thirsted for military glory. After all, when the war was over, a politician with his connections in both political parties, who was also a war hero, could look to anything. Alas, there had been precious little opportunity for glory. The brave old salt, Commodore Farragut, had blown past the forts, protecting the mouth of the Mississippi, with Butler's little army not much more than terrified spectators, while the Navy's ships sailed to victory. The Confederacy had relied completely on the forts, which were not, in fact, as powerful as supposed. There were literally no gray troops in New Orleans when Butler's transports tied up at the docks.

Cheated of the chance for the military fame he felt he deserved, Butler had been in a savage mood. His first act had been to hang a gambler who had torn down the first Union flag Farragut's men raised, without even the pretense of a trial. New Orleans and the South were outraged, but the act had restored Butler to his usual cynical good humor.

As Butler approached his headquarters, he surveyed approvingly all that surrounded him. Upon arrival, New Orleans had been a disgustingly dirty, diseased city: the streets filled with garbage, the air reeking with indescribable stenches. Immediately drafting outraged citizens willy-nilly to do work they would not have asked of slaves, he succeeded in weeks in bringing a New England sense of orderly cleanliness to the city. Of course, the citizens had been livid, especially the women, who had taken to various acts of defiance, including emptying chamber pots from upper story windows on the heads of Union officers passing in the street. One woman had even fouled the courtly, upright Farragut, who literally cried when he told Butler of what had befallen him. Butler had a fondness for Farragut that the corrupt sometimes have for the innocently honorable, and he was genuinely outraged at such treatment to a brave and decent warrior who never offered the slightest offense to those without weapons in their hands. With cold deliberation and in his own hand, General Butler had drafted General Order No. 28, which stated the following: "Any woman who by word or deed, insulted the Union flag, uniform, or army made herself liable to be treated as a woman of the town, plying her vocation." This presented a lewd riddle to the women of New Orleans. Just how is a woman of the town plying her vocation to be treated? Apparently, no woman of New Orleans cared to learn the answer. The overt offense stopped, and if General Butler noticed the occasional glance of naked hatred, he'd endured worse in the rough-and-tumble of Massachusetts politics.

As Butler reached the entrance of his headquarters, Old Glory waving fitfully in the light morning breeze over the door, he stopped and swept his eyes back down the clean, empty streets. A few curtains hastily closed on upper story windows. Some of the traitorous cows had been watching him and were frightened that he might see them watching.

Butler grinned savagely. *Let them hate*, he thought. They were just like those pious frauds back in Boston who snubbed his wife because she had been an actress when Butler found her. She had been beautiful, and he had wanted her as an addition to his collection of nice things. Briskly, he offered her a share of his growing wealth for her hand. Quite to his amazement, he realized, one day, she genuinely loved him, despite his being a doppelganger to a frog. And, after his wife presented him with an adorable daughter, he realized lust had been replaced by love in the cold space that answered for his heart. Butler chuckled to himself at the thought. *Wonders never cease.*

The pair of Negro sentries at the door snapped smartly to attention as Butler passed, smiling proudly at his most recent innovation and cause for further Southern hatred. Lincoln was still disclaiming any intent to free the slaves, telling anyone who would listen that this war was about Union, not slavery, and would not even accept free Northern blacks into the army. But Butler realized, to paraphrase a Russian saying, 'God is in Heaven and Lincoln is far from Louisiana.' Short of troops, Butler had come up with his 'contraband' theory: that the slaves of those in revolt were contraband property, and under the rules of war, they could be seized for the use of the government. In truth, Butler had done no seizing. When word spread he had established the "Native

Guard" for black soldiers, slaves began pouring in as fast as he could arm and train them.

The few slaveholders with guts enough to complain personally to Butler were laughed at and told that since they considered themselves no longer to be under the jurisdiction of the United States government, they would be taken at their word and could expect no legal redress from Washington. News Butler was arming escaped slaves had reached Washington long ago, and there had been no response. Butler could only assume Lincoln tacitly approved.

Saber clanking at his side, Butler marched into his large ground-floor office, contentedly taking in the opulent hardwood and plush velvet furnishings surrounding his enormous mahogany desk. He had no idea what the desk had cost, as it had been seized from the townhouse of a wealthy Creole planter serving in faraway Virginia.

He noted that the tall, lean Major Alan Howard, his precisely efficient operations officer, was already hard at work at his much more modest desk on the far side of the room, alongside a massive pigeon-hole bureau filled with neatly cataloged documents. Butler regarded Howard as a real find—an intelligent, well-educated, efficient Rhode Islander, with a burning Puritan hatred of the sinning traitors of the South. Howard was an administrative wizard. The only thing Butler found hard to take was Howard's tendency to unleash impromptu sermons at a moment's notice.

It's well worth tolerating his boring piousness in exchange for his tireless efficiency, reflected Butler.

Howard stood up and saluted formally.

"Morning, Alan," Butler said casually in acknowledgement, moving behind his desk to sit down in the high-backed leather chair, anxious to take the pressure off his corns. "How goes the fight against the rebellion this morning?"

Major Howard continued to stand stiffly, dark eyes staring at the improbable figure of Benjamin Butler. "General, sir, something has come to my attention." He cleared his throat. "You know I have not approved of certain practices of yours—and how the proceeds of those actions accrue to your private benefit. I have tolerated it, sir, because I understand the Lord God moves in mysterious ways, and He may chastise the wicked with an unworthy instrument. But in this case, your brother has gone *too* far. I have learned, along with your protection, he is crossing enemy lines northeast of the city and receiving cotton from the Confederacy in return for supplying them with salt, sir. With salt!"

Butler affected casual indifference. "So? The Union needs cotton. The mills of New England would grind to a halt without Southern-grown cotton. There is nothing new in such trade." He failed to mention he had substantial investments in several of those mills.

"Sir! You, of all people, are fully aware salt is in a different category than money or trade goods. Salt is the only way to preserve the meat the Rebel armies must have to survive, and the South has little salt of its own. This is outright rank treason, sir. Treason as sure as if they were being given rifles and cannon! I intend to denounce him to Washington, where he will face the penalties of treason. I earnestly hope he has engaged in this trade without your knowledge, so you will not share his fate."

With surprising speed, and despite the tortuous pain in his feet, the ungainly Butler sprang from behind his desk and lunged to within an inch of Major Howard. To Howard's credit, he did not flinch. "You will tell no one about my brother's activities, and I will tell you why," rasped Butler, sweat and spittle flinging with each word. "Should they come to light, then it might also come to light how a certain Union major has been issuing orders to seize certain plantations, ostensibly for failure to pay taxes. It will come to light a certain Union major has misused soldiers of the United States to keep all bidders but him away from the auctions. It will come to light a certain Union major has been quickly selling the plantations and sending the proceeds to Boston."

Howard had paled and was nervously stroking his long lantern jaw. "There is nothing too unusual in spoiling the Egyptians, as the Good Book says. Many do it. Certainly, you do, sir. At worst, it would be a scandal requiring my resignation, nothing more."

"Ah, but Major, once you are forced to resign, the money stops. The private doctors and nurses for your mother would have to go. She would have to go back to the asylum at Danvers, wouldn't she?"

Howard looked as if he had been gut-shot. He staggered wordlessly to the nearest chair and buried his head in his hands.

Butler was relentless, strolling over to the now-weeping man and resumed in a cold, chilling voice, "You really don't think much of my brains, do you? Did you really think I would not find out? I know it all. I know how your father's manufacturing business was ruined in the crash of '57, *and* how he shot himself. I know you paid what little money was left to the coroner to falsify the death certificate to show heart failure, and save your family from public disgrace. I have connections throughout government in Providence, and the coroner talked. Then your mother went idiot. I hear she had always had a melancholic disposition, and since there was no more money in the family, she had to go to the Danvers asylum. Do they still allow curiosity seekers to view the lunatics for a fee? I know they chain them to the walls and whip them or throw cold water on them when they're excited. I sure wouldn't want anyone I love in Danvers. She must really be feeling a lot better now, what with being at home with constant medical supervision. I'd hate to think what kind of relapse she would have if she had to go back to Danvers." Butler tsk-tsked and shook his head sympathetically.

Howard had ceased weeping and was now gazing at Butler with devastated, red-rimmed eyes.

Heartless, Butler could not help himself. "And let's not forget your sister, Letitia, to whom you've been sending large sums. She just married that high-flying businessman, Phillips, didn't she? He thinks there's money in the family. Wonder what it will do to dear Letitia's happy home for him to find out he was tricked into marrying the daughter of a bankrupt."

"It was the South, the cursed South," said Howard unexpectedly in a low monotone, staring blankly. "The spineless, wicked Democratic Party leaders tried to appease the soulless slavers by giving them a tariff, letting in the cheap foreign goods, which were all the sweat their victims could earn them. Many God-fearing merchants of the North, like my father, were ruined." He cut his dark eyes to Butler, pleadingly. "Please understand; he was a good, kind man, always full of laughs and jokes, always having time for Letitia and myself as we grew, always showing infinite patience with my mother's melancholia. I do not know what demons of perdition had fastened on his soul nor why he didn't take the short trip to Harvard to tell me of his agony. I would have cheerfully left Harvard, begged in the streets, worked at the most menial jobs . . ." Howard broke off, racked with silent sobs.

Butler patted the lean man's shoulder, absently wondering why Howard had been so affected by the death of his father. He, on the other hand, was proud of the fact he'd never known his own father, which had not affected him in the slightest.

"It must have been hard for you, to reconcile what you needed to with your religion. Very hard. Then you had your revelation, didn't you? In your sick mind, God meant the wealth of the South to compensate the Howard family for what they had suffered. Your mother could have decent care and your sister maintain her happy home, and, after the war, Alan Howard could restore his father's business to its rightful prominence in New England. But there can be even more, Alan, much more. You think I care what you take from traitors? You're not like the other rogues around headquarters, spending it on gaming and fancy women. The money you take goes to good use, *just* like the money I take."

Butler paused, and focused his crossed eyes as best he could on Howard. "You think I need more for my personal use? I'm not a pig. I was rich enough before all this started. Money is a tool. Money is the visible expression of power. The power that comes with money can translate into political power. The more money, the more power. Enough money, and all power flows into the hands of he who has that money. Alan, this war is shaking up the nation. When it is over and the slavocracy crushed, Americans will be, for a short time, like a ship without a compass, uncertain of what direction to go. If the right man is there at the right time, he can push this nation in remarkable directions. Remarkable. Alan, I will let you in on a little secret. I intend to be *that* man. You can help me be *that* man."

Howard's dark eyes were now black holes. "Why should I help a sinner such as you?" he asked in a low voice.

Butler grinned crookedly. "Because, as you yourself have said, the Lord moves in mysterious ways. I need someone I can trust, someone who is capable, someone who is—in most respects—incorruptible, to help me establish the new order. And that new kind of new order is *not* incompatible with the kind of country you would like to see. You think the country has degenerated from the ideals of the Puritans: their Godliness, their industrious-ness, their intolerance for the foreign and the alien. What do you think they would make of the mongrel hoards in New York and Boston these days, eh? Those jabbering idolaters that are diluting America's purity? I, too, want the American people to be Godly, orderly, obedient, and hard working. Alan, I know you don't want the goods of this Earth. How would you like to be one of those who helped bring the kingdom of God to America?"

Howard stroked his jowls, his eyes experiencing a landscape few others could imagine. "It is tempting, sir. A nation free of foreigners, traitors, slavers, Jews, Mormons, Papists—a true kingdom of the elect." He abruptly stood, his eyes lighting up. "Yes, yes, I believe it could happen. I did not know you shared in this vision. And if you possess such a vision of the city on the hill, then there is yet hope for your soul."

A stone atheist, Butler suppressed his inner satisfaction. "Then, we have a deal. No more talk about my brother, whose activities are giving employment to the mills in New England and, indirectly, putting clothes on our soldiers' backs. And if you continue to find a need to smite the traitors by dispossessing their goods, all the better for Old Glory."

"Yes, for God and Old Glory," amended the saturnine Howard, but hesitated, saying, "Sir, there is another matter demanding your attention this morning. Action must be taken immediately over Captain Clay. You know I do not care what the traitors think of our forces, but what happened at Deveraux plantation goes beyond all bounds of morality, much less military discipline, and we may have riots in the streets if he is not immediately punished."

Butler scowled. "Alphonso Clay? Damn fine quartermaster—one of the few goods things Washington has sent us in a long time. What's he done to get you so riled up?"

Howard stared at his superior. "You really don't know? Word has been spreading all morning since he was brought in at daylight by a Negro sergeant."

"No, I don't know," snarled Butler unpleasantly. He prided himself on knowing everything important that happened in his command before most everyone else.

Howard walked over to his desk and picked up a piece of paper. The morning light slanting in through the window made the ink glisten wetly, proving it to be freshly written. "Sir, it may save time if you read this document." He handed the paper to the corpulent general.

"What is it?" asked Butler as he eased his bulk into the chair behind his massive desk and focused his crossed eyes on the paper.

"Captain Clay's confession. I was with him as he wrote it in the cell we use in the basement for temporary prisoners. He finished it just five minutes before you arrived."

Despite his crossed eyes, Butler was a swift reader and began to quickly scan the document. Then something apparently caught his eye. "Jesus," the agnostic Butler said with genuine reverence. He read on until another section caused him to pause and say slowly, "Sweet Jesus, Mary, and Joseph!" He finished the document, leaned back in his chair, and exclaimed, "The stupid bastard signed this? It's his death warrant if it gets into a court. I don't care what connections he has, he's a dead man once a court martial sees this. It can't be true! He has to have gone crazy."

"The sergeant who brought him in has confirmed the truth of what is there. He was an eyewitness."

"This has to have been beaten out of him. Is that what happened? Not that I would blame—"

"No general, it was completely voluntary. After the sentries brought him to me, and I heard what happened, I took him down to the basement cell. He went quietly, only requesting paper, pen, and ink. He wrote that document in less than ten minutes, gave it to me without a word, and then turned to the wall."

"Damn it, Alan, this can't be the true story! You know the man—Kentucky bluegrass aristocrat, polite, well mannered, intelligent—he's covering for someone. Bring him up here! We have to get to the bottom of this."

Major Howard bowed slightly and left the room. Shortly, he re-entered the room, followed by a short, slight man in a dirty captain's uniform, who was shadowed by a wiry black man of equal stature in an ill-fitting sergeant's uniform. The captain saluted, then stood at attention, not stiffly but with the deceptive ease of a natural athlete. Butler did not speak at first. For a few moments, he studied the man who stood in front of him—severely stained, filthy uniform and all.

Alphonso Clay stared placidly at his commanding officer through wire-rimmed spectacles. His long, blonde hair and sky-blue eyes, combined with his small frame and precise way of moving, made him look almost effeminate. Butler gave Clay his best trial lawyer stare; the practiced look had caused many a witness to become nervous within moments, but there was no visible response from the calm junior officer. On the contrary, it was Butler who became uneasy as he noticed the dark stains on Clay's blue tunic, realizing it was blood—a great quantity of blood.

Butler collected himself. "All right Clay, what does this fool document mean?"

"It is a confession, of course," replied the captain in a soft, calm voice.

"You can't be serious! No one would voluntarily write something like this. You're covering for someone, aren't you?"

Clay moved not a muscle. "Every word in my confession is strictly true. It can be verified by Sergeant Lot there; others, if necessary."

For the first time, Butler truly noticed the black sergeant who had accompanied Clay into the room. The lightly colored Negro was obviously a mulatto; almost identical to Clay in height and build, but did not share Clay's placidity. Struggling to control his emotions, he fidgeted nervously with both the hilt of a heavy officer sword, which had surely been strapped on hurriedly, and the butt of an unusual revolver jammed into his belt.

"Sergeant, what is your name and unit?" demanded Butler.

"General, sir, Jeremiah Lot, Company D, 1st Regiment, Native

Guard." Lot spoke cultured, educated English, a surprise to Butler. Even the free blacks in Boston with whom Butler dealt did not usually speak in that fashion.

"What is your relationship with Captain Clay, and how did you come to witness the events described in this paper? He is a staff officer and you are in a line regiment."

Lot hesitated before speaking, gathering his thoughts. "Sir, I was born to a house slave on the plantation owned by the brother of Captain Clay's father and have known the captain since we were both small children. When his uncle died, I came to be ... owned by the captain's father. When the elder Mr. Clay himself passed in August of last year, I came to the captain along with all his father's other ... property. The captain gave me my freedom immediately, as he did all his father's other slaves, whom were registered regular-like with Kentucky. When the captain took his commission, I went as his personal servant. When we got down here and I saw you were allowing Negroes to join the fight, he helped me sign up with the Native Guard. Last night, he asked me as a personal favor to accompany him to the Devereaux plantation with my squad. My lieutenant wasn't available to ask permission, but I didn't feel it was necessary since Captain Clay is on your staff."

"Are you fond of Captain Clay?" asked Howard unexpectedly.

The sergeant turned his attention to the sullen major, and then spoke carefully, "The captain did more than free me. He persuaded his father to keep my sister and me from the fields. He guaranteed we'd receive a decent education, despite the fact it was a criminal offense under Kentucky law. What is most important, he treated me as an equal; most abolitionists wouldn't do as much."

There was a moment of silence in the room, and then Butler asked, "Sergeant, do you know what is in this document?"

"General, sir, I read it as he wrote it. It is the truth. I would give my life if it were not."

"Are you aware this is his death warrant? No military or civil court will be able to keep him from hanging?"

"General, he is out of his senses and can't be held responsible. There are circumstances not in that paper, which if you knew—"

"Enough, Sergeant," said Clay loudly. Then addressing Butler, he said, "The circumstances to which Sergeant Lot alludes are irrelevant. You are a trained lawyer, as am I. You know the only defense under the circumstances set forth in my confession would be legal insanity under the McNaughton Rule, which would only apply if I did not know what I was doing was wrong, or did not understand others would believe it to be wrong. I will testify I knew both to be the case. I would suggest you convene a court martial as soon as may be, so we can dispose of this matter expeditiously."

"Goddamnit man, you will hang!" exploded Butler. "What is your game? Are you trying to convince me you're insane by seeming to commit legal suicide?"

"It would not be suicide!" Clay shouted with the first hint of displayed passion. "It would be operation of law. Clays do not gamble, do not use foul language, do not drink to excess, *and* do not seek easy ways out of difficulties. Clays *do* take responsibility for their actions. Suicide is a coward's evasion."

"Yet, if you tell the truth in this document, Clays can do unspeakable things," said Butler brutally.

Clay's sky-blue eyes narrowed chillingly. "Sir, I said Clays take responsibility for their actions. I am prepared to take responsibility for mine."

"Damn you, I won't give the rebels the satisfaction of seeing me hang one of my own staff officers. I'm going to dispose of this insane document of yours and ship you back East. Nothing you can say is going to persuade me to hang you."

Clay smiled. It was chilling enough to Butler and Howard,

but Lot actually got goose bumps and shivered. "Oh, I think I can persuade you to convene a court martial when I tell you—"

At that moment, a flustered aide burst into the room.

"*What is it*, Lieutenant? Can't you see I'm occupied?" Butler berated the already-upset man.

"Sir, the ship that just docked . . . I asked the General to give me time to let you prepare . . ."

A small, puffy man in a major general's uniform shouldered past the lieutenant, followed by three immaculate staff officers. Butler beheld the newcomer with incomprehension, then growing anger. "Banks," he growled, making it sound like a curse. "What the hell are you doing here?"

"General Butler," Nathaniel Banks acknowledged disdainfully, making it sound as if he had discovered a horse apple in the parlor, then addressed Captain Clay. "Ah, Alphonso, I didn't expect to see you quite yet. I must apologize; I never had a chance to send you a note of condolence on the passing of your father. Despite his being a slaveholder, he was a good man and a loyal American."

Clay cordially replied, "Thank you, General, he was all those things."

Butler could not believe his ears. "You know Captain Clay?"

"Of course. His family is well known to several of my key political supporters. I've known Alphonso ever since he came out of Harvard; the *same* year I blocked your bid for Governor," said Banks with deliberate emphasis.

"I remember." Venom dripped from Butler's voice. "The voters deserved your holier-than-thou tenure in the governor's mansion."

"They did," replied Banks arrogantly. "People know their money is safe with me, and I am flattered the President trusts my honesty absolutely."

"Better than he trusts your military competency," snarled Butler at his fellow political general. "He had to take you out of the

Shenandoah command after Stonewall Jackson chased you all over the map. I heard Jackson seized so many of your supply depots, his soldiers referred to you as 'Jackson's Commissary Officer.'"

Banks froze for just a moment. "Well, the President thought I might do better in a different command. As a matter of fact, the reports of your *questionable* dealings have persuaded him an officer with higher moral standards was called for in New Orleans. That is why he has sent me to relieve you." Banks certainly was enjoying this moment a great deal.

Butler shouted a vile oath, and then more coherently said, "What reports? Why didn't Lincoln ask me? I could explain everything—"

"Oh, you will have the chance to explain, *Ben*," said Banks, giving ironic emphasis to Butler's nickname. "You are relieved immediately, and are hereby ordered to report to the President as soon as a ship can get you back east. The reports Captain Clay, here, have been sending to Washington made it very clear there are some rotten dealings in your department. I am flattered the President thinks me able to set things right."

Butler shifted his attention to Clay, his visage contorting murderously. "You son-of-a-bitch! You've been writing to Washington behind my back, making up lies—"

"Hardly lies, General," responded Clay. "Lincoln already had his suspicions. That's why he ordered General Meigs to send me out here and quietly look into matters. I must admit, you've been clever. I was unable to come up with enough evidence to construct an ironclad case, but I was able to show enough hints of civilian property theft, misuse of government stores, and trading with the enemy to make the President think perhaps he would like you closer to him, where he could keep an eye on you."

Major Howard involuntarily gasped.

"By God, you are not getting away with this Scot-free! You're going to have your court-martial and hang before sunset!"

Banks protested, "What court martial? What hanging?"

The ungainly Butler lurched to his feet with Clay's confession in his hands, strode over to Banks, and thrust the document into his hands. "Here, you sanctimonious bastard, read this! Do you really think any reports against me, written by a man who could do what is put down there, could possibly harm me?"

Banks snatched the paper and commenced to read, wincing at several points. By the time he finished, he was white as a sheet. "Alphonso, this cannot be true! Can it?"

"I wish it were not, but it is. After it was over, I surrendered myself to Sergeant Lot, giving him my sword and pistol. I have nothing more to say, nothing in extenuation."

"General Banks, sir, if I may—" began Lot.

"Sergeant!" Clay threatened. "I order you to silence on this matter. Nothing you can say will alter what happened. You swore to me you would be a superlative soldier when I agreed to help you get in uniform; now prove it by demonstrating your discipline!"

Agonizingly, Lot resumed his silent pose.

Butler self-righteously announced, "Now, let me gather some officers together and we will have ourselves a little court martial."

"Just a moment," said Banks slowly. "Perhaps you did not hear me. You are relieved. You no longer have authority in this department to convene a military court martial."

With a trace of anxiety, Clay said, "General Banks, there is no need for delay. You can convene the court and get this out of the way to everyone's satisfaction."

Banks disagreed, "Alphonso, something here isn't right. I can't believe what is described in this document is the whole story. We must investigate this matter. Washington will—yes, Washington will need to be involved. The ship I came in on will be setting out tomorrow morning. You will be on it, informally under arrest. Sergeant Lot, you should accompany him as guard. According to this paper, you were a witness. Washington will want to hear what you have to say." He extended the confession to Lot, who accepted it reluctantly. "I hold you personally responsible for delivering Captain Clay to Washington. Guard this paper carefully. You *do* realize that was just a formality. If he were inclined to escape, he would never have written a document such as this. See he gets his personal possessions together in time for tomorrow morning's departure." Rotating to Clay, he asked, "Do I have your personal word of honor you will attempt no escape?"

"You do, General. Nevertheless, I must again urge you to convene the court. The end result will be the same in Washington. All this is merely deferring the matter."

Banks shook his head sadly, puzzled. "You are not being perfectly candid with me, Alphonso. I know you well enough to recognize there is some deeper reason. But, we will let Washington decide this matter."

"Hold on there!" Butler howled. "You are actually going to let him go home in informal arrest, with no manacles or irons?"

"Yes, I believe I am, *Ben*," responded Banks mildly, but with a steel gaze. "Alphonso's word he will not try to escape is enough for me. And, by the way, although you and your operations officer are relieved, you are not to attempt to return on the same boat as Clay but wait for the next one. I have a feeling having you on the same ship with Alphonso for several weeks might be . . . unlucky for him. Now, General, Major, you are to leave this office immediately. We would not want any key documents to be *misfiled* in the last minutes of your tenure."

As Butler and Howard trudged down the road toward Butler's hotel, Howard twittered, "That hypocritical Pontius Pilot doesn't want Clay's blood on his hands, so he sends the case to Herod. We are both in serious trouble, which means trouble for my mother and my sister, also."

Surprisingly, Butler snickered. "Alan, it is good to remember, some days are better than others, and there is a world of tomorrows. I'm pretty sure there is nothing beyond hearsay and suspicion they can make stick to me. I'll get clear of this, and I'll make sure you get clear of it, too. And if by some miracle they don't hang Clay, well . . . Butler left the statement hanging in the air as he contemplated a future with infinite possibilities.

CHAPTER TWO

THE FATHER'S BURDEN

"Damn you Clay! You are a low monster and a disgrace to the uniform!" shouted Quartermaster General Montgomery Meigs, staring with rage across his desk at the docile captain sitting quietly in front of him. Meigs clutched the confession he'd just finished reading, his heart racing and nostrils flaring. The dim, early-morning light from a drizzling winter sky filtered fitfully through his window in the War Department Building, setting the scene—dreary.

Most people would have quailed before the fury of Montgomery Meigs, a large bull of a man with a grizzled beard shot through with gray: the spitting image of an Old Testament prophet. Not Alphonso Clay. Immaculately dressed in a perfectly tailored new uniform, acquired immediately upon arrival in Washington, he wasn't the least intimidated.

Sergeant Lot stood rigidly near the door, his eyes focused on a point somewhere over the middle of Meigs's well-organized desk.

"Damn you, Clay! Damn you—" Meigs choked off a worse curse. Even in his rage, the Georgia-born Southerner, and good friend of Robert E. Lee, could not entirely forget the artificial code of gentility he'd been taught to revere since birth. Finally, under some control, Meigs questioned, "Why, Clay? Why? In the name of God, tell me this doesn't mean what I *think* it means."

"It does, General," replied Clay in his soft, rather high voice. "I will not demean you or myself by offering any excuses. The matter is inexcusable, and the military code of justice should be allowed to follow its course."

"If it were up to me, you would hang before tomorrow noon, Clay! It's not just the monstrosity described in this paper, it's the shame and dishonor you brought on me personally. I selected you for New Orleans, thinking you would be perfect for a discreet, politically delicate assignment—a Harvard man who had traveled in Europe, from one of the wealthiest families in Kentucky, first cousin to Cassius Clay, and second cousin to Henry Clay himself. But if I hadn't chosen you, this wouldn't have happened!" Meigs threw the offending piece of paper onto his desk, furious with himself.

"There has been absolutely *no* dereliction on your part, General," comforted Clay. "The fault is mine completely, morally as well as legally. As you recall, I asked for an assignment, any assignment, in New Orleans. It is doubtful you would have chosen me without my request. As it happens, my wishes coincide with yours. I believe by noon tomorrow, this matter can be resolved as it should be."

"As I said, if it were up to me, you would hang, but Lincoln learned of your behavior from the newspapers and told me to set up this meeting. He is already late, but—"

Unmistakably, argumentative voices sounded directly outside the door, which was flung open to reveal the tall, angular figure of Abraham Lincoln, sporting a look of wry amusement.

A small man, floridly dressed in checked trousers, a loud vest, and a somewhat frayed frock coat was tugging insistently at Lincoln's elbow. "Mr. President, you can't just walk away from me! I broker cotton for some of the largest mills in New England, and I'm ruined if I can't come up with at least a thousand bales by next month," said the insistent man. "I've got a Treasury permit from Secretary Chase, all legal of course, allowing me to trade for Southern cotton, but it's no good if the Secretary of War doesn't give me a pass to cross the lines, and Stanton refuses to do so. Why, Mr. President, he actually threatened me! Just minutes ago, I spoke to him in this building, and Stanton said if I asked him again, he would have me hanged!"

"Mars truly said he would hang you?" Lincoln enjoyed using his favorite nickname for the mercurial, hard-charging Edwin Stanton. "*If* he said that, then I would be careful if I were you. He generally does what he says he will do."

The blustering little man was discernably deflated. No doubt, he did, indeed, expect to endure financial ruin if he did not obtain enough cotton to meet his contractual commitments to the mills.

Lincoln smiled sadly at the crestfallen broker, saying, "Oh, come on, it won't be as bad as all that. I have an idea for you. Rather than trying to go through Stanton, hop a steamer down to New Orleans and talk to General Banks. I have given him special dispensation to permit trade in cotton, so long as certain military goods are not part of the trade. Show him Chase's permit, and you will have no trouble obtaining cotton for your customers."

With cringing gratitude, the broker thanked the President for his suggestion and left the room.

Sighing, the President eased himself into an armchair in front of Meigs' desk.

Captain Clay's face had lost some of its tranquility; his lips had thinned, and his piercing blue eyes, glittering behind spectacles, focused on Lincoln with a cold intensity. "Mr. President, I can hardly believe you are encouraging this trade with traitors and slavers," said Clay. "I expected this sort of thing from a corrupt creature like Butler, but not from you. Prohibiting military goods is a fiction. One way or another, the South will convert the proceeds of such trade into arms, and good men will die. It is outrageous!"

"Clay, you will treat your commander-in-chief with respect!" grated Meigs.

"Now, General Meigs, go easy on the young man," reprimanded the President, tipping his head to Clay. "Captain, it's a funny thing. Several times in the middle of the night, I have thought the same thing you just said. Despite everything Jeff Davis says and does in Richmond, we are one country. The North cannot prosper without Southern cotton, and the South cannot produce the goods the North can make. If I tried to prohibit such trade outright, it would simply take place illegally. Better to have some controls on it than leave it totally unrestrained. That broker fellow was trying to do it right, rather than finding some hungry officer who would take money to look the other way. Seemed a shame to ruin him because he was honest."

"Honest!" exclaimed Clay. "That *tradesman's* like one of Mr. Darwin's apes; he wouldn't be walking upright if he hadn't found there was money in it."

Lincoln looked levelly at the blonde officer. There was something terribly unsettling about his gaze. "I have to admit I am disappointed in you, Captain Clay. Your lack of compassion for people, like that feller, is only the least of my reasons why. That New Orleans business . . . and yet, after your association with my son, Robert, in '61, I thought you were capable of finer feelings."

"Mr. President, there is no need to trouble General Meigs with that piece of history," said Clay hurriedly, an intensified anxiety showing whereas he was ordinarily composed.

"Captain Clay, *I am* the President, though there are many who would wish otherwise, and not all of them down South. And although we both saw the need to keep it out of the papers at the time, I want General Meigs to understand why I don't want military justice to take you, at least right yet."

"Mr. President, I don't understand," said a befuddled Meigs.

Lincoln slouched deeper into his chair, until only his shoulder-blades touched the back, now staring moodily at the ceiling. He spoke without looking at any of the room's occupants. "It is normal to love your son, isn't it Meigs? For instance, I see that photograph displayed proudly on your desk, obviously your son. Only a man who loved his son would keep a constant reminder on his desk. You must be very proud of that young man."

Meigs beheld the tinted photo in its elaborate frame: the distinctive marking of "Brady" in the corner signifying it was a product of the most fashionable studio in Washington. The soldier in the picture was dressed in an immaculate cavalry lieutenant's uniform. Brady had captured a twinkling eye and a hint of mischievousness, indicating an easy-going, charming nature. In a curiously unemotional voice, Meigs said, "He is everything I would ever have wished for in a son." Then, with much effort, he pulled his gaze away from the picture to focus on the President.

"Meigs, I have never been close to my eldest, Robert. He is a decent young man, even if he's too serious and a bit too aware he is a Todd on his mother's side. It troubles me I could never warm to him. Maybe it was little Eddie, Mrs. Lincoln's favorite, dying while he lived. In any case, I've never stinted on Robert. I've given him everything I never had—the finest schools, Harvard, everything. Everything but my love, I fear.

"Now then, you remember when John Brown—the Providence detective, not the deluded abolitionist—broke up the Starry Wisdom cult?"

"I do," replied Meigs solemnly. "I don't believe the Providence authorities were ever able to determine the total number of children's bodies buried in the basement of their hellish church. Most people assumed Starry Wisdom was a ring of monstrous pederasts, but a few of the penny dreadfulls hint the madmen had some insane notion that the sacrifice of those innocents would actually give them some sort of powers. Claptrap."

"They believed certain sacrifices would give them knowledge that would lead to power and wealth in this world," said Clay unexpectedly. "A number of rich and powerful figures, even a few from outside New England, were members of the Church. When Brown first began to suspect Professor Slaughter and his unusual group of being behind the disappearances, they used their connections to try to have him dismissed. They nearly succeeded."

"Yes sir, that was some right sharp detection on the part of Mr. Brown," said Lincoln. "Meigs, I later met Brown when he came down to offer his services to your department. Isn't much to look at—scared of his own shadow. I guess that's why Slaughter didn't take him seriously until it was too late. I was interested in that Starry Wisdom stuff. I had seen and heard many fantastic stories in my years practicing law, but that one took the prize. Anyway, one of the strangest about the story was how Clay here showed up after the first arrests, demanding to speak to the prisoners."

A displeased Meigs shifted to Clay. "*Why*? What interest did you have? Some morbid, sick curiosity? After New Orleans, I can believe it."

Clay, evidently uncomfortable, was silent.

The President took advantage of it. "Had something to do with your grandpappy, didn't it Clay?"

"His grandfather?" asked Meigs, eyebrows arched, sitting straighter.

"You didn't know? The father of Clay's mother was German philosopher Friedrich von Juntz, the professor who wrote a book on outlandish religious beliefs. It had one of those mouthful German titles—"

"*Unaussprechlichen Kulten*," supplied Clay. "Roughly translated, it means 'Unspeakable Cults.' It was very controversial in Germany, especially after my grandfather's murder. Instead of horror at a learned man being torn literally to pieces, with no sign of who committed the atrocity, nor one ounce of pity for his orphaned only child, the ignorant rabble of Weimar spread the most outrageous rumors about him. Then they commenced to persecute my mother, who had no place to go. Indeed, if not for fate, of my father stopping to visit the university and his seeing a cowardly mob pelting a frightened young woman with rocks and filth . . ." Clay's calmness had completely dissolved; his blue eyes gleamed fiercely, making everyone in the room uneasy. Visibly agitated, he pulled out a large pocket watch, opened it, and stared intently at it. Gradually, he calmed, then carefully closed the watch and restored it to an inner pocket of his blue tunic.

Lincoln's voice boomed in the quietness of the room. "Even in Illinois, people talked about what happened then. How the wealthy, well-known, young bluegrass aristocrat offered the penniless foreigner his protection, and his hand in marriage. How people talked when he brought his extraordinarily beautiful wife home, and how he horsewhipped a man in the main street of Louisville for not paying her proper respect. How she died giving birth to a still-born daughter, and how he never looked at another woman again, not even his slave women."

"Clays never abused their servants," responded the captain automatically. "It has always been beneath us to exploit power over those less fortunate than ourselves, at least in that way."

"You must have missed having your mother very much as you grew up," said Lincoln, with much compassion.

"I appreciate your sentiments, sir, but it was hardly a tragedy. I was barely four and can scarcely remember her."

"It must mean more to you than you say," said Lincoln gently.

"After all, you showed up in Providence to see if Starry Wisdom was, in some way, related to the work of your mother's father. Brown told me you were quite insistent on talking to two of Slaughter's inner circle. He said you got quite *enthusiastic* in your questioning. In point, he blamed himself for the fact that one of them had to be carried to the gallows, you hurt him so bad. Odd, his sympathy for people who had done what they had."

"I found Detective Brown to be not only intelligent and determined, but a genuinely good man. A rare combination, especially in police work. He is truly admirable," Clay commented sincerely.

"I believe you to be right, which brings us to the reason I am here, General Meigs." Lincoln shifted himself to the glowering Quartermaster General. "General, you have done good service to this country. I have heard—never mind how—you feel I won't give you a field command because I doubt your loyalty—that I hold your Georgian birth and your lifelong friendship with Robert E. Lee against you."

The grim old soldier literally blushed like a schoolgirl and began to stammer, his mouth moving like a fish out of water.

Lincoln waived him away. "Now, now, general, some may have questioned your loyalty, but not me. I've seen a lot of scoundrels over the years; hard to say where I have seen more of them, in the criminal courts or in the legislature at Springfield. After seeing the worst of human nature, I've become quite good at reading the human heart. I can tell this rebellion has hurt you, hurt you bad, but you would never waiver in your devotion to the United States."

With simple dignity, Meigs explained, "On two separate occasions, I took the oath before God to defend this country against all its enemies, foreign and domestic. There was no special clause for Georgia, no special exception for friends who betrayed both my country and my faith in them."

"I have never doubted it, Montgomery. Never for a moment

think I have. But I need you here, in this office, to keep the armies in the field supplied, and to keep the crooks and sharpers from giving them inferior food and weapons. Former Secretary Simon Cameron had an unfortunate tendency to give contracts at high prices to friends and relatives who delivered inferior goods, *if* they delivered at all."

"You should have hanged that bastard," muttered Meigs. "It was murder, pure murder, what he did to the brave men in the field."

Lincoln took a deep breath and let it out slowly. "Probably should have, Meigs, probably should have. But the people of the Commonwealth of Pennsylvania do think the world of the former Secretary, and I must keep them happy. So, I saved him much embarrassment and sent him off as Minister to Russia—at the same time, sending a private warning to the Tsar to bring in his things at night." Lincoln chuckled for a moment in remembrance and then became serious. "Cameron left a God-awful mess for Stanton to sort out, and Stanton is the first to say he couldn't do it without you. In fact, when Congress reconvenes, he wants me to put you in for a second star as Major General of the Volunteers. That should let the world know what I think of the slanders on your loyalty."

"Sir, I do not remain loyal in hope of promotion!" said an indignant Meigs.

"I know, General, I know. That is one of the principle reasons to promote you. Now, I am going to tell you something no one outside this room except Brown himself knows, as proof of just how much faith I put in your loyalty." The president sat up straight. "You understand this does not leave the room. Sergeant, you, too."

Lot, who had been like a fly on the wall up to then, nodded with the others.

Lincoln resumed speaking, "Brown told me one of the things mentioned after Clay here had his *conversation* with the prisoners was that Wade Hampton, a rich, fire-eating South Carolinian, has been a long-distance member of Starry Wisdom—that he paid a couple of the members to go up to Harvard, kidnap my son Robert, and hold him for ransom. His life for my acceptance of secession, a price I could never have paid." Lincoln became infinitely sad. Although he spoke to Meigs, his eyes focused on some inward place. "Clay left the jail without saying anything to anybody, while Brown furiously worked the telegraphs to the Boston and Massachusetts authorities to hunt down the two kidnappers and hold them for extradition. But you know how hard that kind of thing is between states. The Boston police proved surprisingly co-operative. In only two days, they had traced down the pair to a run-down hotel by the docks, both freshly dead, shot twice each with a Colt pocket revolver left lying on the floor. No one in that seedy place had heard or seen anything. I gather no one there ever hears or sees anything. Brown saw no point in publicizing the matter, nor did I, and Robert never knew of the risk to his life—that his father would let him . . . well, he never knew, and I do not want him to know."

Clay's masked face showed no visible sign of anxiety. "I do not see what that has to do with me, sir. I am, of course, glad some chance criminal dispute prevented them from either disrupting this country or inflicting an unfortunate tragedy on you and your family. It was really very fortunate. The inevitable delays afflicting police matters between states virtually guaranteed the authorities would not have been in time to thwart the plot."

Lincoln gave Clay a penetrating look. "Captain Clay, I owe someone more than I can ever repay. I suspect that person is you, although I will not insult your intelligence by attempting to get you to admit it. That is one reason why I will not allow General Meigs to hang you, at least not yet. The other reason is I need you to go to General Grant's headquarters near Vicksburg. Brown is now a lieutenant on the staff of W. T. Sherman, commanding the 15th Corps in Grant's army, and he has specifically asked for you, bypassing all protocol."

He had Clay's full attention now. "Asked for me? Asked for me for what?"

"That's what's puzzling. Although the telegram he sent was in military code, and he sent it directly to Stanton, it only said, 'Treason at highest levels. Dare not go out. Send Alphonso Clay. He will confirm all.' I checked up on it, and there *is* a little scandal brewing. Brown has locked himself up in a stateroom in the riverboat Sherman is using as his headquarters, ordering meals and necessities left outside the door. Sherman is showing great forbearance. From what I know of him, he had Grant telegraph in a request as to whether Brown should be put under restraints as a madman or left as he is until you get there."

"Until I get there?"

"I assume you are willing to go. It's obvious you respect Brown as an investigator. His refusal to send his request through the chain of command gives me a bad feeling about how high the treason to which he alludes goes. I propose to dismiss the charges, free you from arrest, and send you out to help Brown with whatever he has found."

Clay contemplated the matter for a moment. "Yes, sir, Mr. President. But with respect, I have two conditions of my own. One, Sergeant Lot accompanies me, and two, when the matter is concluded, General Grant will go forward with my court-martial on the New Orleans incident."

Lincoln looked at the adamant captain for a long moment, considering it all. "Very well, Clay, I will leave the details in Meigs' hands. I have a meeting with Senator Wade very soon, so I must be off. Do your best out West, Clay. I hope Brown has let his imagination run away with him, but I fear he has not." All stood quickly as Lincoln unfolded his lanky frame from the chair, stretched, and ambled over to the door, opening it to a startled corporal and private about to knock.

"Ach, Herr—Mr. President," said the corporal, a squat, swarthy man with a strong German accent, "I know not with General Meigs you be."

Behind the corporal, a tall private with a shock of unruly red hair visibly gulped.

Lincoln, amused, reassured them, "Please, gentlemen, I don't bite. May I have the pleasure of an introduction?"

The corporal clicked his heels, European style. "Corporal Johannes Schnetzer."

The private saluted sloppily, accompanied by a silly grin. "Beggin' ye pardon, Private Patrick O'Malley," he answered in a thick brogue.

Lincoln beamed. "New Americans, both." Then the joy faded. "And fighting for an adopted country. You, and those like you, have my respect. You are the truest Americans." Lincoln ambled out, putting on his top hat, with the two immigrant soldiers looking after him in awe. Those few carefully-chosen words had converted the two loyal immigrants into worshipers.

Corporal Schnetzer gave Meigs a crisp salute. "My general, the box from Virginia arrived has. On a buckboard, it is loaded. You told me to report when happened, and one other soldier bring."

Meigs remained motionless an unaccountably long time. Then, sweeping up Clay's confession, he sprang from behind his desk. "I must do this. Captain, Sergeant, come with me and these soldiers. I will give you your final instructions on the way to this other matter."

A quick trip along a corridor and down two flights of stairs led the small party out into the rear courtyard of the War Department Building where a passel of horses were tethered, including the two army mounts Clay and Lot had borrowed from the army stable near the train depot. In addition, there was now a buckboard, pulled by a single, tired horse. In the back, lay a single crude army-style coffin, a pick, and two shovels.

Briskly, Meigs turned to Sergeant Lot. "Sergeant, restore Captain Clay's sword and pistol to him. He is no longer under formal arrest. And take this document, being sure to present it to General Grant when you get out West."

With reluctance, Lot took the document, carefully folded it, and placed it in an inner pocket of his tunic, then awkwardly handed the heavy sword stuck through his belt to Clay, who swiftly and wordlessly slotted it into his empty scabbard. As it sheathed and clinked, he passed the odd-looking pistol to Clay.

Confused, Meigs asked, "That's not a Colt. What kind of gun is it?"

"A Model 2 from Messrs. Smith and Wesson," said Clay as he secured the firearm into his holster. "Quite a triumph of military science. It fires a self-contained metallic cartridge, with percussion cap, gunpowder, and bullet all rolled up into one waterproof container. We really should be adopting metallic cartridge repeating rifles for the army. Several firms have good prototypes, but they seem to have trouble getting contracts from the War Department."

Meigs, Clay, and Lot swung into the saddles of their respective horses, and Schnetzer and O'Malley got onto the seat of the buckboard. The conversation picked back up as the small procession trotted down Pennsylvania Avenue toward the Chain Bridge, the most direct route into Virginia.

"I'm not the problem, Clay. As it happens, I agree and think it's criminal to not be buying more Spencers and Henrys, but the Quartermaster Department can approve no contracts for firearms until the Ordinance Department authorizes us to do so. Despite my repeated requests and demonstrations of the combat superiority of cartridge-repeating rifles, the old fossils in Ordinance refuse to authorize. The fools think it will encourage soldiers to *waste* ammunition! But that is an issue for another day."

The procession had reached the Chain Bridge. Although the sentries were supposed to allow no traffic in either direction without a formal pass, they recognized Meigs and were not so foolish as to demand identification from a general. The party crossed over without pause to Virginia, sentries at attention, eyes straight ahead, saluting.

Meigs talked, staring at the landscape, the trotting of his horse giving a staccato quality to his words, "There is a train leaving tonight at seven-thirty-five that, with connections, will get you into St. Louis in three days. By the time you get your effects together and reach the station, my office will have made all the arrangements, and your tickets and passes will be awaiting you and your sergeant." Meigs briefly considered Lot: an unspoken question as to how the railroad would treat a black passenger, in uniform or not, in his eyes. Then a foreboding shadow crossed his features. He hoped no railway official tried to make an issue of it, for his own sake. "There are several steamboats down the river to where Grant and his army are camping each day. Your passes will guarantee you passage on the first available one. Stay in contact by *coded* telegraph, letting me know if you or Brown need anything. If it is within my power, I will see you get it."

The party had now passed through the gates of an apparently abandoned plantation. Although out of cultivation, it had been well maintained. As they ascended a gentle road toward a beautiful plantation house on top of a hill, they could see the estate commanded a spectacular view of the nation's capital. Despite the drizzle, the distant, incomplete dome of the Capitol was visible, as was the stump of the under-construction Washington Monument; even the White House and the sheep grazing on its lawn could be clearly seen.

Drawing up to the side of the plantation house, Clay asked, "I hope you will forgive my curiosity, sir, but what is this place?"

"The home of Robert E. Lee, traitor to our nation, and the best friend I ever had," Meigs stated in a carefully controlled, neutral voice. He swung out of his saddle and strode over to the buckboard, grabbed a shovel, and walked quickly the few steps to the northeast corner of the pillared mansion, where a small rose garden showed signs of past glory.

The four other soldiers exchanged puzzlement.

Clay boldly approached him, "Once again, please forgive my questions, sir. I know we are about to do a burial here, but why here?"

Meigs opened his tunic to have greater freedom of movement and commenced digging in the garden at a measured, mechanical pace. "We are here because Abraham Lincoln is a good man, a forgiving man, and because I am not. This property was seized for failure to pay taxes and came into the possession of the army. It is only right and proper traitors lose both their property and their lives." Meigs stopped talking while digging like a metronome.

The witnesses to this inexplicable ritual felt chilled, and not just because the cold winter drizzle had increased in strength.

"Lincoln is already talking about an amnesty when the war is over. Not only that, but a restoration of the traitors' properties. It is insupportable, but I am certain he will try to do it. Well, Robert Lee *will not* have this property back. He and his family will *never* have it back, no matter what Abe proclaims. The President asked me to create a national cemetery for the war dead here in Washington, but he doesn't yet know that I have selected Lee's estate of Arlington for that cemetery. The officer in that coffin is the first of hundreds already on their way here—hundreds that will be interred before Lincoln learns of this, many thousands more before this war is over. No matter what he decrees, no government could possibly stand that would give back to traitors' land containing the bones of patriots."

"My general, let the private and me this do," said Schnetzer from the seat of the buckboard. "Fit it is not for someone of your rank."

Meigs did not respond, but kept shoveling earth.

Meanwhile, O'Malley had slid off the seat to go around to the back of the buckboard to ease the coffin out of the back. As he grabbed the edge of the rough box, his eyes lit on the crude stenciling that had been applied when this object had started its journey north. He moved his lips slowly as he deciphered the blurred letters. Comprehending, he started and stumbled backwards with a blurted, "Jaysus, Mary, and Joseph!"

Schnetzer leapt down from the buckboard's seat and strode over to the now-quaking private, who was busily crossing himself, glancing repeatedly from coffin to general and back again. "O'Malley, you ill-mannered Irish pig!" chastised the corporal. "Manners for the general show!"

"Oh, Jaysus, Hans! Oh, Jaysus, look!" stuttered O'Malley, pointing to the words on the box.

With an angry scowl, the stocky corporal went over to the coffin and read to himself, jerking bolt upright: his response even less reverent than his subordinate's.

"*Scheisse!*" he hissed, making the 's' seem to go on forever. Then he strode to where Clay sat on his horse, saluted formally, and said, "*Herr Hauptmann—ach*, Captain, sir, this must you see."

Clay dismounted in a fluid motion, approached the coffin to see the message that had so discomfited the soldiers, but did not react so extremely when he read aloud, "Lt. John L. Meigs." Carefully, he studied Meigs. Given it was misting so hard and his spectacles were somewhat blurred by the weather, it could very well have been only water coursing down the furrows of the old man's cheeks into his tangled beard as he dug, or not.

Meigs muttered incoherently, "Destroy the traitor, Clay! Destroy him! Destroy him!"

Slowly, reverently, Clay saluted the general whose task had all consumed him. Ignoring Lot's questioning eyebrow, he swiftly mounted his horse, and without another word, Clay and Lot rode down the road leading to the Potomac, leaving only the two newly-minted Americans to watch Montgomery Meigs bury his hate, his grief, and his love into the beautiful hillside by his best friend's home.

CHAPTER THREE

"JOHN BROWN'S BODY LIES A'OLDERING IN THE GRAVE . . ."

Clay and Lot stood together in the bow of the riverboat as it chugged wheezily toward the western shore of the Mississippi. The side-wheeler's goal was clearly a series of rickety piers where several nondescript steamers were berthed, with a sporadic leavening of the ugly, deadly ironclads. Near the piers displayed a cluster of tumbledown, unpainted wooden buildings—what remained of the original little river town of Young's Point, Louisiana. In the muddy acres surrounding them set evenly a sea of army tents. Blue-clad figures, mostly on foot but sometimes on horseback, scurried with apparent randomness, dodging the random lumbering army wagon.

"Not much to look at, is it, Captain?" commented Lot, peering at his friend for confirmation.

Clay responded not, only grimaced slightly, intently studying the approaching chaos as if trying to solve a deceptively difficult equation in mathematics. Clay, who was never very talkative at the best of times, had said little since the incident just outside Cincinnati. A conductor had made some rude remarks about

Lot's ancestry and attempted to eject him from the train. Without speaking a word or blinking, Clay had punched the heavy man in the stomach, rabbit-punched him in the temple as he leaned over retching, and threw him unceremoniously from the train. Sd the train was moving slow at the time, the conductor would undoubtedly recover, so Lot felt he could gloat with a clear conscience, but the incident had depressed Clay, resulting in one of his moody, prolonged silences.

Lot tried again to draw Clay out. "Why do you suppose Grant has his army here? This is the west bank of the Mississippi, and Vicksburg is on the east bank—about ten miles downstream. Doesn't make much sense to me."

"Nor to me," replied Clay, eliminating the awkwardness. "Yet, there must be some reason. You can ignore the nonsense the newspapers say. I don't know if Grant is a drunk, but so far, he has shown no sign of being a fool. I must confess; it will be intriguing to see what the man is really like, especially after reading all the rubbish the scribblers have been putting out."

Bumping and scraping, the riverboat slid slowly along one of the piers, then the paddles came to a stop and reversed, killing most of the forward motion, and some soldiers helped the crew with the mooring ropes. Clay and Lot gathered up the large carpetbags containing their few belongings, mainly changes of garments, and were the first of the varied passengers, mostly soldiers of various ranks, to cross the fragile gangway onto the pier.

They just set foot on the pier when the air was split by a booming shout. "Captain Clay! Captain Alphonso Clay!"

Both Clay and Lot looked around, locating the source of the ruckus, a tall, broad-shouldered major cupping his hands around his mouth to magnify the force of his voice.

The two friends went directly to him, saluting formally. "I am Clay. This is Sergeant Lot, who is acting as my personal aide."

The major returned the salutes. "Ely Parker, staff officer, Army of the Tennessee Headquarters. General Sherman is engaged with General Grant and unable to get away. He asked me to meet you and conduct you to him, so he may speak with you as soon as possible."

Clay emotionlessly scrutinized the burly major. Parker, a full-blooded Indian, wore an immaculate major's uniform with easy grace, and his deep, cultured voice, completely without an accent of any kind, indicated a college-educated man.

Parker noticed Clay's puzzlement but only responded grimly, saying, "Gentlemen, if you will follow me, I will conduct you to General Grant's tent."

The three Federal soldiers navigated the muddy byways surrounding the docks, dodging the occasional galloping courier whose horse would splatter mud for yards in every direction.

Clay muttered under his breath as his immaculate boots became encrusted, then asked, "Major, is it always this muddy in these parts?"

Very solemnly, Parker replied, "Oh no, Captain, we've had quite a dry spell the last week." Then more seriously, "You cannot imagine how we have come to despise the mud. An unusually wet winter has developed into an equally wet spring. The rebels have destroyed the dikes in many areas in an effort to impede, forcing us to crowd the army onto scarce dry ground and the levies. General Grant tries to keep the men from dwelling on their discomforts by giving them constant tasks and drills. Even so, morale is not what it should be."

"Because of the mud, sir?" asked Lot.

Parker hesitated. "That, and the sheer frustration of not being able to come to grips with the enemy.

"Nevertheless, that's not why you are here. On top of all his other concerns, General Grant is beginning to lose patience with the insane antics of General Sherman's man Brown. I, too, am losing mine. He's been locked in a stateroom on Sherman's riverboat, refusing to open the door for anyone, even demanding his meals be left on the floor in the corridor, *and* the steward leave the corridor, before opening the door. It is passing strange. He is doing something for Sherman, but I will be damned if I can figure out what it is. General Grant is quite fond of Sherman and indulges him in most things, but I think that is coming to an end. Ah, here we are."

They had reached a large tent pitched on a relatively dry knoll.

"Leave your bags here with the sentry. I will see they are delivered to wherever we end up quartering you." Parker nodded to a sentry, threw back a flap, and led his guests into the center of a furious argument. An agitated Sherman was half-shouting, half-pleading with a slightly built, bearded general, as four other officers watched in uncomfortable, quiet respect.

"Damnit Grant, I need more time! I know Brown is acting crazy, but hell, the papers call me crazy, too! You know his reputation. Half the damned country knows what he did back in Providence, even if most don't know the details."

"Sherman, I have been patient long enough," said General Ulysses Grant in a tone as calm as he could muster. "The whole army is beginning to talk about the madman we have on your headquarters boat. Rawlins tells me everywhere he goes he hears the wildest rumors, each more curious than the last, and all concerning what a demented detective could be doing in that stateroom."

"Grant, you know neither of us has any reason to pay attention to what—" Sherman halted, noting the new arrivals. His baleful, restless eyes opened wide as they lit upon Sergeant Lot. "Son-of-a-bitch! What is that *nigger* doing in the uniform of the United States?"

Lot looked as if he had been slapped. He'd, of course, heard the epithet many times but did not expect it to be hurled at him by a general in the very army he served. With controlled effort, he did not respond; he simply stiffened his posture and stared straight ahead.

In the embarrassing silence that followed, Clay spoke softly but clearly, "General Sherman, I assume? General, you have insulted a serving noncommissioned officer of the United States. Further, you have insulted my friend. It is obvious manners were not taught to Ohio scrubs, but I assure you they were taught to Kentucky gentlemen. If these were times of peace, and if it were not for the disparity of our ranks, I would know how to deal with such disrespect."

The horrendous shock in the tent was palpable. Lot touched Clay's elbow, saying urgently, "It's nothing, Captain, nothing. I don't mind, so let it be."

"Damn you, you pipsqueak bastard!" the enraged Sherman managed to choke out. "Just who the hell do you think you are?"

"Captain Alphonso Clay, United States Quartermaster Bureau, on detached service, at your disposal for whatever purpose." The pale blue eyes behind the spectacles blazed. making those in the tent uneasy, for no reason they could easily name.

Grant pulled his beard. "Alphonso Clay . . . that name's familiar. Something to do with New Orlea . . ." he trailed off with the memory of what he'd read, considering the new arrival with a combination of loathing and interest, but perhaps surprisingly, without a trace of fear. Grant was a man of many strong emotions, but fear was not among them. He chastised his favorite general. "Sherman, you were out of line. You knew the day was coming when free Negroes would be allowed in our army. Stanton is authorizing colored regiments for rear-echelon duty. Why not? They can take bullets as well as white men."

"So can sandbags, and they aren't half the trouble," muttered Sherman sullenly.

"Cump, you know what's right," said Grant in a low voice, staring at him, waiting.

Sherman eyeballed Grant strangely. More than one person in the tent thought of how a loyal dog would look at a beloved master after an unpleasant command. Then he squared his shoulders, faced Clay and Lot, and said in a surly voice, "I offer my apologies, Captain and . . . Sergeant. The disrespect was unintentional. There is much on my mind at present."

Lot replied most respectfully, refusing to make eye contact, "It is nothing, General."

Clay, on the other hand, said in an even tone, eyes forward, "I accept the apology in the spirit with which it was offered." The words were perfectly correct, but Sherman had not missed the underlying sarcasm.

"General Sherman told me someone was coming out from Washington on the Brown matter," Grant spoke directly to Clay in a blatant attempt to diffuse the tension.

"No need for a damn, paper-collar soldier from back East," said a craggy major general, with a crawling beard high up on his cheekbones and narrow, cold eyes. "Grant, you and Sherman are playing something close to the vest, and I suppose it's your business, but it's time to break into that cabin and send the little lunatic off to the nearest Bedlam!"

"General McClernand, perhaps we can keep everyone happy." There was something cold and distant in Grant's voice, subtle but unmistakable, indicating that Grant did not care terribly much for him. "Captain Clay is here at the request of Lieutenant Brown, as relayed through Sherman. We will respect his rank, *and* his duty." With a nod of his head in the direction of the general, he continued, "Captain Clay, the officer who has just indicated a preference for Western over Eastern soldiers is John McClernand, Commander of the 13th Corps, Army of the Tennessee and my senior corps commander, who commands the army in my absence. General Sherman commands the 15th Corps, while *this* gentleman is General James McPherson, commander of the 17th Corps." Grant gestured to the younger, prematurely balding officer to his right. His voice had softened. Clearly, he liked the cheerful McPherson as much as he disliked the morose McClernand. "Major Parker you've already met, which only leaves my Chief of Staff, Colonel John Rawlins." Grant cocked his head to the emaciated Rawlins whose deadly-pale skin and dark, burning eyes gazed at the world with feverish intentness.

Introductions over, Grant let everyone know, "All right, we'll have Clay go and try to pry Sherman's man out. Clay, if he won't come out, I would like you to break down the door and see what ails our nervous lieutenant. Major Parker, show Captain Clay and Sergeant Lot to Sherman's boat."

"One thing, General Grant, sir," said Lot nervously.

"Yes, Sergeant?" Grant looked directly at Lot, who realized there was a subtle but disturbing asymmetry to Grant's eyes. They were quite uneven. Through some trick of placement, one eye appeared very melancholy, the other fierce and pitiless. Lot wondered briefly if this reflected Grant's true character, or was simply a coincidence.

"General, General Meigs strictly charged me to place a document directly in your hands. With your permission, I will now do so." With reluctance, he drew the paper from the inside pocket of his tunic.

Grant took the paper, unfolded it, and read the contents. A quick reader, in less than a minute, he was done. His thoughts illegible, he stared deep in to Clay's eyes, trying to decipher, to break him, but Clay did not even blink. Grant carefully refolded the document and placed it inside his own tunic. "Captain Clay, we will discuss the contents of this remarkable document at another time, in private. Major Parker, please conduct this gentleman to Lieutenant Brown."

"Yes, General," said the tall Indian, saluting smartly. Clay and Lot saluted as well.

As they followed Parker out of the tent, they heard Sherman say, "Back to the matter at hand, Grant. It's mandatory we pull the army back to Memphis and start over. Take the overland path on east bank of the Mississippi. We're doing no good here."

"Sherman, what makes you think we wouldn't have the same supply-line problems we had last year with Bedford Forrest?" Clay stopped so abruptly Lot nearly ran into him; being so close, he was the only one who heard Clay breath the word "Forrest." Clay recovered immediately, and the last thing they heard as they left the tent was Grant saying, "What is the point of trying to maintain a supply line with Forrest's cavalry able to cut it at will?"

As the three churned their way through the muddy paths leading to the docks, Parker made some small talk. "You heard what they've been saying about Bedford Forrest. A cold, dangerous cavalry leader, they say he is almost illiterate, yet, oddly, a genius for mounted operations behind *our* lines. Made millions before the war trading slaves and speculating in real estate, and pays for much of his outfit's equipment out of his own pocket. Grant was trying to come down the east bank last year, having built up a huge supply depot at Holly Springs, when Forrest came out of nowhere and sacked the whole town, burned everything we could use, shot several of our local supporters, and fled before we could turn around. Grant had to go back to Memphis and come down the west bank of the Mississippi; at least his supplies were safe from Forrest, with the river between us. Of course, now we're on the wrong side of the river. Grant's big problem is where and when to cross." Parker was leading the way and did not notice how Clay's eyes burned and lips pressed so together they were devoid of color, but Sergeant Lot did, and concealed his unease as best he could.

The three had reached one of the rickety docks and ascended the frail gangway leading to a riverboat that had seen better days.

As they entered a narrow corridor leading to the first-level staterooms, Parker said, "As nearly as I can tell, it has been more than a week since anyone has laid eyes on Brown, except for Sherman, who got into the cabin once or twice to talk to him. It will probably be necessary to . . ." The major trailed off and came to a halt. A flimsy cabin door stood ajar in front of them, the area around the small knob shattered. "That's Brown's room. Looks like someone lost patience before us."

The three entered the cabin.

A small man in a lieutenant's uniform lay on the floor, feet to the open porthole, and what was left of his head pulped blood and bone toward the door; the rest coated the walls and floor. Standing over the body, staring at it with calm contemplation, a tall, handsome, sandy-haired lieutenant's posture and manner were weirdly incongruous with the gruesomeness of the cabin.

Before anyone could react, Clay moved with the shocking speed of a striking rattlesnake, ramming the surprised lieutenant up against the wall of the cabin. Deftly extracting the young officer's Colt revolver from its holster, he jammed the barrel under the lieutenant's jaw and cocked it.

"Don't Alphonso! Don't!" screamed Lot. "Smell the pistol!"

Clay paused then brought the gun up to his nose. "Quite right, Sergeant. This revolver has not been recently fired." He lowered the pistol and sniffed again. "No gun has been fired in this room." Clay questioned the lieutenant without releasing him. "Who are you, sir, and what are you doing in here?"

Parker answered for him, "He is Ambrose Bierce, a mapmaker on loan from the Army of the Cumberland, who arrived here just last month. We have found the local maps to be almost useless. General Grant asked Rosecrans to send us an experienced cartographer."

"And just what is he doing on this boat?" asked Clay, never taking his eyes off the lieutenant but releasing him.

"I am quartered here," replied Bierce in a mellow, baritone voice. "They couldn't find a dry tent for me to share with a fellow officer. I have papers and instruments that do not respond well to moisture. A very disgruntled second lieutenant is now shivering in the sloppy tent, which originally was to be mine."

"Very well, sir. Can you explain your calm presence in a room with a murdered man?"

Bierce readjusted his uniform. "My cabin is the next one down, so I was all too aware of Lieutenant Brown's abnormal behavior. In fact, I never saw the man in life, just heard weird comings and goings in the middle of the night. Be that as it may, a few minutes ago, I heard a loud cry, then the sound of a heavy object falling. I came out of my cabin and knocked on the door. Although it really was none of my business, I feared perhaps he'd had some lunatic fit and had done himself an injury. There was no response to my repeated knocking, no sound at all. So thinking he was in need of some help, I put my shoulder to the door. The builder of this boat certainly did not lose any money on its fittings, as the door gave way at the lock as if it were made of paper." He looked down at the body. "A very curious sight, indeed. At first, I thought he'd shot himself, but I heard no gunshot. And besides, his revolver is still in its holster."

Clay glared coldly at him. "Very plausible, Lieutenant Bierce, but we all saw you calmly standing over a murdered man—your only reaction to be one of quizzical interest. A very peculiar reaction under the circumstances."

Bierce sniggered, an odd thing to do in such a grave scene. "Ah, that. I was trying to commit every nuance to memory. Quite unusual. I have seen many men killed by horrific violence in the field of battle but never one in the snugness of his bedroom. I wanted to be certain I could later remember every aspect of this sight."

Parker, repulsed, asked, "And just why would you wish that, Lieutenant?"

Bierce smiled broadly, bizarre how diabolical a response could be from such a handsome man. "The war will not last forever. Should I live, I intend to earn my bread by writing. Already, I have found this wonderful war a literal gold mine of inspiration for stories, and of unforgettable scenes to put in them. I was in the act of speculating how I might use this incident in a work of fiction at the very moment you saw fit to manhandle me."

Clay tilted his head in a most distasteful manner. "Wonderful? You find this national catastrophe wonderful?"

Bierce appeared amused at Clay's question. "Of course, it's wonderful, Captain. Look at the folly of it, the endless opportunity to view human stupidity and vice at close hand. Look at all those Confederate soldiers who bravely throw away their lives, thinking they are dying for states' rights and liberty when, in fact, they are protecting the financial interests of the one-in-twenty-five Southerners who own slaves. Look at the ignorant Midwestern farm boys and jabbering immigrants who are nobly sacrificing themselves so industrialists in tall hats can become rich, and corrupt suppliers can buy seaside mansions with the proceeds of rotten salt pork and weevily crackers. And do those farm boys and immigrants care about making the darkies free? They would sooner die than live next door to one. Look at the women on both sides who encourage their men folk to run off and make them impoverished widows. Look at it all! Look at it all! Is not it all a wonderful source of material for literature?"

Parker shook his head with disgust. "You can see, Captain Clay, why those who deal with the Lieutenant have taken to calling him

"Bitter Bierce." All I can say is he has the reputation of doing his duty admirably."

Bierce examined Clay with renewed interest. "Captain Clay? Captain Alphonso Clay? The one who taught the slavers such a lesson at Devereaux plantation? It is a genuine pleasure, Captain." He extended his hand to Clay who ignored the gesture. "I followed story in the papers, but I would really like the opportunity to hear more of the details—" Bierce stopped midsentence. Behind Clay's spectacles, his eyes were glowing weirdly, and the pistol in his hand was rotating toward the center of Bierce's chest.

Gently, Lot touched his friend's shoulder and calmly said, "Captain, it looks like the Lieutenant had nothing to do with this. Return his revolver to him."

Clay snapped out of it and silently handed the Colt, butt-first, to the lieutenant, then contemplated the mutilated body on the floor of the cabin. Without looking at Parker, he said, "Major, I would suggest you notify the provost and General Sherman. They will need to know of this immediately. Sergeant Lot and I will stay with the body, to see what can be learned while we wait."

"Captain, I must confess, I do not look forward to that. General Sherman was quite fond of Lieutenant Brown."

"That is the first thing I have heard of General Sherman that impresses me," said Clay, his eyes glued to the corpse.

Bierce appeared amused at Clay's question. "Of course, it's wonderful, Captain. Look at the folly of it, the endless opportunity to view human stupidity and vice at close hand. Look at all those Confederate soldiers who bravely throw away their lives, thinking they are dying for states' rights and liberty when, in fact, they are protecting the financial interests of the one-in-twenty-five Southerners who own slaves. Look at the ignorant Midwestern farm boys and jabbering immigrants who are nobly sacrificing themselves so industrialists in tall hats can become rich, and corrupt suppliers can buy seaside mansions with the proceeds of rotten salt pork and weevily crackers. And do those farm boys and immigrants care about making the darkies free? They would sooner die than live next door to one. Look at the women on both sides who encourage their men folk to run off and make them impoverished widows. Look at it all! Look at it all! Is not it all a wonderful source of material for literature?"

Parker shook his head with disgust. "You can see, Captain Clay, why those who deal with the Lieutenant have taken to calling him "Bitter Bierce." All I can say is he has the reputation of doing his duty admirably."

Bierce examined Clay with renewed interest. "Captain Clay? Captain Alphonso Clay? The one who taught the slavers such a lesson at Devereaux plantation? It is a genuine pleasure, Captain." He extended his hand to Clay who ignored the gesture. "I followed story in the papers, but I would really like the opportunity to hear more of the details—" Bierce stopped midsentence. Behind Clay's spectacles, his eyes were glowing weirdly, and the pistol in his hand was rotating toward the center of Bierce's chest.

Gently, Lot touched his friend's shoulder and calmly said, "Captain, it looks like the Lieutenant had nothing to do with this. Return his revolver to him."

Clay snapped out of it and silently handed the Colt, butt-first, to the lieutenant, then contemplated the mutilated body on the floor of the cabin. Without looking at Parker, he said, "Major, I would suggest you notify the provost and General Sherman. They will need to know of this immediately. Sergeant Lot and I will stay with the body, to see what can be learned while we wait."

"Captain, I must confess, I do not look forward to that. General Sherman was quite fond of Lieutenant Brown."

"That is the first thing I have heard of General Sherman that impresses me," said Clay, his eyes glued to the corpse.

Parker threw the captain a scandalized glance, but saying nothing more, he left the cabin.

"Five minutes, Jeremiah! Five minutes! If I had been five minutes earlier, I might have prevented this," said Clay in a low voice. "On such small things does human fate ride—a boat is slow leaving the dock, a train is delayed briefly on a siding, and a good human being dies . . ." Back in the moment, he held up his forefinger. "Now, let us see if we can determine how this happened."

"Do you mind if I stay to observe?" asked Bierce with sordid eagerness in his voice.

"Not only do I not mind, I would *insist* you stay," said Clay coldly, squatting on his haunches, intently scrutinizing what was left of Brown.

"Captain, do you suppose there is any chance this is *not* Brown?" asked Lot. "The features are so mutilated, it could be almost anybody."

Clay paused. "Quite a valid question, Sergeant, but I am afraid there can be no doubt. The size of the man is the same I knew. And besides, I remember noting the ear.

"Some years ago, I read a paper by a German researcher citing certain characteristics of the human body that are truly individualistic. He theorized every human being had a specific structure to his ear. More subtlety, he suggested the patterns of skin ridges on fingertips are unique and might be of use in tracking criminals who try to change their identities to evade capture. I am not sure patterns on fingers will ever be a practical method of identification. But since reading the paper, I have been observing people's ears, and, to my surprise, the theory is profoundly valid. So far, I have not seen one I could not have distinguished from anyone else. I remember the particular patterns of cartilage in Brown's ears. Much as I regret saying it, there is no question: this *is* John Brown of Providence."

Clay stood and examined the porthole from across the room. "No one else in the room, the door locked, and no weapon fired within the room," he mused aloud. "The bullet must have come through the porthole and struck him in the face—note how he fell backward. He had gone to the window, but why? An accident, or had he heard or seen something drawing him to the porthole? Questions with no obvious answers, Sergeant." Crossing the small room quickly, he fearlessly peered out the opening, apparently not considering or caring that where one bullet had entered, another might do the same. "No boats or structures nearby, over one hundred yards to the shore, and quite a jumble of trees and brush. The bullet probably passed through his head." He swiftly shouldered an amused Bierce out of the way and inspected the splattered wall, door, and doorjamb. All at once, Clay exclaimed, "There, Sergeant! See that hole in the jamb? About five feet up? I see the bullet. Please remove it."

Lot stepped forward, removing a pocketknife from his trousers and began to dig out the bullet. It did not take much effort. The sergeant peered at the flattened lump of lead, then stated, "A rifle bullet, probably from one of the British Enfields the rebels prefer but similar caliber to the one fired by our Springfields. Yet, there is enough of a difference that I am pretty sure this came from a Confederate Enfield. Must have been fired from quite a distance, though. The Enfield packs quite a wallop, and this thing was close to spent when it went through Brown, or it would have gone clean through the jamb into the corridor." He handed the lump of metal to Clay, asking, "I don't suppose this was just a stray shot that by pure accident killed the man we were about to see?"

With melancholy contemplation, Clay pocketed the deadly fragment. "No. No chance whatsoever. Brown acts like a man in fear of his life, telegraphs a desperate message mentioning treason to Washington, asking especially for me, barricades himself in a room, and is shot to death minutes before I reach him. No, that stretches coincidence far past the breaking point. Let us see what papers or other source evidence of his fears he may have left."

A few minutes search of the small cabin revealed nothing of relevance. Reluctantly, Clay informed the two men, "I fear we must search the body. Help me, Sergeant."

Bierce excitedly volunteered, "I can be of help here."

"No! You shall not touch this man. You just make sure no curiosity seekers get a view through that door. One of your ilk is quite enough."

"Surprisingly, Captain, I have often thought *one* like me is more than enough."

Both Clay and Lot spared the ghoulish Bierce a disgusted look but quickly and gently went through the dead man's pockets. When they were done, all they had to show were two handkerchiefs, a dog-earned notebook half-filled with cryptic jottings difficult to decipher, three pencil stubs, $27.35 in a combination of greenbacks and coins, and a pocketsize portrait case.

Clay undid the clasp of the case and found a heartbreaking family portrait. John Brown was staring nervously straight into the camera, slick hair parted down the middle. Seated directly in front of him was a petite, blonde woman, who would have been pretty, save for an over-generous nose, and four little girls, two on each side of their mother, varying in age from two to eight.

"I did not know he had a family," admitted Clay in a low voice. "He never mentioned it. A widow and four orphans. After all he did for his country. People think they know all he did; people are wrong. It wasn't just a matter of all the children who will now have a chance to grow up and grow old because he fearlessly pursued the rich and powerful. No, the world will never fully realize what they owe this man, and the fact he never realized the full extent of what he had done does not lessen the world's debt to him."

Both Bierce and Lot were puzzled by Clay's enigmatic comments, but only Bierce chose to speak. "Just what do you mean by the world's debt, Captain? I mean, everyone knows how he put paid to Slaughter and his thuggish child killers. What more is there to know beyond his exposure of Starry Wisdom?"

Clay looked at Bierce with distaste. "Nothing, Lieutenant, nothing. My mind wandered for a moment, is all."

Just then, Parker came back, followed by Sherman and Rawlins. The wild-eyed Sherman took in the scene in an instant and then did the most surprising thing—he began to cry—not a quiet trickle of tears, not a couple of sobs, but a bawling, howling, cursing stream of grief. He crossed to the cabin's far wall and punched it repeatedly until his knuckles bled, all the time crying incoherently. The other soldiers in the room exchanged shocked uneasiness. Now they understood how some questioned the sanity of the commander of the 15th Corps.

Gradually the storm subsided, and Sherman noisily blew his nose repeatedly on a handkerchief. Then, yet further astonishing the others in the room, he screamed, "I killed him! Damn me to hell! I killed this man!"

The pale, intense Rawlins was totally taken aback. "General Sherman, you cannot mean that."

"I believe the general is speaking metaphorically," replied Clay logically.

"I don't give a *shit* what you call it!" Sherman's spittle flew as he spoke. "I knew there was a traitor—knew the traitor would be desperate—and yet, what did I do? I put this man, this nonprofessional soldier, in harm's way. Brown was a good man, with a good family, and now he is dead. If it isn't my fault, whose fault is it?"

"It is the fault of the man who pulled the trigger, and whoever was *behind* that man," Clay stated with cold reason. "I was too late to save his life; blame me if you like. Regrets are pointless. But to find his murderer, is to find the traitor he sought. That will at least give some meaning to his death. We owe him nothing less.

"With respect General, your extravagant grief is an indulgence. You are a general whose duty is to place men in positions where they may be killed. I know far better than you what is owed to John Brown. It is insupportable, *absolutely insupportable*, that this should happen to him, of all men. It is . . . It is . . ." Clay's voice cracked and trailed off as he quickly drew the large pocket watch from his tunic, opened it, and stared intently at it far longer than was necessary to ascertain the time. In the span of less than ten heartbeats, Clay closed the watch, stuck it in his tunic pocket, and spoke as if nothing had happened. For everyone there, time stood still until words proceeded again from his mouth. "The bullet came from outside. If you will excuse Sergeant Lot and myself, we must see what can be learned before evidence is disturbed. I am sure the murderer is long gone, but we may just find something that will lead us to him."

"Of course, Captain." Sherman cleared his throat and composed himself. "I will take care of Brown's body. Dismissed."

Leading Lot out into the corridor, Clay reflected on the door opening to the outside stairs and the second level of the boat. "Before we go ashore, I want to see up there. Come."

They shouldered past a growing knot of soldiers and civilians attracted by the commotion surrounding Brown's cabin. Swiftly ascending the stairs, Clay paced off careful steps along the upper level deck. At a certain spot, he commented, "I believe we are now directly above Brown's cabin," then leaned over the rail, listening. Sherman's distinctive voice could be heard coming from the cabin directly below him.

Tossing his forage cap on the deck, Clay commanded, "I need your help, Sergeant. Hold my legs as I examine the area around Brown's window." Lot firmly grasped his booted legs, and Clay leveraged himself over the rail. Showing no doubt in his friend's hold, Clay hung full-length upside-down. The murmur of voices coming from the open porthole showed no signs the officers inside had any idea Captain Clay was hanging like a bat at rest just outside their window.

Clay thoroughly assessed the wood around the top and sides of the window, running his fingers lightly along the surface. When satisfied, he softly instructed, "I'm done, Sergeant. Help me up." With some difficulty, Lot pulled Clay back onto the deck. Picking up his forage cap and fitting it snugly on his head, he headed toward the stairs. "Now we will examine the shoreline in direct line to Brown's window."

Clay and Lot swiftly descended to the main deck, crossed the gangplank, and gained the shore. At point, Clay turned right and picked his way along the muddy paths and clearings nearby, regularly looking back to see how Brown's porthole lined up with his position. His destination was unmistakably the dense patch of second-growth trees and bushes he'd spotted from the riverboat.

"Captain, why are you so sure the assassin fired from that patch of trees?" asked Lot as they made their way.

"Simple geometry. The bullet came through a rather small porthole and entered the doorjamb almost directly opposite. The trajectory of the shot creates, roughly, a right angle with the side of the boat. Tracing the imaginary line back indicates to me the shot must have been fired from that patch of wilderness. The fact it is the only place in a crowded camp someone could fire without being clearly seen reinforces my hypothesis."

"Perhaps no one saw the murderer, but surely someone would have heard the shot."

"Of course, they heard it, Sergeant, but whoever heard it would not realize its significance. There are over twenty thousand armed soldiers in this immediate area. Sentries could accidentally discharge their weapons, and individual companies engage in target practice all the time.

"Here we are." They paused at the edge of the little thicket. "Whoever used this firing position was not far back since foliage would interfere with aim. We will investigate the area just opposite the boat, a short ways in. Please walk directly behind me to minimize disturbance of the area. We are looking for boot prints, perhaps used cartridge paper, anything out of the ordinary."

Blue eyes darting behind his spectacles, Clay cautiously, carefully led the way, scanning the turf and bushes. After a few minutes, passing around trees and bushes, near the very edge of the river, Clay froze. "There, Sergeant! You see? Footprints."

Lot studied the markings in the muddy soil uncertainly. "Captain, are you sure they have anything to do with this? Whoever made those marks wasn't wearing boots *or* brogans. Might have been Indian moccasins. Also, look at the size; those marks belong to a young boy, not a man."

"Good points, Sergeant. Let's file this information away in our brains and see where it leads us." Just then, Clay spied something stuck in the packed grass, a shredded piece of paper; he picked it up between two fingers. "Ah, part of a paper cartridge. We cannot tell the caliber; it's only a scrap. But without a doubt, this is where the killer stood, regardless of the footprints. You see how it must have been. The assassin chose this point with a clear view of Sherman's riverboat, and the crook of this small tree made an excellent firing position on which to rest the barrel of his weapon for greater steadiness. There!" Clay virtually leapt at the tree to which he referred. "Look, Jeremiah! Look!" he exclaimed, pointing to the crook of a branch about four feet from the ground. "See the slight abrasions in the bark? This might have been done by some animal, but I am certain it was done by the murderer as he adjusted his aim during a long wait."

"How do you know the wait was long?"

"Do you see all the blurred footprints just around this tree? Some are no doubt yours, but others are too smeared to tell what kind of foot made them. Point being, someone stood here for a long time. He must have carefully loaded the Enfield right here. He bit off the top of the cardboard cartridge, spat out that bit of paper you saw me recover before pouring the gunpowder down the barrel, ramming the bullet down, using the remainder of the paper cartridge as wadding. A further mystery is how he knew which window to shoot through. The marksman was expertly trained to kill at this distance, but at this range, he could not possibly have identified Brown as Brown. How did he know which porthole, out of the dozen or so facing him, was the one where Brown might show his face? A question with no answer, at least none I care to think about at this moment. Now, from where did the killer come, and where did he go?"

Once again, his eyes glued to the ground, Clay scoured every square foot of the surrounding area. Confounded, he said, "All I see coming or going are your prints. Could the killer be a redskin child? I understand the Confederates have been successfully recruiting Indians to their cause under Chief Stand Watie. Yet, his troops are not known to be active in this area."

"Just because someone wears Indian moccasins doesn't make him an Indian."

"True enough, Sergeant," Clay agreed, eyebrows scrunched together. "Damn! It is as I feared!" He gestured to a confused patch of muddy ground at the edge of the river. "This is where our trail ends, at least for the time being. A small vessel landed here: either a rowboat or a canoe. The murderer could have come from downriver . . ." he directed his gaze one way, then another, ". . . or upriver for that matter, which is officially under Federal control. *And*, of course, there are bushwhackers and irregulars freely operating behind our lines. They even could have come from across the river, although that is a long haul. We need to make inquiries, but I doubt we'd get anything useful from eyewitnesses; you've seen for yourself how many small boats are going back and forth in this vicinity. Alright, back to Sherman's boat."

By the time Clay and Lot trod the rickety dock, Brown's body had been brought out on a canvas stretcher and laid on the forward deck next to an empty oblong crate: one constructed to ship rifles. Sherman was gone. Only Rawlins, Parker, Bierce, and a couple of idle soldiers stood as witnesses. Clay bounded up the gangplank just in time to hear Rawlins give the order to place Brown in the box.

"What are you doing with Lieutenant Brown?" asked Clay in an ominous voice.

"We can't leave the body lying around," replied Grant's pale chief of staff. "Human remains do not do well in here. Sad but necessary, we must get him over to where the burial details are currently working." He indicated an area on the shore where several soldiers were lowering another rifle box into a muddy hole. "I'm glad for my faith, or otherwise I would despair. Even without combat, we have several burials a day. Brave, patriotic, young farm boys who volunteered to serve their country." He inhaled deeply through his nose, holding his composure. "If they thought they might die, it was hoped to be gloriously in battle. Most don't even get that consolation. How glorious is it to die of bloody flux, or malaria, or measles? Measles, in the name of the Lord!" Without warning, Rawlins was racked with a round of coughing, not loudly but deeply and repeatedly. He drew out a handkerchief and coughed several times into it. When the fit passed, he stared intently at the piece of linen as if it were a cryptic message of vast import. As he restored it to his pocket, melancholic relief flitted across his face.

"You *are not* burying John Brown in a Louisiana riverbank," said

Clay with cold intensity. "That is unacceptable, sir, unacceptable. He shall be sent home. His family should not have the final insult of having nothing to grieve, nothing to bury."

Parker gently tried to intervene, "I understand your concern, Captain, but the body will not keep without embalming, and the army simply has no money for that."

Clay glared up at the tall Indian, insulted on Brown's behalf. "This army must have a number of those parasitic sutlers, those *unscrupulous* civilians who provide small luxuries at outrageous prices to homesick soldiers, hanging about camp. It is my understanding, at times, one will make available undertaking services for well-to-do officers. Is there such an individual in the area? I shall take it upon myself to pay for this."

"I know one," said Bierce unexpectedly, diverting all eyes in his direction. "Paid a visit to him not long ago—thought it would be instructive to see the process. I can take you there, but I must warn you, his services are not inexpensive by any means. Are you sure you can afford them?"

"I assure you, I can afford them," he said with confidence. "Lieutenant Bierce, I would like you to help me. Major Parker, if you would be kind enough to help Sergeant Lot, the lieutenant, and myself, I think we can handle this matter."

"Certainly, Captain Clay," replied Ely Parker. Some majors might have regarded this as beneath their dignity, but Parker was not among them.

Together, they gently lowered Brown's remains into the rifle box. He was so frail and light, there was no need to call for a wagon. The four easily carried the box the short distance to where a slovenly civilian in filthy clothes stood outside a tent reeking of formaldehyde.

"How much to preserve this officer?" demanded Clay in a peremptory manner as they set the box down.

The gaunt civilian appraised the remains inside the box and rubbed a stubbled chin, pretending to consider the matter. "$200 in paper or $100 in gold."

It was an *outrageous* price. Privates received a meager $18 in *depreciated* greenbacks per month. Nevertheless, Clay did not haggle. Wordlessly, he reached into his tunic and withdrew a leather satchel, from which he removed five gold coins, dropping them ceremoniously, one at a time, into the civilian's outstretched, filthy hand.

Unable to believe his good fortune, the sutler grinned broadly. "Yes sir, Captain. Pleasure doing business with a real gentleman. I'll see your officer friend here gets a real smart job. He'll look handsome enough to marry a month from now; I guarantee it."

Parker and Lot were repulsed by the ghoulish merchant, knowing Brown hadn't anything left *to* make better.

Clay glared at him with an emotion that was hard to define, then drug his eyes away and addressed Parker, "Major, I understand there is a regular, evening steamboat departing for St. Louis from the southernmost pier. Is this information correct?"

"Yes, Captain Clay, in about two hours' time."

Clay asked the mortician, "Can you have Lieutenant Brown's remains delivered to the southernmost pier, without fail, in two hours?"

"Oh, without doubt, sir, without doubt! Best undertaking services to be found in the Army of the Tennessee. You have my word on that!"

"Then please be so good as to do so. Major Parker, please take us to the St. Louis boat. I need to make certain arrangements with its captain."

Nearing sunset, Parker introduced Clay to the side-wheeler's skipper, a grizzled but capable man. Clay asked for pen and paper, scribbling out instructions for the captain, authorizing him to obtain the best coffin money could buy for Brown in St. Louis and arrange for its shipment by rail to Rhode Island, billing all costs to his bank in Louisville. He then wrote and sealed a short letter to the Louisville bank, sanctioning them to pay, without question, all bills relating to Brown the captain might submit. Last, but not least, he wrote a long letter to Mrs. John Brown of Providence, allowing no one to catch a glimpse of its contents. He gave this to the captain as well, who gravely promised to see it posted in St. Louis; you could clearly see he'd performed such duties in the past.

With the business concluded, Clay, Lot, Parker, and Bierce stood on the dock, impatiently waiting for the undertaker. The time for the boat to cast off was rapidly approaching, and Clay was heating up by the minute.

Just as the deck hands were about to cast off the ropes, the gaunt civilian galloped up, the rifle box jouncing on the bed of a rickety buckboard drawn by an overworked horse. He greeted the waiting officers gaily. "See Captain, a great job done, and on time." He jumped down and threw open the box—the wafting odor of embalming fluid nauseating everyone. "Not much I could do for the face, I'm afraid. His missus should have a closed casket service."

"Thank you for your advice," snarled Clay, on the verge of losing control.

Oblivious to the blonde captain's rage, the sutler gestured to some deckhands who unloaded the box and carried it up the gangplank, then down into the hold. Smiling and tipping his hat, he backed off the pier, directing his rig back toward his place of business, clearly cheered by the hope of more such custom.

The deckhands emerged from the hold and quickly threw off the mooring ropes. Slowly the paddles began to turn, and the boat edged away from the dock. Gradually, they gained purchase, the water under them churning with white froth as the vessel headed north. It was then Alphonso Clay began to do the most peculiar thing. He began to sing. The song was the abolitionist anthem "John Brown's Body," set to the tune of "The Battle Hymn of The Republic."

"John Brown's Body lies a-mouldering in the grave,
John Brown's body lies a-mouldering in the grave,
John Brown's Body lies a-mouldering in the grave,
But his soul goes marching on.

Glory, glory hallelujah,
Glory, glory hallelujah,
Glory, glory hallelujah,
His soul goes marching on."

Lot, Parker, and Bierce looked uneasily at one another. Clay was singing in a clear, attractive tenor, eyes riveted on the rapidly moving riverboat. It was not just the weirdness of the singing—it was apparent to all: Clay was not with them. None were sure they would like to be exactly where Alphonso Clay was either.

Clay started singing the second verse, and for some reason, which he would never be able to describe, Jeremiah Lot joined in with his own clear tenor.

"He's gone to be a soldier in the Army of the Lord,
He's gone to be a soldier in the Army of the Lord,
He's gone to be a soldier in the Army of the Lord,
His soul goes marching on.

Glory, glory hallelujah,
Glory, glory hallelujah,
Glory, glory hallelujah,
His soul goes marching on."

As the northern-bound riverboat briefly caught the last rays of the setting sun, the running lamps began to shine. For reasons he would never be able to clearly articulate, Ely Parker added his uncertain baritone to the next verse.

> "*John Brown's knapsack is strapped upon his back,*
> *John Brown's knapsack is strapped upon his back,*
> *John Brown's knapsack is strapped upon his back,*
> *His soul goes marching on.*
>
> *Glory, glory hallelujah,*
> *Glory, glory hallelujah,*
> *Glory, glory hallelujah,*
> *His soul goes marching on.*"

The St. Louis boat was now just a twinkling light in the descending dusk. For the sheer hell of it, an amused Ambrose Bierce joined his unpleasant voice in the final verse.

> "*John Brown died that the slaves might be free,*
> *John Brown died that the slaves might be free,*
> *John Brown died that the slaves might be free,*
> *His soul goes marching on.*
>
> *Glory, glory hallelujah,*
> *Glory, glory hallelujah,*
> *Glory, glory hallelujah,*
> *His soul goes marching on.*"

The boat to St. Louis was gone.

CHAPTER FOUR

FIRE ON THE WATER

Jeremiah Lot's eyes jerked open. Images of flame and blood and a round horror sailing through the air remained briefly before his eyes. It took a moment to realize he was in the narrow bunk in what had been John Brown's cabin on Sherman's riverboat. He recalled Clay's insistence that the cabin be assigned to them both the moment the gore was cleaned from the planks. Despite the general lack of sleeping facilities in Grant's crowded encampment, no one asserted a prior claim. Lot had been uneasy about sleeping at the scene of a murder and tried convincing himself his nightmare had arisen from the resulting unease, but in his heart, he was all too aware that was not the case. Blinking sleep from his eyes, he looked over the small distance to the tiny desk under the porthole through which the watery light of early morning filtered, supplementing the fitfully glowing remnants of a candle. Alphonso Clay was staring intently at Brown's notebook, sparing a rare peek at the heartbreaking Brown family portrait carefully displayed on the desk.

Lot noted the blanket on the floor, which Clay had assured him was all he needed for a night's rest, was hardly disturbed. The only sign he'd rested at all was the slight mussing of his long blonde hair.

"Good morning, Sergeant," said Clay, not looking directly at him. "It is a true shame Brown was not writing for others. He seems to have developed his own personal shorthand. I believe there is much significance here, but it is like trying to read ancient Egyptian before the Frenchmen obtained the key. Unlike them, I have no Rosetta stone, and fear there is none to have."

Lot swung his feet onto the cold planks, knuckling his eyes. "Captain, how much sleep did you get last night?"

"Enough, Sergeant, enough. My requirements for those little slices of death seem to be much less than average."

"Didn't use to be, sir."

"Yes, hmmm, many things changed recently."

"So, do you really think you can discover who killed Lieutenant Brown?"

"I will attempt to do so. Whether I succeed depends on factors simply unknown at this time. If you have had enough rest, get dressed and let's get something to eat. I want to meet this morning with Colonel Rawlins. I understand he has been making regular use of our sardonic friend, Lieutenant Bierce, to scout far outside the picketed lines to obtain information for usable maps."

"You suspect Bierce?"

"Interesting, the man who discovered the body is in the habit of ranging far outside our lines into Confederate-held territory. It could, of course, be a coincidence. Very interesting."

While Lot quickly put on his shirt, Clay stuffed Brown's notebook into his side pocket, but with much greater care and gentleness, he closed the picture case and carefully placed it in an inside pocket of his blue tunic.

Lot was uneasy about the family portrait, and as he pulled on his brogans, he said, "Captain, this is not meant as a criticism, but shouldn't you have returned that picture to Mrs. Brown?"

"Possibly, Sergeant, possibly. She shall receive it eventually. I am simply borrowing it as a, well . . . a muse. It is all too easy to put the innocent out of mind when they should never be out of our minds. Would not you agree, Sergeant?"

Lot found it hard to meet Clay's eyes. All he could see was fire and blood and the round horror. "Yes sir, we should not forget the innocent."

"Alright then, let's go put some revolting pork, maggoty crackers, and bitter coffee in our stomachs. Taste is too much to expect; I'll settle for fuel."

The edge taken off their hunger, Clay and Lot strode over to Grant's command tent. Clay viewed his feet intermittently; the ever-present mud had already fouled his expensive boots, souring the disposition of the fastidious captain.

A melancholy Colonel Rawlins stood by the campfire burning near the entrance to the tent, taking sips of coffee from a tin cup while talking to Lieutenant Bierce, who reacted as if it was a private joke.

Clay and Lot saluted formally.

"Good morning," responded the ashen Rawlins, making no move to return the salute—his distaste for Clay palpable. "Frankly, I expected to find you gone this morning. With poor Brown dead, there's no reason to stay."

"With respect, Colonel, there is even more reason to stay. I have already sent a message north for Meigs. As soon as St. Louis is able to telegraph it, I am sure he will ask me to stay. I expect my orders will reflect a change, charging me to investigate why Lieutenant Brown was murdered."

"Captain Clay, this *is* the Army of the Tennessee, *not* the Quartermaster Bureau," replied Rawlins with some heat. "General Grant commands, *not* General Meigs, and General Grant will determine who stays with his army and who *does not*."

"I reckon I will," said a gravelly voice.

All in the little group jumped, except the amused Bierce who'd been the only one who'd noticed Ulysses Grant quietly move out of his tent. To the obvious surprise of both Clay and Lot, Grant was followed by a rather dumpy woman whose pretty features were marred by badly crossed eyes. Clay was irresistibly reminded of Benjamin Butler. Behind her came an intelligent-looking boy of about ten years, who was already showing an uncanny resemblance to Grant.

Noting Clay's mien, Grant said, "Captain, may I introduce my wife, Julia, and my son, Fred? They are here on an extended visit. Julia, let me present Captain Alphonso Clay and Sergeant Lot of the Quartermaster Bureau." Grant's gaze lingered on his wife, and amazingly, his stern features softened. Unconsciously, he reached out and squeezed her hand. The middle-aged matron actually simpered. She and her husband were acting like bashful young lovers, not a married couple in their forties. After allowing her eyes to rest upon her husband for what was an almost embarrassing length of time, she turned to Clay and focused, as best she could, on him.

"Captain Clay, I don't remember you, but for some reason your name is familiar . . ." began Julia Grant.

"Common name, here in the South," interrupted her husband hurriedly. "Anyway, I have no problem with Captain Clay staying on for a bit, so long as he understands it is *my* choice, not *his* right." Grant looked directly at Clay, who could not help but notice that despite his slight build and slouching posture, Grant would brook no interference with his army. "So, Captain Clay, how do you propose to investigate this tragic matter?"

"General, I suspect Lieutenant Bierce is about to go out on one of his mapping excursions. With your permission, Sergeant Lot and I will accompany him. It will be helpful to get a more complete idea of the surrounding area and how an assassin could approach the encampment."

Bierce's cynicism vanished. "Hold up, Captain. I prefer to do my job alone. There may not be organized Confederate forces on this side of the river, but there are plenty of partisans. The job is dangerous enough for a lone rider; it would be much harder for a party of three to be inconspicuous. Besides, I have . . . ah, informers I have to meet. Their position is . . . um, delicate. I am sure they would prefer few know their identities."

"Sergeant Lot and I can keep a secret," responded Clay, a hint of nefariousness written subtly on his face.

"If the captain and the sergeant are to stay, I see no problem with them going with you, Bierce," said Rawlins unexpectedly. "I appreciate your bravery, Lieutenant, but I've never been happy with you going it alone. It would make me feel better if Clay and his sergeant accompanied you while they are our guests. Oh, I almost forgot. Here is the gold you wanted." Reaching into his side pocket, Rawlins came out with five ten-dollar gold coins, which he gave one at a time to Bierce, who casually pocketed them. "I wish you could persuade your informants to accept greenbacks; specie is hard to pry out of Washington."

Bierce made light of the situation. "Sir, the people I deal with do not have much more faith in our paper than Jeff Davis's. Gold is always a more attractive incentive to the ignorant rabble. Captain, Sergeant, since my superior officer thinks it would be a good idea, you are, of course, welcome to accompany me on today's little excursion. Let's see what we can do to scare you up some mounts. General, Colonel, Mrs. Grant." Bierce jauntily saluted each in turn, even though a salute to the General's wife was, strictly speaking, inappropriate. Then, without checking to see if Clay and Lot followed, he began walking toward a corral visible in the distance, casually whistling "The Bonnie Blue Flag," oddly enough a song very popular in the South.

Clearly, Lieutenant Bierce had selected the best of the available horses for himself; it required little urging to pick its way along the muddy corduroyed road. Behind him, the fuming Clay and Lot had to repeatedly urge the sway-backed nags Bierce had chosen for them over the uneven logs laying crosswise in the mud to give marginally better going to heavily-laden wagons. It had taken them nearly an hour to ride merely three miles south of Grant's main encampment.

Ahead, they could see a gang of blue-clad soldiers busily chopping down small trees on either side of the muddy path to lay in the road, giving more solidity to the sticky mire. One bemused private with a musket stood guard over his sweating comrades, smugly delighted to have drawn sentry duty. He noticed the approaching horsemen and recognized Bierce.

"Morning, Lieutenant. Off on another scout? Got more guts than I've got. Another cavalry picket was killed yesterday, not half a mile from this very spot. It's right unhealthy to go by yourself beyond the regular lines."

"Good day, Private," said Bierce, amused by the informal, garrulous soldier. "It's hardly a surprise the Union blue is not beloved by the good people of Mississippi, is it?"

"No, sir, but it's mainly the planter folks who would really like to have our guts for garters. Most of the scrubs are sullen, but no worse. Guess with no slaves, most of 'em figure they got no dog in this fight."

"I wouldn't count on all the white trash being harmless if I were you, Private," warned Bierce. "Why, even up in my native Indiana, you might be surprised how many Copperheads there are, just hoping for a Confederate victory. No slaves up that way, but they'd rather die than see free darkies roaming around."

"Uh-huh, I'll just keep an eye on anyone with a Southern accent. So, who are your friends, Lieutenant? I have to ask. No one's supposed to pass me either way except with regular business, like yourself."

"There is no cause for concern. The good captain and his sergeant are going to be my personal escort." Bierce took in the area. "There's been a lot of progress on this road since I passed here last."

"Surely has, Lieutenant, although I'll be damned if I can figure the sense of it. Sure, it's going to reach past Vicksburg, but the army will still be on the wrong side of the river, and as far as I can see, no closer to taking it than before. Besides, the locals say the soil never really gets dry this close to the river. Even after we've corduroyed it, the road won't be able to take much wagon and cannon traffic until it's all churned up again; with mud deep enough for a mule to go in over its ears. The real strange thing is the boys are saying General McPherson—him of the 17th Corps—laid out the plans for this road. They say he's a first-rate engineer, so he must know we won't be able to make a permanent road to support the army." The private looked closely at Clay, then at Lot, exclaiming, "Lord Almighty, that sergeant's a nigger! Heard rumors Grant was going to put 'em in uniform but didn't really expect to see it."

"Private, that is not the correct way to address a superior," replied Clay in a dangerously soft voice. "You address the sergeant as 'sir,' and salute."

Confused, the private saluted Lot hurriedly. "Lord, Sergeant, I'm sorry. I didn't know calling you a nig—uh, using that word would give offense. Hear it all the time: didn't know anyone cared."

"Oh, a Negro cares, Private," reprimanded Lot. "We hate that word. It's just most of us don't dare say anything about it, and whites never stop to think how we might feel about it."

The private was oddly unafraid, only deeply embarrassed, as if he had belched in church. "I hope you believe I didn't mean any offense, Sergeant. Preacher Rice, back in Lawrence, told us before the war started, we are all God's children, and it was God's will that we join Abe's army and free the slaves."

"So, Private, you would have no trouble taking orders from a Negro?" asked Lot.

The young man rolled his head around, eyed the sky, considering this anomaly. "It would be unusual for a bit, but I reckon I could get used to it. Hell, my captain is a drunken coward—just between us. I suppose better a sober and brave black man than a fool like Captain Welch."

Bierce, displeased at the private's response, changed the topic. "Private, we must be going. What is tonight's password in case we come back through the lines after dark?"

"Julia."

"Julia," responded Bierce, almost judgmentally. "I suppose it came directly from the army commander."

"Wouldn't rightly know. You be careful now, Lieutenant. You, too, Captain, and Sergeant." With no irony, the youth was careful to make his sloppy salute encompass Lot as well as the commissioned officers.

After the party had passed the sweating work gang, the path got smaller but marginally better; it hadn't yet been ruined by heavy traffic. As they trotted along, Bierce's eyes flicked right and left ceaselessly, taking in every detail of the surrounding terrain, memorizing with conceded confidence every nuance. Clay found himself revising his opinion of the lieutenant slightly upwards. Sarcastic and offensive, Bierce might be, but he obviously took his job very seriously.

After a half hour of progress, Bierce wordlessly signaled for a halt. He then drew out a large notebook and some colored pencils from his saddlebag and began swiftly and confidently making notations, untroubled by the fact the notebook was balanced precariously on his pommel. Clay rode up alongside Bierce and stared with fascination at the map that was taking shape. For an initial draft, it was superb. Every curve and rut in the muddy road they'd just ridden were given in accurate detail, along with patches of forest and landmarks in the distance; explanatory notes were scribbled, most prominently "Corduroy!!"

"You do not feel the army will be able to use this path indefinitely without reinforcing it?" asked Clay.

Bierce shot Clay a disgusted eyeful. "Hell, they won't be able to use it for more than a week, even with the corduroy. You have to see to believe what an army of thirty thousand can do to an unpaved road. I keep telling Rawlins it's no damn good this close to the river. Last week, I even scouted a big arc out on higher ground to the west and found some pretty-damn-good country roads that, with a little work, could serve the army forever. Chastising, Rawlins put a real flea in my ear, 'Lieutenant Bierce, it is your job to observe and map, not to think. General Grant has said the path must be the most direct one south. You will kindly confine your efforts to surveying such a path.' When I tried to point out that no matter what we do, this bottomland is so waterlogged we would never be able to keep a road in shape for more than a week or so, Rawlins said, 'Lieutenant, I do not believe you have studied civil engineering. Generals Grant and McPherson have. Kindly let them do their jobs, and you do yours.' After that, I shut up. Let the arrogant fools come to grief. If Grant tries to move his army south along this road, it will be a worse fiasco than Burnside's Mud March last winter." Bierce's opinionated sneer had been ironically replaced with a smugness. "I'll enjoy watching the pompous asses trying to pass off the blame on some poor fool of a junior officer." He was almost looking forward to it: genuinely delighted with the image of a coming disaster for the Union army.

The sound of horses approaching them from ahead, the riders

shielded by a clump of second-growth trees hiding the bend in the road, sent a wave of adrenalin through each person. With shocking speed, Clay's new-fangled revolver was in his hand, while Lot was still fumbling with the clumsy Colt in his holster. Quite the opposite, Bierce made no move to draw his own pistol. Instead, he saluted jauntily as the riders came into view. They were two in number: a man and a woman. The man was compact and athletic, red-haired and handsome, marred only by a slight squint. Dressed in nondescript farmer's clothes with a shapeless felt hat, he had both a rifle and a double-barreled shotgun in scabbards on opposite sides of his saddle. The woman was tall and thin, with raven-black straight hair reaching out from under her straw hat to past her shoulders. Her large eyes were light blue, a jarring contrast to her dark hair, which, along with her high cheekbones and lithe build, spoke of some Indian ancestry, while the pale blue eyes and light freckles shouted Scottish. She wore men's clothes with small, loose Wellington boots, and sat astraddle the horse, rather than sidesaddle. No weapons were visible on her horse, just a large sack with something bulky inside tied to the pommel.

The man peered at the three Federal soldiers and put his hand on the butt of the shotgun. "What's this, Lieutenant?" he asked in a Mississippi drawl. "The deal was only you. Me and my woman are risking getting our necks stretched for you. I don't cotton to sudden changes in the plan."

"Good to see you, too," replied Bierce in a jovial voice. "Don't worry about Captain Clay and Sergeant Lot, here. They're just along to see if they can prove I murdered an officer back in Grant's camp. They can be trusted."

The man and the woman started at the casual statement, as did Lot. Clay only looked speculatively at Bierce, as if he were an algebraic equation to be solved.

With undisguised distaste, the woman discriminately ogled

Lot, then said to the man, "Amos, don't fret. They've got a nigger in uniform. Cain't see as how the Confederates would try to set us up using a darkie."

Bierce leaned toward Clay and Lot. "Gentlemen, you may put your firearms away. This is Amos and Amelia Shea, very valuable sources of information. Mr. and Mrs. Shea, may I present Captain Alphonso Clay, late of New Orleans, and his dusky subordinate, Sergeant Jeremiah Lot. I would suggest you avoid the colloquial for a darkie when addressing the sergeant. They have both shown a tendency to take offense at the phrase." Bierce directed his next explanation to Clay. "They live on a farm near the outskirts of Vicksburg and are extremely well-placed to know what is going on with the Confederates on both sides of the river, especially since their sideline of horse trading gives them a legitimate reason to roam all over this neck of the South."

"Never was much money in trading horses hereabouts, and there's even less now, what with Pemberton requisitioning every horse in sight and giving that worthless paper in exchange," said Amos Shea sourly. "Which brings me to the point, Lieutenant. You got the gold?"

"I do indeed, my mercenary patriot," replied Bierce, putting away his notebook and reaching into his tunic pocket. "Five bright, shiny coins, as a reward in advance from a grateful Abe Lincoln for loyal services rendered to the Republic." Bierce trotted his horse over alongside the man and carefully dropped the coins one at a time into an outstretched hand. "Now my good man, what have you to tell me?"

"Well, we hear a lot, from both sides of the river. Truth to tell, we don't see much with our own eyes and would probably be caught if we tried. But folks, hereabouts, hear all kinds of things and talk about those things, and we both listen real good. They say General Pemberton has about twenty thousand men inside

Vicksburg, with another ten thousand or so scattered around Western Mississippi, from Vicksburg to Jackson.

"This side, they say General Kirby Smith has about fifteen thousand in Western Arkansas, but he's so scared of what Grant will do, he won't go east of Little Rock, no matter how much Jeff Davis screams for him to help Pemberton.

"Hereabouts, there's just an undersized regiment or two here and there—and some bushwhackers. The only thing to really worry about is Chief Stand Watie and his three thousand or so Injuns. They say he's been raising hell generally in Northwestern Louisiana, and though he's supposed to be remindin' the scrubs where their loyalties lie, they say his braves aren't too particular about whether a farmer supports Lincoln or Davis. Red devils have really been having a grand time, and ain't nothin' the Federals can do. They can cross three counties in the time it takes a blue trooper to saddle a horse."

Clay interrupted, an unearthly light in his eyes. "So, the Indian irregulars roam widely. Do you think they could have patrols in this area?"

Amos Shea rubbed his chin thoughtfully. "It don't seem likely. Any idiot who says he don't think there can be an Injun in the neighborhood runs a chance of bein' parted from his hair."

Bierce said, "You are a puzzling man, Captain. The Indians are only a threat to farmers and women. They run at the sight of a blue uniform and showed that clearly enough last year at the battle of Elkhorn Tavern."

Clay replied, "They may run most of the time, Lieutenant, but I would put it to you, an officer who counts on them always running, will come to grief and may not live to profit from the experience. I would advise you to never underestimate an enemy, even if you feel he is inferior to you: perhaps, *especially* if you feel he is inferior to you."

"I will try to keep that in mind, Captain." Bierce adjusted his mount to address the Sheas. "You rode up from crossing the river at Grand Gulf. Any changes in the dispositions from what you told me the last time we met?"

Amelia Shea spoke up, "Naw, Lieutenant, there be only an undersized regiment at Grand Gulf, guarding the eastern side of the ferry crossing. On the western side, all we could see was a single company, near eighty men, guarding the ferry landing. Between here and there, near thirty miles, didn't see nothin' 'cept a farmer and two drovers. Maybe we missed a cavalry patrol or two—can never be sure if they stay off the main road, and maybe one or two of Watie's scouts, but no more than that."

"And the condition of the road?" asked Bierce.

Amos Shea shrugged. "Pretty much what you see here. Wet and muddy, and likely to stay that way clean through August. Not easy for single horsemen; bad for a wagon or two; out of the question for a lot of wagons."

"Thank you; you've been a great help to your country. We will ride back with you to the crossing. I need to survey the ground myself, now that you tell me there is no real danger of running into Rebel troops."

Amos Shea instantly became uneasy. "Now, Lieutenant, I didn't say there was no danger. Lots of folks, hereabouts, who didn't join up, still don't like the sight of a Federal. Some of the farmers you pass, lookin' all peaceable-like, have been spendin' afternoons and evenings bushwhackin'. If you and your friends ride south with us, you're headin' into more trouble than you bargained for. Why hardly a week goes by there ain't a Union picket or cavalryman killed from ambush, and I never hear of the poor soul's friends finding out who pulled the trigger, no matter how much they beat the bushes. Better if we part here, and you and your friends go back direct."

Bierce took the information in stride. "I do appreciate your concern for Federal officers in the performance of their duties, but I still need to see the route. There's matters of elevations and lines-of-sight you are simply not trained to evaluate. Why, we can all do it at the trot—shouldn't take more than three to four hours each way—and my colleagues and I can be back in Grant's camp before dark."

"It's your funeral," said the Mississippian. "If you aim to be back before dark, we better ride."

With no further ado, the oddly assorted party set out to the south at a brisk pace. As the miles slipped by, Bierce would now and then pull out his large notebook and make cryptic markings in it, not even slowing his horse's pace. He had much to write; the road was every bit as poor as had been described. And every time they passed a stand of second-growth timber, Bierce made a notation, apparently interested in sources of logs and branches for corduroying a road. Only rarely did they spy a human figure, always a hardscrabble farmer in some distant field who did not notice nor care that three of the five riders wore the uniform of the Federal Army.

Hours passed, with Bierce and the Sheas taking the lead, Lot behind them, and Clay bringing up the rear. At times, you could catch a murmur between Bierce and Amos Shea, but the others were inclined to keep to themselves.

After more than twenty miles of bad road, Amelia Shea dropped back, leaving her husband and Bierce in the lead. She said nothing to Lot as the sergeant overtook her, merely sparing him a look of disdain, but took up position to the right of Clay's wheezing old nag. "What was all that about, Bierce saying you thought he killed some officer?"

Clay replied without bothering to acknowledge the woman. "Lieutenant Bierce has a peculiar sense of humor."

"But someone thinks he might 'a killed someone?"

"He had the misfortune to be found standing over the body of Lieutenant John Brown. He says he found Brown shot to death. We shall see."

"Funny thing about names," said Amelia lightheartedly. "I know I shouldn't find anybody's death funny, but imagine a Yankee officer with the name John Brown, just like that crazy feller they hanged in Virginia. But I reckon there are plenty 'a fellers with that name. Why, that policeman who caught them bastard child-killers back east had the same name."

Emotionlessly, Clay stated, "The Lieutenant Brown who was murdered is the same as the brave man who destroyed the Starry Wisdom cult."

Amelia Shea jerked with surprise, causing her horse to toss its head. "You're shittin' me!"

"I presume your colorful phrase means you doubt my word. Sadly, it is true. Mrs. Shea, you do surprise me. I did not expect someone of your background to have followed his doings in Rhode Island."

Amelia bristled at Clay's implications, pulling back her shoulders. "I got my letters and follow the papers when I can get 'em. Ain't my fault Pappy ran away and Ma couldn't afford to send me to school. I'm right proud I learned readin' and cipherin' with only a little help from the parson. I'm better at it than Amos, that's for sure, and he's right proud of that."

"Perhaps he should be," said Clay in an indifferent voice.

They rode on awkwardly until Amelia attempted to breach the chasm. "You don't sound like no Yankee captain. That's Kentucky in your voice, ain't it? Crazy to hear a Southern voice comin' from a blue uniform."

Clay cocked his head, sizing the woman up and down. Some might have thought it prurient, but Amelia Shea was perceptive enough to realize she was being appraised as a person, not a woman, and had been found wanting. "Yes, I hail from Kentucky." It was remarkable how such a banal statement could be so charged with distaste.

"Never understood why Kentucky stayed in the Union, what with all the slaves and such," Amelia said, feeding the conversation. "Your people own slaves?"

"Yes, my father owned twenty-three servants." Clay's eyes were fixed straight ahead on Lot's back.

"Then your pappy must've been pro-South."

As Clay cut his eyes at her, a coldness touched her bones. He looked forward before responding. "My father was a Clay, a cousin to Henry Clay himself. Our family helped build the western part of this country. My father served in Mexico and was wounded at Buena Vista. He took the oath to defend this country against all its enemies. The issue of how he felt on slavery is irrelevant. Clays do not go back on their oaths, and they did not help to build this republic only to tear it down."

"Is your father proud about you fighting to preserve the Union?"

"My father is dead," responded Clay curtly, and then he spurred his horse forward until he was riding alongside Lot.

Amelia Shea blushed red. An attractive woman, she was not used to men snubbing her and felt a growing anger toward the slightly built captain, mixed with a curious interest.

Suddenly her husband raised a hand, signaling a stop. They all gathered where he sat on his horse on a slight rise. About a mile away, they could see a cluster of buildings and a small ferry tied up at a rickety wharf; a passel of tiny figures that may or may not have been soldiers bustled about. Across the wide Mississippi, they could see on the far bank an assortment of buildings pretentiously named Grand Gulf.

"Okay, this is where we part," said Amos Shea. "Any closer and they are sure to see you as Federals. When do we meet again, Lieutenant?"

"I will get word to you through our friend in Vicksburg when I need you again. Stay safe, Mr. Shea, Mrs. Shea. You're too valuable to the Republic to see the business end of a rope."

"And you three hurry back to where you came from, 'lessen you want to be crammed into Libby Prison in Richmond," said Amos Shea, referring to the converted tobacco warehouses where Union prisoners were known to be kept in unbelievable squalor.

With that, the Sheas urged their horses into a trot, and the three Federals pivoted their horses and began the long ride back to Grant's encampment.

They had been on the road for about an hour when a tree branch under which Clay was passing snapped and fell to the ground. At the same time, the sharp crack of a rifle report echoed, startling the horses of all three riders. As the shot came from behind, none hesitated. but spurred their mounts into a furious gallop. Riding wildly down the muddy trail, clods slinging helter-skelter from the horses' hooves, each expected to feel the sickening impact of a bullet at any moment, although in their hearts, each rider had somewhat different emotions concerning that expectation. But there were no further shots, and after half an hour, they slowed to a trot, trying to conserve the strength of their horses, but prudence dictated they go no slower, as they had no idea what kind of pursuit, if any, their unknown assailants were making. Because of the accelerated pace, they reached Grant's lines long before dark and had experienced no trouble with the pickets.

The trio rode straight to Grant's tent, horses lathered and near to dropping. Under a nearby tree, they could see the cross-eyed Julia Grant seated on a camp chair, reading aloud to young Fred Grant.

Bierce spoke to the sentry outside the tent entrance. "Private, let Colonel Rawlins know Lieutenant Bierce and company are ready to report." As the private saluted and entered the large tent, the three exhausted Federals swung off their even more exhausted mounts. The private emerged from the tent, followed by both Rawlins and Grant, the latter clutching the smoldering stump of a cigar in his right hand. Rawlins, white as a sheet, was thankfully and unusually relieved to see them, but Grant spent a moment studying the horses with blatant disdain toward the new arrivals.

"Thank the Lord you are back early! The General has decided on a course of action and only wishes some confirmation from your scouting before issuing the necessary orders," said Rawlins.

"You better have a doggone good reason for having treated those horses that way," said Grant ominously.

Clay stared at the general with unconcealed curiosity, finding Grant's anger at the perceived abuse of the animals astonishing.

Bierce moved to defuse the tension. "General, sir, we had the pleasure and the glory of nearly being killed by ambush this afternoon in the service of our country. Ordinarily, we would have put the health of these noble steeds above our own survival, but we were aware the Army of the Tennessee waited for our report with breathless anticipation."

Grant studied Bierce for a long moment, taking a pull on his cigar, slowly expelling the smoke. "It's lucky you are darn good at what you do, Lieutenant." He spit a piece of tobacco and pointed the cigar at him. "Someday that sharp tongue of yours will be the death of you. Now, I've pretty much decided what I'm going to do, but I would sure like to hear what you saw today before I give the final orders. All of you, come in here."

Grant led them into his command tent. Despite its large size, it was quite crowded. Standing around a folding table cluttered with maps were Generals Sherman, McPherson, McClernand, Major Parker, and a young, heavily-bearded naval officer, who Grant introduced to the newcomers. "Captain Clay, Lieutenant Bierce, Sergeant Lot, this is Commodore David Porter. He's in charge of the ironclads and commercial ships we're leasing from upriver. What I have in mind won't work unless Commodore Porter can hold up his end."

"Grant, I'm begging you, don't do this," interrupted Sherman, his hard eyes radiating with wildness. "Let's go upriver to Memphis and start overland on the east bank of the river. Yes, I know Forrest will play hell with our supply lines, and I know it's the obvious move, and Pemberton will be waiting for us, but this war won't end until we kill every Rebel who feels like bearing arms, and we might as well do that killing on our way to Vicksburg as anywhere else."

"Here, here!" exclaimed McClernand. "Wipe the traitors out, I say. Resettle with good, loyal stock from the East and Midwest. Hell, bring in Micks and Dutchmen from overseas."

Clay noted, although McPherson looked upon McClernand with distaste, he said nothing. Recalling Grant had promoted the engineer rapidly, Clay wondered if it had been so fast the officer lacked the confidence to take on his elders when they were wrong.

"Gentlemen, I am fully prepared to do whatever it takes to preserve the Union," said Grant meekly. "At the same time, I've seen enough death already to last a lifetime, more than a lifetime. I want to win this war with few casualties to our people, and as few as are necessary to the enemy. Remember, nice as it sounds, we are not going to depopulate the South. These are our fellow citizens; that's what this war is about. Now, Lieutenant Bierce, tell me what you saw today."

Placing his hastily sketched drawings on the table, Bierce gave a swift, accurate and succinct summary of what they had seen, pointing out key features on the maps. Grant intermittently asked for confirming details from Clay and Lot.

As Bierce finished his presentation, Clay admitted to himself he would have to revise his opinion of Bierce, upward, yet again. He'd been dragged, without warning, into a high-level war council, with officers far superior in rank, yet he had conducted himself with coolness and professionalism. *Of course*, thought Clay, *such self-possession would make him a perfect traitor and murderer.*

"Gentlemen, it's about what I expected," said Grant when Bierce had finished. The general paused to light a new cigar, then asked, "What do you think, McPherson?"

"It's what I feared from the beginning," replied the commander of the 17th Corps. "We won't be able to move the army at all until we have corduroyed the road. Even then, just sending the army down it once with wagons and cannon will tear it up so it won't be useable to anything but the lightest kind of traffic for months to come. There will be no possibility of supplying the army along that road."

"I guess it won't be necessary. Commodore Porter, after our private talk of last week, have you examined the matter we discussed?"

The commodore ground his teeth, eyes darting to the various generals in the tent. For some odd reason, he gave Clay the impression of the "lean and hungry" Cassius in Shakespeare's *Julius Caesar*. "I believe it can be done, if the night is dark, and we have reasonable luck."

"What can be done?" sternly asked McPherson, who was apparently not in on the secret.

"Running a fleet of warships downriver past Vicksburg," replied Porter gruffly.

"Yep," said Grant. "This is what we are going to do. McPherson's boys will drop everything they are doing and corduroy the road down to the ferry crossing at Grand Gulf. With the whole 17th Corps pitching in, it should only take a couple of days. Then we'll leave only a skeleton force to hold this camp; everyone else marches down to the ferry crossing, where we will cross the Mississippi and march up to Vicksburg *from the south*. Using five ironclad gunboats as escorts, for about eight requisitioned transports carrying supplies, we will run right past Vicksburg and its cannon. The gunboats will protect the transports as they ferry the army across the river. The land beyond the east bank of the river is flat and dry, and there aren't any good defensive positions for Pemberton short of Vicksburg itself."

"I must warn everyone, there will be no going back," said Porter solemnly. "Even at night, this will only work because of the element of surprise, combined with the fact that we will be adding the speed of the current to the speed of our engines. We should be blowing past Vicksburg at close to twelve knots, which will make the ships harder to hit, and keep them in range a shorter period. Yet, you do realize, fighting the current upstream, we would be lucky to make four knots. The Vicksburg batteries would be ready and waiting and have three times as long to shoot at slower moving targets. To try to bring the fleet back upriver would be a massacre."

"Damnit, Sam, you can't be serious!" exclaimed Sherman. "Maybe the gunboats have a chance, what with the iron plate armor, but one shell through one of those riverboats would surely blow it to hell!"

Porter explained to Sherman, "General, all the ships will have barges lashed to their port sides, facing the Vicksburg batteries, loaded with bulky supplies: coal, fodder for the horses, things of that nature. Not only will the barges carry much of the necessities of the army downriver, but they will absorb many shots that would otherwise hit the ships themselves."

"Sam, I know military theory and logistics," said Sherman to Grant. "Yes, the boats may be able to run one big load of supplies past Vicksburg, but we will have no line of supplies after that. And even a dozen barges of supplies are nowhere near enough to keep the army going until we are able to get up to Vicksburg and capture it, or at least Chickasaw Bluffs just north of it, and re-establish a river supply line with Memphis."

Grant took a pull on his cigar, a calm satisfaction on his face. "Gentlemen, I'm not concerned with our lines of supply because I intend to have none."

Everyone else in the tent was instantaneously shocked except for Rawlins and Parker, who must have been in on the commanding general's planning.

McClernand's dark eyes narrowed. "Grant, have you lost your mind? All the books say you must protect your lines of communication."

Grant favored the group with a slight upward turn of the lips. "Certainly, the books *Pemberton* reads. We will live off the land, take what we need from the good people of Mississippi—cattle, poultry, hay, whatever we need. The only things we will take with us are the things we will not be able to find in the countryside— ammunition, hardtack, medicine, and the like. It'll be hard on the people of Mississippi, but war is hard. Their elected representatives helped bring on this war. They've sown the wind and will reap the whirlwind. Pemberton will spend his time trying to cut my lines of supply, unaware I have none to cut. By the time he realizes that, our army will be at Vicksburg."

An appalled Sherman stated, "Sam, you do realize, even if we live off the civilians, the army will die if it can't keep moving. Thirty thousand men and their animals will eat out the most bountiful district in nothing flat."

"Then, we will just have to keep moving until we get to Vicksburg. General McPherson, put your entire corps into improving the road; drop everything else. General McClernand, Cump, do everything to have your boys ready. The night after next, Porter is going to make the run past Vicksburg. After that, everyone is in motion until this campaign is at an end."

All but two of the people in the tent showed various degrees of unease. Clay was one of the two exceptions, as he appraised Grant with much interest. The other exception was Grant himself, who calmly puffed on his cigar, staring through the smoke as if he saw something interesting in the distance.

Dusk had fallen, the night moonless and overcast, perfect for what the Union forces were about to do. Soldiers scurried about the poorly-lit, rickety wharves at the Young's Point docks, making last-minute checks on the cables that lashed heavily-loaded barges to the sides of the ugly armored gunboats and the more elegant riverboats.

Grant, Porter, Rawlins, and Parker stood on the wharf next to a gunboat, *Benton*, Porter's flagship. Briefly, the group illuminated by the flare of a match as Grant lit a new cigar, the shadows creating faces even more strained than they were.

"Grant, sir, it's time to cast off," said Porter.

The tip of Grant's cigar flared as he took a long pull. "You know, there is no need for you to actually be on board, Commodore. *Benton* will be the first in line, and the Rebs will probably concentrate most of their fire on it, at least to start. It might be better for you to be on one of the ships further back."

There was just light enough for Porter's wide grin to be clearly visible. "Nothing on earth could keep me off the lead vessel. I swore to myself I would end this war an admiral, and this is my chance."

"Go to it, Porter!" ordered Grant proudly. "See you south of Vicksburg." The two men shook hands firmly, knowing it may be the last time. Porter bounded up the gangway to his flagship as Grant and his aids took off toward his command tent.

"Rawlins, have you checked to see about the order of march?" asked Grant.

"Yes, General. McClernand's 13th Corps will be in the lead, and Sherman's 15th behind him. McPherson's boys will keep the road in good repair, guarding the rear and flanks, and generally watching our backs."

"Parker, I know you've packed up headquarters. Is everything all right with Mrs. Grant and Fred?"

"Everything is in hand, General," said the tall, proud Indian.

"I appreciate it, Ely. I know it's not what you signed on for, taking care of my family."

"No trouble at all, sir. Mrs. Grant travels light, and the boy is no worse than rambunctious." Parker hesitated. "However, I am concerned for your sake, sir. You know Stanton has forbidden all officers to have their wives along during campaign, much less children. Should the Secretary of War find out, he could make things hot for you."

Grant took another pull on his cigar, letting the smoke out with his words. "Sometimes we bend rules a bit in the army, and Stanton is far away. I like having them near. They make the other burdens of my job bearable. Don't you worry about Stanton. If he raises a fuss, I'll tell him I ordered everyone to be quiet on the matter. When we take Vicksburg, he won't dare do anything to me." He locked eyes with the major. "Should we not succeed, perfect obedience won't save me."

As they approached the tent, three horsemen trotted out of the gloom—Clay, Lot, and Bierce reigned up their horses and saluted.

"General Grant, sir," complimented Bierce gaily, waving his open hand toward the waterfront, "a wonderfully ominous scene: powerful warships preparing for battle, thirty thousand soldiers preparing to move, and all in perfect darkness. Someday I would hope to put in writing how gothic all this played out."

"If you write it up, I'll read it," replied Grant mildly. "What brings you three up this way? I thought you would be scouting the flanks of the army as we march."

"With respect, General, there is no threat to worry about north of Vicksburg; it's only to the south my services are needed. Knowing how concerned you are with the health of horses, I would like to request permission to ride one of the transports. That way, the animals will be fresh when they are most needed. Besides, I expect the run past Vicksburg to be spectacular, and I would like to see it close to hand."

"It will also be quite dangerous, Lieutenant," warned Rawlins.

"Ah, one must die of something. And when we do, even more interesting mysteries may await." Bierce was overtly cocky for some reason, most likely selfish.

"It's your choice, Lieutenant," said Grant, a tone of disapproval creeping into his voice. "But is it the choice of Captain Clay and Sergeant Lot?"

In the darkness, Clay was hard to read—not that he was ever *easy* to read. "I have found the last few days in Lieutenant Bierce's company quite instructive. I feel much can be learned by remaining in his company. I offered the sergeant the choice of meeting us south of Vicksburg, but he, too, feels the experience will be worth the risk."

Grant's body language was visible in the darkness. "It's your funeral. Go to the riverboat right behind the *Benton*, and tell the captain I have said it is all right. We will meet in a few hours."

The three horsemen saluted and trotted off, and as they did so, they heard Grant say, "So Parker, where is Fred? I'd like him to ride with me."

Dismounting at the dock, with some difficulty, the three Federals led their reluctant mounts up the gangplank onto the riverboat *Albina*, just before the soldiers removed it and cast off the lines. They had some difficulty securing the horses behind the bales of fodder piled high on the rear deck, as no lights were permitted on this or any of the other vessels. By the time they'd safely tethered the horses and made their way, largely by feel, up to the pilothouse, the ship had taken its place behind Porter's flagship in a dark, ungainly line of vessels chugging its way down the curving Mississippi. A small bulls-eye lantern, placed on the floor, gave barely enough light for the captain and his pilot to see what they were doing. The low placement of the light cast exaggerated shadows on everyone's faces, making them unreal and ghostly.

The captain, a sour man with flowing sideburns and a clean-shaven chin, inspected the new arrivals. "So, you are the fools who wanted to come when you didn't have to. Ha! You're more than welcome! I wish you could take my place. Should've read that damn contract before I signed it back in St. Louis. I thought I was just signing my ship up to haul supplies and troops up and down the river; never dreamed of this. Told Porter to go to hell when he told me what he wanted me to do. But then he brought some damned redskin in who showed me a clause in the contract that said I was under army jurisdiction; claimed a court martial could send me to prison if I didn't go where the army said."

The weird lighting gave Clay a sinister air about him. "Sir, I have some knowledge of what the army is paying for civilian transports. Many people have risked their lives for much less, never mind the issue of patriotism."

Lot attempted to diffuse the tension. "Captain, why are we not under full power? I thought you would be going as fast as you possibly could."

"It *was* something that Porter bastard insisted upon, and I have to admit it makes sense. The faster we run the engines, the noisier they are, and the more sparks they send out the smokestacks. That makes it easier to hear and see us from further off. So, he says we go under reduced power. When we're seen, he'll hit his steam whistle, and then everyone runs the boilers for all they're worth—Oh, God!"

The boat captain's last exclamation was odd, out of place,

and got everyone's attention. The others in the pilothouse saw he was staring fixedly ahead and followed the direction of his gaze. The inky outline of the banks of the Mississippi was hardly visible, but about a mile ahead, the river made a slow turn to the right. Around the bend of the river, a constellation of lights on the eastern bank was becoming visible. It could only be one thing—Vicksburg. Vicksburg and its scores of cannons, some the monstrous Whitworths imported from England, a single shell from which could blow an unarmored ship to atoms.

The skipper's eyes darted wildly about, searching for an escape, any escape. The pilot at the wheel, scarcely less frightened in the dim light of the pilothouse, gripped the wheel fiercely, his knuckles devoid of circulation.

Yet none of the Confederates manning the batteries noticed the fleet approaching the city. No cannon opened fire, and there was no shriek of a steam-whistle from Porter's flagship. Slowly, the dark column of ships drew up to Vicksburg. Passing right by, through the open window on the left side of the pilothouse, they could hear the various sounds of a city at night—horses neighing, a woman's laugh, some man singing off-key to the accompaniment of a banjo. At first, they thought they would pass completely undetected. Then, without warning or cause, hell opened its gates.

Flashes, too numerous to count, erupted from the bluffs on which Vicksburg rested. The crashing booms of cannon reached the ears of those in the pilothouse—a single, continuous roar that physically beat on the skin. Shells cut through the air, screaming like banshees, so hard you could not distinguish them from the steam whistle of Porter's *Benton*, but the boat's captain correctly assumed Porter had given the command for full power. He screamed into the communication tube for the boiler crew to give him maximum power. The ship vibrated as the paddles picked up speed, but still, the cannon-studded bluffs of Vicksburg passed with maddening slowness. All at once, the boat shuddered, and from somewhere aft came the sound of wood being splintered with gigantic force. At the same time, through the front window, they saw a streak of fire as a solid shot struck the armor of the *Benton* and careened into the woods on the western bank of the river.

"This is suicide!" yelled the skipper to the pilot. "Hard starboard and make for the west shore! We'll ground the ship and make for the woods!"

"That is not an option, sir," said Clay in a quiet voice that, nonetheless, cut through the pandemonium. "You will throw the rest of the line into confusion, perhaps cause the vessels behind us to slow. The mission may fail, and more people will die. You must maintain your course."

Oddly, Bierce hadn't heard a word of the argument. Entranced by the total destruction of war, he was talking to himself. "Beautiful, just beautiful. See how the flashes and explosions play across the surface of the river. It's like fire on the water. Marvelous."

Even the terrified captain paused to stare at Bierce and his reaction to their situation, but his fear rapidly reasserted itself, and he spoke to the pilot. "To hell with the little pipsqueak, Jake! I'm the captain, make for the shore!"

Somehow, Clay's revolver appeared in his hand, with no noticeable movement. "Turn to the shore, and you will die at *my* hand. Stay on course, and you *may* live."

"You little turd!" screamed the skipper. "How dare you?"

"The same statement applies to you, pilot," said Clay calmly.

"Alphonso, please, this is getting out of hand, like the other time," pleaded Lot urgently.

"Beautiful," murmured Bierce, entranced by the violent spectacle outside.

"Why, Captain Clay, what is going on here?" asked a high voice. Everyone, even the mesmerized Bierce, turned to see the new arrival at the head of the stairs. Little Fred Grant skipped into the room, childish excitement on his face. "Why are you pointing a gun at them, Captain? Are they Reb spies?"

Clay lost his composure; his eyes widened, and his mouth opened, but not an utterance came forth. Finally, in a hoarse and horrified tone, he said, "Child, what in the name of God are you doing here?"

"I stowed away. Pa wouldn't let me see any of the fun, of course. I asked him if I could ride with the fleet, and he got angry with me. Imagine! He wants a general's son to hide away when the greatest battle of the war is going on. Well, I can show him I'm not scared. He'll see that—"

With a noise like the end of the world, a Whitworth shell tore through the pilothouse. For some reason, it didn't explode during its passage and went on to bury its force in the far bank of the river. Even so, during impact, deadly fragments of wood had gone careening about the pilothouse. A large jagged piece transfixed the skipper's left thigh, and he screamed like a hog being gelded. A piping-high cry went up from Fred Grant, who fell to the deck, clutching his right shin. Stunned, the pilot held on fearfully to the wheel and did not attempt to turn to the shore. He had decided for himself there was less danger in running full bore downriver, as Vicksburg was already slowly slipping behind the boat.

Clay uttered a cry—part shriek, part moan. Holstering his pistol, he dropped to the deck beside the child, uttering unintelligible noises of grief. Using a pocketknife, he cut away Fred's lower trouser leg, revealing a serious gash. He giggled with relief to see there was no arterial spurts, no sign of broken bone. Drawing out a hipflask, he doused the wound liberally with the cheap whiskey he never drank, keeping it only for disinfecting purposes he had learned about while in Europe. He bound the wound tightly with a clean handkerchief, then told the lad, "This will hold you until we can get you to a proper doctor, you fool."

Having regained his composure, he noticed the hellish noise was much diminished and getting fainter every moment. They were out of the range of danger! He looked around the damaged pilothouse, to see Lot in the process of carefully extracting the splinter from the moaning skipper. Wordlessly, Clay passed his friend the flask so he could disinfect the man's more serious wound.

Fred was over his fright and was now excited. "My pa is going to be so proud. Imagine, only ten and wounded fighting for the Union."

Clay giggled nervously, then saw Bierce watching him with the purest amusement. "My, my Clay, there *is* more to you than meets the eye."

"Kindly mind your own affairs," Clay muttered, standing up and brushing himself off.

Meanwhile, the ships had drawn up to the temporary anchorage McPherson's industrious men had prepared.

The pilot searched deeply into the gloom behind them and commented, "Looks like all but one got through. Better than anticipated. For a while, I thought none of us would make it."

Clay peered through the jagged hole on the right side of the pilothouse. "I see they have jury-rigged a gangplank. Let us get young Fred and our captain friend some real medical aide."

Fred Grant was happily moving under his own power, but the skipper had to be helped by both Lot and Bierce to the shore. There, a couple of medical orderlies put him on a stretcher to allow his easy transport to a temporary hospital tent. They clucked over his wound, but as the skipper was being carried away, he could be heard to say, "Ah, it's nothing boys, nothing. Takes more than a little flesh wound like this to slow me down. Why even after it happened, I refused to let myself give up command. I forced myself, cool as ice, to keep to the course, knowing Grant was depending on me."

Bierce and Lot laughed aloud; even Clay allowed himself a moment of amusement.

"By the time he gets home, he will have been responsible for winning the whole campaign," said Lot, and guffawed again.

In the pitch blackness, there arose a commotion as three riders approached. They resolved themselves into Grant, Parker, and Mrs. Grant, the latter riding expertly sidesaddle.

"There he is!" exclaimed Parker. "The corporal who thought he saw him sneak onto the ship was right."

With a cry, Julia Grant slipped out of her saddle and ran to her son. Going to her knees, she examined with motherly concern the bloody bandage around Fred's shin.

"It is not serious, Mrs. Grant," replied Clay calmly. "I would recommend the wound be stitched and kept clean." Then to Grant, who had leapt off his huge black horse and was hurrying to his son, "It could have been much worse, general, much worse. It is inexcusable for you to keep your family with an army in the field. Inexcusable! You must send them away now. I insist on it!"

Grant ignored the insubordinate outburst and went to his son, hugging him fiercely.

"You proud of me, Pa? I got wounded for Union. It was great!"

Even in the dim light from the scattered lanterns, those nearby could see the glistening of tears in the general's eyes. "Yes, Fred, yes, I am very proud of you. Very proud. And now I have another duty for you. I need you to help guard your mother as she goes back to St. Louis. Major Parker will take you both to the old camp and put you on the steamer to St. Louis. There may be spies there, and in St. Louis. I want you to stay very close to her and protect her for me. Can you do that, son?" Grant's admiration for his wife was self-evident as he glanced over to see how tears rolled freely down her cheeks.

"Why sure, Pa. I'll keep an eye peeled. No dirty, old Rebel spy will get near Ma while I'm around."

"Thank you, my brave young soldier," said Grant in a tight voice. He led his son over to his wife, shared a few words with her, and then, without hesitation, kissed her passionately. Wordlessly, he nodded to Parker, who mounted his horse, then reached down and effortlessly swung Fred up into the saddle in front of him. Mrs. Grant smoothly mounted her own steed. General Grant watched them fade into the night that was slowly beginning to lighten; sunrise was not far off.

After they had gone, Grant walked over to Clay, drew out a cigar, and lit it with careful deliberation. He inhaled, pondering, staring across the water. "Captain, I will forget the deliberate insubordination with which you just addressed me. I will forget it because the fundamental fault is mine. For personal, even selfish reasons, I brought those I love into danger. It was wrong, and if the way you reminded me of my impropriety was impertinent, the sentiment was not. Now Clay, Lieutenant Bierce, Sergeant Lot, I suggest you retrieve your horses and commence your scouting."

Bierce, outright surprised, asked incredulously if not respectfully, "Now sir, with no rest?"

Grant took another pull on his cigar. "You're alert enough to me. Wait until you are ready to drop; then rest. There will not be much rest for any of us short of Vicksburg now."

"What if we don't reach Vicksburg quickly?" asked Bierce.

"Then the army will be destroyed, and the Union will die," replied Grant. He took another pull on his cigar, enjoying it in the wake of chaos.

CHAPTER FIVE

IN MOTION IN ALL DIRECTIONS

Seated on an empty army cracker box, Alphonso Clay made a further notation in a blank page at the end of John Brown's notebook. He carefully restored his pencil to the inner pocket of his tunic, removed his spectacles, and rubbed his eyes tiredly. He had been pouring over the notebook for the hundredth time, trying to tease some clue out of Brown's cryptic, near illegible scrawl, with only the flickering light of the small campfire. He restored his eyeglasses and peered up at the clear sky, where the stars were beginning to retreat before the early hints of sunrise. Searching his soul, he felt nothing at the sight of the starry void overhead except a distant intellectual curiosity, which saddened him deeply in a dispassionate way. He recalled a time, not so long ago, when he could spend hours staring at the awesome majesty of the night sky, thrilled and humbled at the contemplation of the great mysteries hinted at by the tiny lights above. Of course, that was before . . .

Urgently, he drew out his pocket watch, opened it, and stared fixedly as the second hand ticked around for over a minute before gently closing it and returning it to his pocket. Glancing in their direction, he was glad Bierce and Lot could sleep. Despite the odd rustles, muttered curses, and occasional neighing of horses from all sides, an army is never truly silent. For a moment, his eyes glistened, and, for very different reasons, he wished neither of them to see that. A Clay must be composed at all times. Allowing himself a soft sigh, he went back to the notes he'd made over the past week.

Those notes were precious few. Brown had repeatedly jotted, "Who benefits, and what is the benefit?" Clay found this puzzling. Of course, the Confederacy would benefit from treason. What a stupid question upon which to obsess! Yet, Clay knew John Brown had not been a stupid man. Another comment read, "Bierce— cavalrymen shot—connection?" This was a most significant piece of evidence to Clay who would have paid gold to see Ambrose Bierce hang. He discounted the fact Bierce claimed never to have met Brown; even after repeated questioning of everyone familiar with the two, he failed to come up with a single instance in which they had even been present in the same group, but that might merely be proof of Bierce's deviousness.

Of course, Brown could have known Bierce, but not vice-versa; a good policeman could become expert at shadowing a subject without the subject's knowledge. One entry read, "Viewed cavalry body—no money!" Try as he may, Clay could not assign a clear meaning to that jotting, yet it was pertinent, as Brown was sparing in his use of exclamation points. The next entry was, "Moccasins— Indian?" This made more sense, confirming what Clay had seen at the spot where Brown's assassin had stood. Then on the last page, marking the end of John Brown's life, there were only two entries; if the writing was unusually clear, the meaning was not: "Scout Vicksburg March 13th!" and "Small boots!!!!" The series of exclamation marks were apparently the last products of John Brown's thoughts.

Discordant bugles sounded, and various regiments began

to rouse themselves. Grant was insistent everyone be on the move before sunrise. Speed. Speed above everything was what Grant demanded.

The Confederates, dazed by the brazen passage of an entire fleet past Vicksburg, concentrated what forces they had at the town of Grand Gulf, on the east bank of the Mississippi. It was the logical move. Grand Gulf was the only town for fifty miles south of Vicksburg with wharves and facilities able to handle the supplies necessary to support an army of thirty thousand. In spite of this, Grant had marched his army south of Grand Gulf and had Porter's ships ferry his army across at the insignificant hamlet of Bruinsburg. The moment the men were across, along with the field artillery and a few wagons filled to bursting with ammunition, salt, medicine, and not much else, Grant started driving his men, not north to Vicksburg, but east toward the state capital of Jackson, a suicidal goal for an army without a secure supply line, deep in enemy territory. The forces were ordered to travel so light, there were tents only for Grant himself and his three corps commanders. Sherman had impulsively thrown his own tent in the river, determined to sleep on the ground like his men until the campaign was over.

The two figures wrapped in blankets near the fire began to stir. Lot jolted upright, a wild fear in his eyes, before he could adjust to his surroundings. Only Clay knew what his friend had dreamed.

Bierce stretched and yawned in an elaborate manner, looking around in an alert way that belied his yawn. "Ah, a surprisingly restful night," said the lieutenant sleepily. "And I thought I'd been spoiled by all those luxurious evenings aboard the riverboat, disturbed by only a killing every now and then. When Grant said we would have no tents, I anticipated some miserable nights."

"Mississippi in April," commented Clay. "I don't imagine your home in Indiana has springs where it is comfortable to sleep outdoors. Just wait for summer. The Deep South will have an unpleasant surprise for those not raised in its extreme climate."

"I've read England pays its diplomats in Washington extra because summers there are considered a hardship assignment," added Lot. "And Washington is considerably north of where we are now. Breakfast, Captain? Lieutenant?"

"God no, Sergeant Samb—I mean Sergeant Lot." Bierce was unaffected by Clay's cold stare—both perfectly aware the mistake had been no mistake. "Give the stomach a chance to adjust. Also, it's best to get my orders from Rawlins first thing. He is busy in the best of times. You need not be a fortune-teller to guess he'll want me far out front. Pity for you, Captain. There is an excellent chance you will never see me again, at least if the CSA is lucky and I am not." He shook his army-issued blanket and started rolling it in anticipation of a day without an escort.

"Oh, I think *I will* accompany you this morning. I find observing your scouting techniques quite educational."

Bierce's face drooped, and he stopped moving. "See here, it may not be my business what you do with your life, but there is considerable danger in what I do."

"I am touched by your concern of my well-being, sir."

"Damn you! I do not care whether you live or die, but if a sniper kills you, and I come back alone, I know what will be thought! Without saying a word, you'd give headquarters the impression I had something to do with Brown's death! Admit it; that's what you think."

Clay pondered and filed Bierce's words before speaking. "I have not yet made up my mind. In any event, I will be coming with you."

"That's fine; you are the captain, sir. Let us see Rawlins." Bierce brushed off his uniform and ran his hand through his scraggly curls, preparing to leave.

"One moment." Clay led Lot just out of earshot and then said, "I don't want you on this patrol."

"I'm not afraid of going out in front."

"I never thought you to be. I want you to talk to all the staffers and any aides that might have been on Sherman's command boat the night Brown died."

"But you talked to them yourself already."

"True. But you are as intelligent as I, and sometimes you see things in original ways, ways that would not occur to me. Carefully question them again, and take good notes. We will discuss the results when I return." Clay stepped back, then said in a louder voice, "Dismissed, Sergeant!" Approaching Bierce, he said, "Alright, let us see Colonel Rawlins."

It was easy to find Grant's tent, even in the predawn light, as it was the only one for half a mile. Grant stood near the campfire outside the tent's entrance, facing his three corps commanders; Rawlins and Parker stood respectfully behind Grant. Clay and Bierce approached, saluted smartly, and waited for their superiors to acknowledge their existence.

". . . so I can't emphasize the need for speed enough, General McClernand," said Ulysses Grant. "Your corps must drive with all dispatch on the town of Port Gibson. Cavalry patrols report only a brigade or two there, so you should sweep over them."

Sporting a grim visage, McClernand looked nervous—in conferences, he breathed fire, but when faced with actual battle, he showed a certain agitation. "Ah, Grant, don't you think it's best I bring up a couple of batteries, soften up Port Gibson, and shell 'em to hell? While that's happening, I can round up stragglers, get the men better organized, and scout out all the ground. That's the ticket! You should listen to me; I'm next in line for command if anything happens to you!"

"There is no time for that." Grant was cold as ice. "By all means, try to bring up all the cannon you can with your units, but don't wait for them. Double-team what batteries you can to keep up with the advance troops, and leave the rest behind. Pemberton is probably sending everything within reach to Port Gibson. If we can get stronger with a pause, so can they. General McClernand, see to your corps. You are dismissed."

You could almost see the steam spewing from McClernand's ears as he barely saluted and stomped away.

When he was out of earshot, Grant said to Sherman, "Cump, I want you on McClernand's left, between him and Vicksburg. He has absolutely no military ability and would never have been given a general's commission if he wasn't an important Illinois Democrat. Taking Port Gibson will be easy enough; his division commanders will be able to handle anything the few Rebs in town can throw at him. My concern is what Pemberton will do if he decides to bring his whole army out of Vicksburg. You and your corps are the best I have. Keep in touch with McClernand, but always be feeling for Pemberton. You can kill two birds with one stone by having your men spread out to take what we need to the left of Port Gibson.

"Seize whatever wagons and horses you find, load them up with whatever grain and meat you see, and have your boys herd back to their regiments any living cattle and pigs they find to be slaughtered in the evenings.

"McPherson, you will be on McClernand's right. Do the same foraging. You can do more since there'll be less of a Confederate threat coming from that direction. Make sure all foraging parties are under the direct command of experienced field officers. I only want material the army can use, and I will not tolerate this descending into random pillaging. Court-martial anyone who offers unprovoked violence to civilians.

"I've ordered General Ord to make a demonstration at Chickasaw Bluffs, so some of Pemberton's men will be tied up down there. And I've told Colonel Grierson to take a thousand cavalry from

Tennessee to Louisiana, burning bridges and cutting telegraph wires all the way. This should keep Pemberton so confused he won't dare concentrate all his forces against the main body."

This disturbed McPherson. "Even if we don't molest the civilians, it's going to be a hard year with their livestock and food gone. I mean no disrespect when I say, I *am* distressed by this."

"No choice, McPherson," said Sherman impatiently. "We didn't ask for this war. The South seceded, the South fired the first shots at Sumter, and the South seized all Federal property and installations within its borders. I was running a small college down in Baton Rouge when secession started, and I remember how all the whites were enthusiastic for war, saying how glorious it was all going to be. Well, now they have war: war stomping into their parlors, muddy boots and all. You're a good man and a good general, McPherson. If something happens to Grant or me, you'll be the one to carry on. But never forget, our profession is necessary but terrible. War is absolute hell—organized murder—and it's merciful to leave these people their lives."

"Gentlemen," said Grant, looking directly at each man, "you have your orders. Dismissed." As the two corps commanders made their way to their waiting horses, Grant drew out a cigar, bit off the end, and busied himself with lighting it. After thoughtfully expelling his first puff, he said to the four remaining officers. "Major Parker, see to it headquarters is packed up and ready to move. I want to stay close to where McClernand is operating—to make sure he doesn't stop to crow after taking Port Gibson. I want him to drive without pause on to Jackson."

"You're not worried about Generals Sherman and McPherson?" asked Parker.

"Of course, I worry about them! I worry about every doggone man in this army!" Grant pushed his jacket aside and put his hand on his hip, his cigar poised between the fingers of his other hand, pointing at Parker. "But they are good and won't need me in an emergency nearly as much as that—as McClernand.

"Rawlins, I want you to make sure cavalry patrols are covering all the roads on our flanks. I want you to personally debrief each patrol, and then combine their reports into a single picture for me. I was surprised once by an unexpected Reb army; I'm not going to be surprised again."

Parker saluted and moved away, preparing to break camp.

Grant paused moodily. Anyone could tell, for a moment, he was back at the bloody fields of Shiloh, where the Rebel army had seemingly come out of nowhere. He shook his head as if to dispel some thought, then tilted it to Clay and Bierce. "And so, Lieutenant Bierce, Rawlins told me he wants you out making maps of the roads between Port Gibson and Jackson."

"Yes, sir," Bierce replied with great respect. "There will be cavalry and foraging parties well in advance of the main body, but Lord knows they don't know how to make a map or tell a mapmaker enough detail for a usable product."

Clay was puzzled. "Is it really so necessary to rely on such people as Lieutenant Bierce? Would it not be more efficient to acquire commercial maps of the areas?"

"You would think so, Captain," replied Grant in a disgusted tone of voice, "but they're about worthless for an army on the move. Oh, the main roads and towns are marked accurately enough, but they fail to show creeks and streams that would impede an army's movement, indicate side roads where none exist, or vice-versa, and have next to nothing to say about how rough or broken the terrain is.

"Lieutenant Bierce, your maps have always been accurate. I realize you undergo considerable risk in scouting out ahead of the army to do this. Our country owes you a great debt." Taking a long pull on his cigar, Grant looked away, as it pained him to compliment the uncouth lieutenant.

"Why thank you, sir," said Bierce breezily, bowing his head slightly. "And with your permission, I believe Captain Clay and myself should be on our way. If the army is going to move as fast as you say, I'll need to move even faster if I'm to have maps to you in time to be useful."

Grant positioned himself in front of Clay, asking, "And Captain Clay will accompany you?"

Bierce lifted his shoulders with indifference. "It's his funeral."

Grant stared for a long moment at Clay, trying to feel him out. "Captain, you have a peculiar way of investigating Lieutenant Brown's death."

Clay was nonplussed. "It was a peculiar death, sir."

Grant's eyes never left Clays, reminding Clay someone had once said, 'General Grant can be silent in seven languages.'

"Captain, I never liked it when my superiors didn't trust me to know my own business," said the general, honestly. "I guess you may be the best judge of yours. Get about it."

Clay and Bierce paused at the steep banks of a stream where the rutted road made a steep plunge down to the water, only to show itself again fifty yards later to make an equally steep climb up the opposite bank. Both officers could benefit from a rest. Although it was only the first of May, the noonday Mississippi sun made riders and horses sweaty and uncomfortable.

They could hear dull booms from far behind them to their right. Port Gibson was more than ten miles away, but the stagnant air let the discharge of cannon be heard over incredible distances.

Bierce stared fiercely at the stream before them, then, uttering a vile curse, opened his map folio and began to sketch with sharp, angry strokes.

"Grant isn't a complete fool, you know," Bierce commented to Clay as he sketched. "This is exactly what he was talking about this morning. The cursed maps of Mississippi they sent me from St. Louis are supposed to be the best you can buy, yet they show no sign of this stream."

"I can see the cause for your anger. This stream is not going to be much of a barrier for a few men on foot or horseback, but it could significantly delay an army of thirty thousand especially when encumbered with wagons and cannon."

"Damn right, Clay! Well, at least I will be able to warn Grant. He plans, I'll give him that. There's a special bridging regiment in McPherson's Corps that can throw up bridges faster than you would ever imagine. The delay will be minimal, as long as they know where they will have to work." Bierce made some annotations on the page, closed the folio, and restored it to his saddlebag.

Several more booms far to their rear were audible.

"Sounds like the Confederates are putting up some resistance at Port Gibson," commented Clay.

"It won't last long," Bierce snorted. "They can't possibly have enough men there to defeat McClernand, no matter how incompetent he may be. But that's the Rebs for you; they fight even when there is no chance of victory."

"Seems you admire them."

Bierce set forth a sharp, unlovely laugh. "Admire them? They are romantic fools, sir. What is to admire in a fool going foolishly to his death?"

Clay made a stance just to see his reaction. "Traitors they may be; death they deserve. Yet somehow, the willingness to die for a cause, even a bad one, is deserving of some respect."

"Why Captain Clay, you should be careful. You are in danger of becoming a romantic."

Instead of answering Bierce, Clay pointed with his gaze. "Do you see those figures on the far side of the stream? There, where the road comes out of that stand of trees?"

Bierce's eyes followed the direction Clay indicated. "Will you look at that! Ten, no twelve Union cavalrymen, with two civilians on horseback, and another two people on foot in front of them. They're leading three wagons full of supplies. It's surprising for the horse soldiers to get further out than me. Grant must have really lit a fire under their commanders. About time, too. Let's see what they can tell us of what is ahead. Hell, they may even save us some effort."

The two officers spurred their mounts down the near bank, splashed through water that reached their stirrups at its deepest point and climbed the far bank. The small column quickly pulled in the reins at the sight of the two approaching riders. The cavalrymen were wary. Despite the fact that Clay and Bierce wore blue uniforms, they held their weapons at the ready. The two figures in front, wearing tattered butternut, had their hands tied behind their back. The two civilians on horseback were more interesting; one was an angular, red-haired white man, the other a massive coal-black African, both showing the signs of a recent, terrible beating. The officers drew up their horses before the lieutenant at the end of the column, who saluted the higher-ranking Clay.

"At ease, Lieutenant," said Clay. "I am Clay of the Quartermaster Bureau, on assignment to the Army of the Tennessee. This is Lieutenant Bierce of Grant's headquarters. To whom do I have the pleasure of talking?"

The cavalry officer was skinny with a prominent Adam's apple—hardly old enough to shave. "Lieutenant Ole Nickerson, 2nd Minnesota Cavalry, sir. You are very far out in front for headquarters officers, if you don't mind me saying so. What's your business?"

"Lieutenant Bierce makes maps for the army—very good ones, I might add. I am learning from watching him in action. I take it you have been foraging."

"Yes, sir. Thought the generals were crazy when they said we would find provisions enough on the road, but damned if they weren't right—good land and good farms almost everywhere. There's more food and forage to take than we can carry." The young officer paused, worried. "Um, just isn't right to me and the boys. Yes, I know they're all traitors, hereabouts, but they're Americans. It's like we're stealing from our own people."

Clay stated factually, "Their leaders chose this war. The best we can do for these people is end the war quickly. Lieutenant, those carbines your men have are new, aren't they?"

"Ah, those." Nickerson's tone lightened a bit. "They're the new Spencer repeating rifles. We have your boss to thank for them. Old Meigs couldn't talk the fools in Ordinance into adopting it as the new standard rifle, but he pried some money out of Stanton to buy a few thousand. He's sent them out to certain selected units for "field trials" in hopes the results will make Ordinance change their hide-bound, old minds. Our regiment is one of the lucky few that got 'em."

"How do you like them?" asked Bierce.

"They're great!" exclaimed the lieutenant, with agreeing murmurs from his men. "You can see the proof in those two Johnnies there." He pointed to the surly prisoners on foot. "They're all that's left of a Reb cavalry patrol we ran into at a farm near here. There were sixteen of them and twelve of us. It was a wild minute or two, but in the end, eleven of 'em were dead or dying, and three so badly wounded we had to leave them with a farmwoman who was grief-stricken to see the boys in gray ground to dust by 'damn Yankees.' Only these two were left whole enough to take along as prisoners. All the harm we suffered was Sergeant Jeffries getting creased along the top of his hand."

"Damn fight wasn't fair," muttered the taller of the lean prisoners.

"You Goddamn Yanks got off six or seven shots for every one of ours. Never heard of any rifle that could fire like a Colt pistol. Waren't no fight at all." He spat with disgust.

Clay ignored this exchange, more interested in the massive black man on horseback who'd been beaten unmercifully—one eye was almost swollen shut, dried blood crusted his lips, and the back of his tattered shirt showed dark stains where blood had seeped through in several places. He recognized Clay and spoke to him directly, "Cap'n, it's a small world, ain't it? Bottom rail's back on bottom. I expected it to be that way."

"What happened to this man?" asked Clay in a mild voice, never taking his eyes from the Negro.

"They were prisoners of the patrol we ran into," responded Nickerson. "After the rumpus, we didn't know what to do with them and decided to take 'em back to regimental headquarters. They both need a doctor, even the white man, but not as much as the darkie."

"They beat the poor bugger near to death," said the white civilian with a noticeable Scottish burr.

"Why?" Clay demanded of the speaker.

The lanky redhead lifted his filthy palms up. He had a split lip and a shiner and held himself as if he were made of glass. "The wee lieutenant in charge of the Reb patrol was a bad man—one of them officers who only feels good when he's hurtin' somethin'. They'd already picked me up and were on the road to Vicksburg when one of his men noticed the poor sod there hiden' in some brush by the road. They figured he was a runaway, an' told him he was now goin' to Vicksburg to dig trenches before he went back to his master. He drew himself up like a man, an' said Mr. Lincoln's Proclamation meant there be slaves no more in America. The lieutenant laughed and said Mr. Lincoln could come and read the Proclamation to him in person. But until then, he was property—and insolent property at that. Then he ordered his men to teach the moor to show respect for his masters." The Scot made a face. "I mayn't have much book larnin', but I can tell the difference between respect an' fear, which was more than the little bastard could do. He laughed while his men held down the darkie and . . . Sir, I served in Her Majesty's army in the Crimea in '56 and saw how our Turkish allies treated their Russian prisoners. It was like that. A sin, sir, a sin."

"How came you by your injuries?" asked Clay quietly.

"Mon, they be nothin'. Had worse in barracks brawls on Satra'day nights."

"Mr. McFeely is modest," said the former slave. "There was no need for him to get involved, but he threw himself on the Reb officer and got in a couple of good blows before the others beat him down."

"That's your name?" asked Bierce.

"Andrew McFeely at your service, sir. Me dusky acquaintance goes by the name of Samson."

"I know," said Clay unexpectedly. "And how came you to be with these Rebels, sir? You're not in uniform."

"Me soldierin' days are over. After I saw the inside of Sevastopol in the Crimea, and what our siege had done, I was through with takin' up arms against me fellow man, especially for gilded lordlings what don't value a soldier's life more'n that of a dog. There was nothing for me in Britain, so I came to the land of promise where I heard ever' man was the equal of another." He shook his head sadly. "No doubt, I was misinformed. Was makin' a poor livin' in Vicksburg when the war broke out. Wouldn't join, no matter how the lasses and bairns would taunt me in the streets. Then Jeff Davis says there will no longer be a choice in the matter, and a conscription officer came for me. I decided to leave—to disguise meself in Jackson under a new name. There be none to care what becomes of Andrew McFeely. Twern't quite quick enough. The conscript officer turned me over to the nasty little bugger of a lieutenant from Forrest's cavalry to go back to Vicksburg, where he said I would have a choice between joinin' or hangin'. Hadn't quite decided which it would be when your friends with their bonny new guns arrived."

At the mention of "Forrest," Clay twitched, then stilled. Slowly, he pivoted his head to the two captured cavalrymen, one tall and one short, both lean, dirty, and unshaven. "Are you in service with Nathan Bedford Forrest's cavalry?"

"Yep, Billy Yank and proud of it, too," replied the taller of the prisoners. "Best damn cavalryman this side of Jeb Stuart. Ain't nothing them fools Grant or Rosecrans can do against old Forrest."

"And when were you conscripted into his service?" asked Clay, his voice controlled, but behind his spectacles, his ice-blue eyes began to glow.

"Conscripted, hell!" exclaimed the shorter of the two. "We joined, and figured ourselves lucky to get in. No one better at killin' Yanks and keepin' down the nig—"

Casually, Clay drew his revolver and shot the short prisoner through the forehead. He fell backwards, kicked once, and was dead. Clay shifted his aim to the tall prisoner, who, eyes widening, attempted to run. Clay shot him in the side, but his aim was slightly off; Clay's horse startled from the noise of the rapport. The bullet entered the Confederate but did not immediately kill him. He lay gasping on the ground, drawing up into a fetal position, crying in pain. Clay, who had regained control of his horse, trotted closer and fired a third time. The rebel shuddered and died.

There was a shocked silence; then the cavalrymen in a flurry of motion pointed carbines and revolvers at Clay, uncertain as to what had happened or how to respond. Bierce was neither shocked nor afraid, only amused, in wonderment at the captain.

"You bastard!" shouted the red-faced, furious Nickerson. "Those men were my prisoners! Their war was over! You murdered them! By God, I'll see you hang for this!"

Clay ignored the weapons pointed at him. He broke open his revolver, and, one at a time removed the three expended brass shells, replacing them with fresh bullets from a pouch at his belt. "The one drawback to the Smith & Wesson Number 2 is its small caliber," he commented to no one in particular. "A .32 caliber bullet simply will not guarantee an immediate kill unless it strikes a vital organ. I believe I will write to Messrs. Smith and Wesson and urge them to market a .44 caliber version. The heavier bullet will assure more satisfactory results." He finished reloading, closed the revolver, and carefully restored it to its holster.

"Sir, you are under arrest!" yelled Nickerson. "Give me your sword and sidearm!"

"I think not, Lieutenant," replied Clay, completely unconcerned with his fate. "Forrest and his men do not comply with the laws of war, as formulated by various German and French authorities. They have murdered loyal citizens, slaughtered freed blacks serving the Army, and seldom appear in full uniform. Although the United States has not decided officially to adopt the developing international standards on the laws of war, it, in fact, abides by them. General-in-Chief Halleck has written a book containing approved passages on these standards. Even most Confederate units follow them. Under such rules, I believe anyone serving Forrest qualifies as an 'unlawful combatant,' subject to summary execution in the field if captured. As the ranking officer present, I performed that duty."

"I don't give a damn what some Frenchie or Dutchman says! I know murder when I see it. You will surrender, or by God—"

"Ye might want to think on this, laddie," interrupted McFeely. "I'm not sayin' I ken to it, but in Russia, that's how the Cossacks acted to the Turks, *and* the other way around." This obviously bothered him a great deal. "And I helped hang some irregulars we captured behind our lines. One was only about sixteen and cried for his mother. War is a cruel thing, laddie, which is why I'll have no more of it. I had no reason to love them who lie there now. I like what the captain did little more than you. But ponder this, I am not sure the captain went beyond the rights the high and mighty generals will say he has."

Nickerson stared furiously at Clay, heart racing. Even after McFeely's interjection, he was inclined to escalate the confrontation.

Surprisingly, it was his own sergeant who defused the situation. "Ah, hell, Lieutenant, it ain't worth a dust-up. Remember what them Johnnies and their friends, we already put paid to, did to the Scotchman and the darkie. I wouldn't have done that to a dog, much less a Christian."

Nickerson considered the grizzled, burly Sergeant Jeffries. Apparently, the lieutenant had the sense to depend on his more experienced subordinate. "Very well," he said reluctantly. "Go about your business. But be warned, I will file a report with Grant and demand a court-martial on you."

"Do that," replied Clay satisfied. "I will dispute no fact you assert and willingly will surrender to his judgment on the matter. Good day, Lieutenant. Good day, Mr. McFeely." He hesitated for a moment, then advised the former slave, "Samson, when they get back to camp with you, you might want to think about joining one of the colored regiments Grant's forming. It will give you a chance to kill slavers with no consequences. Would you like that?"

The powerfully built Samson bowed his battered body slightly in reverence to Clay. "Oh, yes, Cap'n. I would like that a whole lot."

Clay nodded thoughtfully. "Then we will meet again, soon. Bierce, the road to Jackson awaits."

Clay and Bierce trotted away from the group of soldiers and freed prisoners clustered around the two lifeless bodies in the road.

As soon as they were out of earshot of Nickerson's men, Bierce spoke. "You knew Samson from somewhere, didn't you?"

Clay did not respond.

"Another thing, Clay, I could tell you were indifferent to those two Johnnies you killed until you found they rode with Forrest. What you did back there had nothing to do with how they treated the Scot and the darkie, did it? It has something to do with Forrest. What is it about Forrest? What did he do to you?"

"I would suggest you focus on the road to Jackson. You have a duty to Grant, as, in a different way, so do I. Let us concentrate on our respective duties."

Although curious, Bierce said respectfully, "Yes, Captain, let's."

The two Union officers quietly rode eastward, toward the capital of Mississippi.

It was about noon on the 14th of May when Clay and Lot rode into the chaotic streets of Jackson. Bierce's maps had proven accurate, and Grant had driven his army by the shortest route forward through successive lines of Confederate resistance, never giving the rebels time to organize, never giving gray reinforcements time to arrive.

The new overall Confederate commander for Mississippi, Joseph Johnston, a scholarly, cautious soldier, had been furiously scraping troops from wherever he could find them, ordering them to assemble in Jackson where all the railroads in the state seemed to meet. Indubitably, his intention was to meld his patchwork forces into the semblance of an army, then march west to Vicksburg and combine his force with Pemberton's. Together, there might be enough troops to destroy Grant and recover all the Confederacy had lost in the Mississippi Valley. It was a long shot, but it was the only plan that gave Johnston any hope of victory. The trouble with being an only hope is that the other side can often see it.

Indeed, Grant had seen it and was not giving Johnston time to grasp that hope. He drove his officers forward relentlessly, putting more and more trust in Sherman and his 15th Corps, who alone of his three corps commanders truly felt the need for speed.

Johnston had thrown up the best defensive line he could with the troops he had on the outskirts of Jackson. Not enough. Sherman's corps hammered through the line, not even waiting for McPherson and McClernand, killing and capturing thousands of rebels, sending disorganized thousands more fleeing eastward. Scarcely more organized blue troops poured victoriously through the streets of Jackson, shouting and laughing, drunk on victory. Terrified civilians huddled in their homes, fearing the murder and rape they had been told would be their lot. In truth, the only real danger was to their liquor and to the overworked girls in the brothels.

Lot had already given the results of his inquiries to Clay. Nothing decisive had been uncovered. Bierce was widely disliked but was acknowledged to be brave, intelligent, and resourceful, and no one had ever seen him with the late John Brown. The only thing Lot found that had much relevance was a higher-than-expected number of solitary pickets and cavalrymen shot to death. Soldiers were frightened of drawing picket duty, preferring straightforward combat to being killed by ambush. Some blamed bandits rather than Confederate snipers for the deaths, as several of the dead had been found with their pockets emptied and their weapons left behind; Union arms were generally better than Confederate, and hard-pressed Confederate soldiers would be loath to leave perfectly good weapons.

The sergeant rode alongside his friend in silent disapproval as they weaved their way among exuberant, unsteady troops—many of whom had liberated the alcoholic contents of bars and stores.

Clay disapproved vehemently. "The provost should be more active. This kind of disorder is bad for discipline."

Looking straight ahead, Lot replied, "They are alive and victorious; some of their comrades are neither, Captain. Let them blow off steam. They deserve it. I am more concerned with what Rawlins said when he ordered me to fetch you." He paused and took a deep breath. "Why? In the name of God, Alphonso, why? Do you honestly think *she* would have wanted that, *or* what happened back in New Orleans? Do you think she would be pleased about an inevitable court martial?"

"I regret nothing." Clay told the truth, for his heart was numb. "As for the court martial, I doubt it will occur. The atrocities Forrest's men have committed place them beyond the pale. Although, if there is a trial, I am perfectly prepared to accept whatever punishment it imposes."

"This isn't about any 'law of nations' violation, and you know it! This is personal, sir! Those two men you slaughtered had done nothing to you. They were innocent."

Clay analyzed his words for a moment, and then he curled his lips slightly at the sergeant. "You are a good man, Jeremiah, far better than me—certainly far better than those two pieces of low-born white trash I dispatched. Once I ascertained they joined Forrest of their own free will, I killed them with no more thought than I would give to the slaying of mad dogs. How can you believe there is such a thing as innocence, after what . . . after New Orleans? My motivations may have been personal, but they were nonetheless traitors and criminals deserving of death."

They ambled past the graceful state capitol building, constructed in the Greek revival style. Shouting, blue-clad soldiers cheerfully threw records and books out of upper-story windows, where laughing comrades shoveled them into several bonfires. They drew up in front of a modest hotel at which the presence of sentries and banners indicated Grant had established his temporary head-quarters there. Clay and Lot dismounted, tied their reins to the hitching post, and entered.

Uniformed officers scurried back and forth through the lobby; cheerful confusion ruled. There was no sign of Rawlins, but they did spy Major Parker, standing behind the front desk, going through copies of telegraph messages. He acknowledged them as they approached. At the site of Clay, the major went from cordial to granite, an impenetrable mask.

Clay saluted his superior. "Sergeant Lot has indicated Colonel Rawlins would like to see me. I am here as ordered."

"It is not only Rawlins; the General would like to talk to you as well. The business with Forrest's cavalrymen has traveled all through the army. The men approve; the officers, especially Grant, have a somewhat different opinion."

"And what do you think, Major?"

"I think Forrest and his men treat blacks, and even whites, as the whites were always content to see Indians treated," said Parker evenly. "People realize the barbarity of such tactics, now that it has been directed at the civilized. Perhaps this will open their eyes to what inspired the Indian rage that led to scalpings, burnings, and less pleasant retaliations during the Indian wars."

"Ah, you feel actions such as mine were justified."

The black, unreadable eyes bored into Clay for a long moment before he replied. "It is not for me to judge your actions. I have no idea what has driven you to your attitudes demonstrated on the road to Jackson and elsewhere. All I can say is, for a savage, they are perfectly justifiable; for a civilized man, they are more troubling."

To control swiftly impending violence, Clay drew out his pocket-watch, opened it, and stared at it to the count of ten, then snapped it shut, saying, "I have abandoned some standards of civilization, just as they have abandoned me—my personal choice. If you continue to respect such standards, in the midst of a war such as this, I can only salute you. In any event, I did not come here to debate philosophy. Where may we find Colonel Rawlins?"

Perplexed at his actions, Parker simply said, "He went with Grant and Sherman to inspect a factory we learned about on the northern outskirts of town, right after they had an early dinner here." Parker's impassive stance morphed mischievously into delight. "The meal had been prepared for General Johnston, but he had to flee with the remainder of his army before he could enjoy it. It tickled Grant and Sherman to no end to eat a dinner prepared for the Confederate commander.

"Hey, you can do me a service if you are going right out there. Our boys seized copies of the recent army messages from the local telegraph office. Many of Pemberton's messages were not coded and contain very valuable information, which the General should see post haste. I was just sorting out the most urgent." He thrust towards Clay a small pile of flimsies.

Clay read the message on top and burst into laughter.

Parker and Lot exchanged an uneasy glance.

"What's so funny, Captain?" asked Lot.

Clay held the message aloft. "This, this is what is funny, a message from Pemberton to the War Department in Richmond, implying the Confederate commander is an incompetent fool and that Grant is winning . . . and the Rebel general is totally clueless."

Parker nodded. "I deduced that as well."

Lot's curiosity was aroused. "What exactly does it say?"

Chuckling, Clay replied "I'll read you the relevant part. 'ENEMY ACROSS RIVER IN FORCE STOP THREAT AGAINST CHICKASAW BLUFFS RENEWED STOP CAVALRY OPERATING FREELY IN INTERIOR STOP GOAL OF MAIN BODY MAY BE VICKSBURG OR MOBILE OR JACKSON OR ALL THREE STOP GRANT IS IN MOTION IN ALL DIRECTIONS STOP'.

This is a statement from a confused and demoralized commander. It will not matter how many reinforcements are sent to such a general; his defeat will be virtually inevitable, unless a strong army commanded by another comes to his aid. Yes, Major Parker, I will be happy to deliver such a message to Grant. If he is half the general I suspect he is, he will appreciate what this means."

Parker resumed his former position and defensively stood straight. "I believe he is a great deal more than half the general you suspect he is."

Clay and Lot saluted Parker, who casually returned their salutes and went back to scanning the telegrams he had not yet evaluated.

Although the capital of Mississippi, Jackson was a small town, and it only took a few minute's ride to reach the northern outskirts. A huge, barn-like building was the only structure deemed to be a factory. This was affirmed by the presence of a small cavalry escort outside the large sliding doors that stood open, apparently to admit a breeze.

Clay and Lot dismounted, secured their mounts, and confirmed with the bored horse-soldiers that Rawlins, Sherman, and Grant were inside. They walked through the open doors into an amazing spectacle.

The interior of the sprawling wooden building was filled with a confusing number of rapidly moving belts, which powered scores of huge looms and machines of less certain purpose. Bustling about the interior, their motions frantic despite the heat and humidity, were scores of harried young women, faces perspiring, sweat soaking their thin dresses. It initially appeared they were acting as the servant of the machines, but upon reflection, Clay concluded this was a silly notion. No living being could be subservient to machines! Somewhere to the back of the building, the hisses and chugs of a steam engine could be heard, clearly the source of power for the devices spitting out huge bolts of cloth, regularly marked

"CSA," denoting the material was the property of the Confederate States of America. Women scurried past Clay and Lot, staggering under heavy loads of finished material, taking them to growing stacks along the walls; then, they literally ran back for more.

After a few moments, it dawned on him. The women were working in a plant catering to the Confederate army, yet they spared nothing more than fearful glimpses as they repeatedly passed two Union soldiers, one of them black.

Frustrated and furious, Clay stepped directly in front of one of the frantic workers heading for a fresh load of cloth, so she could not easily move around him without coming dangerously close to the flying belts. "My apologies, madam," said Clay, bowing slightly. "I am hoping you could satisfy my curiosity. It could not possibly have escaped your notice that this factory is now under the jurisdiction of the United States government, yet you continue to work frantically on Confederate material that will *never* be delivered. I would like to understand why."

The worker, a handsome woman whose beauty was already being eroded by hard work, glared at Clay with undisguised hatred. She hissed, "Will you get out of my way, sir? You *damn* Yankees killed my husband at Shiloh. The *damn* bank took the farm. The *damn* foreman knows that this is the only place around Jackson where a woman can earn a decent wage, and he fires anyone he thinks is slacking. I've got three little ones who will go hungry if I lose this job. Now kindly move, sir! *Damn* you!"

A shadow passed over Clay's features. He raised his hat, bowed to the woman, and moved out of her way. With an angry swirl of skirts, she moved into the bowels of the factory without a backward glance—tears of fear, lament, and loathing streaming down her cheeks.

Lot moved alongside Clay, who was watching the receding back of the Confederate widow, and remarked, "I imagine most of the women in this factory have a similar story. Those who aren't widows have their men folk in the army and cannot work the farms themselves. The management of this charming establishment knows there is an endless stream of desperate young women and must drive them mercilessly with the threat of instant dismissal." He paused. "There are all kinds of slavery—not all of which involve physical chains and formal bills of sale."

Clay ignored his friend. "She was not speaking theoretically or for effect. Her children are hungry. The children. The people who started this war have much to answer for." He shook his head as if to clear it and saw, down a parallel aisle, three Union officers arguing with a thin, greasy-haired civilian. Clay and Lot walked to where the foreman was arguing frantically with Grant, as Sherman and Rawlins watched.

"There's no need to burn this place, General," whined the man. "The owners just take their business where they can find it. They's good Union men I swear!"

"Good Union men who supply the Confederacy with cloth!" exclaimed Grant, who then took an angry puff on one of his ever-present cigars.

"But sir, I can speak for the owners. They'll be happy to make cloth for the Union. Happier! They always opposed this unpleasantness."

Clay and Lot arrived at the group, saluted, and wordlessly handed the telegrams to Rawlins. Grant was the only one of the three officers who returned the salute, and that was with some reluctance.

Sherman acted like someone had just lit a fire under his ass; wildly he screamed, "Clay, this is it, damn you! This is it! I don't give a shit who you know or if you're Abe's bastard son! You have dishonored the uniform of the United States. You are a mad dog who needs to be put down, and by God, I'll see you put down!"

The deathly ashen Rawlins solicited Grant's attention, "General, with your permission I will place Captain Clay under arrest."

Grant instantly became as serious as the muzzle of a cannon. "Captain Clay, what shall I do with you? Lt. Nickerson insisted on filing charges formally. In fact, he bypassed his brigade commander to do so, a serious breach of military etiquette." He took a long pull on his cigar, letting it out slowly, never taking his eyes from Clay's face. "He is a passionate fellow and apparently an honest one. Despite his rage at you, he reported your statements about Forrest's men being unlawful combatants. That is an argument with some merit! I saw what Forrest's people did to the loyalists in Holly Springs and other places.

"Whether your action was intended to do so or not, it sends a message that Forrest has to rein in some of his wilder people and start leaving loyal civilians alone. Court-martialing you would dilute the force of that message, so I told the him there would be no trial. He wasn't happy and told me so to my face." A hint of delight flitted across Grant's features. "Can't have that with regulars but have to make an allowance for volunteers, especially one with such a good combat record. Promoted him to captain and gave him a company in the new colored regiment McPherson's organizing. Be a good thing to have an idealistic officer in charge of freed slaves being shown how to fight."

Sherman looked as if he was going to explode; in fact, a vein visibly throbbed at his temple, beet red. "Sam, I beg you to reconsider! Our people are falling into Confederate hands all the time. What if they don't see this as retaliation for Forrest stepping out of bounds, and start hanging our prisoners?"

"Then I will start hanging their prisoners we hold two to one. Those fine gentlemen, who pretend to be so chivalrous, know Forrest is a not gentleman. They will not press the point, Cump." Grant shifted the conversation back to Clay. "Captain, our point has now been made. There will be no more killing of unresisting prisoners. Do you understand? I realize, for some reason, you have no fear of punishment, or even death. Therefore, I want your word as a gentleman. I don't know why, but, despite everything you've done, I figure I can count on that."

This disturbed Clay greatly, causing him to make a calculated response, "Sir, I can give you my word, *except* as to Nathan Bedford Forrest. If you insist I promise not to take his life, under whatever circumstances I encounter him, then regretfully, I cannot offer you my word."

Grant threw his head back and laughed heartily. Then he asked Sherman, "What do you say, Cump? Do we give Captain Clay permission to kill General Forrest whenever he can?"

The mercurial Sherman had shifted from blind rage to giggling amusement. "I think we should give him that exception. I've always said there will never be peace in the Mississippi Valley until Forrest is dead. Perhaps Captain Clay will give us that peace."

"Then you have my word, General."

Pivoting toward the manager of the textiles factory, Grant's merriment dropped from his face. "As for you and your owners, I am now giving you an opportunity to show your devotion to the Union by an economic sacrifice. We are staying in Jackson just long enough to tear up the railroads and take what supplies we need. After we are gone, I *suspect* you will be back to making supplies for Jeff Davis. I am sure you will be willing to prove your devotion to our cause by standing by while I see this place is burned to the ground." Without breaking eye contact with the Rebel supporter, he shouted, "Captain Clay!"

"Sir."

Grant prepared his order with bitter distaste. "You had some experience with this kind of thing outside New Orleans, I believe.

Let's put that experience to use. Make sure all the women get out, and burn this building to the ground."

"Sir, I will *gladly* perform that function. However, it has come to my attention that some of the workers here are in want. I know war is hard, but could they be permitted to take as much of the finished cloth as they could carry? They could sell it for enough to meet the immediate needs of . . . well, their immediate needs."

"They will undoubtedly sell it to the Confederacy, so it will go on equipping our enemies," observed Rawlins.

"True," conceded Clay, "but in the grand scheme of things, the amounts they will be able to carry away in their arms will make no difference."

Grant took a long moment, observing Clay, chewing on the stub of his cigar. "I can't quite make you out Clay. You assemble the women, tell them their services are no longer required, and let them carry away as much as they can. Then burn this place."

"No, you can't do this!" screeched the factory manager.

Clay stepped forward, knocked him down with a blow to the jaw, and then kicked him viciously in the ribs several times with his elegant, hand-made boots. "You are fortunate I gave my word to General Grant," said the small captain, standing over the huddled, sobbing manager. "Your days of profiting on the misery of the weak are *over*. Now pick yourself up and order the workers assembled before you find out how far I can go without causing death."

"Clay!" exclaimed Grant menacingly as the groaning man staggered off down the aisle.

"My apologies, sir," said Clay. "I never would have seriously hurt that . . . that . . . It was necessary to frighten the blackguard to get him moving."

"If you were directly under my command, Clay, I would . . . All I can say is you better put the Brown matter to rest before we attain

Vicksburg, or I'm sending you back to Meigs in chains! Sherman, Rawlins, let's get out of here. I need fresh air." The three left Clay and Lot to supervise the act of destruction.

The fearful factory manager assembled his workers quickly in an open space at the rear of the large structure, near the chugging steam engine. Clay briefly and unemotionally told them their employment had ended, but they could leave with whatever they could carry. Amidst tears and some sobbing, the women fell on the finished cloth and staggered out of the building with their pitiful spoils. Clay spotted the woman who had cursed him earlier, who staggered under a load larger than those of her sisters. She neither sobbed nor cried but simply spared Clay daggers of naked hatred as she left the building.

When the last of the women had gone, Clay went to the engine, inspecting it carefully. "The label says this device was manufactured in Pittsburgh," he said to himself. "So much for the South. They transported a simple, factory device *six hundred miles*! No place in the whole South could make a reliable steam engine."

Lot watched as Clay gathered a large pile of cloth scraps and rags and doused them with lubricating grease from a bucket near the puffing machine. He then opened the firebox, stuffed the flammable rags inside, and closed it. Using a leather harness left lying nearby, he tied down the safety valve that released steam when the internal pressure exceeded a certain level. Then he took two oil lamps from a wooden table, lit them both with a friction match, and picked them up.

"Come, Sergeant, it is time we left." They walked the long corridor to the front of the factory building. Behind them, the steam engine began to make louder and louder pounding noises. About halfway to the entrance, Clay hurled one of the lamps at a wall just above a pile of raw cloth. It shattered, and the oil caught fire, dripping in flaming globs onto the cotton material. Near the entrance, he flung the other one in a similar manner. Clay and Lot stepped into the hot afternoon sunlight as flames began to flicker and the wheezing noises of the steam engine grew.

A lone Union officer trotted up on horseback. To the surprise of both Clay and Lot, it was Ambrose Bierce, who clumsily dismounted, staggered slightly, and then gave Clay an exaggeratedly precise salute. There was a silly gin on Bierce's face, and Clay noted with disgust that Bierce reeked of cheap whiskey and cheaper perfume.

"Ah, Captain Clay and his blackamoor companion!" Bierce declared in a loud, slightly slurred voice. "I was directed here in my search for Colonel Rawlins. Should've reported sooner, but I found myself ensnared by the charms of the capital of the sovereign state of Mississippi."

"Rawlins departed with Generals Grant and Sherman only a few minutes ago. I imagine they went directly back to the hotel. It is fortunate for you. I suspect Rawlins would not approve of your present state."

"Damn Bible thumper! He's a typical Puritan—lives in dread fear that someone, somewhere, may be having a good time. The Good Lord created alcohol and women for the delight and enjoyment of man." His lips curled and puckered out. "Wonderful things, liquor and women! They make a man forget things." At once, the drunkenness evaporated from Bierce, and, for a moment, was replaced by fear, almost as if he'd seen haints. "Yes, forget . . . things. Damn, Indiana!" His head rattled back and forth, trying to rid himself of the relentless memories. "I was saying something . . . What was I. . . ?"

With a loud, tearing boom, the steam engine exploded, and a moment later, the walls of the wooden structure bulged, and then obliterated. Wooden boards and pieces of flaming debris hurled in all directions, deadly projectiles, some narrowly missing the three soldiers. Clay and Lot staggered under the force of the blast, as the less balanced Bierce fell on his ass.

"My apologies for putting you at unnecessary risk, Jeremiah," apologized Clay. "I seriously underestimated the force with which the engine would explode. I should have made you move further away."

Then, in the middle of total chaos, Clay and Lot heard hands clapping. Bierce was happily applauding from the dry, dusty, ground, watching the flaming ruins of the textile factory like a kid seeing fireworks for the first time. "Wonderful, Clay, wonderful. You are a card. There's never a dull moment where you are."

They refocused from the amused drunk back to the remains of the building. Both knew without saying, they were thinking of the same thing—flames, blood, and a round horror sailing through the air.

The Army of the Tennessee had been driving westward from Jackson for three days, a relentless juggernaut, pushing irresistibly toward Vicksburg. Intercepted messages from General Joseph Johnston showed him to be frantically ordering Pemberton to march his garrison northwards out of Vicksburg to join the forces being hurriedly assembled near the Tennessee border. Johnston repeatedly stressed that even if Vicksburg fell, their combined forces could crush Grant and easily regain the fortress. Yet, Pemberton refused to follow Johnston's orders. Instead, he threw small detachments forward to try to impede Grant's triumphant army. The brave soldiers he sent simply died or were captured to no purpose, not even materially delaying the blue horde.

"It makes no sense," commented Lot to Clay as they rode alongside Lieutenant Bierce in front of a ragged but jaunty regiment from Sherman's 15th Corps. "It is basic tactics; his only chance would be to join up with Johnston. It's stupid of him not to try.

I can't believe a man could rise to the rank of lieutenant general and be that stupid."

"Ah, you underestimate just how far a person can go with no brains, Sergeant," replied Bierce, who had recently rejoined the column after a successful scouting expedition. "Take our own McDowell, McClellan, and Burnside; do you really think the South has cornered the market on stupid generals?"

Clay regarded Bierce. "Do you have any particular basis for thinking Pemberton is unintelligent?"

Bierce laughed unpleasantly. "Once I was at headquarters, waiting to talk to Rawlins, and caught the tail end of a story Grant was telling his staff. Seems the only time he actually met Pemberton was in the Mexican War, during the siege of Mexico City. Grant was a quartermaster and really had no business in the front line, but he had wandered forward and assumed command of a squad that had lost its lieutenant to a sniper. Got to give that bastard credit; he has ice in his veins. Back to what I was saying, lots of greasers were on rooftops picking our boys off one at a time. Grant found an abandoned mountain howitzer, broke into a church, had it manhandled up into the bell tower, and then started dropping shells on those rooftops. With nowhere to hide from someone above them, the Mexicans cleared out real fast. You see, Pemberton was on General Scott's staff at that time, and as Grant tells it, in the middle of his shelling of the enemy positions, he popped into the bell tower, congratulated Grant on his initiative, and said he was going to get him four more howitzers."

Lot said, "Sir, I don't see how that shows Pemberton's lack of intelligence."

"Neither did I, until Grant went on to explain that the platform in the bell tower was tiny, and with himself, the howitzer, and the four soldiers working it, there was barely room for Pemberton himself to squeeze in, much less another cannon. Grant said it would have been plain to a blind man that nothing more would fit in the tower, yet there was Pemberton promising another four howitzers!"

"Pemberton's reluctance to abandon Vicksburg could also have something to do with the fact that he is a Pennsylvanian," Clay said, unexpectedly. "He allowed his Southern-born wife and his good friend Jefferson Davis to persuade him to betray his country. He must know that no one trusts a traitor, even one they create. He must be fearful that if he abandons Vicksburg, even for strategic advantage, he will be accused of disloyalty to his adopted homeland."

Bierce inclined his head. "Better and better, the leader of our opponents is not only stupid, but he is weak-willed and henpecked by his wife." Changing the subject, he said, "I understand Grant is with the 15th Corps on the right flank, which should be reaching Chickasaw Bluffs today. I'd better ride over and get my latest orders. Coming?"

"I will be along presently," replied Clay.

"How about that! Trusted on my own for once. I am touched by your faith in my loyalty." Bierce guffawed, spurring his horse into a gallop, and then melded into a cloud of dust.

"Do you trust him?" asked Lot after the mocking lieutenant could no longer be seen.

"Of course not, but there is nothing decisive. During this campaign, you and I have been interviewing everyone we can find who was on that steamboat the night Brown died. Nothing either of us has found either clearly implicates Bierce or clearly points to anyone else as the murderer. He claims he never actual met Brown, and no one can testify to the contrary. Seeing as it was Sherman's headquarters boat, people were constantly coming and going. The sentries apparently were letting on anyone who claimed to belong. The people they remember coming on board that night before Brown was shot constitutes a long list—Rawlins, Parker, all three of the Corps commanders—just to begin."

"Many civilians were allowed on as well," added Lot. "One wonders why they even bothered with sentries. One of the guards I talked to remembers that sutler, who embalmed poor Brown, and even the spy, Amos Shea, Bierce employs."

"Really?" responded Clay. "That is very interesting, given how nervous Shea acted about the possibility of being noticed when we met him on the road."

"I wouldn't make too much of it; Captain. Bierce confirms Shea came to him unbidden with information on Confederate cavalry movements, for which he demanded and received payment on the spot. Besides, he acted nervous, according to what Bierce told me the other night because he had left his wife behind, unlike his usual practice of taking her along. And remember, Brown was convinced there was treason at a high level. It would be stretching things to the breaking point to call Lieutenant Bierce a 'high level,' and my impression of Shea is that all he was interested in was money."

"The more I think about it, the more I am certain we should not ignore the possibility that Bierce may be the tool of a higher-ranking traitor. This bothers me greatly. We should make haste to wherever Ambrose Bierce is."

"He won't be hard to find, Captain," said Lot. "Look at that."

The column had broken through the woods. Across cultivated fields, at a distance of about four miles, a cluster of buildings could be dimly seen—Vicksburg at last. In the fields in front of them, soldiers pointed, laughed, and cheered, as their smiling officers restrained them from immediately charging forward. The steadfast danger from the thousands of troops Pemberton had in there reminded the leaders they must wait for orders from Grant.

"Chickasaw bluffs will only be a short distance to the right," observed Lot.

"Indeed. Let us make haste."

They drove their exhausted horses northwest across gently rolling fields, until, with surprising suddenness, they reached the bluffs overlooking the Mississippi. Spotting a group of horses with the pennants of the Army of the Tennessee and the 15th Corps, they knew their goal had been found. The friends rode up to the group, dismounted, and secured the reins of their horses to the branches of a small tree. Grant and Sherman stood silently side-by-side at the edge of the bluff, while, a short distance away, Bierce conversed quietly with Rawlins and Parker.

As they approached the two generals, Clay and Lot could hear Sherman, "Down there, Sam, down there. I was down there on the 27th of December, looking up at these heights, watching my boys fall by the hundreds. It's so peaceful now. We've come so far to go such a short distance." Sherman faced Grant full on. "Sam, I always thought this campaign was a mistake. I told you at the time it was mistake. I was sure we were doomed to destruction and only followed you because I owed it to the man who had faith in me when I had none in myself. Now, I see it. Your plan was brilliant—its execution superb. This campaign will be taught in military academies for centuries to come, and deservedly so. You are the man who will win this war."

An embarrassed Grant said, "It was the men and their officers, Cump. History always talks about the generals, but without good men, the generals are nothing. And without good officers, the men are nothing. You and your 15th have been the point of my spear. We would not be here without them and without you. In fact, I'm not sure I could do what needs to be done without you as my right arm."

"Bullshit, Sam! You don't need me! The men are great; I'll give you that, but what does their bravery count for when fools like McClellan, Burnside, and Pope throw their sacrifice away! It is you they will remember! It is you history will remember!"

"Doggone it, Cump, stop that! The campaign isn't over yet. Pemberton remains in Vicksburg with close onto thirty thousand troops, and the scouts report some pretty impressive earthworks."

"Its fall is inevitable now. The only question is whether we charge right in or settle down to a siege and starve them out."

"It's a hard decision. We'll lose a lot of people going over the top and might be repulsed altogether and have to settle into a siege after all. On the other hand, over a long siege, we might lose even more men, especially from fevers and disease; a lot of our boys are not accustomed to Southern summers and how unhealthy they can be."

"Do you want my advice, Sam?"

"No, I guess not. Whatever I decide, a lot of good men will die; the decision should be completely mine." Grant stared into the distance. "I guess we'll make a run at them. All three corps will attack at dawn tomorrow. We'll need that much time to get units organized and sorted out." He pointed down the slope toward the Mississippi. "Just detail one regiment to start working up piers down there, and a good wagon road to the top. We want to start getting regular supplies from Memphis as soon as may be. But aside from that regiment, everyone goes into the attack tomorrow, except for the standard reserves."

"Even McClernand, Sam? His performance on this campaign has been damn poor."

"I know, Cump, but he did well enough at Port Gibson, which just required straightforward slugging; that's what this will be. And besides, we will need every man we've got. But I want you to know one thing, Cump. You are my right hand; you are the one I depend on above all others. I cannot do what needs to be done without you."

Grant noticed Clay and Lot waiting quietly. "Captain, any closer to finding Lieutenant Brown's killer?"

"I am not certain, but circumstances point to the possibility of Lieutenant Bierce's involvement. I must strongly recommend you not allow him near headquarters without the presence of either Sergeant Lot or myself."

Grant listened to Bierce's animated discussion with Rawlins and Parker; studied the mapmaker for a good minute before saying, "Bierce is not a very lovable man, but his work has been flawless, and if he were a traitor, he would have had plenty of opportunity before now to strike a blow."

"Perhaps he is waiting until such a blow would be the most disruptive," replied Clay.

"Stay close to him, but I will not permit any action against him until the proof is decisive." He paused, then said moodily, "I know what it is to be the victim of rumors and suppositions."

The cannon had fired for half an hour before 30,000 yelling men charged enthusiastically forward toward the trenches surrounding Vicksburg on the landward side. For a moment, it looked as if the cannonade had stampeded demoralized troops and that in one glorious rush, the Union would reclaim Vicksburg.

But looks can be deceiving, and Grant was about to learn that artillery was seldom conclusive against troops defending a prepared position. As soon as the Union guns stopped firing, to avoid hitting their own soldiers as they advanced, the ragged Confederates rose from their trenches, screaming their Rebel yell, and emptied volley after volley into the attackers. The surviving Federals came to a sudden halt, falling on their stomachs, returning fire from prone positions as best they could. Field officers strode among them, screaming at them, brandishing swords, trying to get them to resume the charge. Their bravery was often rewarded with death or mutilation as Rebel bullets found conspicuous targets.

Grant had made his headquarters with Sherman, who was fidgeting with increasing nervousness, seeing the assault stall. Grant sat stolidly on horseback beside Sherman, forcing himself to watch the carnage from a distance that was still not safe, as the whines of random bullets passed through the air. Among the others surrounding the two generals, only Rawlins and Lot showed any unease: Rawlins showing concern for Grant; Lot fearfully watching Clay. Clay and Parker displayed complete indifference to the whizzing pieces of lead. Bierce, on the other hand, unnaturally enjoyed the whole experience: bright eyed, smiling as if witnessing some secret joke.

Sherman twisted in his saddle to address his commander, "Grant, this is Chickasaw all over again. It was worth the try, but it's not working. Call this off. These men are needed for greater work later on."

Grant hesitated and was about to speak, when one of John McClernand's staff officers galloped up. "Compliments of General McClernand, sir!" he announced breathlessly to Grant. "The 13th Corps has staged a breakthrough! We are established on the main parapet, and our flags are seen in the enemy entrenchments, but he needs reinforcements to exploit the breakthrough. He asks you send help from General Sherman's corps immediately!"

"A breakthrough!" exclaimed Sherman excitedly, going from dejection to elation in an instant. "Yes, I have a reserve division that can be committed. We always hold back reserves for the supreme opportunity, and this is it!"

Grant had removed his binoculars and was peering at the distant, dusty slope in front of McClernand's corps. He lowered the binoculars and addressed Sherman. "I don't see any flags. I don't believe a word of it."

Sherman leaned forward, a wild light in his eyes. "Sam, I know you don't like McClernand—hell, I don't like him either—but don't let your dislike rule your head. It's dusty and confused up there—easy to miss what McClernand could see from closer up. If we take time to confirm the breakthrough, Pemberton will shift his own reserves, and the gap will be closed. Send me in! I'll lead them myself. Send me in!"

The normally stone-faced Grant regarded Sherman with deep concern. In a low voice, he said, "Go Cump, but take doggone good care of yourself."

With a wild yell, Sherman spurred his horse into motion.

Grant ordered Rawlins in a much firmer voice, "Colonel, ride for the artillery reserve and tell them to let loose with every long-range piece they got. I know they can't see the roads leading up to the Reb lines, so tell them to fire blind into the town.

"Major Parker, ride like the dickens to McPherson and tell him to support Sherman anyway he can."

The two staff officers saluted and galloped off.

Bierce trotted up to Grant, an eager gleam in his eyes. "General, with your permission, I would like to go up and observe the assault. Perhaps my knowledge of topography could be of some use to General Sherman."

Grant looked at Bierce for a moment, unable to disguise a faint disgust. "I suspect you may have other motives, Lieutenant. Nevertheless, it's your funeral. You may go if you wish."

As Bierce gaily galloped off, Clay spurred his horse to follow, not bothering to request permission. Stifling a curse, Lot grimaced and galloped after his captain.

Within minutes, the three approached a hellish scene. They stopped far back of the front lines, although even there was not an especially safe place to be. The whine of bullets careening through the air sounded continuous; a passing courier cried out and fell from his horse with a heavy thud. They were in time to see the blue-clad column Sherman was waiving on start up the slope to the entrenchments collapse; some fell dead or dying, some ran, and some fell to their stomachs, trying to fight on, unable to go forward, unwilling to run.

Sherman galloped back and forth in front of the prone survivors, screaming in a voice that carried to the three new arrivals.

"Bastards! Whoreson cowards! Victory is up there! Up there! Follow me! Follow me!"

The grim soldiers stayed as stationary as their dead comrades.

The crazed Sherman could be seen from a great distance. "Yellow sons-of-bitches! Call yourselves men! Puking babies! I'll show you how to die like men!" He spurred his horse toward Vicksburg and certain death.

Jeremiah Lot held no love for William Tecumseh Sherman. The sergeant had never grown used to the casual, brutal bigotry of those in power, and Sherman had rubbed salt into wounds that hadn't healed, would never heal. Lot had followed the progress of the war with intense interest. Until Grant had commenced his command, he feared in his heart that military blundering would allow the South to win and keep millions of human beings in bondage forever. Grant was his hope, possibly his last hope, for the victory of freedom.

In his head, he heard Grant say to Sherman, *I'm not sure I can do what needs to be done without you as my right arm.* Unconsciously, he set his spurs to his horse, arrowing straight for the enraged general.

"Jeremiah!" screamed Clay

"Let's go see the elephant!" shouted Bierce, who set off after Lot, like a maniac.

Stifling a rare curse, Clay spurred his own mount into a gallop. All three heard the whine of Minie balls whirling past them as they raced toward Sherman who had stopped halfway between his troops and the entrenchment full of whooping Graybacks, pulling his horse's head toward the Union troops, screaming profanities of surprising creativity and intensity.

In pursuit, Lot wondered whether he would live to reach

Sherman, whether Sherman would live until Lot reached him, and how he would compel the frenzied general to come with him to safety.

He was almost there when the head of Sherman's horse exploded in a spray of blood and brains. As the horse fell, Sherman reflexively threw himself from the dead animal before he could be trapped under its bulk. The general hit the ground hard, his stringy limbs flopping like those of a rag doll. He struggled unsuccessfully to get to his feet, dazed by his fall.

Lot reached Sherman and stretched, offering him a hand. "General, swing up behind me! We must regain our lines!"

Sherman had struggled to his feet but refused the proffered hand, his eyes unfocused. "Get away from me, you goddam nigger! I let Sam down once; I'm not letting him down again! I'm leading those whoresons into Vicksburg! Not again—"

Two rifle bullets struck Lot's horse at nearly the same moment, one barely missing the sergeant's leg. The animal screamed and fell heavily toward the stunned general. Lot hurled himself from the dying animal, knocking Sherman clear of the flailing hoofs. The additional blow further disoriented the already stunned Sherman, who slumped semi-conscious to the ground. Lot grabbed the unresisting general under the armpits and dragged him to his feet as a bullet zinged past his ear. Lot realized, with despair, that they he had about zero chance of surviving the trek back to safety dragging Sherman's weight, when he heard a braying laugh.

"Time to redeploy to the rear, Sergeant Sambo!" shouted Bierce with manic glee. "Throw his arms over my pommel, grab him from the other side, and hang on!"

Quick as lighting, Lot threw Sherman's arms across the top of Bierce's horse, raced to the opposite side, and grabbed them before the general collapsed to the ground. With an exuberant, incoherent yell, Bierce viciously put the spurs to his horse, making straight for the Union lines—Sherman's and Lot's heels dragging in the dirt as the horse struggled with the treble load.

Clay had taken in the situation and made straight for the Confederate lines, then raced parallel to them for several hundred yards, distracting fire from the retreating Bierce and his cargo. If all the enemy soldiers had been firing at Clay, he would have died in moments, regardless the speed with which he raced across the battlefield, but most withheld their fire, astonished at the daring of the lone Union horseman.

When Clay ascertained the other three had reached comparative safety, he jerked his horse's head toward the Federal lines, urging his exhausted mount to a new burst of speed. Achieving his goal, miraculously untouched, cheers broke out. Nearly as many came from Confederate throats as Union ones.

Sherman was sipping a brandy in the shade of a tree, reclined in a camp chair, with Clay, Lot, and Bierce hovering nearby when Grant rode up with McClernand. Grant virtually leapt off the horse and strode over to his subordinate. "Sherman, you doggone fool! I heard what you did. Don't you ever expose yourself like that again!"

"You won't have to worry about that, Grant," replied Sherman morosely. "I'm resigning. I've failed you and my country for the last time."

"You didn't fail, Cump. The failure was mine, and others," Grant said, casting venomous darts at McClernand. "I thought some fool had made a mistake, and yet I went against my better judgment."

"Uh, I'm *sure* I saw our flags in the trenches," said the craggy McClernand, unable to look Grant in the eye. "Now, if Sherman had been quicker—"

"I have had Rawlins and Parker asking around," interrupted Grant, a menacing tone in his voice. "No one, not even your aides, claims to have seen with their own eyes what you said you saw.

The responsibility for all those wasted deaths is mine, as is the responsibility for retaining a vainglorious fool in a high command."

"Now, Grant—" began McClernand.

"I'll tell you what I think," interrupted Grant, a rising note of fury in his voice. "I think perhaps an ambitious Illinois politician wanted the glory of having the corps he commanded be the first into Vicksburg. He selfishly *sacrificed* the lives of hundreds of brave men so he could advance to post-war glory. You are on thin ice, sir, thin ice. You will return to your corps and be very careful how you conduct yourself in the future. If you were not the special pet of President Lincoln, if he didn't need the support of Illinois Democrats who follow your lead, I would have you court-martialed for dereliction of duty. As it is, I will send you home the next time you step the slightest bit out of line and let Abe take what action he may. Now get out of my sight!"

Without saluting, and with a venomous backward glance, McClernand mounted his horse and rode away.

Grant stared grimly after him, and then he faced Sherman, his features softening. "No more talk about resigning, Cump. This is a setback to you, nothing more. Remember how I was about to quit after Shiloh, tired of all the rumors about my drinking, and you talked me out of it."

Sherman smiled wanly. "Best day's work I ever did, Sam. But the Union needed you; it doesn't need me."

"General Sherman, I am giving you an order," said Grant with mock severity. "I order you to consider yourself my most valuable general. I order you to help me win this war."

Sherman laughed, although he was shaking all over. "All right, Sam. I guess I should stay with you, especially if it's turning into a siege for Vicksburg. With Pemberton and his thirty thousand inside trying to get out, and Johnston and his twenty thousand on the outside trying to get in, you're going to need someone who thinks fast. McPherson is good enough. But if there's one thing McClernand can't do, it's think fast." Sherman hesitated, then said, "Sam I want you to witness something." He raised his voice and shouted, "Bierce, Lot, and Clay, front and center!"

The three approached the two generals and saluted.

"Captain Clay and Lieutenant Bierce, your actions went far beyond what was necessary. You exposed yourselves to extreme danger to protect a superior officer, who had behaved foolishly and was undeserving of that protection. And Sergeant Lot, you behaved the same. This is something I want to acknowledge before the Army Commander—that I have treated you repeatedly with disrespect and used rude phrases. I doubted the suitability of members of your race to be citizens and soldiers. You have proven me to be wrong, at least in your case. Sergeant Lot, I am a fouled-mouthed bastard and won't be changing my ways, but I want you to know you have earned my respect and admiration. I will try to contain my language toward persons of color in the future." He shot his hand out, and gingerly, Lot took it. Then, for the first time in his life, William Tecumseh Sherman shook the hand of a black man.

"Now, dismissed, all of you," said Sherman gruffly. "Grant and I have things to discuss in private."

The three dismissed soldiers strolled to a nearby copse of trees.

When they got there, a worried Clay grabbed Lot by the shoulder. "Jeremiah, don't you ever take a foolish risk like that again!" Clay exclaimed with fierce intensity. "You are the only living soul for whom I care. The world would simply be . . . be . . ." Clay broke off and drew out his pocket watch, the only thing to calm him. Bierce happened to be standing close behind him, and casually peeked over Clay's shoulder. He saw the inside cover of the lid to the watch contained a small but elegant photograph. The woman was a mulatto of astounding beauty and regal bearing. It might have been a trick of the photographer, but her countenance presented intelligent, haughtiness, and sensuality, all at once.

"A striking wench, Clay. Someone you spent the lonely evenings with on the old plantation?"

Clay whirled around with shocking speed. Bierce, who feared little in the way of physical danger, surprisingly took a step backward in alarm at the look on the captain's face. The ice-blue eyes behind the spectacles glowed with an unearthly light.

Neither spoke for nearly a minute, but it was Clay who broke the silence. "If you were any kind of gentleman, I would call you out for that remark," he said in a frighteningly unemotional voice. "As you are not a gentleman, I would ordinarily take action preventing you from ever repeating that offense. But *only* because of your service to Sergeant Lot today, I will overlook it *this once*. I would advise you against repeating any such remark in the future. It would really be an unlucky thing to do." Clay restored his watch to his pocket and walked quickly away.

"What the hell was all that about?" Bierce asked Lot. "Everyone knows these Southern bucks have a quadroon or two on the side. It's expected of them."

Lot's gaze sadly followed Clay, then to Bierce. "I probably owe you my life today, so I will give you a warning and an explanation I have never given anyone else. Do not mention her, and do not mention Clay's possession of her portrait. It *will* cost you your life." He paused, took a deep breath, and let it out controlled, choosing his words carefully. "Her name is Arabella, the only woman Alphonso ever loved. She is my sister."

"Ah, is that why you stick so close to Clay?" His curiosity had peaked.

Lot hesitated. "I only tell you this to impress on you the danger if you play your taunting games with Alphonso. Arabella and I are his cousins; his uncle was our father."

This genuinely startled Bierce. "At least he will be able to rejoin her when all this fighting is over."

With infinite despair, Lot replied, "I'm afraid not, Lieutenant. My sister is dead."

Bierce uttered a low whistle. "I'll be damned!"

"That is not for me to say, Lieutenant," said Jeremiah Lot.

CHAPTER SIX

WHAT'S THE MOST FRIGHTENED YOU'VE EVER BEEN?

"Now, Cap'n, I *was* on that boat the evenin' that little feller was killed, rest his soul, but I don't recall seeing either him nor Bierce." Sergeant David Larson wiped the sweat off his forehead with the sleeve of his tunic. June in Vicksburg was hot and humid to begin with, and he and Alphonso Clay were crouched down in a shadeless trench under the broiling Mississippi sun, scarcely twenty yards downhill from a similar Confederate trench filled with desperate, armed men anxious to kill anything wearing blue.

Sighing, Sergeant Larson slid to a sitting position, back braced against one wall of the trench, feet braced against the opposite wall. The fastidious Clay, disdaining to sit in the dirt, squatted uncomfortably on his haunches. On either side of them, sweating young men in wool uniforms clutched their rifles, waiting with a combination of nervousness and boredom for something to happen.

"Yep, I'd come back from a long trip by myself," he explained. Using the butt of his telescope-equipped Springfield, he dug repeatedly at an itching shin. "I'd gone to Grant's headquarters to see Major Parker."

"Why Parker?" asked Clay.

"See, officially, I'm with the 8th Iowa, and supposed to be on temporary assignment out of headquarters. My colonel won't let me go permanent-like, only for a month at a time, so at the end of each month, I have to go to Parker who cuts an order for another month. I suppose Parker could order the colonel to make it permanent, if I asked, but the colonel's a good man, and I don't want to be doing what I'm doing for the rest of the war."

"And what are you doing for Parker?"

"Killin' fellers. I's a talent for it."

Clay exceedingly disliked what the man just said. "We are all killers in this war."

"Yeah, but some more'n others, Cap'n." He patted the stock of his Springfield. "With this little sweety here, I can kill a feller at near half mile, weather permittin'."

Clay sought to see if the weather-beaten sergeant was serious. "That's incredible, unbelievable if you don't mind my saying so."

"Nope Cap'n, I don't take no offense. It ain't boastin' for me to say I was the best shot around when I was a little tyke back near Rolla in Missoura. Pappy moved us to Iowa when I was sixteen. Had some trouble with the Injuns at first. Didn't last long, though they did kill my sister before the neighborhood was cleared." The lean man's eyes were dead for a few moments. Clay understood where his thoughts had taken him and guessed who had done much of the "clearing."

Larson shook his head for a moment. "Don't mind sayin' ever'one in the regiment said I was the best shot any had ever seen. Word got 'round to that Injun major, and he came to see me: said he needed someone to scout. I told him I didn' know much 'bout maps. He told me not to worry; there was a feller named Bierce for that, but he needed someone to go out quiet-like and kill Confederate pickets, without gettin' caught."

"A sniper."

"Yep. I guess that's what they call it. So's he says someone's been killin' our fellers from ambush and makin' the others real nervous, and it was time they got some of their own medicine. You should have seen that red major when he told me what he wanted." He shook his head side to side, like he could hardly believe it. "Don't show it much, but you can tell he's a good hater. Never liked Injuns, but I understan' *that*. I think we're kinda alike."

"So how many have you killed?" asked Clay with interest.

"Twenty-nine since April, for sure. They're three others I'm not so sure about. They could'a lived."

Clay stared in frank amazement at the matter-of-fact sergeant. This was an incredible performance for one man armed with a Springfield. Then Clay forced himself back to the subject. "So, you didn't find Major Parker at Grant's headquarters that evening?"

"Yep. That sickly colonel said he'd gone to Sherman's boat. Made my way over to the boat, but he waren't there; at least no one I asked had seen him. Then I went back to Grant's headquarters to wait for him."

"Did you see anyone out of the ordinary on the boat?"

"Don't recollect so, Cap'n. Oh, there were Generals McPherson and McClernand; you sort of notice major generals. Several junior officer types, lookin' soft and important. A couple of civilians. That's about it. Sorry you had to spend so much time trackin' me down for so little. That darkie sergeant of yours said you'd been lookin' for me since before Jackson."

"Well, before we established who you were and that you had been on the boat the night of the murder, you had gone off on one of your solitary patrols, *and* things have been fairly disorganized ever since. Only when I learned Parker had sent you up to this portion of the earthworks could I catch up with you. Incidentally, why did Parker send you here?"

"Yep, this part of the line is losin' more'n its share of fellers to snipers and Parker wants some payback. Course, it's easy to see from here why they lose so many; this is where the lines come closest, and a feller can almost spit into the Reb trenches. Anyone who sticks an eye over the edge is likely to have a Johnnie shoot it out. I'm the best there is at long distance, but this close almost any straw-foot recruit could hit the target. Hell, even with a pistol—"

A black cylinder rolled over the edge of the trench and plopped into the dirt beside Clay, a short length of fuse sputtering. The soldiers on either side of Clay and Larson stared frozen at the three-inch shell, which some Confederate had rigged to be a large, crude hand grenade, counting on gravity to roll it into the Union trench once the fuse was lit and thrown over the lip of their own earthwork. Moving with the speed of a mongoose, Clay scooped up the heavy bomb and heaved it back toward the enemy line. It was inconceivable, illogical for so slight a man to throw a twenty-pound object as far as the Confederate trench, but Clay had *surprising* strength for his size. *Surprising*. He ducked back below the lip of the trench just as half a dozen Confederate riflemen shot at him. None of their bullets found purchase, although several kicked up dust at the edge of the earthwork. The flurry of shots was followed almost instantly by an explosion. Screams emitted from more than one throat, but they rapidly subsided into one voice, continuously sobbing. Vengeful bullets began to patter the edge of the trench from where Clay had lobbed back the bomb.

In a crouching run, Larson had run a dozen paces down the trench in a direction opposite from Clay, shouldering one pasty-faced recruit aside. He took a deep breath, held it, then popped up, steadied his rifle, and took a shot, immediately dropping to the floor of the trench an instant before a flurry of bullets passed through where he had stood just a moment before. Then came a horrible, gurgling scream, a scream trying to force its way through something liquid.

Crouching down, Clay moved to where Larson sat, calmly reloading his Springfield. "Quick thinking, Captain," he said, not interrupting the process of loading. "I guess I owe you my life. Quick as I am, I'm not as quick as you were. You ever need Dave Larson for anythin', let me know. You've got credit with me."

Clay cocked his head in the enemy's direction. "They cut the fuse too long. It takes real nerve to cut it so short that an object like this cannot be thrown back at you."

They heard the horrible, gurgling scream give way to a choking sound, which was followed by a silence only broken by the sobbing of the man injured by the shell.

Larson leaned his ear to listen, but, for the moment, the sobbing was the only thing audible. "Reckon that's thirty, for sure," stated Larson matter-of-factly as he calmly loaded his rifle for the next kill.

After a long, hot trek through the zigzagging, sheltered approach trenches, Clay was relieved to be able to stand erect, stretching the cramped muscles in his back. He walked the short distance to a grove of shady trees where Grant had pitched his headquarters tents. He had ordered Lot to wait there for him: seeing no point in both of them running the risks inherent in a daytime trip to the front trenches. He was mildly surprised to see Lot and Bierce sitting on adjacent cracker boxes under a large tree, the sergeant engrossed in a copy of *Harper's Magazine*, while Bierce was writing furiously in a notebook. Ever since they had retrieved the temporarily deranged Sherman, the two had gotten on comfortably with each other, despite all expectations. Clay was not sure he approved of this development.

Lot noticed Clay's approach and stood, rapidly folded up the political magazine, and saluted formally. Bierce merely cut his eyes at Clay, touched the bill of his kepi absently, and wrote rapidly in the notebook.

"Did you find Sergeant Larson?" Lot asked.

"Yes, I did. A dangerous soldier. In any event, he saw nothing decisive. Tonight, I will write down everything he said; one can never tell when subsequent events may lend significance to what was assumed insignificant at the time."

With a flourish, Bierce underlined his last line and snapped his notebook shut. "That's a good stopping point. Are you ready, Captain? I saw little point in meeting with Rawlins until you were back; thought you'd undoubtedly want to know where I was and what I was doing."

"I am sure everyone appreciates your consideration. Were you writing a report for Colonel Rawlins there?"

"The notebook? Oh, that's something personal," Bierce replied as he restored the book to his haversack. "A work of fiction I hope to sell to the magazines someday. I'm thinking of calling it, 'An Occurrence at Owl Creek Bridge.' A Confederate spy is being hanged, and imagines a lengthy escape in the interval between the drop of the trap and the snap of his neck. The reader does not know the escape is imaginary until the last paragraph. I view it as a comedy."

"Ready to see Rawlins?"

A short walk took the three soldiers past the sentries and into Grant's large command tent. Grant, himself, was not there, but Rawlins and Parker were there, pouring over a pile of documents and dispatches together.

The three saluted formally, and then Bierce petitioned, "Colonel Rawlins, I would like a pass to go outside our lines. One of my sources of information lives in the neighborhood, in fact only a half-mile from our lines, but he fears his Confederate neighbors and would rather not be seen entering our camp."

"I suppose that means you'll be needing some more gold," replied the pale Rawlins.

"Of course, my source is a very *mercenary* individual, and, also, very old-fashioned; doesn't hold with greenbacks."

Rawlins stared at Bierce for a moment—his large, eyes underlined boldly with dark circles made even darker by his pasty, sickly pallor the whites somewhat jaundiced—contemplating the consequences. "Ordinarily, I would check with the General, but he has gone up to Memphis for two days, trying to unsnarl the confusion in our supply arrangement. I don't think he would object if I used my judgment in this matter. You've given us good results. I imagine it's money well spent." With swift bold strokes, Rawlins wrote and signed a pass, handed it to Bierce, and proceeded to open a wooden chest beside Grant's camp cot. The others heard the heavy chinking of coins, and when Rawlings turned around, he had five double-eagles in his hand.

"One hundred in gold, Lieutenant Bierce. Hard to get specie out of Washington, but your scouts have saved lives, and so I suppose it is worth it."

Clay changed the atmosphere of the tent when he addressed Major Parker, who had been silently watching the transaction. "Major, I had the pleasure of meeting Sergeant David Larson this afternoon."

The broad-shouldered, intimidating man—giving no outward sign of acknowledgement.

"Apparently, he has quite an unusual commission from you to engage in wide-ranging sniping activities. It seems very unusual for a staff officer to be controlling such assignments. Can you tell me whether General Grant has any knowledge of this?"

Parker continued to stare blankly at Clay, who wondered if he had even heard him. Then he said, "With the concurrence of Colonel Rawlins, I have not bothered the General with this particular matter, and I would take it as personal favor if you did not bother him with it either."

"If you insist. Be that as it may, I cannot restrain my curiosity. Why have you exercised your discretion in such an *affirmative* way?"

Parker's eyes bored into Clay. "Because General Grant is the finest man I know."

Clay countered, "An unusual response, if you don't mind my saying so."

Parker thought through his response before speaking, "You will never truly understand Sam Grant until you are aware of these two things: he is the greatest man you are ever likely to meet, and he hates being a soldier."

Clay leered. "He chose the wrong profession in that case."

Parker squared his shoulders in defense of his leader. "Fate chose him for the profession. He is a brilliant general. What he would like to have done has no more to do with it than the color of my skin has to do with my druthers."

"A strange attitude, Major."

"If you had been born an Indian, you would understand better." He announced to Grant's chief of staff, "Rawlins, I will see our guests over to the corral for their horses. I'll be back in a few minutes." Motioning to the trio, he said, "Gentlemen, come with me."

Parker led the three out of the tent and out of earshot of the brace of sentries. Abruptly, he stopped and ordered Lot, "Sergeant, retrieve the best three you can find from the sorry nags in the headquarters corral. I need to speak to Captain Clay and Lieutenant Bierce."

Concerned, Lot saluted and strode off.

When out of earshot, Parker lit into the two officers, enraged, which made him all the more terrifying for the calm quiet words he issued forth. "I will only say this once, so listen well. In your different ways, and for different reasons, you may be able to bring grief on Sam. If either of you harm him in any way, I will keep you dying for two weeks. My father and grandfather taught me *interesting* ways to deal with enemies.

"Sam Grant treated me like a man when every white I knew either spurned me as a savage or treated me with condescending contempt. I bore it, for my father's sake. He told me this was now the white man's country and that I should go to his schools and learn his ways, for it was no sense to wish for yesterday to come again. It was years before I understood fully what he meant when he said it would take more courage to live than to die in battle. It didn't matter that I had a college degree, that I became a skilled architect, that I spoke better English than most whites. I was a filthy, heathen savage wherever I went.

"When I first met Grant in Galena, he treated me fairly, unlike everyone else, but he was going through hard times and could not be choosy about his friends. When he received his general's star, I was certain he would want no more to do with the redskin." He paused, laboring under strong emotion, caught up in the memory.

"Then the most astonishing thing happened. Sam sauntered into my office, resplendent in a brigadier's uniform, and casually said he was holding a commission open for me. Thinking he was making an empty gesture, I said I was sure he could find a better staff officer. Then he said, quite calmly, he knew of no one he trusted more, and only one person he trusted as much, and he would consider it a personal favor if I would join his staff as a major. I have been with him ever since and have seen for myself that he is a great man and a great general.

"His only flaw as a general is his essential goodness. Bothered enough by the need to kill outright, he has trouble with the notion that you must fill the enemy's soul with terror. I save him that trouble wherever I can. In this case, word has gotten back to me a sniper has been unusually active against our men on the march. Many are filled with unease; make excuses not to go on patrol; spooked at shadows. Thinking this is a game that can be played by two, I found a superb marksman in the scrub Larson and told him to 'Go thou, and do likewise.' There was no need to bother the General with this; so much is already weighing down his soul. Evidently, it worked. The loss of our pickets due to snipers has significantly fallen off. Be that as it may, if either of you burden Sam Grant, I will remove your power to do so, by whatever means necessary."

"Very pretty sentiments, Major," responded Clay, "but you cannot hide the hatred you must feel to the white man and the white man's government, for a number of excellent reasons. Unkind people might suggest this could give you a motive for wishing ill on its armies, even to insinuate yourself into the confidence of a top commander, so at a key moment you could help to destroy it. A very potent vengeance."

Parker had become as immobile as a statue, his black eyes focused unwaveringly on the small, blonde captain. Then in a voice, barely above a whisper, he said, "If I did not think you might possibly be of use to Sam, you would die for that remark. As it is, pray to God I never come to believe you are of no use to him. Now, both of you have been warned. Go about your business." The proud Indian/Union warrior strode briskly away, back ramrod straight, the very picture of stoic dignity.

Bierce could hold back no longer, bleating, "Clay, you are a corker. That redskin is a dangerous man to cross at several levels; watching you provoke him was a *treat*."

Staring thoughtfully at Parker's retreating back, Clay never wavered. "The major holds much inside himself and must find it hard to hold it there. I wondered if a provocation might cause him to inadvertently reveal something of interest. It certainly did. He is filled with loathing and resentment for the white man. Perfectly understandable, but a probable motive for treason nonetheless."

"I guess that means I am no longer your chief suspect in the death of Brown."

"Oh, you still have a place of honor on my private list, Lieutenant Bierce. You are one of several men who might have had a very good motive."

"Come, sir, what motive could I have?"

"You are from southern Indiana, an area rife with Copperhead sympathizers to the Confederacy, and it just may be you enjoy the thrill of treason."

Suddenly quite sober, Bierce's stance became much more formal. "You don't like me very much. Fair enough, *I* don't like me very much. Nevertheless, I have always tried to conduct myself as a gentleman, but I do not regard betraying my country gentlemanly. You can believe it or not, as you please, and be damned, either way!" Bierce's cordial demeanor morphed into a fury oddly mingled with pain.

The confrontation was interrupted by the arrival of Lot, skillfully leading three horses by a tangle of reins. "Captain, is everything all right?" he asked, sensing the tension in the air.

Bierce answered for Clay. "Of course, Sergeant, everything is dandy. Now you can both come with me or not, as you choose. I have work to do."

The three mounted and rode off without a word.

The ramshackle cabin had seen better days. Although sufficiently shaded by mature trees, its condition spoke of poverty, but you could tell much effort had been spent in keeping it from sliding in total decay. Chickens pecked randomly at the ground in front of the cabin; from somewhere behind, a cow lowed. From the west came the sound of rifle reports, the Vicksburg lines scarcely a mile away.

They dismounted and loosely wrapped their horses' reins around a crude hitching post. The door was propped open in hopes of catching the rare summer breezes. Bierce strolled through the entrance without knocking, followed by Clay and Lot.

Two people were inside, seated in crude chairs on opposite sides of a plank table, frozen in the midst of what had been a comfortable conversation. One was Amelia Shea, the thin, lithe wife of Bierce's mercenary spy. Oddly enough, the man *was not* Amos Shea, as expected, but Andrew McFeely, the Scot soldier turned pacifist, and to all appearances fully recovered from his vicious beating. Near the hearth, a small redheaded child of about five played with a wheeled toy horse. McFeely leapt to his feet and automatically saluted British-style, palm outward, then quickly dropped his hand in embarrassment.

"Lieutenant Bierce, Captain Clay, I dinna know how you ken where I'd be, since I didna decide until this mornin' to visit the Sheas. Glad I be to see you. I've been tellin' Mrs. Shea what happened on the road to Jackson, and of the debt I owe you."

Bierce returned McFeely's involuntary salute in a breezy manner. "Pure coincidence, McFeely. We're here to see Amos Shea. I am glad to see your experience has left you with no ill effects."

"Still a wee stiff, Lieutenant. I had worse serving the little queen, but I was younger then and could shake it off easier. D'ya know Mrs. Shea?"

"We had the pleasure of meeting her in the company of her husband, last April," replied Clay, the tone of his voice suggesting the pleasure had been minimal.

"Captain Clay, Lieutenant Bierce, I owe you for what you do on Andy's behalf," replied Amelia Shea, deliberately ignoring Lot. "He's an old friend from before my marriage. Of course, I would have—I mean, he should have taken up arms, but I respect his refusal to do so. Not many hereabouts did. But was it necessary to shoot those two Rebs, Captain?"

"It was not necessary, madam, although, it was very much a pleasure," responded Clay brutally.

The muteness that followed was broken by Lieutenant Bierce, clearing his throat. "In any event, Mrs. Shea, I came here to receive a report from your husband, and to pay him his lucre."

"Amos is over at 13th Corps headquarters. He heard the general there might need some scoutin' and figured to pick up more work along this line."

Bierce threw his hand to his head, affecting a melodramatic pose of despair. "Unfaithful wretch! Damn! And he told me I was his only one!"

"You don't pay that much, Lieutenant, an' I want a good life for little Zach there," she said gesturing to the boy, who looked up from his play upon hearing his name. "And anyways, it don't interfere with what Amos does for you."

"Thanks for the toy, Uncle Andy," said the child fondly.

"You shouldn't have brought him a store-bought toy," said Amelia in a scolding tone. "I know how little you've been able to earn, what with those hereabouts spurning you, except for the worst kind of day work."

"Ach, couldn't spend it better than on the bairn. He's a bonny lad. He'll grow up soon enough and find out what a hard world it is. Let him enjoy the spring of his years."

Subtly angry, she changed the subject, addressing Bierce, "Amos thought you might be by. He had me write down what he larnt recently and expects to be paid for it." She went to the simple mantelpiece over the fireplace and took down a ceramic pot in the shape of a castle. Clay was reminded of the castle looming over Edinburgh, although the workman-ship was so crude it was impossible to be sure. Holding it in her oddly small, fine-boned hands, she brought it over to the table, partly lifted the lid, and extracted a crumpled paper so quickly no one could have seen what else was inside before the lid was back on.

Bierce quickly scanned the document. "Nothing to set the world ablaze, but some useful information on Johnston's strength and the movements of Forrest's cavalry, assuming it's true. As your husband has generally been accurate, I think this is worth some of Uncle Sam's gold." He casually dropped the coins on a copy of *Harper's* laying on the table.

"That is an unusual magazine to find in a household such as this," commented Clay, gesturing toward the illustrated periodical. It was open to an inner page, where an article was entitled "Rebel Sniper Takes Life of Wizard of Providence." There was an accompanying woodcut. Although grainy, it was recognizably Lieutenant John Brown.

"I like knowin' what's happenin' in the world beyond Mississipp," replied Amelia, insulted by the implied slur on her social status. "Even an ignorant cracker likes to know things. For instance, the article on that feller Brown, I had no notion of what them bastards in Starry Wisdom were doin' to the tykes. If that poor feller hadn't put an end to it, an' seen 'em hanged, no tellin' how long it would have gone on. What a shame for a man who done all that to die such a way. That picture there is not very good. Wonder what he really looked like?"

Wordlessly, Clay removed the picture case from the inner pocket of his tunic, opened it, and placed the family portrait near the magazine illustration. "I would say it is a fair likeness."

"Jesus!" exclaimed Amelia. "That the feller's wife and daughters?"

"Yes, his widow and four fatherless children, condemned to start life on the government's generous grant of fifteen dollars per month." Clay, kept his voice carefully neutral.

Amelia Shea behaved curiously agitated. "Close that thing up! I don't want little Zach seein' such things!"

Clay complied with her demand, carefully closing the picture case, and sticking it in his inner pocket, although there was little chance the child was paying any attention, as he focused on his new muse. He started towards the door, hesitated, then asked, "Mr. McFeely, are you literate and experienced in mathematics?"

The Scot laughed heartily. "Did ya ever see a Scot who didna know his sums, couldna calculate interest, or had trouble in writin' a dunnin' letter to a defaultin' debtor?"

Clay favored McFeely with the curl of the corner of his mouth. "It has indeed been my experience that the inhabitants of Scotland place a proper emphasis on the value of education. In any event, I have substantial property and business interests in Kentucky. I attempt to regulate them by letters while serving the army, but as you can imagine, that is not entirely satisfactory. Mrs. Shea has indicated hostility toward your lack of enthusiasm for the Confederacy is hindering your ability to earn a living. If you are willing, I would be able to pay you a sum to personally run some documents up to Kentucky and to return here with an eyewitness report on how my agents are handling my interests. Would such employment be agreeable to you?"

"If the money be ready, then I be your man."

"Come to my tent tonight then, and we will settle on terms. You'll have no trouble finding it; it is near General Grant's." As he led Bierce and Lot out of the cabin, he did not fail to note the remorseful yet sinister Amelia Shea.

Late that night, a furious Colonel Rawlins stormed into the tent Clay and Lot shared. Clay had been quietly reviewing Brown's notebook for the hundredth time, while Lot polished his boots; both were astonished at the enraged actions of the normally self-contained Rawlins.

"Have you seen Bierce?" he demanded loudly. "I need him, and he's nowhere to be found!"

"If he is not in his tent, then I have no idea where to find the lieutenant," Clay said calmly.

Rawlins rounded on Lot. "You. You have been pretty thick with our free-ranging spirit lately. Where do you think he might be?"

Lot could not meet the enraged colonel's eyes. "I have no idea, sir."

"May I ask the reason for the urgency?" Clay asked.

"The upriver station has signaled Grant's boat is about to dock. Whenever he's been away like this, the first thing he demands is a complete intelligence briefing. I need Bierce there, and no one can find him!"

Clay could read his friend's moods well enough to deduce Lot knew exactly where Bierce had gone, but revealing it could cause trouble for the lieutenant. Clay decided to save his conscientious friend further agony. As it happened, Clay was fairly certain himself where Bierce was.

"Colonel Rawlins, a sutler has set up a series of tents outside our patrolled lines. In those tents are reputed to be women of great physical charms and little virtue. Our Lieutenant Bierce has been a regular habitué of this establishment; the passes he has for his duties allowing him to pretty much come and go as he pleases."

The normally pale colonel flamed to blood red. "That whore-master! I hope he dies of the pox! I'll have his sorry carcass in the stockade before the night is out!"

"I would advise against that," said Clay in a reasonable tone of voice. "I believe he only indulges himself carnally when there are no immediate duties. Also, I have reason to believe some of the most useful information he has been providing to you recently has come from *talkative* employees in the establishment in question.

He has just made sure you were not burdened with the knowledge of the source. And, I have not been able to entirely eliminate him as a suspect in the murder of Lieutenant Brown. His sustained freedom may give him a sense of security, which could lead to a misstep."

Rawlins glared at Clay, considering the force of his arguments. "All that is as may be, Captain, but I still need—"

"Lieutenant Ambrose G. Bierce, reporting for duty, sir!" came a loud voice from the entrance of the tent. His uniform was neat enough, his eyes clear enough, but a faint, decadent odor wafted into the tent, a combination of liquor and perfume. Clay was amazed Bierce had somehow been alerted to the rampaging Rawlins; the lieutenant did indeed have a natural gift for intelligence.

"Bierce, where in the name of the Lord have you been?" grated Rawlins.

"Combining business with pleasure, sir, definitely pleasure," replied Bierce just short of insolent.

"I will deal with you later, Lieutenant. Right now, you come with me. You, too, Captain. I would not be surprised if General Grant would want to hear of your progress on the Brown matter immediately."

"There is sadly little to report, but of course I will comply with your wishes, Colonel. Sergeant, come with us."

The foursome set out for the steamboat landing, winding their way through the organized confusion of the army encampment. It was surprisingly easy to avoid obstacles; the night sky was clear, the moon near full. They reached the top of the bluffs just in time to watch the deck crew of a side-wheeler finish tying up to one of the docks down below. Setting a quick pace, Rawlins led the others down the steep path to the docks.

Just as they reached the newly arrived vessel, a familiar figure could be ascertained at the top of the gangway. Grant descended unsteadily and tripped on nothing obvious on the bottom, barely saving himself from a bad fall by clutching the rail. He straightened himself with difficulty, swung his head toward his chief of staff, then said in a slurred voice, "Howdy, John. Missed you. Nothin' to do. Would've liked to talk. Jus' like old times. Who's that with you? Ah, Bierce. Bitter Bierce. Good soldier, sorry excuse for a man. Have to take what we can get in war. Oh, Clay. Darn shame; dis- dis-grace to the army. Hard to stand the sight of man who did . . . Ah, children are all we have in the end, aren't they?"

Rawlins was literally frozen in shock. Clay and Lot frowned, while Bierce grinned from ear to ear.

In a low voice, which carried in the silence, Rawlins said, "Sam, you told me never again. You promised me."

Grant's eyes would not leave his feet as he mumbled, "Meant it, John, truly meant it. Trouble sleeping . . . dreams . . . no one to talk to." He shook his head as if to clear it, then started walking unsteadily up the path. "Ah, got to get to headquarters. Good old headquarters. Got to get back to planning deaths of good men. Who's gonna do it, if I don't? Sherman, good man, smart man but needs someone to hold his reins or he'll run away with you and himself. McPherson's too young, needs experience. Darn McClernand's a fool; would kill more'n me an' still manage to lose war. It's all up to me, all up to me . . ." Grant's voice trailed off. As he trudged unsteadily along, he fumbled with a cigar, taking a long time to get it lit with a curious mechanical flint device an admirer had recently sent to him.

Rawlins swiftly moved to Grant's side, holding his left arm to steady the tipsy commanding general, whispering fierce words into his ear the others could not quite catch.

Not having been dismissed, they trailed behind Grant, heading to the command tent. As they approached his tent, guarded by two stolid sentries, Grant veered to the right, shaking off Rawlins' hold, making for the small corral where his favorite horse was penned.

Dimly lit by a nearby campfire, Jeff Davis unerringly sensed his master and trotted up to the gate. The horse was a recent gift of Sherman's to Grant, winning its name from Sherman's foragers who'd seized it from a plantation owned by the Confederate president's brother.

Affectionately, Grant stroked the animal's forehead, growling, "Jeff hasn't been exercised. Can tell. Don't doggone fools around headquarters know you can't leave a fine creature like this penned up with nothing to do for days on end? Ruins his spirit. Horses love freedom; all creatures do. Get me a saddle and tack. Gonna take Jeff for a ride."

Rawlins was appalled. "Sir, you are in no cond—It is dangerous to ride at night."

"Non-nonsense. Night's best time for a good ride. It's dark. Can melt into the dark, an' feel free."

"Sam, I don't think—"

"Colonel Rawlins, get me a saddle and tack!" bellowed Grant in a commanding voice none of those present had heard him use before. Stiffening as if struck in the face, Rawlins hesitated, then formally saluted and moved off wordlessly.

Clumsily, Grant undid the gate and led Jeff Davis out. "Darn fine animal," he said. "Sherman knows horseflesh." Absently stroking the animal's mane, Grant became aware of his scout. "Ah, Bierce. I believe you're a feller who likes taking a nip. I need some hair of the dog. Let me have a pull from what you've got."

Albeit amused, Bierce's eyes darted around wary, uncertain. "General, sir, I'm not sure if what I carry is of good enough quality for a man of your rank. And besides, I wouldn't want to get Colonel Rawlins on my back. He has a bee in his—"

"Never mind Raw-Rawlins! I'm the general, not him. Hand over what you've got. I'll make it good for you later."

Cordially but with visible reluctance, the lieutenant drew a battered silver flask from an inner pocket and handed it wordlessly to the already inebriated general. Grant uncapped it, and putting it to his mouth, he drank enthusiastically. A faint odor of cheap whiskey wafted to the reluctant witnesses, who watched with increasing concern as the army's commander drained the entire flask without taking it from his lips, without a single shiver. When done, Grant recapped the container with difficulty, then fumbled in his trousers pocket until he fished out a large coin. "Here's a half dollar, Lieutenant. Should be about right to get that thing filled again."

Glaring, nostrils flaring, Rawlins reluctantly but quietly began to saddle the animal and fit the reins.

Astonishingly, it was Clay who maintained Rawlins' plea. "General Grant, sir. With deepest respect, I must urge you not to do this. If you are injured, who will provide the leadership the army needs?"

Grant refused to look at the captain. "Suppose you're right. But sometimes, I need to run. Sometimes memories are too real."

"Memories, sir?" Clay inquired.

"Memories. Things a feller shouldn't have in his head. Didn't need to drink when I was young. But sometimes it's only the thing that can make memories go away." His steely gaze, regardless of the deep shadows surrounding them, penetrated Bierce. "I take it you understand such needs, Lieutenant."

Bierce stood there solemnly. "Yes, sir, I do," he said simply.

Grant's eyes lost their focus. "Mexico was bad enough. Saw awful things, plumb awful. Saw men, Mexicans and Americans, dead and bloated. Saw fellers still alive with their guts on the ground, tryin' to stuff 'em back into their bellies. Saw an officer live a full day after his lower jaw was carried clean away by a cannon ball. But bad as that was, it couldn't hold a candle to Panama."

Clay had not heard of this. "Panama, sir? What happened there?"

"Panama. After Mexico, I was assigned to an infantry company being transported to California. Commander was a puffed up major named Bonneville. Should've taken the long way, round the Horn. Everyone knew the fever was in Panama. But takin' a boat from New Orleans to Panama, marchin' across, an' catching a boat on the far side was quicker and cheaper. Figured on lookin' like a hero to Washington, I guess. Anyway, eighty-some-odd soldiers, many of whom brought wives and children, about two hundred all told."

Rawlins, who had finished saddling the horse, joined Clay and Lot in staring at Grant with rapt attention. It was clear he'd not heard this either. Grant disregarded their reactions, and all else, as he was reliving that time a dozen years before.

"Told 'em to boil the water. Told 'em all, and kept telling 'em! But the jungle was so darn hot and humid, and the water in the streams looked so clear and pure. Couldn't be everywhere at once. Company was spread out along the narrow trail. Bonneville didn't care. Womenfolk and children started sneaking drinks, and then their men folk started figuring it was safe. Didn't matter how clear it was. Guess that Frenchie doctor is right about little bugs you can't see. Told 'em. Told 'em! Should've done more. No excuses, and Bonneville was useless. I was second in command. Should've . . . should've . . .

"First signs of cholera didn't show up until we reached the Pacific Coast. Then Columbian port authorities quarantined us. Can't blame them, I suppose, though I did at the time. Then the dying started. First children, then joined by women and their men. Bonneville ran. I was only officer left. Did what I could. Organized shelter on the beach where they forced us to stay. Those who weren't sick were scared out of their minds. Suppose they were right to be scared. I was sure scared. Couldn't let it show, though. They were all looking to me, and I had to set an example. They depended on me, and there was nothing I could do to make any difference. Did what I could. I helped clean the ill, sponge their bodies, try to keep liquid in them while their traitor bowels leaked their lives away. Poor fools thought if their officer was changing the fouled sheets, it couldn't be quite as dangerous as they thought. I expected to catch it any day. I *hoped* I would catch it. Then, I was *angry* I wasn't catching it, so I could be delivered from a living hell. But for some reason, I'll never understand why, I didn't catch it.

"About half of them ended up getting it. Of those who got infected, about one-third recovered. But it really hit the children hard. All caught it, and all died. Lord, the wailing when I would take the bodies out to the beach and arrange the cremation the port authorities demanded for those dead from the cholera. And the smell! I thought the smell of my pappy's tannery was the worst there could be—Oh, no. When those who were going to die had died, and the remainder had recovered enough to travel, I led them onto a leased boat, which took us up to the fort on the coast north of San Francisco. I expected they would hate me, blame me for not saving their nearest and dearest. Do you know the most horrible thing? They all adored me, depended on me. I couldn't stand it! I failed them, and they treated me like some kind of hero!

"One night a grizzled, old veteran of Mexico, a sergeant who would gut an Indian with a bayonet just for the practice, came up to me when I was alone on the deck of the ship. His skinny little wife and tiny daughter had both died in my arms. I expected him to try to throw me over the side, and half of me wouldn't have minded. But instead of assaulting me, he hugged me and started bawling. Between sobs, he thanked me over and over again for trying my best, saying he couldn't do it before the men but wanted me to know how much what I had done meant to him, and told me whatever I needed that he could give was mine. It made me feel as bad as could be.

"When I got to the fort, the dreams started coming. The dreams always ended the same way: in a tent, on a tropical beach, with the old sergeant's wife and daughter dying horribly in my arms. Then something happens, and they are Julia and little Fred, and they're dying, and there isn't a doggone thing I can do. Sometimes the dreams would torment me during the day. Fort doctor said a man can't dream while he's awake, but I know different. Started drinking real heavy; the dreams didn't come as often. The more I drank, the less often they came. Pretty soon, I was drinking pretty much all the time. Colonel Buchanan, the fort commander, didn't care much for officers who drank; told me I could choose to resign or face a court martial. I resigned."

The witnesses to this drunken monologue were so entranced they scarcely noticed the four Provost General horsemen who rode up to Grant's tent and were greeted by Major Parker; no doubt rendering some late report relating to the security of the encampments.

Grant lurched over to the horse and lay the side of his head along the animal's neck, eyes completely unfocused, lost in bygone night-mares. "Very strange," he muttered in a slurred voice. "Moment I got back to 'em, dreams stopped. Was real hard-scrabble; wasn't much good at anything but soldierin'. Didn't matter. Julia put up with the hard times, bless her. And, as long as I was with her and Fred, the thoughts, dreams, whatever were right out of my head. Then war came, and the country needed every officer it could get, even washed up drunks. It's really a para-paradox. When I was real busy dealing out death and destruction, everything was all right. Only when things were quiet-like did I need Julia and Fred to keep away . . . to keep away . . ."

All at once, Grant became terrified, white as a sheet. Those who saw it would later find it hard to describe—fear, loneliness, panic, regret—all a human being could stand concentrated in one man.

"Gotta run! Gotta leave it all behind. Gotta run!" he shouted in a piercing voice. With a surprisingly athletic leap for someone so drunk, he was in the saddle and spurring Jeff Davis into a wild gallop.

"Sam!" screamed Rawlins at the top of his lungs. "Stop! You'll kill yourself!"

The commanding general paid no heed, charging rapidly into the darkness.

Without a sound, Clay sprinted the short distance to where the four mounted soldiers were quietly conversing with Parker. They had jerked their heads around in surprise at Rawlins's screams, but much less expected Clay, who shoved a corporal out of his saddle, sending him sprawling. Vaulting into the saddle, he frantically urged the animal into pursuit of Grant.

Rawlins, Lot, and Bierce were only steps behind. At a shouted command from the chief of staff, the other three tumbled voluntarily from their mounts. Astonished, Parker watched the three take off into the night after Clay.

With reason, Clay considered himself a superb horseman. But as he chased after the galloping general, he realized with amazement that Grant drunk was a better rider than Clay sober. The moon shone bright, but not bright enough to illuminate all the obstacles and pitfalls. Heedless, Grant urged his mount around, over, and through every conceivable barrier. At one point, Clay was gaining on the general, only to see him effortlessly jump his steed clean over a buckboard in his path. He dared not attempt the same maneuver in the dark, and he lost precious seconds going around the wagon. Soon after, a large campfire, lit by a Union infantry company, stood in the way, a stew kettle bubbling merrily over it. Grant effortless cleared the large fire, kettle and all. Knowing he could not be sure of equal success, Clay fell further behind, then even further as he slew through the surrounding tents and surprised soldiers who were clueless of what was transpiring. Fearing a Confederate raid, they seized their rifles and began to fire. A bullet whizzed past Clay's ear. Ignoring Rawlins' shouts of cease-fire behind him, he concentrated all his senses on gaining on the general. Several more encampments were rudely disturbed in rapid succession; only the darkness kept them from realizing it was their commanding general causing their temporary fright.

Clay was certain Jeff Davis would, at any moment, step into some hole or trip on some obstruction obscured in the shadows, sending Grant flying to break his neck on a tree or crush his skull on a rock. Then, by a combination of luck and superb horsemanship that even drink could not eclipse, Grant unerringly avoided all such deathtraps.

It was at that moment, a tent with a small fire nearby came into view, and Clay realized Grant had led them in a huge circle, bringing them back to his headquarters. Parker, two sentries, and the four forlorn soldiers from the Provost's office had not moved from the front of the tent. Seeing a figure approaching he knew must be Grant, in no fit state to be seen by casual witnesses, Parker barked an order to the horseless troopers, who scurried off into the darkness so quickly they forgot to salute.

Grant brought his exhausted animal to a stop directly in front on Parker and slid smoothly off his back. He was patting the heaving sides of the tired beast with affection when Clay rode up and swiftly dismounted, followed in a few moments by Rawlins, Bierce, and Lot.

"Major, I wouldn't ordinarily ask this of you . . ." started Grant, much soberer than when he commenced his wild gallop. "I'm tired from the trip, and this magnificent animal needs to be toweled off and watered. Could you handle that for me?"

"Yes, sir," said Parker most respectfully, eyeing the furious Rawlins over Grant's shoulder.

In an appalling breach of military etiquette, Rawlins grabbed his commander's arm and dragged him into the tent. Angry words were immediately audible.

Clay only hesitated for a moment before saying, "Major Parker, have our horses tended for as well; then join the lieutenant and the sergeant in my tent for a few hours. I think Colonel Rawlins will only require my help him with the general."

Parker could not believe his ears. He thought the captain had less right than himself to aid Ulysses Grant. But then he remembered his own binge drinking, a secret from all but Grant, which made him an appallingly stereotypical drunken redskin and knew he was not the one to give help to Grant this time.

"Fine, Captain. Send for me when you feel the general is rested."

Clay saluted, then entered the tent, leaving the others to swiftly care for their horses, grateful to have left the scene of what could have been a career-destroying scandal.

Inside the tent, Rawlins was speaking to Grant in a low voice charged with more emotion than other people's screams. "Sam, you may have thrown it all away! How could you? How in the name of the Lord could you?" He gasped for air. "You told me that was all behind you: that you would never—never—" Rawlins could not go on and began coughing a series of deep, rasping coughs that could not manage to clear his lungs. After an especially violent series, he quickly brought a handkerchief to his mouth. When the coughs subsided, he removed the cloth and stared at the crimson it contained. He hurled the bloody garment into a far corner of the tent and collapsed, silently weeping into a camp chair.

In a controlled effort, Grant walked over to his dear friend and put a hand on his shoulder, at a loss as to what to say.

"There isn't much time left, Sam," said Rawlins miserably between sobs. "I had to work myself into ill health when the worthless alcoholic I had for a father drank himself into an early grave, and Mother and all my brothers and sisters became *my* responsibility. And I met that responsibility! But Lord, it was hard. The work was unrelenting, but no one dependent on me was ever in want. I know pride is a sin, but I confess I was proud of that. Now I have children of my own, children without a mother, and I support them like I supported my worthless father's offspring. As much as I worry about leaving them, I worry about leaving no mark in this world. When we met, back in Galena, I could tell there was more to you than a weak-willed drunk, Sam. And when the war started, I realized we both were going to leave a legacy behind. You were going to win this war, and I was going to help you to win it."

"That's true," said Grant quietly. "Even when I got my first star, the most I hoped for was a cavalry division. You and Ely, and of course Julia, were the only ones who thought I would ever rise to command a great army."

"And you have been brilliant, Sam! You've justified all the faith I ever had in you. That's why I weep when I see you slip back into the bottle. That's why I stormed and raged that other time and made you swear before the Lord God not again! It's not even that you're addicted. You know you're not! You can go *months* without touching a drop. No, you *choose* the bottle!"

"Yes, I do, John." His voice cleared, as did his eyes, except for the moisture. He grunted and swallowed. "I've hurt those I care about more than I care to think. I was so wrapped up in self-pity, I didn't stop to think what it would do to them. I know it is hard for you to believe after tonight, but I promise this will *never* happen again. *Never.*" Grant released Rawlins' shoulder, and an infinite weariness washed over him. "I need to sleep. Tomorrow will be time enough to start planning the deaths of fine young fellers. Just do me one favor, John . . ." Grant hesitated with embarrassment. "Stay here until I'm fast asleep. I may need to . . . talk to someone."

It was then he noticed Clay, who had witnessed the whole drama emotionlessly. "Captain Clay, you are in a position to do me two favors. One, stay with Colonel Rawlins for a spell. As you have seen, he is not in good health. I would rest easier if someone was here to make sure he has aid if needed. Two, on your honor as a gentleman, never breathe a word of what you have seen to another soul."

The response was immediate. "You have my word, sir."

Grant nodded, but said nothing. Without removing any clothing, not even his hat, he collapsed onto the camp bed, and in moments was softly snoring.

Clay drew the tent's remaining camp chair up alongside Rawlins. Reverently, they watched the commander of the Army of the Tennessee sleep for some time, until Clay spoke. "I was wrong, Colonel Rawlins, in demanding Mrs. Grant and Fred Grant be sent away. I demanded that as much for reasons of my own as for concern over their safety. You should telegraph Mrs. Grant at first light and let her know her husband needs his family."

Rawlins nodded silently, staring at the sleeping form on the cot.

After thinking for a moment, Clay spoke again. "I suppose it is a weakness in a great commander to need his family so. Still, as weaknesses go, it speaks well of him that alcohol is his second choice."

The petite captain and the pale, gaunt colonel remained vigilant over their sleeping commander for the rest of the night.

Jeremiah Lot and Ely Parker shuddered involuntarily as Ambrose Bierce finished his gruesome tale of a man literally frightened to death by the ghosts of the wife and children he had murdered years before. They were seated on empty cracker boxes around a small campfire in front of the tent Clay and Lot shared. All three had been concerned about what was happening back at headquarters, so Bierce had decided to divert them by telling them a story he was thinking of putting into writing, to take their minds off things.

Lot chortled, "Lord, Lieutenant, when I was a child, the stories of haints the old slaves told frightened me nearly to death, but they couldn't hold a candle to you. You really should write that down and sell it to one of the magazines."

Parker drew out a pipe and began to absently fill and light. "Bierce, I admit you can spin a yarn better than most, but after all, you are only talking about fiction. At some level, we know it isn't real, so it doesn't truly frighten us."

"So, Major, you've heard more frightening stories around the tribal campfire?" Bierce challenged.

"As a matter of fact, I did, as a youth. Of course, there were stories made up to frighten little ones, which had no effect on the braves. But late at night, when the children could not hear, sometimes tales would be told by those who believed them to be true. Some may have been originally lies, but some were undoubtedly true."

Bierce guffawed at Parkers revelation. "Ignorant savages scared of thunder and cringing at the wind."

Parker *did not* laugh. "Perhaps, Lieutenant, but there were many things braves, who were not fools and were afraid of nothing, feared: things the white man did not fear because they had not read of them in books and because college professors laughed. Things like the Manitou."

"What's a Manitou?" asked Lot.

"No one knows for sure because no one who gets close to one

ever comes back. It is said he is an evil spirit who eats human flesh, can disguise himself as any animal, and cross the forests with the speed of the wind. It is said that among many of his snares, he can assume the form of a deer and lead a lone hunter far away from his people. Then he lets the hunter come close, and only then, in his last moments, does the hunter see the true shape of the Manitou."

Lot felt a chill creep up his spine. It must have shown on his face, for Bierce laughed. "You two are a pretty pair," he said. "It is amusing to tell tales of monsters and ghosts, but we live in the 19th Century, an era of science, of steam, of physics. Ghosts and goblins are now banished to the nursery and used to frighten misbehaving children into obedience. Why, I will bet either of you twenty dollars in gold you could not tell me a true story that would really frighten me."

"That is hardly a fair bet," said Parker. "You would be the sole judge of what frightened you."

"True enough. You would have to trust my sense of honor, and you *can* trust it since I don't require you to cover the bet. You win, I pay twenty dollars; I win, you pay nothing." In the flickering light of the campfire, a cloud could be seen passing over Bierce's face. "But be warned, I saw something truly horrible in Indiana, more horrible in certain respects than anything you have seen in this war so far. After that, I don't think any tale could truly frighten me. Alright, gentlemen, what do you say? Do you have a true story up to the challenge? What's the most frightened you've ever been?"

Sergeant Lot stared anxiously into the fire, poking it with a stick, before speaking. "Lieutenant Bierce, I can tell you a story of the most frightened I have been that will terrify you to your marrow. But I'm not doing it to win a bet. I must ask both of you, what do you think of Captain Clay?"

"A bad man," Parker said without hesitation. "Brave of course; there are uses in war for bad men. But what the newspapers said about New Orleans . . ." Parker shook his head in disgust.

"Oh, clearly a candidate for Bedlam. Ought to be in a cage, but he's very entertaining to be around," added Bierce cheerfully.

"He is none of those things," said Lot sadly. "He is ever so much more complicated than the newspapers said."

"Are you saying the papers lied about the incident at the Devereaux plantation?" asked Parker.

"Oh, the accounts were accurate enough. It just wasn't the whole story. I am about to break confidence with Alphonso, so as hypocritical as it sounds, I want you to swear you will never repeat the story I am about to tell you."

"Why break the confidence then?" asked Bierce, amusement in his voice.

"Because I am the only living man who knows there is more to what happened than what was printed in the newspapers. Death comes unexpectedly in war. I want there to be someone who knows that if Alphonso Clay is a monster, there are reasons for it. Do I have your word?"

A solemn Parker and an amused Bierce both nodded their heads.

Lot then stared into the fire for a long time, marshalling his thoughts. "I have to go back quite a ways, to set the stage, so to speak. You must first understand, it is a very hard thing, being a Clay. Very hard. The family has high standards, very high. Many live up to them, but those who fail, fail spectacularly. There is light and dark in the family. On the one hand, you have those like Henry Clay, who, although a slaveholder, rejected the South to help preserve the Union, and, hence, lost forever the chance to be President. And, there is Cassius Clay, who survived decades of being an abolitionist crusader in Kentucky only through a proficiency with pistol and Bowie knife. On the other hand, you have those like my father."

Lot could not tear his eyes from the embers. "Of course, you can tell I have white blood. I and my sister Arabella was fathered on an unwilling slave by Decimus Clay, younger brother to Alphonso's father, Cicero. Our mother died giving birth to the stillborn result of yet another drunken outrage by Decimus."

The silence of the listeners was absolute, but Lot was completely unaware of how he had riveted them in their seats.

"The death of my mother caused Cicero to descend on his brother like the wrath of God. I was only eight at the time, but I distinctly remember when the enraged elder Clay arrived at the plantation, accompanied by the superintendent of the state asylum and a sheriff holding a court order for the commitment of Decimus as a "moral lunatic" and appointing Cicero as conservator for Decimus's estate. Decimus was drunk, as usual, and hardly understood what was happening. But to Cicero, it didn't matter whether his brother understood. In truth, he acted more like a madman than his brother did, shouting repeatedly of the disgrace his brother had brought on the family name by his drunkenness and fornication with inferiors. The befuddled alcoholic was led off unresisting to the madhouse, where he would hang himself six months later, completing his disgrace as far as Cicero was concerned, who would never mention him by name again.

"After his brother had been taken away, old Clay began to examine the slaves and the other property, limping along with the aid of his heavy cane. I never heard for sure how he had been lamed. Later on, some slaves said they believed he had been bayoneted in the leg by a Mexican grenadier at the battle of Buena Vista. They also said they believed the Mexican was dead.

"His stay ended by a detailed examination of the estate papers in the library. In my short life, I had known nothing but the arbitrary, drunken neglect of Decimus and his overseers, and I feared things would get worse.

"Slaves learn early to spy on their masters; knowing their moods, strengths and weaknesses is the key to survival. I snuck into the house and peeked around the corner of the library, wanting to get a close look at my new owner. I saw a short, heavy-set man, red-faced and angry, muttering with disgust over documents that apparently were not arranged, as they should have been. I was holding my seven-year-old sister's hand. To my amazement and dismay, Arabella shook off my grip, and, before I could react, she entered the room confidently. She stopped in front of the desk where Clay worked, curtseyed in an amazingly adult manner, and said, 'Good afternoon, sir. I believe you are our new master.'" Lot's eyes misted over at the image of his little sister, so sweet, so innocent.

"Clay dropped the papers in his hands and leaned back in surprise at the display of adult manners in a child of seven. Not wanting to leave her to solitary punishment, I entered the room and stood beside her, trying to keep from trembling. He probably only studied us for a few moments, but it so felt like an eternity.

"'Ah, you must be the two—You are the ones of which I have heard. Very adult, very adult. Blood will tell.' He paused, then said, almost to himself. 'What shall I do with you? Clay blood should not have been so mixed. But it is done.'"

"Face downcast, I mumbled, 'Sir, when will the master be back?'

"'That—He is *never* coming back,' responded old Clay in a furious voice.

"That scared me. As the offspring of his favorite concubine, Decimus had allowed us to live in the big house. I was old enough to realize we would now be sent to the miserable hovels Decimus had allotted to the field hands, and the prospect of losing the little comfort we had, on top of our mother's death, frightened me.

"'Once I have settled the affairs here, you two will be coming with me. My son recently lost his mother and is an only child. You will be his companions.'

"Two days later, after appointing an overseer for his brother's estate, known to be both honest and reluctant to use the whip, the elder Clay loaded us into his buggy and took us on the twenty-mile trip to his own plantation. Arabella and I had discussed running away, but even at our tender ages, we knew we would not get far. He squeezed us into the one-horse buggy on either side of him, and in five hours, we were at the estate he had named Dignitas.

"It was not what I had expected. No tobacco or cotton cultivated, the large fields had been designated primarily to grazing and horse paddocks. Much later, I learned Dignitas produced the finest thoroughbreds in the Bluegrass, the income from which would have by itself supported the expenses of the estate. Here and there were small buildings with chugging steam engines at their rears. I would find each of them was a small factory manufacturing some form of high-quality commercial product—cutlery, steel pens, cigar cases, that kind of thing. It was the most unusual plantation I was ever to see, although I didn't know it at the time.

"The main house was surprisingly modest, considering the estate encompassed nearly 6,000 acres: a three-story brick structure in the old-fashioned Federal style, unadorned by the pretentious pillars and porticos so common in plantation architecture. A middle-aged black woman came out, saw us pulling up to the front door, and hurriedly retreated inside, shouting something. By the time we clambered stiffly out of the buggy, and old Clay had secured the horse to the hitching post, a small, blonde child, not above nine years of age, had emerged from the house, impeccably dressed in miniature adult clothes. This was the first time I laid eyes on Alphonso Clay.

"The child acted incredibly mature and formal for one of his youth. He bowed slightly to his father, saying, 'Welcome home. Nothing serious happened in your absence. Who are these children?'

"'Good afternoon, Alphonso. This is Jeremiah and Arabella. They will be staying in the house with us.'

"Alphonso gravely shook my hand, then took Arabella's and kissed it lightly, European-style. He stepped back, scrutinizing. 'We're related to them, Father. You can tell from their build and faces. Has Uncle Decimus been naughty?' It was only several years later, I realized what an astonishing performance this was from a child of nine.

"'Alphonso, you will never mention him to me again. He is dead to me, Son, dead. Arabella and Jeremiah will be living with us in the main house as companions for you. It is not right that a child be on his own all the time, and my business will keep me occupied more than I would like.'

"'That should be interesting. Tell me, Father, what is their last name?'

"'People who are, uh, servants are discouraged from having last names by Kentucky, Son.'

"'Father, they really should have one. They *are* Clays.'

"'Perhaps you are right, Son. However, it cannot be Clay.'

"'Why not, Father? They *are* Clays.'

"The old man was most uncomfortable. 'Someday I will explain it to you. Notwithstanding, they shall have a last name.' He thought for a moment, then asked my sister and me, 'Do you have any objection to being called Lot?'

"'No sir,' Arabella said, replying for both of us. 'But why Lot?'

"'Do you know your Holy Bible?'

"'A little sir,' I responded.

"'You see, Lot was a righteous man who suffered for his righteousness at the hands of an evil city's people. The Lord had decided to destroy the evil city but told Lot in time for he and his family to flee. However, the Lord also warned them never to look back at what they had left behind, no matter what they heard. As the Lord began to destroy the evil city, Lot's wife could not help herself. For her defiance, she was turned into a pillar of salt. Let that be a warning to you. You are leaving one kind of life and entering another; never look back. Henceforth, you shall be Jeremiah and Arabella Lot.'

"And so, our life at Dignitas began. Swiftly, strong bonds formed between us children. It's not uncommon for white children to be friends of slave children when very young, but it usually ends abruptly at about the age of ten or twelve. My sister and I did not realize how privileged we were until much later. Old Clay did not put Alphonso in public schools, but hired, at great expense, a series of excellent tutors. To the amazement of most of them, Alphonso's father permitted my sister and me to attend. We found we had a thirst for knowledge and never sought to evade what others would have regarded as boring drudgery. Not that it was all education; there was hunting, fishing, riding. We grew very close, during those years; Alphonso and Arabella closest of all. I wasn't jealous of that. No, I saw them as affectionate brother and sister. Would that it had remained so . . .

"Dignitas was a very unusual place. Cicero Clay *was not* loved by the slaves; he was a cold, distant man. In any event, rare is the slave who can love his owner, no matter how well treated, even though he was respected. The slave quarters were clean and well-maintained; the overseers forbidden the use of the whip although harsh words permitted. Work was expected and demanded, but old Clay had set up a phased emancipation system. If you worked hard and loyally for a certain number of years, and otherwise showed yourself of good character, he would grant you your freedom and set you up in a small business of some sort in Louisville or Frankfurt. It was a hard-headed investment; he expected half the profits of the new businesses. But even so, a slave could have far worse masters than Cicero Clay. I don't believe he felt black people were his equal, but to be fair, I don't think he thought most white people were his equal. Although he felt chattel slavery was becoming obsolete, and, in a few generations, would diminish of its own accord, he was no abolitionist. He disagreed violently with his cousin Cassius. Yet, several times, I heard him express grudging admiration for his bravery in agitating for the end of slavery so publicly in a slave state.

"We grew up almost forgetting for long periods our status as blacks and as slaves, but then something would happen to remind us. A simple trip to Louisville would lead to a snide comment or offensive phrase. Usually, we just ignored the offender, no matter how much the words stung. Then just after Alphonso's 18th birthday, we had gone into town to buy something, I truly don't remember what. Abner Laing, the son of a prominent tobacco-grower, known for his wild ways, whistled at Arabella and then said . . . he said something that proved beyond doubt he was no gentleman, no matter how much money his daddy had. I started toward the young buck, intending to pound him into a pulp, but Alphonso grabbed my arm with a grip of iron and hissed, 'You know what happens if a black man strikes a white man in public.'

"'Let it go, Jeremiah,' Arabella added.

"With a great act of will, I turned back in the direction we had been heading, feeling humiliation, shame, and anger, all at the same time.

"When we got back to Dignitas, I spent the evening muttering and cursing under my breath. I was so wrapped up in my humili-ation and shame that when Alphonso slipped out that evening, I never noticed.

"The following afternoon, word reached Dignitas: Abner Laing had been killed that morning in a duel. The word around town was that Alphonso had challenged Laing and shot him through the heart. Dueling was illegal under Kentucky law, but there was no concern about the law; such 'affairs of honor' among the landed gentry were generally ignored.

"Old Clay took Alphonso into the library and had a long

discussion with him. When they emerged after an hour, the old man fairly glowed with pride and satisfaction. He told a servant to bring a horse and soon was galloping off, no doubt to boast about his son's success in an affair of honor.

"We were left standing in the parlor, with Arabella bestowing Alphonso the purest adoration. As for myself, my feelings were conflicted. I had wanted Laing hurt, but not dead. To my own surprise, I found myself sorry for what Alphonso had done.

"'Alphonso, it was not necessary for you to defend Arabella's honor, or my own, at least against an ill-bred wastrel,' I said to him.

"'It was not just your honor. Any insult to a Clay is an insult to me personally; I was defending my own honor as well.'

"'That's as may be, but I want you to swear on your honor you will not duel in the future. It's murder; I don't care whether the sheriff ignores it or no.'

"I was the recipient of a furious glare from Arabella, who apparently had no qualms about what had taken place.

"Alphonso studied me calmly with a faint sign of emotion. 'You are a better man than I. Jeremiah, you have my word; no more such affairs of honor. In any event, a further one would probably be unnecessary. I am sure the gossips and idlers are busily spreading the word of what happens to those who insult someone with Clay blood.'

"He was, in fact, correct. Verbal insults became a very rare thing when we ventured into public. Somehow, it did not please me as much as it should.

"The distinctions caused by our black ancestry became most apparent when it was time for Alphonso to go to college. Not even the wealth and connections of Cicero Clay could get a mulatto into a fine university. So, when Alphonso went away for his undergraduate work at Miskatonic College in Massachusetts, he made an unusual arrangement with Arabella and me. He promised to send us copies of every book and every lesson plan he received, so we could follow the process of his education, with only a lag caused by the mails. He was as good as his word. In effect, we received the benefit of a university education without ever leaving Dignitas. Somewhat to my surprise, old Clay thoroughly approved, especially when he saw how his niece and nephew kept up with the most abstract subjects without the help of a professor. If Clays have an overriding sin, it is pride in their blood and themselves.

"Not that it was all study. The old man was getting weary and forgetful, often complaining of blinding headaches. I asked if I could take some of the burden off him. Gratefully, he gave me more and more of the responsibilities of running the estate, until by '58, I was virtually the manager of Dignitas, at only the age of twenty-one. You should have seen the faces of some of the merchants when they saw a mulatto handling transactions in the thousands of dollars! Some refused to deal with me. I did not make a scene; I simply took the considerable business of Dignitas elsewhere. Most found their greed could override their bigotry. The only part of my responsibilities I hated was the need to give orders to the slaves. Usually, it was the overseer who did it, but sometimes I needed to get personally involved. Physical cruelty was not permitted at Dignitas, and yet, I felt disgust with myself at lording it over people with skins no darker than mine. Occasionally, I could conjure up a bit of naked hatred, but I never did anything. Truthfully, I didn't blame them.

"Arabella developed into the old widower's hostess. Cicero Clay had lost his wife when Alphonso was four, and apparently never felt the need to remarry. Naturally, he did miss a woman's light touch around the home, the kind of touch a mere servant could not provide. As she grew up, Arabella blossomed into perfection. Her beauty was remarked on by all who saw her;

her intelligence far surpassed that of myself, or, for that matter, her uncle. Only Alphonso was her equal, and none her superior. Her taste was faultless and used to perfection within the great house. Old Clay gave her leave to decorate as she would, and all acknowledged the house had become the most beautiful in the county. As if this was not enough, she became an accomplished musician. On vacations from college, Alphonso encouraged her to learn the piano and hired her tutors, although before long, they were not necessary. I remember many an evening when she played Beethoven, Mozart, and Mendelssohn to perfection, while Cicero Clay and myself listened with rapt admiration. During those times, Alphonso would bring back with him scores for the latest music arranged for piano, especially that new German fellow Richard Wagner. I never really liked Wagner's music; there was something decadent in it, but Alphonso and Arabella felt the German was ushering in a new musical age.

"I suppose our privileged life couldn't have lasted forever, but the coming of the war made it end sooner than it otherwise would. In the summer of '59, Alphonso came back from his first year at Harvard law school, where he had gone after graduating Miskatonic summa cum laude. He was ever so glad to be home, despite the fact he was coldly furious at something. Only gradually did Arabella and I worm it out of him. According to Alphonso, as sectional tensions increased, the sons of New England aristocrats at Harvard had been making insulting remarks to him about coming from a slave-holding family, and casting doubt on his devotion to the Union. Apparently, he had knocked one of the offenders down and had almost been expelled. I found out later it was only through pressure from Governor Nathaniel Banks, an old friend of the family, that his expulsion was avoided. The following year was even worse. Even though he held his temper in check, when he came home to Dignitas for the summer break in

'60, he raved for days about the dishonor of listening to the sons of lucky tradesmen doubt the patriotism of a Clay."

Lot took up a stick and stirred the fire. You could hear every crackle and pop, every cricket and rustle from the wind. Neither man in audience dared to utter a sound.

"That summer was when it all began; even I had no way of realizing it at that time. Alphonso's anger and rage just wouldn't go away, and nothing I was able to say or do made it any better. His father could do nothing. I am sure Cicero Clay loved his son, but he was a cold man with many secrets and had difficulty talking about personal matters. It was Arabella who could comfort Alphonso, could calm him. During that summer—it seems so long ago, even though only three years have passed—Alphonso and my sister grew closer and closer. More and more often, they rode out together by themselves across the estate; more and more often, no one could say where they were. At first, I was uneasy, and then I was frightened. Living the way we did, it was easy to forget there was a barrier that could be crossed only at one's peril. Clays did not engage in casual affairs with slaves; the unmentioned Uncle Decimus was the exception that proved the rule. If things went too far, Alphonso would want marriage, and that simply wasn't acceptable. Arabella knew that as well as I, which is why I *could not* understand why she did not insist on a respectable distance.

"Old man Clay was very worried, but then he was worried about many things, not least of which was the coming election victory of the Republicans, where he said publicly, and at every opportunity, would lead to a long and bloody war. Alphonso was back at Harvard for his final year during the election in November of '60. Almost immediately, neighbors began to choose up sides. Old Cicero began mobilizing what support and influence he had to keep Kentucky in the Union. As you know, he was one of key people who prevented a secession vote from coming up in Frankfurt.

"About the time it was clear Kentucky wouldn't secede, Alphonso came home from Harvard, a fresh law degree in hand, and a new anger in his heart. He had just . . ." Here Lot remembered the promise of secrecy he had taken to the weary President in the office of General Meigs and amended his story in midstream. ". . . performed a great service for an important man, and in performing that service had learned something of the Starry Wisdom cult that upset him very much. I never learned what it was; the one time I asked him, he laughed and said, 'Jeremiah, I am too fond of you to burden you with this knowledge. Just know, it is not a question of whether you would respect a confidence; I will not make your life uneasy where it is not necessary.' What I do know is that Arabella and Cicero knew something of it, and whatever it was, involved his German grandfather, Friedrich von Junzt, dead for a quarter of a century.

"One evening shortly after his return, I heard raised voices in argument, coming from the old man's library. It was unpardonable, I know, but I crept close enough to hear some of the dispute.

"'Son, there is no need for this. Slaughter and his minions were depraved degenerates, nothing more. The ravings of those two prisoners mean nothing!' said the old man.

"'Sir, I will not live in suspense on this matter. I will not! I will see it confirmed, one way or the other,' said Alphonso.

"Arabella said in a soothing voice, 'Your father is right, dear. This is an age of science. You trouble yourself to no purpose.'

"'My mind is quite made up. I have booked passage on the Cunard liner leaving New York five days from tomorrow. With fair weather and good rail connections on the continent, I should be in Weimar in about two weeks.'

"'You'll find nothing; there's nothing to find!' spluttered the old man.

"'Nevertheless, I must see for myself if there is nothing to find.

There must be dozens still alive who knew von Juntz. I will start with them. Good night, sir. I wish you a pleasant evening.'

"I rapidly retreated from the door and down a darkened hall where I could see but not be seen. Alphonso opened the door and held it for my sister, who swept from her uncle's library in a swirl of skirts. Alphonso then stepped out and closed the door behind him with a bang; he apparently did not notice the door did not catch and left an inch of opening. The two of them walked only a short distance into the central hall before they grabbed each other and began kissing in the most frenzied, passionate way, almost like they were attacking each other. I was so shocked I could not move, but felt dirty watching this scene.

"When they paused for breath, Alphonso asked huskily, 'You still desire me, even when you know about my ancestry?'

"'I would desire you no matter what, my love. And if what you suspect is true, you haven't really thought what it would mean for our children. Think of what they could be!' Leading Alphonso over to the large bureau in the entry hall, she opened a drawer, removed a small box, and opened the box. 'Love, I was saving this for your birthday, but I want you to have with you during your journey. It is a gold pocket-watch, with my photograph set on the inner lid. I want you to always hold my image near.' My sister fiercely kissed Alphonso with the wanton abandon of a Louisville crib girl.

"Shocked, I started to creep down the hall and away from the scene when my eye passed over the inch of open library door, and lit upon a single cold blue eye and a bit of furious red face. Frankly, I was frightened. I fled.

"But of course, that isn't the fear of which I wanted to tell. Alphonso left two days later, and I was in an agony of indecision. It was obvious Arabella's relationship with Alphonso had gone too far. She would destroy herself and Alphonso if it was allowed to persist. Yet I hesitated, trying to think how best to approach a sister who, despite her legal status as a slave, was very much aware of her superiority, and proud to the point of sin.

"As fate would have it, the decision was taken out of my hands. About a week after Alphonso departed for Germany, old man Clay summoned me to his library, where he stood behind his desk coldly staring at a stranger who was calmly smoking a small cigar.

"This man sent a jolt of fear through me the moment I first laid eyes on him. He was tall, and his thinness made him seem even taller; not an ounce of fat on him, but not from the result of ill-health. Indeed, he projected an air of strength and energy. It was his face that inspired unease, I finally decided. The sharp angles of his cheekbones, the pointed chin the black goatee could not hide, the unruly black hair that streamed away from his high forehead, gave the impression of Lucifer personified. As I entered the room, he looked at me; his eyes were black, piercing, and dead. If ever I had seen an evil man, this was he.

"'Mr. Clay, I apologize for the interruption. I can come back after your guest has departed,' I said.

"'No, you may as well stay,' said old Clay in a strained voice. 'Your sister has been summoned. When she arrives, there is something I must tell the both of you.'

"Immediately my sister entered the room with stately elegance. 'Sir, you wished to see me?'

"My uncle could not bring himself to meet his niece's eyes, or mine. 'Arabella, Jeremiah, this is Mr. Nathan Bedford Forrest. He provides certain services and has agreed to offer those services to me.'

"Forrest raked my sister up-and-down insolently; it reminded me of the way one looks over a horse before making an offer. 'A very comely nigger,' he said. 'The fancy houses in New Orleans pay extra for the light ones. I could get you five, maybe even six thousand dollars for her. After seeing her in person, I find it even more outlandish you're selling her to me for one dollar.'

"My sister froze in shock; I don't even want to think of what my face revealed. Before I could I could say a word, my uncle responded in the grating voice that always indicated he was one short step from uncontrollable fury. 'Mr. Forrest, sir, I have told you I care not where you send her, so long as it is to a good family who will not abuse her! I will not profit from this transaction; anything you can extract at the other end is yours, and you are welcome to it! And let me warn you, sir. She has been brought up as a lady. If you do not place her where that is respected, you will answer to me!'

"He leaned over his desk, scribbled his signature on a document, and thrust the paper at the despicable Forrest. The latter reviewed the document, folded it, and placed it in an inner coat pocket. He then reached into his vest pocket, extracted a large silver coin, and tossed it casually onto my uncle's desk.

"'I really don't know why I'm bothering with this,' commented Forrest in his chilling voice. 'This is my last trip up the river. When I get back to Memphis, I'm going to organize a cavalry regiment for the Confederacy. I have money enough to do it on my own. It's about time the nigger-loving Republicans were taught what it means to try to dictate to Southern gentlemen. Ordinarily, I wouldn't give you the time of day, what with your efforts to keep Kentucky from its rightful place in the Confederacy, but I owe you for that time in Bowling Green, so I suppose I will have to swallow my pride and make a little money that will go to the benefit of the Confederacy.' He then regarded my dumfounded sister. 'Well, missy, this going to be easy or hard? I've got chains out in my buggy. A gag, too, if you feel inclined to be loud about it.'

"Old Cicero's eyes were nearly bulging from his head, but before he could speak, my sister said with regal, icy calm, 'The chains will not be necessary. Under the circumstances, I would have no desire to stay here in any event.' She squared her shoulders and confronted our uncle with furious disdain, who seemed to wilt under such a contemptuous stare. 'Mr. Forrest, I am ready to go immediately.'

"With much amusement, Forrest said, 'No little trinkets from the old homestead that you would like to take along?'

"Arabella refused to look directly at the slave trader. Her eyes boring into our uncle, she said, 'There is *nothing* I would care to take from this place. And sir, I am not 'missy.' I am Arabella Lot. If you are ready, let us depart.' She glided royally toward me and the library door, leading an amused Forrest. As she reached me, she paused briefly and gave me a fierce hug. Then, without a word, she swept down the hall and out the front door, followed by the satanic Forrest.

"In a few moments, I heard the rattle of hooves, which rapidly faded to loud cicadas. With murderous fury, I faced Cicero Clay, who had collapsed into the chair behind his desk. Before I could utter the first of the obscene curses that had welled up inside me, he began to speak in a voice little above a hoarse whisper. 'You will now hate me forever. Good, that's as it should be. What I have done can never be forgiven.'

"'Why, damn you, why?'

"'Because she was about to bring ruin down on Alphonso, and on herself. They are both Clays, you see, and a private fornication would not suit them. They would demand marriage, which is criminal in Kentucky, and socially destructive in the few Northern states that permit it. Slavery may be ending; in fact, I believe the fools in Richmond have guaranteed its end. Nonetheless, the races simply cannot mix in that way. Perhaps someday, but not in our lifetimes.'

"'Society accepted your brother ravishing our mother,' I said, grief and rage making me say unthinkable things to the man who legally owned me.

"'If society did, I did not,' he responded sadly. "I loved Decimus like a son, but when he—He became dead to me long before he brought further disgrace on the Clay name by hanging himself.'

"'Damn you. I don't care what society thinks or the damned name of Clay! You sold your niece. You sold your flesh and blood! God damn you!' I said, running from the room. As I hurled myself into the dark hallway, I thought I heard the old man say sadly, 'Yes, I believe He will.'

"The next few days, I avoided the old man like the plague. I thought of running away and retrieving Arabella, but I realized a black man would have no chance in penetrating into the Deep South, finding and freeing another slave, and fleeing through the Confederate lines that were being rapidly organized. Alphonso could go places and do things I could not, so in the end, I did my regular duties mechanically, and waited for Alphonso, knowing he would not rest until Arabella was free.

"I did not have long to wait. Three weeks after Arabella was taken, he was back at Dignitas. I had been at one of the outlying shops and was not at the house when he arrived. As I approached the house at dusk, I could hear voices shouting long before I was inside. Joyfully, I recognized one of the voices as Alphonso. I broke into a run and burst into the library in the middle of a furious exchange. To my amazement, they were not discussing the sale of my sister; that must have happened before I arrived. They were discussing something else, something cryptic with overtones about which I didn't like to think. Don't ask me to explain the confusing or incomplete parts. I once asked Alphonso to do that, and all he did was laugh, saying again, he cared too much for me to burden me with certain knowledge.

"As I entered, my cousin was furiously berating his father. They both ignored my arrival. 'You knew, sir, you knew! It was no coincidence you were passing through Weimar when you rescued my mother from the mob of German peasants!'

"'My son, you shouldn't believe the ignorant rumors that certain—'

"'Don't insult my intelligence, sir! You had been an early member of Starry Wisdom. Admit it!'

"'Yes, yes, to my shame, before your birth. They promised all kinds of wonders. But I give you my word, the moment I found out how they intended to provide those wonders, I withdrew.'

"'A very pretty morality you have! Why didn't you tell the authorities? Think of all those children!'

"'I only suspected. I wasn't sure. Besides, who would believe such a thing?'

"'But you were still tempted, weren't you? You thought to get what you wanted without dirtying your hands. You disgust me! Look what Starry Wisdom did, and they failed. Grandfather von Junzt succeeded! Did you ever stop to think what he had to do to succeed?'

"The old man was breathing hard, his hands shaking. 'Son, what was done was done. His daughter was there. Don't you see? This country is the hope of the world, but it needs strong leaders, leaders like the Clays. But Clay blood is weakening over the generations. Think what von Junzt's daughter brought into our bloodline. Think of your accomplishments. In part, that must come from what she brought. You and your children could be the guardians of this Republic! But not if you bring African blood into the line to defile us. That's why I did what had to be done.'

"'Defiled? You dare to say Arabella would defile us when you know what von Junzt and his nameless bride have brought into our bloodline? By God, sir, if Arabella's African ancestors were the lowliest cannibals, she could do nothing but elevate us, after the corrupt, unspeakable thing you allowed to happen!'

"The old man opened his mouth to speak, but nothing emerged. His head jerked once, and he fell to the floor. Alphonso stood there in shock. I rushed over to the old man, whom I had come to hate more than I thought I could hate any human being. Glassy open eyes stared upward; he was dead before he struck the floor. Almost certainly apoplexy: the origin of his persistent headaches explained.

"Then his son, who a moment before had been cursing him, sank to floor beside him, took his father's lifeless body in his arms, and began to cry, with weird, keening noises coming from his throat from time to time. In that moment, and only for that reason, I was sorry the old man was dead.

"Afterwards, I took Alphonso by the shoulders, made him look at me, and told him, 'You can grieve later. We must bury him within the next day or so, and then seek out Arabella.'

"He nodded his agreement.

"In two days, Cicero Clay was buried in the vault at Dignitas, and all the slaves he owned were legally freed, including me. Two days later, Alphonso and I were on our way to Washington.

"He reasoned there was no sense trying to go as civilians through Confederate lines and attempting to force Forrest to reveal where he had sent Arabella. Then, sources in Louisville told Alphonso Forrest had literally "sold south" his last shipment of human cargo to Louisiana.

"General Butler had just taken New Orleans, and we reasoned the best way to proceed was to get on Butler's staff and use the resources of the occupation army to trace her down. Alphonso pulled some strings, got a captain's commission out of General Meigs, and winkled an assignment down to New Orleans.

"Once there, it didn't prove too hard to run down where Arabella had been sent. Martial law was in place, and the slave dealers could be encouraged to talk without much difficulty. We found she had been sold to the Devereaux family, who ran a plantation about twenty miles northwest of New Orleans. It was a relief to hear they had a reputation for being firm but not brutal to their slaves.

"By this time, I had sergeant's stripes. Alphonso ordered me to assemble my squad of eight soldiers, and one afternoon, we set out for the Devereaux plantation.

"When we got there, we gathered the whole family in the main hall of the plantation house: Gasper Devereux, his wife Isabel, their two small children of about six and three, an overseer named Longacre, and a few nervous household slaves.

"Clay glared at the assembled people and stated, 'Arabella Lot arrived here three to four months ago. I want her. I realize the United States government still recognizes slavery, so I will pay you whatever you paid for her, in gold. Now produce her, immediately!'

"None of the adults said anything; they simply exchanged nervous, questioning looks. I had an awful presentiment, which Alphonso must have shared.

"He strode up to a hefty black woman, the 'mammy' to the children and demanded, 'Tell me where Arabella is. I guarantee your masters will not touch you. If necessary, I will buy your freedom as well.'

"The woman sought approval to speak from her owners, who glared back at her threateningly. With great fear and reluctance, she decided to speak, her hands wringing her apron. 'Well, suh, ya gotta undastan' dat one was a problem since she gots here. De Devereaux be good peoples, in de main, but dey don' like colored who are upp'ty. An' Miss Arabella was upp'ty. Proud as Satan, she be. Her pride grow'd eben mo' when she realize she be pregnant.'

"'Pregnant!' exclaimed Alphonso. I was shocked and expected

he would be, but all he showed was pure joy. 'We must be married as soon as may be! Where is she?'

"The old woman would not meet his eyes; she stared straight at the floor, rubbing her hands together. 'Hmmm, yuh see, dat chil' seem ta drive huh plumb outta huh mind. She be ravin', suh. She say de child be great, great as can be. Dat someday de whole country would bow down ta dat chil'. Madness, Cap'n. Poor girl be outta huh head. Marse Devereaux, he thank she need ta be brought ta reason, so he tell huh moment dat child be born, he be taken' it away an' sellin' it. She rave dat he cain't do dat; dat she won' a'cept such dishonah; dat he cain't treat a great lady like huhsef in dat way.' Tears flowed freely down her cheeks and snot over her large lips. She sniffled back and wiped her face with the back of her hand. 'Marse Devereaux, he say she be a prop'ty, no more dan a cow o' a horse, an' he'd be teachin' huh place, an' dat de child was his prop'ty, and he be doin' what he liked wid it. He had Mr. Longacre lock huh in de garden shed, 'spected huh ta shout huhsef horse, an' be mo' reasonable-like in de mornin'. De po' girl went clean off huh head. Dere be arsenic in de shed, which we use ta kill de rats, and . . ." the old woman trailed off.

"My stomach had become a block of ice. Alphonso was now a deathly stone. In a quiet voice, he said, 'Where is she?' When no response was immediately forthcoming, he screamed, '*Where is she?*'

"Frightened by the intensity of Alphonso's scream, shaking like a leaf, she blurted, 'It be de freshest one behin' de slave quarters. Ain't been no mo' dan a week.'

"Alphonso was glowing in terror. 'Sergeant, post your men, make sure no one leaves.'

"'Sir, wouldn't you rather I come, too?' I asked.

"'No, Sergeant. I know you loved her also, but this, I must do alone.'

"The family stood in sullen silence, while my squad cheerfully talked among themselves. They enjoyed seeing a white family discomfited, and I could not blame them.

"After this had gone on for nearly an hour, one of the house slaves, a powerfully-built man named appropriately enough Samson, walked over to me and said, 'Uh-huh, nice un'form. Bottom rail be on top; wonder how long till bottom rail back on bottom.'

"'Never, Samson. This war will end slavery forever.'

"'Den why ain't Lincoln—'

"He was interrupted by the most blood-curdling scream I had ever heard. It didn't sound human. Imagine the noise a wolf might make being skinned alive, and you might understand the fear it induced in that hallway. Everyone—prisoners and soldiers, frozen in place.

"Disregarding my orders, I rushed out into the fading light of sunset. I found the crude graveyard where the mammy had said it would be. A recent grave had been disturbed; a shovel, which had undoubtedly been obtained from an outbuilding, lay cast on a huge pile of fresh dirt. On the edge of the grave, making bizarre, unearthly sounds, sat Alphonso Clay, holding the decaying body of my sister. Periodically he kissed the dead face and gabbled meaningless endearments and pleas for forgiveness. I stood by him, appalled by the ghastly scene, thinking in a distant part of my mind that nothing could be worse than what I was witnessing.

"But I was wrong.

"At once, Clay lay her body tenderly on the ground. Opening the flap of his holster, he slowly drew his revolver, cocked it, and began to raise it to his temple. I lunged forward and knocked the barrel skyward just as he pulled the trigger. There was a bang, and the bullet went harmlessly into the air.

"Wrenching the gun from his unresisting fingers, I asked, 'How dare you? Do you think she would have wanted that? What do you think she would have thought of you being so weak as to destroy yourself? She took pride in being a Clay. Would you disgrace that?'

"In an emotionless voice he said, 'No, you are right. A Clay does not commit suicide. It is dishonorable.' Mechanically, with leaden steps and vacant gaze, he began walking in the direction of the plantation house. Loosely holding the revolver in my hand, I stared at my sister's decaying corpse. Tears welled into my eyes, and I sobbed unashamedly.

"In less than a minute, I became aware of screaming coming from the direction of the plantation house. Shocked out of my grief, I ran toward the entrance. As I approached, I saw a crowd pouring out the door: a mix of black servants and soldiers. Some of the soldiers were walking backwards, clutching their rifles, wide eyes focused on the opening; others had simply thrown down their weapons and were running into the growing shadows as fast as their legs could carry them. The fat mammy came tumbling out, screaming over and over, 'Lawd save us! Dat blued-eyed devil! Lawd save us!'

"I shoved past her and Samson, and into the hallway, where hell awaited me.

"Mrs. Devereaux and her children were screaming and screaming as Alphonso methodically swung away with his silver-hilted German sword at two mounds of flesh that, it took me a moment to realize, were Gasper Devereaux and his overseer. They were dead, in fact almost unrecognizable, but Alphonso kept slashing away, each blow sending gore flying. The worst of it was the calmness, as if he were peacefully solving a problem in mathematics.

"Knowing it would do her husband no good, Mrs. Devereaux launched herself at Alphonso, screaming curses in French. As she was about to reach him, he swung around and severed her head in a single blow."

Lot paused in his story; he closed his eyes for a long moment. Bierce and Parker hardly dared to breathe.

With his eyes still shut, he said, "You've probably heard tales of the French guillotine, and of how the severed head will remain conscious for some time. It is true. Alphonso's blow had such force, it sent Mrs. Devereaux's head sailing across the room. As it did so, I saw the eyes dart around wildly, and the lips tried to form words. And God help them, her two children saw it, too. They screamed and screamed and screamed.

"Then Alphonso began to walk toward the children, bloody sword held out like a Bowie knife. I found I was still clutching his revolver and raised it, but then I lowered it. I found I could not fire at Alphonso, no matter how merciful it might be. Instead, I dove at the children, gathered them in my arms, and placed my back to the advancing form of my best friend. I prayed he would leave the children alone if it meant killing me to get at them. I heard his steps stop right behind me, and I closed my eyes, waiting for the blow of the sword. I thought I was as frightened as I could ever be.

"But I was wrong.

"At last, I heard his voice behind me saying, 'Take the children away,' and the sound of a sword being slid into a scabbard. I opened my eyes, and saw Alphonso's figure exiting into the twilight. I hurried the children outside, shielding their eyes as best I could from the ghastly remains of their parents, knowing they would nevertheless retain images that would blight their lives.

"Outside, two of the most reliable members of my squad remained. I handed over the crying youngsters and ordered them taken to the Catholic orphanage in New Orleans. They hurried off, undoubtedly glad to have a reason to leave the scene of such carnage. I watched them ride off into the dusk and then caught sight Alphonso walking calmly toward the house with Arabella's body in his arms."

Lot looked directly at Bierce and Parker, eyes wide with remembrance. "One can be frightened by phantoms of the mind. Remember what I had just seen; it must have driven me mad for a moment, and my mad brain hallucinated. As Alphonso walked by me, I thought I heard him muttering in a language I could not recognize, and I know something of French, German, Latin, and Spanish. I actually *thought* I saw my sister's arms reach up to clutch Alphonso's shoulders. Of course, it had to be some delusion, based on some trick of the on-coming night. No matter how great the love, the dead do not reach across the great divide—not this side of Judgment Day. At the time, it frightened me more than anything I had ever been through, even though it was a delusion, a hallucination . . . Yes . . . Yes . . ."

Lot refocused to the slow-burning embers, his heart racing just as it did that day, trembling. He never thought he would ever be able to unburden himself of the visions plaguing him for so long. To do so now was living it all over again.

"I remained rooted to the spot at the thought of what I had imagined I had seen as Clay carried my sister's corpse into the plantation house. My head jerked up as I heard two crashing noises coming from inside. The sound released me, and I ran to see. I passed through the slaughtered remains in the hallway on into the parlor. Alphonso had arranged Arabella's body on the luxurious sofa, with flowers on her distended stomach. He was seated in a large armchair facing her. Flames were beginning to lick at the curtains and at the stairway at the far end of the parlor; two smashed oil lamps beneath the growing blazes explained it all.

"He knew I was in the room, and without looking up, he said, 'You must go, Jeremiah. You are a good man. In the coming days, the country will need every good man that can be found. As for myself, when my friend, Wagner, reads about this in Germany, perhaps he will honor this story with one of his operas.'

"'Alphonso, please come out. None of this will do any good.'

"'I have chosen my path, my friend. Do me the honor of leaving me to it. I have no wish—'

"'Sergeant!' came a tremulous voice from the doorway. At the entrance, the terrified mammy, with a scowling Samson behind her, screamed, but she kept panic-stricken eyes on the figure in the armchair, 'Sergeant, de baby be upstairs! De fire! Dose stairs be de only ones!'

"Alphonso stirred as if awakening from a deep sleep. He swung his gaze toward the black woman, who cowered. 'Baby? What baby?'

"'Deir youngest,' coughed Samson. 'Dey figure it be safa up dere when yo'soldiers began shoutin' deir orders.'"

"Clay leaped from the chair and stared at the path to the upper floor, which was rapidly becoming a sea of fire. 'A baby. God, a baby!' He threw himself at the growing wall of flame, but involuntarily cringed back, took a few steps backward, and began to breathe deeply. Without hesitation, he was about to plunge directly into the fire.

"I leaped forward and grabbed his arm, screaming, 'For God's sake, Alphonso, it's too late! You can't save the child! All you can do is die!'

"'Then I'll die! A Clay who kills infants does not deserve to live.'

I struggled with him, but he had always been stronger than me. He was about to break free and plunge up the flaming stairs to his death when the huge form of Samson appeared alongside. He threw a swift blow to Alphonso's temple, who fell as if pole-axed. He scooped my friend up effortlessly and carried him outside. I followed.

"In the yard, he lay Alphonso's insensible form under a tree, then said, 'Well, dis be good-bye. I be hittin' de road. When white folk die an' dere only be black folk 'round, some nigga gonna hang.' He regarded Alphonso, saying, 'I got some idea a' what went on.

Neva thought I'd say I'd feel sorry fuh no white man, but I feel sorry fuh dis one.' With that, Samson faded into the night.

"I sat down next to Alphonso and watched the mansion burn to the ground during the night.

"Sometime around dawn, when the last of the flames were flickering out, Alphonso awoke, covered in sticky, drying blood and gore. For the longest time, he simply watched the smoldering ruins; the love of his life was in there. When he did speak, it was an order, 'Sergeant, you are to place me under arrest for the crime of murder, four specifications thereof: Mr. and Mrs. Devereaux, the overseer Longacre, and an infant child, name unknown.'

"My cousin and best friend . . . I thought of what he'd done, what he'd become, and what I had witnessed, and truly believed it could be no worse.

"But I was wrong."

In his mind, Jeremiah Lot was still in the yard of the Devereaux plantation.

Bierce was entranced, picturing it all.

Parker nodded solemnly and asked, "You said you were wrong; what could possibly have frightened you more than what you had already seen?"

Refusing to look at his two companions, Lot replied, "I realized if I was so scared of him, when I loved him as much as I did, then how much more must he be of himself when he hates himself as much as he does. The possibilities petrified me."

Parker nodded in deep understanding, but said nothing.

Bierce rose to his feet, stretched, and walked over to where Lot sat. He was about to say something, but in the end, he silently produced a twenty-dollar gold piece and put it on the edge of the cracker-box on which Lot was seated and walked off into to the darkness, somberly.

Lot seized the coin and threw it into the night so far the sound of its impact could not be heard.

CHAPTER SEVEN

TREASON DOTH NEVER PROSER;
WHAT'S THE REASON?

"I ain't sayin' nothin' to no damn Yankees," said the dirty, starved man in butternut, sitting on a cracker box in Grant's tent. "I knows my rights. I be a prisoner, an' ain't gotta say nothin.'"

Around the prisoner stood Generals Grant and McPherson, Colonel Rawlins, Major Parker, Lieutenant Bierce, Captain Clay, and Sergeant Lot. Even with the flaps of Grant's large command tent folded wide open, the interior was stifling; it was near noon on a cloudless day in a Mississippi June. Yet despite their blue woolen uniforms, the assembled Federal soldiers were sweating less than the prisoner.

While the others glowered at the captured Confederate, pondering his fate, Bierce ruefully welcomed the newly-arrived Clay and Lot. "I need to apologize for interrupting your oh-so-important work of interviewing everyone who may have seen a rat go on Sherman's boat just before Brown was shot, *but* I thought you might be interested in seeing something of what this army is up against. Colonel Rawlins and I have been trying to open a meaningful discussion with our friend for most of this morning, but he has remained disappointingly uncommunicative.

"Our friend here was picked up last night trying to crawl past General McPherson's boys in the dark. Crawled right into the hands of some alert Iowa soldiers. They saw he was carrying dispatches from General Pemberton to General Johnston and immediately brought him to General McPherson; then McPherson brought him over here. Those dispatches are valuable enough, giving us a picture of the number of men in Vicksburg and the state of their supplies, but it would be most beneficial to obtain our friend's personal impressions of what is happening inside Vicksburg."

A loud boom sounded, followed a few seconds later by the sound of a distant explosion. The sides of the tent waved slightly with the force. It was one of Grant's huge, thirteen-inch mortars, which, at quarter-hour intervals, hurled a two-hundred-pound explosive shell into the besieged city. General Grant, seeking some way to compel an early surrender of Vicksburg, short of starvation, had ordered the bombardment, feeling it would deprive the Confederate defenders of rest and attack their morale, and it worked. Used to it, the Federal soldiers did not respond at all to the sound of the artillery, but the surly Confederate cringed pitiably at the noise.

Bierce turned back to the prisoner, thrilled; the Rebel shrank visibly in his sight. "Ah, my friend, you have behaved quite courageously. Alas, only in dime novels does courage triumph. You have failed and are in the hands of the Federal government. We need to know information not included in those dispatches: the morale, the rumors, the attitude of soldiers toward their officers, all that kind of thing."

"I ain't a traitor," responded the soldier sullenly.

"No, but you may be a spy."

All the others in the room watched on in great interest.

The prisoner's head jerked up. "What the hell do you mean? I'm a soldier, not some sneakin' spy!"

"Very interesting," Bierce said, deducing aloud. "To deserve treatment as a prisoner of war requires you be in full uniform." He gently ran his fingers along the collar of the shapeless butternut coat. "Parker, Rawlins, what say you? This look like a uniform to you?"

Parker simply shook his head; while after a hesitation, Rawlins said reluctantly, "No."

The prisoner's eyes had gone wide with a combination of fear and rage. "Goddamn you, Billy Yank! You knows this is all the uniforms we gets! Gotta be an officer to get them stripes and stuff!"

"An argument could be made for that rationalization, my friend," said Bierce agreeably. "But remember, this is a time of war, and it is better to err on the side of caution. The way I see it, if you cooperate fully with us, I can persuade these gentlemen to see your point of view, and you will find your way to a prisoner of war camp, and perhaps to an early exchange. Should you not choose such cooperation, we will reluctantly be forced to conclude this stems from guilt—knowledge that you are a spy—and with the greatest of reluctance, I would have to ask Colonel Rawlins here to cut an order for your execution by firing squad."

The gaunt prisoner gawked at the smiling Bierce, then hid his face. "I ain't no traitor. I ain't got nothin' to say."

Bierce sighed theatrically, slapped his gloves on his thighs, and addressed Rawlins and Grant. "Sirs, I think further efforts are a waste of time all around. If you concur, we can have a firing squad assembled within the hour."

General McPherson, normally sunny of disposition, became angrier and angrier during the interrogation. At this, he burst out, "General Grant, sir, this is too much! I have swallowed a lot during this campaign. I have swallowed the looting of innocent people's farms. I have swallowed your shelling of Vicksburg with no regard for whether the explosions destroy armed Rebels or little children. I have swallowed your refusal to allow the civilians to pass through our lines so Pemberton would use his supplies quicker in keeping women and children alive. But this is too much sir, too much! I refuse to swallow this! You know this prisoner is not a spy, and yet you would kill him! This is dishonorable! If this is what America has come to, if this is what it takes to save America, I swear before God, America is not worth saving!"

All motion ceased within the tent; even the Confederate prisoner stared at McPherson.

Grant took a last pull on his cigar and threw the stub to the ground; then he came nose to nose with the insubordinate officer, saying, "General McPherson, you forget yourself. I will do what I judge best to save this country. If this man's death will advance that goal, he will die; if his life will advance it, he will live."

"And who decides what advances the Union?" blurted McPherson angrily.

"I do," responded Grant levelly, and he spit a bit of cigar.

Before the confrontation between commander and subordinate could spiral completely out of control, Clay decided to intervene. "If I may, gentlemen, I have a suggestion that will finesse this difference of opinion. I assume if our guest cooperates, the issue of a firing squad will become moot?"

"Of course," replied Grant.

"Well then, I believe Major Parker and I can assure such cooperation." Clay then turned to the prisoner, saying coldly, "Major Ely Parker is a full-blooded Seneca Indian."

"I can see he is some sort of redskin," came the surly reply. "Seems, tradition runs deep in ya, does it not, Major?"

Parker, who'd divined Clay's game, settled into his role fiercely.

"I believe if you leave our guest alone with Major Parker and myself for one hour, we could assure the prisoner's cooperation."

The Rebel looked at Parker with undisguised terror; he was from a frontier community, and had been raised on stories of Indian atrocities, some false, others all too true. He spit at Clay, saying, "Just who the hell are you to threaten a white man with a savage like this?"

Clay favored the prisoner guardedly, straightening his posture, and tipping his head. "I am Captain Alphonso Clay, late of New Orleans, at your service."

The soldier crinkled his brow in concentration; the name somehow rang a bell. Then the remaining color drained from his face. "Jesus! You're him! You're the one who burned, who . . . who . . ." The half-starved man crumbled, close to collapse.

Clay suggested to Parker, "With your permission, Major, let us take him outside. No sense making a mess all over the General's things."

"No! No!" screamed the prisoner, looking wildly around to the other Federal soldiers. "All right, all right! I'll tell you what I can. Only don't leave me alone with those two! For God's sake, don't!" The prisoner, already weak from a month of half-rations, on the verge passing out, trembled incessantly.

"The gentleman is quite overcome," commented Clay, as if he was scrutinizing a specimen. "I would suggest some crackers and salt pork, water, perhaps, with some stimulant in the form of whiskey. He should then be in a more comfortable frame of mind to continue our discussions."

"I'll get him something," offered Lot, who moved off without waiting to receive formal permission. Despite being black, and the prisoner being a Confederate, surprisingly, Lot found he had genuine pity for the broken Rebel soldier.

Rawlins focus on the generals. "Sirs, it will take some time to refresh this man. It's stifling in here; if you like, you could rest under the shade trees. Parker and I will watch the prisoner."

"Good idea, John," replied Grant. "General McPherson and I need to talk about some things anyway." Grant, lighting yet another of his ever-present cigars, led the furious McPherson from the tent.

The exhausted prisoner looked at Parker and Clay and unconsciously edged toward the more sympathetic Rawlins. Smiling contemptuously, Clay decided to give the Rebel prisoner a modicum of relief and strolled out of the tent.

Without intending to eavesdrop, he therefore became witness to a furious argument between Grant and McPherson, who stood in the shade of a nearby tree, with Grant's sentries trying desperately to pretend they were hearing nothing.

"Damnit, sir, this is too much. I can't take what I'm doing. I went to West Point to learn to defend this country against the Europeans and the Indians, and here I am fighting our own, Americans!"

Instead of responding with rage to the rebellious outburst, Grant reached out and placed his hand on the younger general's shoulder. "You think I don't think about the things that are bothering you?" he asked quietly. "I hate the political leaders who started this rebellion, but not the people I'm forced to kill. You are absolutely right, Mac; they are Americans. We are fighting to keep them just that. You ever been to Europe? To Mexico?"

"You know I was too young for the Mexican War."

"An unjust war, brought on by Southern slave-owners. Oh, Texas, New Mexico, maybe even California, would have come to us eventually; were never that many Mexicans there, and Americans would have kept pouring over the borders until it would have happened peacefully. But most of the settlers were Free Soil and wouldn't have allowed slavery, and that didn't suit the Jeff Davises and their ilk. I did my duty and fought the Mexicans without ever hating them. They are a wonderful people, the best of them. But I saw a lot of how they lived during the war, and it angered me more than the injustice of the war had done. Mexico is rich, in land, minerals and climate; you can't judge it by the deserts of the north. Yet the people live in the most abject poverty, few owning their land, working themselves into early graves for the hundred or so families that own most of the country. These wonderful people live in squalor, without hope. Just like the people in most places in Europe; slaves in all but name to a small, useless, arrogant aristocracy, living off the sweat of people they treat like animals. That's what the leaders of the Confederacy want to create, and they are willing to break apart our noble experiment to do so. They talk a lot about rights and freedom, but the truth is they want to make sure only the select few have rights or freedom. McPherson, they're close to realizing their sadistic dream. And it's not because their boys are better fighters than ours; man for man, Billy Yank can knock the stuffing out of Johnnie Reb any day of the week. No, the problem is they have better generals, in the main. We don't have many who have the belly and the brains to lead a corps; you've proved you're one of the few."

"Yes, sir. But how much blood? How much suffering? It preys on my mind."

"Then let it prey on your mind, but do your duty," responded Grant sternly. "If the Southern aristocrats have their way in this war, do you think this will be the last war? Their jealousy, greed, and ambition will lead to future conflict, as far as history can reach. Many argue it was a good thing to break Rome apart fifteen centuries ago. But look at those fifteen centuries! War after war, rebellion after rebellion, massacre after massacre! Do you want America to be like Europe? Do you?"

"No-no, sir," stuttered McPherson.

"That's exactly what we're going to have if we don't stop this right now, right here!" yelled Grant with unaccustomed anger. He took a deep breath, then resumed more calmly. "I know better than you can imagine the guilt you feel; I go to bed with it every night. But you have no need to bear it. This war is the responsibility of Jeff Davis and his cronies, of Lincoln and Stanton, and yes, of me. Mac, you and I are like surgeons, cutting into the body of this country, wounding it, causing pain that can never be forgotten, but we are doing it to make the body whole, and to save its life.

"If you must go, I won't stop you. But remember this; I will go on, whether you stay or not. But without your help, it could be bloodier and longer than it needs to be. Sherman is a good general, but he is only one man. Who else could I depend on to command your corps? Ord is the only division commander I have hopes for; the others are barely competent in their existing ranks. Without you, I will have to lean even more on that doggone fool McClernand. You think that will make things go easier?"

The young general, extremely troubled, took a long time to answer. "I suppose not," he said reluctantly. "I will stay, but I want you to know it's as much for you as for the country."

"I'm not sure that is a good reason, but I'll take it, General McPherson.

"Well, that poor devil in there probably has some food in him by now. Let's go hear what he has to say before he recovers his nerve." The two generals headed back toward the tent. Grant regarded Clay, but apparently decided the captain had been too far away to overhear the conversation. Little did he know Clay's hearing was unusually acute.

The three Union officers entered the tent to see the Confederate soldier wolfing down the last bits of salt pork like a starved dog, as Bierce, Rawlins, Parker, and Lot looked on with amusement.

The man took a long pull from a canteen and leaned backward from the table, saying, "Lord, I'd forgotten the pleasures of bein' full. Didn't take much to do it; reckon my stomach's clean up against my backbone." He sourly regarded the officers surrounding him. "I'll keep my word, though it don't seem right. No matter, I reckon you Yanks will be in Vicksburg afore long, anyways. What do you want to know?"

"Just give us your impressions of how thing are inside Vicksburg," said Bierce, not unkindly.

The prisoner gave a short, barking laugh. "How things are, Yank? I'll tell you hows they are. If the Lord sees me safe to home, I swears I'm gonna be a good Christian ever after; for I have seen hell and don't want to see it again. May the Lord damn those men in Washington who are doin' these things, and the men in Richmond who swore the Yankees would never fight!"

"How are the supplies?" asked Bierce.

"What supplies? Soldiers are on quarter rations of bread; meat rations was plumb gone weeks ago. Then Pemberton took all the cows and such from the civilians and slaughtered them. Then the mules. Then the horses. Ever eaten horse, Yank? I'll tell you, I was mighty glad to get it but saw my last bit of horse meat eight days ago. Course, caught myself a nice rat night before last. Ever eaten rat, Yank? Being short on food sort of changes your perspective; cook it right, it's mighty tasty, though there ain't much meat on 'em. Besides, couple of fellers in my company had to make do with a cat they caught in this girl's backyard. Poor little tyke cried and cried. Hungry as I am, don't think I could've eaten the cat after that. Her folks must've loved that cat, else they would've et it themselves some time ago. Pemberton won't give the civilians anything more than quarter rations of bread. Ain't many men civilians in Vicksburg, 'cept the old ones; most are off in the army. Lots of kids and womenfolk, though. It's very hard to see 'em beggin' the soldiers in the streets for something to eat. Some soldiers share what little they have with 'em." The man cast his eyes down. "God forgive me, I waren't one of 'em. I was so hungry, so hungry . . ." The Reb trailed off, his mind drifting into an internal valley of regret and remorse.

To snap him back into talking, Bierce asked a different question. "Tell us about the bombardment. What damage are the mortars doing?"

Despite his helplessness, the captive Reb flashed with dark hatred. "Those big guns with the big shells! What kind of fighting is that, huh? Yes, if it makes you proud of yourselves, it's doin' a lot of damage. Everyone's digging caves in the sides of hills, soldiers and civilians, and hidin' in 'em lessen' they have to be out, in the trenches or on errands. We're living like moles. Oh, safe enough in the holes, lessen a shell causes a cave-in. But you cain't really sleep; cain't get any rest. If you do manage to get to sleep, a big shell will wake you up, then you cain't get back to sleep, but just lay there waiting for the next big bang. Sometimes it's the waiting that's the worst. No, that's not right. The worse is when you have to be outside, on duty. A fellow will be out walkin' the perimeter with a couple of other Johnnies, when out of the blue comes one of them big shells and . . ." He closed his eyes and bowed his head. "I'm sure they didn't feel pain. Sometimes there ain't enough left to fill a cigar box; sometimes, cain't find nothing at all. But I suppose the worst is the civilians who won't go into the 'fraidy holes, but try to get a good night's sleep in their homes. Days will go by with no shells landing nearby, and they think it's safe, then 'bang,' and there's some screamin' bit a flesh that shouldn't be alive but is, leastwise for a while."

"Tell us what people think of General Pemberton," urged Bierce.

The prisoner paused to collect his thoughts, swallowed hard. "Uh, he's all right, for a Yankee." He searched his holey brogans, soles falling off, sockless toes sticking through. "All kind of opinions about him. Mostly, the civilians hate him; thinking he's sellin' us out to old Abe. Several of his generals hate him; says he's incompetent and they could've done better, but personally, I don't rightly see how. He's popular enough with the field officers and common soldiers. They figure he's done the best he can; not everyone can be a Bobby Lee."

"Why do you still hold out, with everything as bad as you say?" asked Bierce with genuine puzzlement.

"We waitin' for General Johnston to break through," said the man, his voice unconvinced. "Everyone wonders where Johnston is. That's why they asked for a volunteer to sneak through the lines. I volunteered, but I don't think Johnston's coming. I just wanted to get out and join up with his army. He's a smart man—too smart to move against this huge army y'all have here by himself. He's going to bide his time and catch you Yanks when you least expect it. This war ain't over yet!" he said with sudden force. Then his shoulders slumped, and in a much softer voice that lacked conviction, he repeated, "This war ain't over yet."

"I think we've heard enough." The sternness had left Grant's voice, replaced with something like pity. "Take this man to the holding stockade. Give the attending officer orders that if there is an opportunity for a prisoner exchange, this man gets the first chance at it."

Rawlins nodded and led the dejected man out of the tent, handing him off to a sentry with some murmured instructions.

"Why do they hold on, with no hope at all? Why?" Grant wondered aloud, digging in his pockets until he came up with another cigar, and busied himself in lighting it.

"Because they're Americans, sir," responded McPherson unexpectedly. "Would any of our armies surrender so long as there was a ghost of a chance? Not likely."

Alphonso Clay's blue eyes glittered behind his spectacles. "With respect, sir, they ceased being Americans when they rebelled against this country. The time for surrender has passed. Anyone with arms in their hands should be put to the sword."

Not an utterance was made; all the officers were horrified except for Major Parker, who displayed a small, forbidding satisfaction.

Grant expelled a large puff of smoke, and then asked, "There are near thirty thousand soldiers in Vicksburg. Do you seriously propose to kill them all?"

"Yes, sir. In my opinion, it would so demoralize the South that surrender would come sooner, and centuries would pass before anyone would contemplate treason again." He adjusted his already respectful posture. "Yet, I accept the fact the President will not allow it. He shows a kindness that does more credit to his heart than to his head."

Grant looked at Clay in disbelief. "And I thought I was hard, Captain. No matter what Lincoln thinks, I wouldn't allow it. There's too much blood on our hands already. Besides, I really doubt it would have the effect you suppose. It would just cause a hatred that would never die and create a section of the country always bent on revenge. No, if the misguided souls we fight are going to someday be our fellow citizens, we must let them up easy."

"Sir, I mean no disrespect, but I would pose this question: If someone cannot resist the pull to treason, how can they be expected to show gratitude for mercy?"

"I would answer your question with a question, Captain. If someone has once killed to no purpose, how could they be relied upon not to do so in the future?"

Clay reddened. "My apologies, sir," he said stiffly. "I was out of place in speaking of this matter."

"Captain, if it consoles you, it may come to what you desire. If they surrender, most will live to see their homes again. But if they do not surrender, then I will maintain this siege until every, last one of them starves, if that is what it takes to possess Vicksburg. Someone must want mercy before it can be granted. Let's hope Pemberton realizes the hopelessness of his situation." Grant took a pull on his cigar and grimaced. "I best go over and talk with

Sherman." He threw a half-salute at the assembled officers and slouched out of the tent.

As the meeting broke up, Bierce approached Clay and Lot. "I'm heading out to talk to the Sheas. I assume your investigation of the Brown matter is stalemated. So, unless you have something more pressing to do, you might want to come with me."

"We may as well," replied Clay, searching for motives in the usually resisting lieutenant. "*I am* a bit surprised you are encouraging us to go with you. My impression is you generally like to go about your business alone."

"Generally, I do, but there is something out that way I would like you to see." The handsome lieutenant was a bit uneasy. "Something I would like you to see for yourself."

Clay stared unblinkingly at Bierce for a long moment; it was difficult to tell what was going on behind those placid blue eyes.

"Very well. Sergeant, let us see what Bierce has to show us."

The trio in blue rode up to the dilapidated Shea cabin, from which emanated the sounds of an argument. A high, Scot-accented voice was exclaiming, "Mon, I dinna think you'd behave that way, especially before the bairn. If he weren't here, I'd be given' you a lesson in manners!"

"Mah woman is mah own affair," came the voice of Amos Shea, anger making his Mississippi accent thicker than usual. "She needed correctin' and I'll be damned afore I let some skirt-wearin' foreigner too cowardly to fight tell me how to run mah family!"

Bierce raised one brow at Clay and Lot as they dismounted and loosely tied their horses to the rickety hitching post.

"Skirt-wearin' be it?" came McFeely's voice, softer but charged with violence. "Aye, and the Tsar's men laughed at our kilts, too, before we be putting cold steel up their bums! Touch her again, and I'll serve you like I served them Cossack buggers!"

"It ain't your concern, shirker. She chose the better man, and—"

"Gentlemen, pray forgive the intrusion," interrupted Bierce jovially, leading Clay and Lot into the room.

The angular Scotsman and solidly-built Southerner were virtually nose-to-nose, glaring at each other, hands clenched at their sides. At the table sat Amelia Shea, an angry red welt covering the left side of her face. She cradled her child in her arms, whose wide eyes were silently streaming tears.

"I don't mean to interrupt this touching scene of domestic bliss, but we have Federal business to transact," Bierce solemnly stated.

"Some private as well," added Clay. "Mr. McFeely, I was unaware you had returned from Kentucky. I would have expected you to seek me out immediately."

"Don't blame our friend, Andrew," replied Bierce. "When I came by early this morning, he was just stopping here on his way from the landing to give the happy couple a great, big howdy before seeing you. I asked him to wait here while I brought you to him. The unexpected business with the Reb prisoner threw the schedule off."

"I'm sorry, Captain," said McFeely, angry eyes focused on Amos Shea. "I only agreed with the lieutenant because there is nothing urgent to report. Your estate manager and banker both be canny and honest. If I not be knowin' better, I'd take me oath they were afraid of ya." He reached into an interior pocket of his somewhat shabby coat and produced a neat bundle of papers, extending them to the small captain. "If ya be willing to take me word on these accounts, me thinks ya fair on ya way to being a vera rich man."

Clay took the papers and riffled through them. To an observer, it looked as if he were only glancing at them, but he had, in fact, taken in all the salient details. Speed-reading was one of the less unusual aspects of Alphonso Clay. "McFeely, you've done a thorough job of checking on my affairs." Clay carefully inserted the packet into an inner pocket of his tunic. "Was there anything of interest not reflected in these papers?"

"Oh, aye, there was. A thin, sharp-eyed, young fella came by while I was a' meeting with your manager. John Rockefeller, he calls himself. Had some scheme for commercially exploiting the petroleum they find here and there in Western Pennsylvania; says if he can get enough investors and capital, he could really give the whaling people a run for their money. Was traveling hither and yon through the Ohio River valley, trying to scare up capital in the midst of a war. Didn't see it, myself; the good Lord will always give us enough whales to keep the lanterns lit. Besides, your manager sent him away with a flea in his ear."

"My manager is an honest, efficient man, but sadly lacking in imagination," replied Clay unexpectedly. "Every year the whaling fleet has to go further and further into the far reaches of the ocean, and every year, more and more lamps and machines needing oil and lubricant flood our country. It is possible we are hunting the whales to extinction. I've read petroleum, when properly distilled, can do anything whale oil can. Further, it can be found more places than people suppose. I believe I will write to my manager soon and ask him to find out about this Rockefeller. If he is not a swindler, perhaps I will put some of my spare capital to work in his enterprise. In any event, that is for the future.

"Any issues you may have with Mr. Shea are entirely your own affair, but Lieutenant Bierce and I have business with him, so I must ask you to defer your dispute. Come to my tent tonight, and I will settle your expenses . . ." Clay trailed off as he followed Bierce's line of sight—McFeely's legs.

A quick, fleeting look told him Lot had done the same: quizzically. Clay's eyes cut back at Bierce, who raised an eyebrow ever so slightly toward McFeely. Clay focused for an instant on the Scotsman's footwear and immediately saw what was fixating the lieutenant and the sergeant. McFeely was wearing bright, shiny, near-new Union cavalry boots, extremely difficult to obtain legally, given the needs of the ever-growing army. Of course, such things were often sold by corrupt quartermasters, but at prices McFeely was unlikely to be able to afford, given the general shabbiness of his other clothing *and* the fact that Clay had only advanced him enough for traveling expenses.

McFeely quickly noticed the attention being given his footwear. "What ails ya, sirs? Have ya not seen decent boots afore this?"

"Oh yes, I have," replied Clay quietly, who recognized the difference between the shabby brogans given the infantry and artillery and the footwear cavalry received—nearly as good as the handcrafted, gleaming boots he'd bought for himself in Louisville, at shocking expense. "I am only curious where you could have come across such fine items, which simply aren't available to civilians in the Mississippi Valley."

"Why mon, it be . . . I mean . . ." he started, confusion written all over his face. Amelia Shea, clutching her little Zachary, gazed back at him with an expression that was hard to describe. He tilted his chin to Clay. "Why mon, I bought them off this feller in a tavern in Memphis, a horse-soldier. Said replacements had been issued him and he'd no use for the old articles."

Clay surveyed the boots, which showed very little sign of wear. "I see. Well, there is no need to detain you further. You may go. We will speak further of my affairs tonight."

McFeely caught himself starting to make a salute. Embarrassed, the civilian nodded and left.

As the sound of McFeely's horse beginning to canter away entered the humble cabin, Zachary forcefully shrugged off his mother's embrace and made a dash for the door, shouting "Uncle Andrew, you didn't say . . ."

Amos Shea backhanded his son so hard he fell backward onto

the floor, wailing softly. Shea stepped toward his son and raised his hand again, but the blow never fell. With strength that did not go with his slight build, Clay seized the raised arm in a grip of iron. In a voice scarcely above a whisper, the Union captain said, "Strike that child again, and I will break the hand that landed the blow."

"Yankee bastard!" yelled Shea through gritted teeth, trying to twist his arm free, but Clay simply increased the pressure further, causing Shea to howl with pain.

"Leave my man be," yelled Amelia Shea, in a voice that was more a snarl than a shout. "Our family problems ain't yourn; they be no one else's."

Clay peered at the woman in utter disgust. Reluctantly, he released her husband's arm. "Very well," he said softly. "Bierce, handle your business with these *things*. The sergeant and I will wait outside." Contemptuously, Clay walked out without salutation, followed by Lot.

Behind them, they heard a muttered obscenity from Amos Shea, followed by a soothing series of words from Bierce. Clay stalked to the shade provided by the large tree in the front yard, then with lightning speed punched it, shattering bark. Blood seeped from skinned knuckles, Clay only massaged them absently, lamentingly.

"Alphonso, there's been cruelty and injustice since the Fall," said Lot quietly to his cousin and friend. "You can't solve it all; you can only keep from adding to it."

"Did I keep from adding to it in New Orleans?" he asked without looking at the sergeant.

Lot said nothing.

They remained quiet until Bierce emerged from the cabin and strolled over to join them, worry written all over his face. "Ah, Clay, time for a snap examination. Did you notice what I noticed?"

"McFeely's boots," answered the distraught captain. "I regret where that observation leads. I had a higher opinion of him."

Bierce agreed. "The cavalry scouts stripped of possessions. Oh, losses of scouts have fallen off recently and the looting of the remains of those who are killed have stopped, but who can forget the wonderfully ghoulish stories the horse soldiers told of the Rebel fiends who robbed the dead not only of their weapons, but of their valuables, down to their very boots. I thought only lawyers did that kind of thing."

"Your sense of humor is inappropriate, Lieutenant," said Clay disapprovingly.

"This whole war is *inappropriate*, Captain. One can either jeer at the folly of man or go mad with the tragedy of it. I prefer to jeer. In any event, I hope your personal observation removes me from your list of suspects. When do you propose to take McFeely into custody?"

Clay tilted his head slightly and studied the young cynic for a long moment before asking, "And just why would you assume that, Lieutenant?"

"The boots, of course. He must be a Confederate irregular: his pacifism the merest blind."

"I admit this new evidence is troubling. There *are* ways he could have come into possession of those boots without being a spy and a murderer."

"Come now! You saw how he stumbled through that lame explanation. That was a man with something to hide."

"I did not say Andrew McFeely has nothing to hide. I am just not certain what he's hiding is responsibility for the murder of Lieutenant Brown. Your eagerness to bring this new aspect to light is consistent with a clever traitor and murderer trying to draw attention away from himself."

"Damn you to hell, Clay! I tire of this!" Bierce's angry exclamation was punctuated by a rumbling peel of thunder; one of Mississippi's notorious summer thunderstorms was heading their way. "Arrest me or clear my name! I have enough to bear without your false charges against my personal honor!" With that enigmatic remark, he threw Clay an angry salute, quickly unhitched his horse, vaulted into its saddle, and set the spurs to the tired nag, which broke into a reluctant gallop in the direction of the main encampment.

Clay stared thoughtfully after Bierce.

Sergeant Lot moved to his side. "Do you really think he murdered John Brown?"

"I just don't know. He is one who plays the clown to hide some great feeling or hurt deep inside. If I knew what that feeling or hurt was, I would have a better idea." He spied the lowering skies and hastened, "Let us hurry back to camp, Sergeant. It would not do to be caught out in the storm. We are currently wearing the only presentable clothing either of us possesses."

And yet, in the end, they were both to be soaked, and more. They had no sooner achieved the safety of their tent when the sky opened and dropped rain in buckets. Lightning gave a flash of illumination through the tent cloth every twenty or thirty seconds; the following thunder boomed like shouts of angry gods. They scarcely had time to congratulate themselves on beating the storm when Colonel Rawlins stuck his head in the tent. "Clay, General Grant wants to see you right now. Lot, you may as well come also; this should affect you."

Clay looked regretfully at the storm through the flap of the tent, then even more so at his gleaming, immaculate boots. "Of course, sir."

Shoulders hunched against the driving rain and fierce gusts whipping into their faces, the trio slogged their way the short distance to Grant's command tent. Thoroughly soaked, they arrived to see Grant and Parker seated on opposite sides of a rickety table, closely studying some dispatches by the light of two oil lamps.

Clay whipped out a handkerchief and quickly wiped the moisture from his spectacles. Both the general and the major looked up, and Grant glared.

He stood and began to speak without preamble. "Clay, this has done it. A complaint has reached me through the 13th Corps that you have assaulted a civilian scout while interfering in a personal family matter. As far as I can see, you have caused nothing but trouble since you got here and are no closer to solving the Brown murder than you were in April. I'm ordering you back to Meigs, who can do whatever he wants with you. You and your sergeant pack your duds. By the time you've done that, Major Parker will have cut the necessary orders and passes. Dismissed!"

"General, sir, if I may explain—" began Lot.

"Sergeant!" barked Clay. "The general has spoken, and he is all too right. I have failed in my mission and can present nothing but vague guesses and surmises. We will do as he orders." With slow precision, Clay saluted, spun on his heel, and walked with dignity out the front of the tent, between the two soaked sentries, into the darkness of the worsening thunderstorm.

Lot hurriedly saluted and followed him. Grant grimly strode to the entrance of the tent and stared after them, as if to hurry their departure.

Clay marched steadily through the storm. As the rain was now at his back, his spectacles were clear enough of water for him to easily pick his way through the gloom. For some reason he would never understand, he glanced to his right just as a nearby lightning-strike starkly illuminated the surroundings. In an instant, he took in a tall pine tree about ten yards away, behind which a dark-clothed figure stood. All he could see were hunched shoulders and the back half of the head brilliantly lit on one side of the tree, with a protruding metal object on the other side, pointed straight at the entrance to Grant's tent where the general stood, back-lit by the oil lamps inside.

"Assassin! Assassin!" screamed Clay to alert Grant and his sentries. Clay whipped his revolver out of his holster but found himself temporarily blinded by the afterimage of the lightning. Desperately searching for the figure he'd glimpsed, Clay heard the massive thunderclap from the lightning stroke, embedded in which was a much smaller, closer boom. Fire pierced Clay's upper left arm, and he staggered back into a tree that happened to be right behind him. Shooting blind, Clay loosed three shots into the general direction of the figure he had seen. Furiously wiping the water from his spectacles with the sleeve of his gun arm, Clay peered into the darkness; a new stroke of lightning revealed no sign of the person.

"Alphonso, Alphonso! God, you've been shot!" The dazed Clay instantly sensed the presence of Lot at his side, exclaiming at a small rent in the sleeve of his tunic, from which something dark oozed to mix with the rainwater. Feeling woozy, Clay cocked his head back in the direction of Grant's tent, to see one of the sentries shoulder the general inside, as the other rushed toward him, bayoneted Springfield at the ready.

The doctor thoroughly disapproved of Clay drenching his wounded upper arm in perfectly good whiskey before allowing it to be bandaged. "European humbug," he muttered, but the pale captain, who sat stripped to the waist in a camp chair in Grant's tent, simply ignored him. The bewhiskered surgeon wiped his probe and pincers clean on his stained tunic front and tossed them into his black bag. "You're lucky, Captain," he said, handing Clay a small round metal object. "It was just a piece of buckshot; part of the buck-and-ball load Rebs use in their smoothbore rifles. If it had been the ball itself, it would have done permanent damage to nerve and muscle, maybe even led to amputation. As it is, you should regain complete use of the arm." The grim old doctor snapped his case shut, gave a sloppy salute, encompassing Grant, Rawlins, Parker, and Lot, and stalked off into the late afternoon sunlight breaking through the remains of the thunderstorm.

Grant busied himself in lighting a cigar. Then, unable to look Clay in the eye, he said, "Captain, I probably owe you my life. If you hadn't shouted when you did, the Reb would have made Mrs. Grant a widow and taken Fred's father from him. I just can't understand how a Reb got through our lines and back out again without being detected, even in the storm. The man must move like a ghost."

"With respect, sir, you are not seeing the forest for the trees," said Clay, wincing as he began to pull on his shirt, angrily shrugging off Lot's attempt to help. "That assassin was not a Reb soldier or partisan. A true stranger would have been stopped and challenged before he reached your headquarters. This was someone who was known at sight to at least some of the people here. This was the traitor—the traitor who murdered John Brown.

"It was a risk to make such an attempt in such a way," mused Clay. "I must be close without realizing it. I must—Sir, may Sergeant Lot and I borrow Major Parker for a short period?"

Grant looked at his aide, who nodded in assent, then said, "Take as long as you like, though darn if I can see what you are about."

Clay finished buttoning his tunic one-handed. Jamming his kepi onto his head, he strode out the tent without saluting, intently focused on some goal; the concerned Lot and puzzled Parker following close on his heels.

The late afternoon sun brilliantly lit the wet, gleaming pine trees among which Grant's tent had been pitched. Clay quickly found the tree he'd staggered against after being shot, peering at several gouged marks. "Major, Sergeant, please use your knives to see if you can dig out the bullets. I would do it myself, but my recent injury would require me to work one-handed, which is quite awkward."

Parker and Lot drew camp knives and began digging into the bark. In a few minutes, Parker had recovered one metal object and Lot two, which they handed to Clay.

He stared at the objects closely, then said, thinking verbally, "I see. At last, I see. It will be a matter of proof. This *will be* difficult." Coming to full awareness, he said, "Thank you for your help. There are undoubtedly more, but I shall not need them.

"Major, I understand General Grant has quartered his wife and son in a farmhouse nearby."

"He has. Sam didn't think the camp a healthy place for them. Found a farmhouse abandoned by its owners, who didn't want to be in the vicinity of Federals. Sleeps there most nights; keeps a squad of cavalry there to make sure they're not inconvenienced by bushwhackers."

"Hmmm," said Clay thoughtfully. "I am going to ask a great favor of you, Major. Please persuade General Grant to convene a meeting there for tonight. I suspect he will listen more to you than to me. Dismiss the cavalry escort; there will be enough armed men for safety's sake, and we don't want rumors to get outside of a small circle. I believe I can reveal the identity of the traitor. You must make sure the general orders the following people to attend . . ."

Night had fallen, but the parlor of the snug farmhouse was brightly lit by three oil lamps; the muggy heat of a summer night in Mississippi made the large fireplace out of the question.

Impatiently, Grant sat in a wing chair near the open window, his tunic loosened to reveal a checked shirt and rumpled vest. In an armchair next to him sat the plump, cross-eyed Julia Grant; her son, Fred, leaned on the side of her chair. Impulsively, she reached a hand toward her husband, who clasped it, hardness softening, before kissing it.

Generals Sherman, McPherson, and McClernand occupied

wooden chairs arranged around a sturdy table. Rawlins and Parker stood at one end of the room, talking earnestly on some matter. Bierce stood completely apart, lounging casually against a wall, his complete isolation from the others somehow natural and appropriate. On opposite sides of Bierce, gazing venomously past the derisive lieutenant, stood Andrew McFeely and Amos Shea; the latter had leaned the shotgun he habitually carried along the wall, while McFeely appeared to be unarmed.

Clay and Lot stood by a small side table Clay had placed in front of the fireplace. He directed Lot, "You will know when to bring him in. I rely on your judgment." The black sergeant saluted and went through the front door.

Turning his back to the room's occupants, Clay reached into his left breast pocket and brought out the photo case of John Brown and his family, which he opened and placed on the right side of the table. From his right, he withdrew another case, then opened and placed it on the left side of the table. A crude daguerreotype from the earliest days of photography, it displayed a young, thin Cicero Clay with a possessive hand on the shoulder of a weirdly beautiful woman with a high, narrow forehead and large staring eyes. Clay extracted Brown's notebook and placed it in the center of the table. Digging in again, he gained purchase of four small metal objects, setting them on top of the notebook. He removed his cap and placed it on the table, then adjusted his spectacles and smoothed back his straight blonde hair, which fell nearly to his shoulders. Satisfied, he brought out his pocket watch, opened the case, and stared at it for much longer than was necessary to ascertain the time before closing it and restoring it.

The observant Bierce, who'd been watching these preparations, began to laugh. "By God, Clay, you look like a papist priest commencing Mass. What comes next, elevation of the Host?"

Clay confronted the occupants of the room, slowly clasping his hands behind his back. "I feel a little solemnity is in order here, Lieutenant Bierce. It is owed to the memory of John Brown, and to his family. I did not know him well, but I know what he did. Professor Slaughter and most of the leaders of Starry Wisdom were exposed and hanged due to his efforts, and some retribution obtained for the atrocities committed against those innocent children. Right now, the country sings Brown's praises, but in a hundred years, what he did will be completely forgotten while schools will preserve the memory of incompetent generals and bloodthirsty tyrants. And ironically, as atrocious as Starry Wisdom was, it was nothing, absolutely nothing, compared to what they were going to do. Brown saved us from that. Yet, the fact he died unaware of what he had prevented does not lessen our debt to him in the slightest."

"What do you mean, what they were going to do?" asked McPherson.

Clay shook his head. "It's not important, sir. General Grant, would you please ask Mrs. Grant and your son to wait outside? What will occur here may involve some indelicate matters."

Grant was *not* pleased. "Clay, I keep no secrets from Mrs. Grant, nor, for that matter, from my son. They will stay here. Count yourself lucky I have agreed to inconvenience my best officers for you. If it weren't for the urgent request of Major Parker, and what I may owe you for earlier today, I would not have done so."

"Here, here," chimed in the fidgety Sherman, who was constantly shifting about in his chair, thin fingers drumming incessantly on the table. "I've supply difficulties to attend to. Steamer with all kinds of things destined for my corps blew up today, somewhere south of Memphis. Only good thing about the disaster is there were half a dozen newspapermen aboard. I guess we'll have the news from Hell by breakfast."

The few chuckles in the room died out quickly as everyone focused on Clay.

"It is strange how much of life is divined to be accident or fate," he began, somewhat irrelevantly. "I was only shown the truth of the matter through a chain of incidents that would have been *impossible* to predict. It gives me an *even higher* appreciation of the late Lieutenant Brown, who had come to the truth much earlier than I, but had not yet committed it to paper. He was wise not to do so. If the truth becomes widely known, it could tear this country apart. What he did do is telegraph to Washington for help, warning there was 'incredible treason at the highest levels.' Unfortunately, the traitor had become aware of Brown's knowledge. We will never be certain how the traitor learned or guessed. Nevertheless, he saw to it that a fine and noble man died horribly."

"Then I was right!" exclaimed Sherman. "The assault last December failed because the Rebs were warned!"

"Yes, General, you were right," replied Clay. "A traitor saw to it that your assault failed. To understand who that traitor is, we must go to the motive for treason. I am reminded of some lines of a courtier from the court of Charles II of England: 'Treason doth never prosper; what's the reason? For if treason doth prosper, none dare call it treason!'

"There is a great truth hidden in those lines. People who commit treason seldom admit, even to themselves, they are so doing. They justify it by appeals to 'states' rights,' 'the people's will,' 'the greater good,' etc., and know if they are successful, they will be hailed as great men, not traitors. Regardless of the labels, it is still treason in my eyes. We must consider the motives of the people in this room, motives that the killer in his own mind would believe did not constitute treason, as we consider which one of you is the traitor who murdered John Brown."

An angry babble of voices broke out in which only every other word or so could be heard, like 'madman,' 'nonsense,' 'what can you expect,' 'New Orleans.'

The confusion was cut short by a bellowed, "Silence!" from Grant. Then, one could hear a pin drop. Julia Grant was a bit shocked, having apparently never heard his parade-ground voice. "Let's hear what the captain has to say," added Grant, eyes boring into Clay.

Clay nodded to Grant and resumed speaking, "When I arrived, I started by considering probabilities. Naturally, Lieutenant Bierce came to mind."

All eyes turned to the debonair officer, who merely smiled and tipped his head slightly, an actor on a stage.

"Consider all the following: He is from southern Indiana, a notorious hotbed of pro-Confederate feeling. A man who jeers at all noble feelings and expresses open contempt for the North's goals. A man who has leave to come and go as he pleases and could communicate with the Confederacy at will. A man I first saw standing alone over the freshly-killed body of John Brown."

Bierce bowed again, ironically. "A convincing indictment. Am I to be arrested now?"

Clay only wished but stifled his innermost desires. "Hardly. Having stated what made you a suspect, I must say, close observation has indicated to me you are too proud and conceited to undertake secret treason. I believe you could go south and fight in open conflict against the country, but it is hard to imagine you engaged in secret deception and betrayal. No, you think too highly of yourself for that. Also, you are too smart to be caught standing over the body of someone you murdered. You are keenly aware of how much General Grant relies on General Sherman, yet you risked your life to save him from the consequences of his *indiscreet behavior* during the first assault on Vicksburg."

With that statement, the hairs stood up on the back of Sherman's neck, and he wanted to say something but controlled himself.

"Finally, Brown hinted at treason at the highest levels, and, to be blunt, you are not *important* enough to meet that description."

"Thank you, *I think*," replied Bierce in a sarcastic tone of voice.

"For some time, my suspicions were directed to Major Parker." Clay indicated with the palm of his hand.

The massive, honorable Indian fixed his stoic gaze on Clay.

"An Indian of great intelligence and ability, who has watched his heritage destroyed by the white man; an Indian not given an opportunity to live up to his potential; an Indian who knows most whites despise him as a savage. I could envisage him betraying the North, not for love of the Confederacy but for the glee of seeing white men slaughter each other. Yet in the end, I could dismiss him as a suspect. Even a short acquaintance would see his fierce personal devotion to General Grant, and, in most Indian cultures of which I am aware, the greatest emphasis is placed on such bonds. I could imagine him betraying the government that had so wronged his people, but I *could not* imagine him betraying his friend."

Clay redirected his gaze. "I considered the possibility of Colonel Rawlins being the traitor."

The pale colonel froze and glared at Clay, who went on unperturbed. "A godly man, and a personal friend of General Grant's, he certainly has access to every secret known to the commanding general, by virtue of his position as chief of staff. He is a widower with numerous children and is suffering from a disease where the eventual outcome is all too predictable. One of the oldest motives for treason is money; here, it would not be for his personal benefit but for the support of those dependent on him, which is how a man of high principles would allow himself to be seduced into treason. After I witnessed a scene between the general and Rawlins, upon the former's arrival from Memphis, Rawlins was immediately dismissed as a suspect. The intensity of his protective devotion was *too* unmistakable.

"Then there was of course General McPherson."

The young general's head jerked at Clay with surprised hostility.

"I think most of us in this room heard his angry outburst against the severity of the measures being taken to preserve the Union, and his loudly expressed opinion that the country was not worth saving if only in that fashion. I felt he could be dismissed as a suspect; a man with so squeamish a stomach would hardly take actions to help a government dedicated to the preservation of the monstrous institution of slavery. Besides, if he were the secret traitor, he would hardly have displayed his dissatisfaction with Federal policy so openly.

"So, having dismissed all the other suspects, I was left with only one—one who intended to betray not only the Union but the Confederates, who he was using to advance his insatiable ambition. Isn't that so, General McClernand?"

There was a collective sharp intake of breath in the room; all eyes focused on the melancholy, bearded commander of the 13th Corps. The general's black eyes darted around the room, then lit upon Clay. "You're mad! Absolutely mad! I'm the second-ranking officer in this command, trusted by Lincoln himself! Why would I betray information to the Confederates?"

"It is *because* you are second in command and would take over this army in the event General Grant were removed. In command of this entire army, you would garner all the glory of the conquest of Vicksburg and whatever would follow. In your mind, I'm sure you saw the Presidency as a natural outcome of such victories, especially when your political connections with Lincoln are considered. I fear, sir, you are not as intelligent as you believe yourself to be. You expected Grant to be recalled after the failure at Chickasaw last December, but you had forgotten General Sherman's brother is a pillar of the administration in the Senate. And since Sherman was the commander on the scene, Grant could not be removed without removing Sherman, which Lincoln was not prepared to do. Then, at the first assault on Vicksburg, you thought you saw a way to correct this mistake. You claimed to see a breakthrough when there *was none*, knowing both that Sherman had the *only* reserves and that in his excited frame of mind, he would insist on leading the assault himself, and almost certainly die. With the assault a bloody failure and Sherman dead, Lincoln would have to remove Grant, and you would get credit for the eventual fall of Vicksburg. At least I think that is how you reasoned."

"God damn the whoreson bastard!" exclaimed Sherman with half-crazed eyes. "My boys! My boys! Their lives just thrown away! You better have a goddamn good answer for this, McClernand!"

"Just a moment," said Grant quietly, raising his palm. "How could General McClernand have communicated with the Rebs?"

"That's right!" exclaimed McClernand.

"An excellent question, sir, and one that puzzled me for a time. Let me tell you how I reached the solution. It was clear McClernand was communicating with the Confederacy when you consider how many other times they had detailed, advanced knowledge of your route. It is not flattery to say your clear-minded flexibility in countering their actions is all that kept it from becoming blindingly obvious they were repeatedly receiving advance information of your intentions, which could have led to embarrassing military setbacks.

"Just one example of many: How did Forrest know Holly Springs was your advance supply depot earlier this year, and it was lightly guarded? Yet McClernand could hardly have passed messages himself; he was far too well known, far too noticeable. He must have had a henchman: someone in a humble capacity who was seen around the camps so much he was soon not being noticed. I was mulling the matter over not long ago when I realized a vital clue was contained in a random jotting in Brown's notebook: a jotting

I had misinterpreted. It said, 'Scout March 13th.' Since Brown was writing in April, I assumed it to be some cryptic reference to an action on the 13th of March. But this morning, a chance remark indicated an individual had been in the habit of scouting for the 13th Corps on its march. McClernand's corps. There is nothing too unusual in corps commanders hiring civilian scouts with no reference to army headquarters. Still, it made me think that jotting in Brown's notebook could have meant, 'I am suspicious of a scout for the 13th Corps I encountered during the march,' rather than a date *in* March. As most of you have heard, there was an attempt on the life of the commanding general this afternoon."

Julia Grant started and involuntarily grasped her husband's hand; he had not told her.

Clay, ignorant to the fright of the general's wife, went on, "The assassin was behind a tree, and, even with the illumination from a bolt of lightning, his identity was concealed by the trunk. He shot me with what the doctor assumed was a 'buck and ball' load, a musket ball with two pieces of buckshot Confederates who have not yet received rifled muskets use in their smoothbore guns. After three pieces of buckshot were recovered from the tree behind where I was shot, and added to the one removed from my arm, we deduced the weapon fired at me was a straight shotgun." Clay grabbed the four pieces of metal from the table and displayed them in his open palm to the room. "Also, I obtained a vivid glimpse of his right ear at a distance of less than ten yards. A few of you may have heard my comments on the recent theory out of Europe that no two people have exactly the same pattern and shape of ear and that over the last year, my personal observations have shown this to likely be true. I recognized *that* ear. It belonged to the same man who acted for General McClernand as a scout. It belonged to a man who regularly carried a shotgun. It belonged to a man who, when angered by me, called me a Yankee bastard, which is not only untrue but an absurd curse from a Union scout. It belonged to Amos Shea."

Everyone concentrated on the compact Mississippian who scowled, making his squint even more pronounced. "General McClernand, sir, do ah haf ta put up with this shit? You knowed ah ain't with the Rebellion."

"Of course, you aren't," consoled the commander of 13th Corps. "Clay is a madman, the rabid dog who committed the massacre at the Devereaux place. No one will believe this lunatic's ravings."

"Oh, but there is a further witness from which we need to hear," said Clay with a trace of satisfaction on his lips. "Sergeant Lot!"

Lot entered with another sergeant: David Larson, the unemotional sniper from Iowa. He scanned the room and pointed at Shea. "Yep, I guess that's him. Saw him talking real intent to McClernand the night that little lieutenant was killed on Sherman's boat, rest his soul. Thought it odd—"

With a banshee cry, Shea lunged for his double-barreled shotgun. Instead of trying to make his escape, he began to level it at the wingchair where Grant sat. But before he could fire, McFeely leaped on him, grabbing the twin barrels and twisting them to the ceiling. There was a brief struggle, and one of the barrels discharged alongside the Scot's head; his left ear exploded in a red spray, and the lanky redhead fell screaming to the floor, clutching the bloody smear that was now the left side of his head. Shea again attempted to level the gun at Grant, and both Julia and Fred screamed, as a cursing Sherman tried to lunge for the killer. But before Shea could fire the second barrel, three sharp bangs rang out from Clay's pistol. Shea fell backward, his dying finger pulling the trigger of the remaining barrel, which discharged loudly but harmlessly into the ceiling.

Grant held his family protectively to his chest, shooting death daggers towards McClernand.

Larson had his rifle leveled at the downed assassin; Lot his revolver, I will not dispute within an instant of the blast.

As McFeely's screaming subsided to continuous moaning, Clay bent by his side and gently inspected the wound. "I believe he will live," said Clay after a quick examination. "I do not believe any of the pellets entered the skull—their path being parallel to the bone—but the lost ear and torn scalp could present a risk of death. Bierce, go get a surgeon, quickly."

The pessimistic lieutenant, for once completely somber, nodded and ran out the door.

Clay rose and approached the table where McClernand now sat, a wild-eyed Sherman behind him with an arm around his throat, a furious McPherson gripping his seat to stay under control. Clay cocked his revolver and pointed it straight at the quaking traitor's chest.

"Wait!" commanded Grant. "You can't kill that-that thing."

"Oh, I believe this is best," said Clay, smiling sweetly, the pistol pointing unwaveringly at the general's heart. "There can be no trial on this matter. Lincoln appointed this piece of offal. A public trial would humiliate the administration and weaken it just when it needs to be strongest. Furthermore, imagine how the details of this would demoralize the troops in the field. It's bad enough they often die because of stupidity and incompetence; to suspect you are killed to advance the ambitions of such traitors would sap our strength when we need that most. You can claim I went mad and murdered the general; have me hanged without disputing the charge. It may not be for the correct offense, but in the end, justice will have been done."

Larson and Lot lowered their weapons yet were on the ready in case Clay needed them. Shea had ceased moving: his squint now frozen in infamy.

"Captain Clay, that will not work, and some part of you must know it," responded Grant in an urgent voice, calmly setting his wife and son aside, standing. "Too many questions would be asked, and we could never keep the details of what happened here secret." Grant reached in his tunic pocket for a piece of notepaper and a reservoir pen; he threw them down on the table before McClernand, saying, "If you do not write exactly what I say, I will allow the captain to go forward with his plan. You will write how you betrayed the plans of the Chickasaw assault to the Rebels. You will write how you conspired with the late Amos Shea to murder Lieutenant John Brown, *and* how you tried to have me killed. You will write how you lied about the breakthrough on the first Vicksburg assault with the intent of causing a military disaster. You will date and sign it, and Generals Sherman and McPherson will witness it. You will do it, or you will die right here, right now. I will let Captain Clay end your miserable excuse of an existence."

"Hell, Sam, let me break his scrawny neck," said Sherman through gritted teeth, tightening his arm around McClernand's throat. "Shooting's what you do to a mad dog, and this bastard's worse than a mad dog."

"I'll write it, I'll write it," came McClernand's strained voice. "Only for God's sake keep these two lunatics off me."

Sherman released him, but Clay's revolver barrel remained mere inches from his chest. With fearful glances at the man who could end his pitiful existence in a split second, McClernand scrawled what Grant had demanded. Sherman and McPherson quickly added their signatures as witnesses.

Grant picked up the document, blew on it to dry it, then carefully folded it, and placed it in the inner pocket of his tunic. "Now here is what you are going to do. You are to leave instantly, this night, for St. Louis. I will announce you have been relieved for issuing stories to reporters praising your own performance. Such communications are an offense if they are not first run through the commanding general, and you've done a lot of that. Normally, I wouldn't care, but this gives me an excuse to dismiss you, in a manner sufficiently petty, so no suspicions will be aroused. I will give you, for a short period, a meaningless command where you can't hurt anyone or anything. Then in two or three months, you will quietly resign from Federal service. If you ever try to interfere in this war again, or if you ever run for public office, I will see that this document is released. Yes, I know you can claim it is forged, but many will believe, and believing, people will view you as lower than Benedict Arnold and Aaron Burr. It is a shame the good of the country requires your infamy be concealed. Now get out before I change my mind!"

Stunned, eyes wide with panic, McClernand made for the door, stepping around the pooling blood of Shea and over the moaning McFeely to do so.

At the door, he was roughly accosted by Ely Parker, who fiercely growled in a voice all could hear. "Do you know how much skin can be removed from a man without killing him?"

"N-n-no," stuttered the traitor.

"Breathe one word of what happened here, cause Sam one particle of worry, and I will personally reveal to you the answer to that question." The livid major then hurled McClernand into the darkness.

Grant announced loud enough for all to hear, "Now all of you, *nothing* must ever be said about this—not now, not ever. Not secretly to wives and lovers, not in memoirs to be published in fifty years. Our wounded country has so much that needs to heal. If it learned there was treason so high . . . well, doggone it, I'm not sure it could. You must all swear to abide by this promise." There was a murmur of agreement from everyone but McFeely, who was excused by circumstances.

During this command, Clay had holstered his Smith & Wesson

and walked up to the table, beginning to place the objects he had so carefully displayed back into his pockets.

As he finished, Julia and Fred Grant rushed up to him. "Captain Clay, you have given me my husband, the only man I have ever loved or ever will." Impulsively, she kissed Clay on the cheek; then embarrassed, she blushed and retreated. Fred Grant demanded to shake his hand, complementing him on killing "dirty Reb spies." They then both retreated to a corner of the room as far from the bodies as they could get, clutching one another.

Sherman, McPherson, and Rawlins all solemnly shook hands one at a time.

It was Parker who approached Clay, motioning Sergeants Larson and Lot to join him, allowing the others to murmur quietly among themselves. "A very convincing performance," he said. "You would have made a fine Indian warrior. The finest warriors always possess great cunning along with great bravery." He then coaxed Larson, "Tell me, Sergeant, was it Captain Clay or Sergeant Lot who coached you in that lie about seeing Shea with McClernand?"

The sniper shrugged, nonplussed, his rifle cradled in his arm. "No harm in tellin' about it now, I guess. Sure, it was Sergeant Lot. Course, it wasn't altogether a lie. I'd seen McClernand talkin' to someone, but was too dark and too far away for me to be sure who it was."

Clay smirked confidently. "My chain of evidence was purely circumstantial, pure educated guesswork. If they had possessed the belly to deny everything and stick with it, no jury or court martial could have touched them, but I had seen how poorly Amos Shea controlled his emotions and reasoned he could be shocked into incriminating behavior. I fear I had not expected him to make a suicidal attempt on Grant's life; I blame myself for not planning for that possibility. In the end, Amos Shea was a fanatical Confederate, willing to give his life for his cause."

Jeremiah Lot placed a hand on his cousin's shoulder. "Don't look for reasons to blame yourself. You have done brilliantly. Now, it's all over."

"Yes, it is *almost* over," replied Clay softly. "Almost over." When he raised his head, there was General Grant staring fixedly at him, none too happy.

CHAPTER EIGHT

THE GLORIOUS FAITH

It was an hour before first light on July 4th, 1863. Sergeant Lot had just finished helping Ambrose Bierce pack up his knapsack, carpet bag, and map case by the light of a flickering oil lamp in Bierce's tent. He gave a final tug on the strap securing the knapsack, saying, "There. I didn't think we could do it, but we got everything you have into three pieces of luggage."

"I appreciate your seeing me to the landing. You sure your dangerous little captain can spare you until the boat leaves at nine o'clock?"

"I believe so, Lieutenant. He has been doing little but lying on his cot, staring upwards, ever since that night. Except to write some letters and send a couple of telegrams, he has hardly left the tent. Seeing as I haven't had as much time to talk to you as I would have liked, with your permission, I will stay with you until the steamer casts off."

"Once again, I do appreciate that, Sergeant," replied Bierce. Left unspoken was the fact few people felt comfortable around the map-maker. He knew he was something of an outsider and recognized the same trait in the black sergeant. To his amusement, he felt as comfortable in the former slave's company as Lot was in his.

They lugged the bulging parcels out of the tent and rested them near the blazing campfire, lit more to provide light than to further heat the unpleasantly muggy Mississippi air. In the east, a hint of sunrise lightened the horizon, but the brighter stars still shone clearly overhead.

"Lieutenant, it is more than four hours until the boat leaves. Do you really need to get there that early?"

"Oh, yes. If Pemberton decides to go forward with the formal surrender this morning, there's going to be all kinds of people making a mad dash for the landing—staff officers, couriers, reporters, sutlers—every one of them mad to spread the news. I want to be sure to get comfortable accommodations aboard."

"It's a true shame you cannot stay to witness the surrender, Lieutenant. It will be a truly historic moment."

"I would have preferred it. But, alas, General Thomas is *absolutely* insistent I report immediately. That fool Rosecrans is at long last beginning to move the Army of the Cumberland against General Bragg and his men. Thomas is too good a subordinate to criticize his commander, especially in a telegram, but reading between the lines, you can clearly see he thinks Rosecrans will be reckless and stumble into some sort of trap. He is able enough to know quick, accurate scouting is going to be essential as Old Rosie moves south. I am complemented he thinks highly enough of me to demand me by name."

"It sounds as if you truly respect General Thomas. Praise for a high-ranking officer is something I've not heard from you."

"Sir, he's the only one of Rosecrans's three corps commanders who is worth a damn. Albeit, Rosie himself isn't worth much himself: an excitable man who stays up most nights discussing Popery with his staff, if you will. He would do better to study maps of Tennessee. If Bragg hits him unexpectedly, he'll skedaddle, and be glad he has George Thomas. The man may be slow, but he cannot be surprised or panicked. If attacked, he will stand like a rock. Like a rock!" Bierce caught himself; praising a general, even one deserving, did not fit with the image he liked to project. "Nevertheless, it's not certain Pemberton will surrender. He is to send his final acceptance early this morning, but the damn feather-brained fool may decide the honor of the Confederacy requires his army to starve to the last man."

Both peered toward the noise of two shadowy figures as they approached the campfire.

The light revealed one of them: Alphonso Clay, uniform clean, boots polished to a shine, carefully shaved. Both men wondered for the hundredth time how the captain maintained such an immaculate personage in the filthy confusion of an army camp.

It took a moment to recognize the other figure as Andrew McFeely. Heavy bandages had been wrapped around his head, from under the jaw to the stained wad covering the left side of his head and over the top to meet again under the jaw. He leaned heavily on a walking stick, a wee bit wobbly, and the left side of his face twisted upward into a permanent grimace, a consequence of forming scar tissue drawing toward where his ear had been. He was an unpleasant sight in the flickering light, but nowhere near as hideous as some survivors of this terrible war, whose mutilations were ghastly.

Somewhat shocked, Bierce gave Clay a mocking salute. "Captain, I didn't think you'd be saying goodbye, and after all we have meant to each other." He bowed slightly to the pitiful McFeely, his ironic prose dropping instantly. "Mr. McFeely, I *am* glad to see you. But should you be up and about? That wound you suffered was nasty in the extreme."

"I dinna hear ya well," came the response in a strong voice, contradicting his weak form. "Ya must be speakin' to me right ear. Surgeon said, not only did that bastard's gun cost me outside ear, but the part inside that hears." McFeely stumbled for no reason but caught himself in time with his walking stick. "He thinks the damage to the hearin' is what's made me unsteady on me feet; no one rightly knows why." The Scotsman began to chuckle ruefully.

Being careful to address McFeely's good ear, Bierce said, "What do you find so funny about your wounds?"

McFeely could still display a pleasant smile, twisted as it was. "I was just thinking, Lieutenant, I endured eighteen months in the Crimea without a scratch, and left soldierin' so I would never have to see such violence again. And here I am, marked for life, lucky to not have been blown to pieces. The Lord is usually inscrutable, but I think He can safely say He dinna approve of pacifism."

"I asked Mr. McFeely yesterday if there was anything I could do to show my gratitude for his having saved me from the consequences of my own overconfidence about having Shea under control," explained Clay. "He simply asked if I could arrange to send him *far away*. After a few telegrams, I was able to get him a temporary appointment as a civilian courier. He is to report to Fort Leavenworth, where a small army column is assembling. They will stop at various forts along the way, delivering payroll and mail, until they make their last stop at Fort Tejon in California. California is far from the war, and a place where people find it easy to make a new start. I tried to talk him into waiting until he was stronger, but he is adamant about being on his way now."

"There be nothing holding me here," replied McFeely with force. "It's away I be wanting."

"I would have thought you would want to stay for a spell and console the widow Shea." Clay carefully maintained his neutral face. "She may not yet have been told of her husband's death, although she undoubtedly suspects something by now. As there will never be an official report on the matter, she might appreciate an old family friend holding her hand." Clay gave no sign he was thinking of how he, Bierce, Parker, and Lot had carried Amos Shea's body through the darkness and thrown it into the river, watching the current swirl it away from the bank and down to areas where; even if recovered, it would not be recognized.

"I dinna want to see her!" exclaimed McFeely, refusing eye contact with Clay. "I be wanting her to remember me as I was, not as I am. I wasn't bonny to start, and now I might scare little Zachary. Besides, there be other reasons, and that's all I be saying."

Clay stared silently at him for a long moment, then nodded his head. "Very well. What do you intend to do when you get to California?"

"Ach, odd jobs here and there; enough to keep me in food and a wee drop now and again. I'll be trying to forget what man can do to man. Funny, I joined the army rather than go to work in my late father's dry goods store in Edinburgh, thinking I would die of boredom there. Now, I see the pleasure of boredom."

"Why not set up a dry goods store in Los Angeles—that town not far from Fort Tejon?" asked Bierce. "I hear it's a sleepy little place just beginning to grow; might be a smart thing to get in on the ground floor."

"Mon, it would take at least $500 to start up such a store, and where is a tramp like me to find such money? And, there is little point in striving to be a success when . . . ach, never mind."

"Regardless, I want you to stay in touch with my estate manager at Dignitas," said Clay. "Depending on what I learn about this John Rockefeller, I may wish to start expanding into this petroleum thing, and I hear Southern California has places where it literally bubbles to the surface. If things become promising, the Clay estate would be prepared to pay you handsomely to represent our interests. With it taking weeks to communicate back and forth, having an honest man on the spot would be invaluable."

"Wouldn't you wish me to write you directly?" asked McFeely, most gratefully.

"It will be hard to reliably contact me for some time to come. It is best for you to communicate directly with the estate manager.

"In any case, Mr. McFeely, Lieutenant Bierce, you had best be on your way if you want to secure acceptable accommodations on the St. Louis boat." Clay bowed slightly but did not offer to shake hands. "Sergeant Lot, I understand you would like to help them settle in. Feel free to stay with them until the last moment. I have several matters to attend to this morning and will not require your services for some hours."

Lot saluted. "Thank you, Captain."

Bierce and McFeely muttered their goodbyes. Then the trio trudged off into the darkness, Bierce and Lot in the front with the luggage, McFeely limping behind. Clay stared after them long after they had gone. "Goodbye, my friend. I will be sorry to grieve you."

"Why is that?" came a voice from behind him. Clay whirled around. Beyond the circle of illumination thrown by the fire, all he could see was a small glowing red circle, which advanced toward the fire. The source, a shadowy figure, developed into Ulysses Grant, holding a smoldering cigar.

"General Grant, I was not aware of your presence," replied Clay smoothly, trying to cover up the fact he had actually been startled. "What brings you out so early?"

Grant took a final puff on the stub of his cigar and threw it into the fire. "Never went to sleep. Pounding headache wouldn't let me. Thinking that doggone fool, Pemberton, might go back on his promise to formally surrender this morning weighs on me. If he doesn't, I will have to starve the whole army in Vicksburg to death, along with all civilians. That is a heavy burden, Captain. Too heavy to let a soul sleep without—well, just too heavy to let a soul sleep.

"Rawlins was feeling poorly, so I sent him and Parker off to get what rest they could and have been wandering about, thinking on a number of things. Saw you folks gathered here but didn't want to interrupt your farewells. I had already given my thanks to Mr. McFeely during his recovery, and I don't particularly want to have much to do with Lieutenant Bierce."

"Sir, do you really think Pemberton would be so mad as to renege on the agreement he reached with you under the flag of truce? Blockade or no, word must have gotten through to him that Lee has wrecked his army insanely assaulting General Meade's dug-in forces in Pennsylvania. If Meade moves smartly, this war could be over by winter."

Grant thrust his hands into his trouser pockets and began to jingle loose change and such. "Pemberton was never exactly the fastest rabbit in the forest, so maybe he doesn't see how hopeless it is. Besides, he may have been born a Northerner, but he is a true Southerner now.

"Clay, you are Union-loyal, but you are a Southern aristocrat at heart. Would you surrender while there was fight left in you, even if all deemed hopeless?"

Clay analyzed his answer for several heartbeats. "I suppose not, sir."

Grant began to search his tunic pockets until he eventually produced a cigar. "Anyway, while I'm here, might as well discuss certain matters with you. I've telegraphed General Meigs, asking him to assign you and Sergeant Lot permanently to my staff, and he has agreed to do so." The general fidgeted with the unlit cigar, watching Clay for his reaction.

Clay was quite taken aback. "Sir, this was, um, unexpected. I do not know what I could possibly offer you. There are no vacancies in your official staff, and now that the traitor has been eliminated, there is no function for us."

"If only hoping could make it so. I'd truly like to believe

McClernand was one of a kind. But somehow, I suspect there are others who could do this country injury in our own armies. Before McClernand, I wouldn't have believed it. After him . . . " He waggled his head back and forth. "I can't leave this kind of thing in the hands of the Provost or the Judge Advocate. Too great a risk it would get out, become known to the army and the country. Country is tearing itself apart as is. If the McClernand matter, or anything like it, gets out, it would be a fatal blow to this country, and to the only real hope for a truly free people the world has ever seen. I think we can trust everyone who was in the room when you—They can be trusted.

"But even good people sometimes make mistakes; sometimes leaves things laying around; sometimes sees things by accident." He'd been rummaging through every pocket on himself as he spoke. "Darn, must've left my matches behind." Grant produced a folded document from an inside pocket; Clay recognized it instantly as McClernand's signed confession. The general bent toward the fire and stuck the end of the paper into the flames, where it spontaneously ignited. Bringing the burning end up to the cigar he'd inserted in his mouth, Grant puffed vigorously until the tobacco began to smolder, and then he tossed the remainder of the document into the campfire.

"General!" exclaimed Clay, lunging for the precious paper, but it was too late. It was already curling into blackened ash.

"Could never dare publicize that; would do more harm than a fool like McClernand could do. Course, McClernand doesn't know and will never suspect, the paper no longer exists. He would never give a thought to the good of the country, so he cannot imagine doing what I've just done."

Clay stared at the fire for a moment. "Be that as it may, sir, I must respectfully decline your offer. General Meigs and I have unfinished business, unless, of course, you would care to save everyone time and delay and proceed on that business for him. In any event, the resolution of that business would render it impossible for me to serve on your staff."

"Yes, the resolution of the business . . ." There was something between loathing and impatience in his voice. "You know, Meigs forwarded to me two newspaper accounts, without any explanation. The first one discusses how a trust fund was established for the widow and four girls John Brown left behind. Collections were not going well until an anonymous contribution arrived, in care of a Louisville bank, for $12,500. By itself, it should secure the family from want, if used carefully. On top of that, Mrs. Brown said she was most grateful for the fact the contribution was accompanied by a family photograph, one she thought lost forever. She has pleaded for the benefactor to identify himself, so she may thank him for both the money and the heirloom, but to date, he has not come forward."

Clay was stone-faced.

"The second account Meigs sent me was an article from a newspaper in New Orleans: one so hostile to the military government, it is a wonder General Banks allowed it to publish. It urged the good citizens of Louisiana to come forward and contribute to a trust being formed for the Devereaux children, orphaned by a Union monster who walks unpunished. It encouraged the well-to-do to follow the example of an anonymous Confederate sympathizer who forwarded $7,500."

Clay moved not a muscle.

"You know, at West Point, the only subject I really liked was mathematics. It has a comforting certainty in a world where everything is constantly shifting. Thought at one time I might become a teacher of mathematics at some small college, but somehow that never worked out.

"General Meigs is a pretty fair mathematician, and I'm sure

he noted, like I did, the amounts were multiples of $2,500. In the case of Brown, the four children and the widow made five; multiply that by $2,500, and you have $12,500. Same with the Devereaux contribution."

"There were only two orphans there," said Clay, clearing his strained voice.

"There was the child who died in the fire; that makes three." Grant was almost enjoying toying with the impenetrable Clay.

Clay refused to respond.

"Can't buy your way out of responsibility for what you do, and I don't just mean money. Your death will not bring that child back to life, or the parents of those orphans."

"I would not imagine so," Clay replied barely above a whisper. "It is difficult to endure a number of things, of which my responsibility for New Orleans is only one."

"Don't talk to me of how hard responsibility is! Don't you dare!" exclaimed Grant with fire in his eyes. "You feel responsible for the deaths at the Devereaux plantation, *and even of the slave woman who took her own life!*"

Clay's head snapped up. He could not imagine how the general came to know anything about Arabella.

"So, you can't stand the burden of guilt, huh?" Grant's anger flared as he walked to and fro in front of the fire, never taking his eyes off Clay. "And you would like to tell me about it? Do you know how many men's blood are on my hands? Do you? Well, I don't! How's that for guilt, Captain Clay? I've sent decent young fellers to their deaths and had other decent young fellers killed, and there are so many of them I could not learn all their names if I tried! Fellers with wives, children, parents; fellers with dreams, hopes, ambitions. I guess a lot of generals never think of that; it's my curse *I do*. You've come to the wrong shop to peddle your guilt, Captain Clay."

"Sir, if you feel that way, how can you continue to do what you do?"

Grant stopped to think and fiddle with his cigar, then tilted his head in Clay's direction. "Because without me, I fear this war may be lost. And if lost, all hope for a better world is gone forever. It's beyond patriotism, Clay. America is the only hope for the people of the *whole world*. If we fail, slavery will be the lot of mankind until judgment day: not just the slavery of the black man, but the slavery of the peasant to the aristocrat, the slavery of the good man to the tyrant. I must go on, so long as I can be of use in the cause; and you must go on so long as you can be of use to me."

Grant took a long pull on his cigar, then coughed and looked at it, making a face. "Doggone things will be the death of me; it must have gone out. Suppose it's better than *other things*." Reaching into his inner tunic pocket, Grant came out with another folded document, Clay's own confession. Before the captain could respond, the general thrust the end into the campfire, where it ignited immediately. Stunned, Clay watched Grant apply the burning end to his cigar, and throw the flaming remnant back into the fire.

Clay took a moment to speak. "Sir, you should not have done that. It requires me to go to the trouble of writing the document again."

"Write it as many times as you want, Captain. I will always have more cigars. General Meigs and I have reached an understanding. There will be no court martial, at least while hostilities continue. Afterwards, no one is going to be looking to try you. But if you are bound and determined to hang, then you will have your wish. But until then, you will serve this country by serving me.

"Since we have that out of the way, there is just one thing I would like to know concerning the events of the other night." He took a long, contemplative pull on his cigar, expelled the smoke, staring directly into Clay's eyes. "Just who did shoot Lieutenant John Brown?"

Clay could not believe his ears and took a moment before responding. "I believe that was made clear, sir. General McClernand felt Lieutenant Brown was getting too close to the truth and ordered his minion Shea to arrange the murder."

"Captain Clay, please remember this; I can be wrong, and I can make mistakes, but I am not stupid. The shot that killed Brown was fired by a superb marksman: two hundred yards or so, by your own account. I'm surprised none of my other staff noted the squinty lines around Shea's eyes, the sure sign of the nearsighted. That's why he carried a shotgun, I imagine—to make up for his poor eyesight. Out of character for a scout to carry a short-ranged weapon."

"There could be other explanations, sir," responded Clay slowly.

"And then, of course, there was your own wound," carried on Grant, as if Clay had not spoken. "Only one piece of buckshot hit you, from a load fired from only fifteen paces away; darn-near missed you altogether. He'd been waiting to see me backlit in the entrance to the tent, where even a nearsighted man could hardly miss with a shotgun, but when he heard you shouting from the raining dark, surprise *and* his bad sight saved your life. So, I ask again, Captain Clay, who shot Lieutenant Brown?"

Clay stood as frozen as a statue for nearly a full minute. Then, he said formally, "General Grant, a matter of honor prohibits me from imparting that information to you. Nevertheless, you have my word, as a gentleman, the killer will be of no further threat to the United States or its armies."

Grant stared levelly at Clay for a long moment before saying, "You doggone Southerners and your honor. You are more obsessed with the form of decency instead of its reality." The general sighed and began to massage his temples. "Very well, I guess I owe you this secret for unmasking the traitor, and for saving my life. It's starting to get light. I best get back to headquarters, to be ready for whatever Pemberton has in mind. Wish this doggone headache would go away. We'll talk later, Clay." Grant slouched off into the predawn light.

Clay watched him go, a blankness to his eyes that belied his thoughts.

Amelia Shea sat hunched over the table, eyes red, her crude breakfast untouched, unmindful to the quiet sobbing of her son Zachary. Her head jerked up at the sound of approaching hoof beats, followed by the faint rustling of a horse being tied to a hitching post. Joy spread over her face, and she began to rise. But instead of who she expected, the small, neat figure of Alphonso Clay came through the door. Joy fled, and she collapsed back into her plank chair. "It's you," she said, voice surly and dejected at the same time. "What kin I do for you, Captain?"

Clay glared at the seated woman, lips curled in faint disgust. "Several things, Mrs. Shea. Let us take them in order." He walked over to the seated figure of Zachary Shea. "Child, did you know your Uncle Andy is leaving this morning from the steamboat dock?"

"Uncle Andy's leaving?" the boy asked, even more dejected than before. "When's he comin' back?"

"Not for a long time," answered Clay, an unaccustomed tenderness in his voice. "He is going to California, and that is very, very far away. Do you know the path to the wharfs?"

"Sure. Not much more than a mile from here."

"Then why don't you go on down to see him off? Ask any of the sentries for the nine o'clock boat." He handed the child a piece of paper. "Here is a pass, should any of them give you trouble. Tell them you are just seeing off a relative."

"Ma, is it all right with you?"

"Guess so," said Amelia in a monotone. "Come straight back

when Andrew—when the boat leaves." The child got up and pattered out the door, clueless, making haste to see his beloved uncle. Clay watched him go, then strode over to the table where Amelia remained seated, lost in some private misery.

"The child seems upset," he said, remaining standing.

"His pa ain't been home in a long time. Amos is a hard man, but Zachary loves his pa."

"Indeed, he does, but perhaps not in the way either you or he thinks. Tell me, does he know Andrew McFeely is his real father?"

The tall, thin woman leaped to her feet and glared at Clay. "That's a goddamn lie, you Yankee bastard!"

"Of course, one wonders whether McFeely himself knows, although he certainly suspects." Clay ignored the woman's curse. "The few times I have seen them together, one only had to observe them: the way he gazed at the child. And besides, there is the matter of the shape of the child's ear. It is very similar to McFeely's, but nothing like your late husband's."

Her blue eyes widened with shock. "Late?" was the single word she managed to choke out.

"Yes, Mrs. Shea, I must inform you, your husband is dead. I discovered his treason, you see, and shot him."

The deflated woman landed in her chair, barely.

Clay's informal voice melodiously went on, "I shot him low in the belly and watched him die. It took a long time, and he was in considerable pain, which I must say gave me much satisfaction to witness. After the traitor squealed his last, I drug him by his heels down to the Mississippi and threw him in for the fish and alligators to nibble; no soil in this country is vile enough to warrant holding such a swine."

With a scream that would have done justice to a leaping puma, Amelia snatched a bread knife, knocked the table out of her way, and lunged at Clay. Deftly, the small captain dodged her knife, grabbed the wrist holding the weapon in a grip of iron, and slammed it against the wall. With a howl, she dropped it.

Then in a motion, almost too fast to follow, Clay struck her in the face with such force she staggered to the opposite wall of cabin, hit it hard, and fell to a sitting position, blood flowing from a split lip.

Stepping delicately around the mess from the overturned table, he grabbed one of her loose-fitting boots and tugged mightily, revealing a small foot encased in an Indian moccasin.

"It is as I thought," commented Clay to the dazed woman simmering with animalistic fury. "I noted, when I first met you, the small size of your hands." He stood back, tossed the boot aside, and studied her hands and feet. "I had seen child-size moccasin prints all over the spot from where the shot that killed Lieutenant Brown was fired. The fact your feet were probably proportionately small, along with your apparent Indian blood, set an interesting chain of thought going through my mind. It was really quite clever of you to always wear only the Indian footgear when engaged in your assassinations. How convenient to blame the red man for violence! Tell me; was that your idea, or your late husband's?"

"It were mine," came the mumbled response.

"I thought that likely. I rather suspected you would show more animal cunning than the dim-witted Amos. However, it was Amos that first drew you into this work, wasn't it?"

Seeing nowhere to run nor anywhere to hide, the cornered woman confided, "He came back from a horse-tradin' visit to the camp of the 13th Corps all excited-like, sayin' there was a big general there who saw the justice of our cause an' would pay us big for helping him. Don't rightly know how Amos met him."

"Ah, Amos made the deals, and you did the killing. What a pretty little family you were."

"Amos wouldn' a had me in on it 'cept his eyes were so poorly.

Sides, we were bein' patriots. That Union general said he wanted Grant to look bad by killin' his scouts an' makin' his soldiers scared to go alone in the woods to take a crap. If he paid us to be patriots, what's wrong with that?"

"If you ask such a question, it is a waste of breath to answer. I will say this much; it was not about the justice of the Confederacy's cause, at least for you." Clay strolled over to the crude mantelpiece, where the cheap copy of a Scottish castle rested; he casually picked up the object. "A memento of your short-lived fornication with Andrew McFeely, I am certain. Who else would have given you a Scottish-themed gift? Worthless in monetary terms, but it was as much as his circumstances permitted him to afford, *and* was a gift from the heart." Without hesitation, he hurled it to the floor, shattering it into dozens of pieces, spilling the contents. A few coins rolled into corners, but the large mass of green papers remained where the porcelain had broken.

"Quite a sum in greenbacks, Mrs. Shea. Nearly a thousand dollars in the pay of Union scouts you killed: dead men from which you stole. In this valley, the only people with large sums in Federal paper money are the soldiers, since Washington cannot pay them in gold. You did not stop at the money, of course. You stole anything that was valuable, which could be resold, even boots if they were relatively new. It was a mistake to give that pair to McFeely. Tell me, did you just make a gift to a former lover, or did you intend to divert suspicion upon him, knowing even if arrested, he would go to the gallows rather than implicate the woman he loves?"

Arms now wrapped around her knees, Amelia spoke dejectedly from her place on the floor. "I would never hurt Andy. It's just, when he got back, his shoes were in pieces, and even though I could get a good price for them boots in Jackson, I hated seein' him so ragged. He never cared enough about money and things. That's why—"

"That is why you abandoned him for Amos Shea, the owner of this impressive estate," said Clay sarcastically. "A handsome man, land of his own: security to trash such as you." Amelia spun her head away as Clay went on relentlessly. "You did not need long to persuade yourself that you did not love McFeely but were passionate for Shea. It must have been quite a shock when you discovered how heavily mortgaged the property was to the bank in Jackson."

Amelia snapped her head up sharply but said nothing.

"Yes, Grant ordered all records swept up on our pass through the charming capital of this state. I took the time to examine them recently, which openly disclosed the financial troubles of your husband. So, do not give yourself pious airs of patriotism; you are an assassin for pay."

"Ah believe in the Confederacy!" declared Amelia. "An' if ah can make money bein' patriotic-like, who are you to judge me? A high and mighty traitor to the South, who's never lacked for any luxury, never mind necessity?" She took a breath and huffed. "Ever felt your stomach against your backbone, Yank? Ever go completely without so kin would have a little something in their stomachs? Well, ah have! So don't you go a-judging me!"

Clay walked over to where she was planted and stared down at her. Amelia Shea, who was frightened of very little, was terrified. "Yes, I was born to wealth and privilege," he said. "And yet, the most valuable thing I ever had is now gone and cannot be repurchased at any price. You had that precious item and discarded it. I would give everything I have, my life itself, for one day, just one hour . . ." Clay clamped his mouth shut, the muscles in his neck convulsing. Half-turning from Amelia, he staggered to the corner. Supporting himself against the wall with one hand and with the other, he scrabbled his watch out of his pocket, opened the lid, and forced himself to focus on the picture.

From where she sat, Amelia could see the picture of the beautiful mulatto. Hatred overcoming discretion, she exclaimed, "That's what your precious Union will lead to—white men messin' with nigger wenches!"

In a blur of motion, Clay whirled and lashed out with his elegant, hand-made boot, catching Amelia in the ribs with such fury, she rolled over twice and lay in a huddled heap on the floor, clenching her teeth to keep from crying out.

Clay visibly quivered all over. Gradually, the motion subsided, and restoring the watch to his pocket, he walked over to where she lay, staring at him with naked hatred, gasping like a fish out of water. "My apologies, Mrs. Shea. My actions were unpardonable. Clays try not to do *dishonorable* things. Even though you are in *no sense* a lady, it was provoked by your comment regarding a *true lady*, I must tender my regrets that I failed to better regulate my actions.

"Now, simply satisfy my curiosity. I believe on the day of Lieutenant Brown's murder, after situating yourself where you had a clear view of stateroom windows, your husband went aboard Sherman's boat, to the deck above the level on which Brown could be found and carefully paced off the distances until he was certain he was directly above Brown's quarters. He gave you time to see him with those excellent eyes of yours, so you would know exactly for which window to aim. Then he knocked loudly on the hull just above the window—I found the slight abrasions he left. Brown, despite his nervousness, would have to approach the window to investigate, and with his head clearly framed by the porthole, the shot would not be too difficult for a superb markswoman such as yourself. That is how it happened, is it not?"

"Yes," she said reluctantly.

"Yet your idyll of patriotic murder for profit came shortly to an end. It was easy to hate faceless Yankees—to kill them without compunction and congratulate yourself on a job well done. Equally, your husband had not made clear to you the identity of your latest victim. It must have been a rude shock when you found out it was John Brown of Rhode Island, the man who had put paid to the Starry Wisdom child killers. The whole country, North and South, sang his praises, with better reason than any of them knew. Instantly, your targets became more than targets, did they not? Even if they were not national heroes, it began to occur to you they could be decent people at home—respectful sons, loyal husbands, and kind fathers. It became harder to kill them. Back in April, when I first met you and your husband, it was you who fired the shot that so frightened us on the homeward journey."

"And I missed you," came the hoarse reply, from a cringing body.

"On the contrary, you hit exactly what you aimed for, which is to say, the branch. Your husband was certain he could continue to play Bierce, who was too cynically contemptuous of your husband to suspect him of such dark dealings, but feared I might be a threat. When we left, he ordered you to kill me but had not counted on you losing your belly for this kind of work. So, you aimed for the branch, correct?"

Amelia Shea bit her tongue.

"Then you told your husband you would no longer kill for him, which made him very angry. That is what led to the bruises you'd sustained the last time I visited this charming domicile, was it not?"

"Amos had a bad temper, but he always got over it." Changing the subject, she asked, "So, Captain, what are you going to do to me?"

"Directly, nothing. No one knows better than I how hard it would be to get a court martial to accept my conjectures and suppositions, especially if it led to hanging a woman. Furthermore, now that you know that I know, your reluctance to engage in further murder will be reinforced by caution. Regardless, you *should* suffer some punishment. In my capacity as an officer of the Quartermaster

Bureau, I have found a way to *inflict* that punishment." From an inner pocket of his tunic, he extracted a folded document and dropped it into Amelia Shea's shaky hands. "By my order, this property is seized as contraband owned by a disloyal person."

As Amelia's eyes widened and jaw dropped, Clay bent and picked up the wad of greenbacks, stuffing them into the side pocket of his tunic. "And this, I will contribute to the Sanitary Commission for the care of wounded Federal soldiers; no better use can be imagined, nor, under the circumstances, more ironic."

In a low voice, half-pleading, half-threatening, Amelia said, "Captain, you cain't do this. I don't care so much for myself, but little Zachary will starve, and there ain't no one else to look after him."

"Not necessarily. There are a number of houses of assignation near the camp, set up by enterprising businessmen. I would suggest you offer your services to one of these capitalists. I believe if you tart yourself up properly, you may be able to net a dollar a visit. Perhaps I will call upon you there soon, time permitting. It would be truly entertaining to see just what you will do for money."

Huddled on the floor, missing one boot, in dire pain, Amelia made a noise not unlike a hissing cat.

Her demise was no concern of Clay's. "The most delicious irony of all is if you had stayed with Mr. McFeely, undoubtedly, you would both be happier and more prosperous. It is clear, even though he suspects your true nature, he still loves you, as unworthy as you are of that emotion. You see, he was shot in the face by your husband while defending General Grant . . ."

Amelia gave a small shriek Clay ignored.

". . . which will heal, leaving a scar. I have seen far worse, but he feels his slight disfigurement would render him hideous in your eyes, and so he did not come to see you or *his* son before he left. No doubt, he correctly judges the shallowness of your character. Properly motivated, he will do much better in California. His mooning after you has left him quite unambitious. You see, he is one of those people who cares little for themselves, but much for those whom they love. Perhaps he will fall in love again and open a dry goods store like his late father's. Of course, it will take him a long time to build up the $500 or so it would take to launch such a business; we can only hope he will meet a woman who will properly motivate him.

"In any event, best move your items out of this hovel quickly, Mrs. Shea. One of the cavalry regiments needs a place to quarter their horses, and I told them they could bring their mounts here this afternoon." Clay bowed slightly, clicked his heels, and strode out of the house.

Amelia Shea leaned to peer out the open door, through which she could hear the receding sound of Clay's horse. She leaped to her feet and flung off her other boot, which left her clad in moccasins, allowing her both speed and stealth. She grabbed the Enfield rifle from the corner, the same rifle with which she had killed John Brown and more Federal pickets than she wanted to remember. The rifle was already loaded. Quickly, she extracted a percussion cap from her hiding place in the disheveled kitchen, placed it over the weapon's nipple, and then launched herself out the door at a full run.

She plunged into the second-growth timber, hair flying, heedless, never breaking stride as she dodged trees and saplings. Knowing the path along which Clay was riding took a big loop through the forest, if she was fast enough, she would reach, by a straight line through the woods, a ledge overlooking the trail before Clay had passed it. She ran as never before, the only thought in her mind, *This Yankee monster must die!*

She reached the ledge faster than she'd thought, well ahead of Clay, giving her time to catch her breath and establish her firing position. She found a tree with a branch crook: an ideal brace for the Enfield and an unobstructed view of twenty yards of road. By the time she'd steadied her rifle, she could hear the clopping hoof beats of Clay's horse. Her heart pounding with a combination of rage and excitement, she shifted her left foot slightly, to achieve better balance, and inadvertently kicked a rock—*But rocks do not jingle like . . . metal . . .* She gasped. What she had *thought* a rock was actually a leather coin purse. About a foot away was a single footprint made by someone wearing an elegant, near-new boot. The jingle from the purse sounded suspiciously like gold coins. In a leap of logic, she knew, with absolute certainty, the purse held $500 in gold.

At that precise moment, Clay and his horse came cantering into her field of vision. She steadied her rifle and prepared for a leading shot, but to her amazement, Clay reined in his horse and came to a dead stop. The impeccable captain peered about—an odd air of contentment on his face. Then, from his pocket, he withdrew his watch, opened it, and admired the contents, the love of his life.

Amelia held off firing, hypnotized by the other-worldly spectacle, acutely aware of the small forest sounds all around her. Time passed; she would never be able to say how much. As it did, Clay pouted, as if impatient, then snapped his head up, and stared directly at her, completely aware of her presence. Instantly, she realized the captain's eyes were exactly the same shade of blue as her own. His head shifted slightly, and his spectacles caught the morning sun, making his eyes blazes of fire and Clay a demonic creature. Then his head shifted again, and he was simply a man— an exasperated man.

Amelia Shea held her breath and took aim. Without conscious thought, she waited until the interval between her heartbeats to touch the trigger. The English-made rifle kicked against her shoulder, and the explosion was followed by a scream she would have expected to hear from a soul in torment. Triumphantly, she grabbed the purse and held it aloft. Then uttering a yell that spoke partly of victory and partly of pain, she began running, running for the St. Louis boat, running for California, running to the chance for a new beginning for her and her son, running to the best man she had ever known, and she realized now, the only one she had ever truly loved.

Fighting to control his mount, Alphonso Clay's screams had been reduced to pitiful moans—not of pain, but of inconsolable loss. Amelia's bullet had struck its intended target . . . the watch held in his left hand. That hand was now numb, although pain would soon follow. The bullet had passed harmlessly in the space between thumb and forefinger after going through the watch, but the watch itself had exploded into metallic fragments, lacerating his hand in a dozen places. Frantically, Clay scanned the ground, searching for the picture that had graced its inner lid. All he could see was a fragment showing a bit of shoulder and a muslin sleeve.

Clay giggled maniacally: a sound that would have terrified anyone that heard it. *The whore*, he thought. *She was more intelligent than I gave her credit for. Somehow, she knew I wanted her to kill me; death from a sniper's bullet does not bring the shame of suicide. How did she know the worse thing she could do to me is take Arabella's image from me and leave me alive? Cracker whore! I still have enough feeling in my left hand to handle the reins. With my right, I can handle the saber. Run where she will, I can ride her down and with one blow* . . . In his mind's eye, he saw again a round horror sailing through the air, heard the screams of innocent children. His shoulders slumped slightly. He would not do that again, no matter how richly the slut deserved it. He would not leave a child with a memory of such violence. Then Alphonso Clay reluctantly acquiesced. *The fates have spoken*, he decided. *There'll be no easy, honorable path to rejoin Arabella.* He might have to wait until he died of natural causes. And if what he had learned of his German grandmother was true, that might be a very, very long wait.

It was shameful to allow Amelia Shea to escape unpunished, but Clay was now certain she would not be killing Union soldiers again. And besides, McClernand was escaping retribution for causing the deaths of hundreds *of his own men.*

Very well then, he could serve Grant. There would be much to interest him in the meantime. The work Grant had promised him could prove to be both challenging and vital. *And*, he thought to himself, *fate might yet deliver Nathan Bedford Forrest up to me.* Content, Clay was thinking of the attentions he would like to pay to Forrest when off in the distance the booming of cannon brought him back to the present. Both he and his mount startled.

Did this mean Pemberton had launched some suicidal attack? Did this mean General Johnston had somehow managed to launch a surprise assault on the Union trenches? Clay listened carefully. Instead of the ragged massed volleys one heard in combat, these were single artillery shots, evenly spaced at regular intervals.

He spurred his horse into motion, desperate to be with Grant. He strongly suspected that even with the noise of the cannon fire, Grant's headache had disappeared. The continuous, evenly-spaced shots could only be celebratory, and there was only one thing to celebrate, and that thing meant the beginning of the death of the Confederacy.

Vicksburg had surrendered to General Grant.

AFTERWORD

This is a work of fiction. For entertainment purposes, massive liberties have been taken with the historical record, but where historical characters have appeared, I have tried to make fictional incidents give a flavor of the real individual. What follows are brief descriptions of the historical characters in *Treason on the Mississippi*, and indications where some freedoms have been taken, for which I plead the informed reader's forgiveness.

LT. AMBROSE G. BIERCE
SCOUT AND MAPMAKE

Ambrose G. Bierce (1842–1914?) was not at the siege of Vicksburg, but I needed a sardonic scout for the plot, and Bierce was nothing if not sardonic. Although he did not perform a rescue of General Sherman, as described in this book, on two separate occasions, while with the Army of the Cumberland, he rescued superior officers under similar circumstances, as well as performing numerous other acts of lunatic bravery. His commanders thought so highly of him that although he enlisted as a private, he ended the war as a major of volunteers by brevet.

He miraculously survived being shot through the head during the Atlanta campaign, and within two months, he had returned to combat, despite being plagued by blinding headaches and vertigo that would be with him on and off for the rest of his life. Some people attribute his black view of life to damage from this head wound, but the evidence was abundant that he was a peculiar and difficult personality long before a Confederate bullet injured his brain.

After the war, he earned his living as a journalist, working much of the time for the young William Randolph Hearst. On the side, he wrote fiction on the supernatural and the all-*too*-natural miseries of the Civil War.

His greatest moment of glory, aside from the Civil War, was when he directed Hearst's public relations campaign against the Southern Pacific Railway's attempt to sneak through Congress a bill forgiving some $70 million in back taxes owed to the Federal government. The head of Southern Pacific, old robber baron Huntington, was nothing if not direct. He personally accosted Bierce on a street, informing him that every man had his price, and bluntly asked what Bierce's price would be. Bierce's reply is reputed to have been, "A check for $70 million, made payable to my good friend, the Treasurer of the United States." Eventually, that check was written.

From this point, his life slid downhill, due as much to his own flawed, solitary character as anything else. This is best illustrated by an entry in his "Devil's Dictionary," where he defines "Alone" to mean "In bad company." By 1913, he was seventy-one years old, in constant pain, and divorced by a wife he had genuinely loved, who could no longer tolerate his repeated infidelities. One beloved son had murdered a friend in a sordid fight over a girl, before turning the weapon on himself; another had quietly drunk himself into an early grave; his daughter wanted nothing to do with him. Telling some he intended to go to Mexico to join a revolution, and others he intended to throw himself into the Grand Canyon, he disappeared. No trace of his fate has ever been found. He would have undoubtedly been amused by the mystery he left behind.

MAJOR GEN. BENJAMIN BUTLER
MILITARY GOVERNOR OF NEW ORLEANS

Benjamin F. Butler (1818–1893) was born after the death or abandonment of his father; it is not quite clear which. Relentlessly mocked as a child because of his homeliness, he grew up utterly determined to achieve worldly success, and none too particular as to how it was achieved. He became an attorney: famous throughout his home state of Massachusetts for winning cases by exploiting technicalities of the law, regardless of considerations of justice. He dedicated himself relentlessly to his advancement, and by 1861, he was a political power in Massachusetts, worth the considerable sum of $100,000. He parlayed his political influence into a general's commission, where he demonstrated considerable administrative talent and absolutely no military ability. Serving one year as military governor of Louisiana before being recalled, he had finagled his $100,000 into a fortune of $3 million. To this day, there is no clear proof as to exactly how this was accomplished, although there are many suspicions. After the war, he switched political parties no less than three times in his relentless maneuvering for the Presidency. After all that, the highest office he managed to achieve was Governor of Massachusetts, where he showed surprising concerns for labor, especially on issues of sweatshops, working conditions for women and children, and equal treatment of blacks. He died immensely rich, fat, and old, mourned only by the wife and children who were probably the only people besides himself he ever truly loved.

MAJ. GEN. ULYSESS GRANT
COMMANDER OF UNION FORCES AT VICKSBURG

Ulysses S. Grant (1822–1885) was born Hiram Ulysses Grant. A clerk at West Point made an error in recording his name as Ulysses S. Grant, and he never bothered to have it corrected. His initials of U. S. led to classmates calling him "Uncle Sam," later shorted to "Sam."

Throughout his career, everyone noted the absence of foul language in Grant. All the more puzzling, he never formally joined a church. His foulest epithets really were "darn" and "doggone."

The story of his taking command of the cholera-stricken

company after it was abandoned by the panicked Major Bonneville is perfectly true. Grant rose to the occasion, as he usually did. His heavy drinking started only after Panama. I took the liberty of assuming it was the trauma of this horrible experience, combined with separation from his beloved Julia, which led him to take to the bottle. During the war, there is only one documented instance of his being drunk, which I used as a basis for his wild nighttime ride through the camp at Vicksburg. Despite all the rumors, when he had a task, or when he was with Julia, he simply did not have an overpowering need for alcohol.

Controversy over his political career has obscured the fact that most modern military historians rate him as one of the three greatest American generals (for those who are interested, Winfield Scott and Douglas Macarthur are usually considered the other two). Clearly, he was not happy with his military profession, the only career in which he was completely successful.

One does not need to be Freud to see the significance in his refusal to eat meat unless every sign of pink was cooked out of it, or to eat chicken because he "could not bring himself to consume anything that walked on two legs."

Although often denounced by political opponents as a mind-less butcher interested only in attrition, he in fact was supremely skilled. He lost fewer men in completely defeating Robert E. Lee than his predecessors had in suffered, repeated, abject defeats at the hands of the Confederates.

Although his Presidency is usually considered a failure, historians have been revising his political reputation upward, but it would never equal those of the military. The corruption of his administration was exaggerated by his political enemies. In fact, when he learned of illegal practices, he moved against them relentlessly, even if it involved his own relations. The group called the "Liberal Republicans" criticized him as incompetent and dictatorial, and since many famous writers were members of that group, their hatred has tarnished his political reputation to this day. It should be noted, they meant to be "liberal" to the defeated Confederates and were angry at Grant for using martial law to put down the Ku Klux Klan and to enforce the political rights of blacks. If Grant's successors had continued his policies, the civil rights struggle of the 20th Century would have been unnecessary.

In 1884, his savings was completely wiped out by the failure of a fraudulent Wall Street firm in which he had been persuaded to invest. At the same time, he discovered he was dying of throat cancer; a twenty-cigar-a-day habit had caught up with him. With his family dependent on him for support, he knew the only thing he had to sell was his memoirs. Racing death, unable to eat solid food, refusing more than low doses of painkillers in order to keep his mind clear, he finished the book the day before his death, gaining his family $500,000 and winning his last battle.

MAJ. GEN. JOHN McCLERNAND
CORPS COMMANDER UNDER GRANT

John A. McClernand (1812–1900) had immense influence with Democrats in the state of Illinois and gained a major general's commission from his friend Lincoln as a reward for attracting such large numbers of them into fighting a war many regarded as a Republican war. There is absolutely no reason to believe he engaged in treasonable conduct, but I needed a high-ranking traitor, and so selected him for this role. I feel little guilt to his memory; the scene in the novel where he falsely reports a breakthrough, persuading Grant to throw more men into a doomed assault, is a matter of record. McClernand clearly wanted to lead his corps first into Vicksburg and sacrificed hundreds of brave men in a hopeless attempt to do so. His selfish squandering of his men sealed his fate. Grant dismissed him on a technicality, and McClernand's appeals to his friend Lincoln went unanswered. He spent the rest of his life in well-deserved obscurity.

MAJ. GEN. JAMES McPHERSON
CORPS COMMANDER UNDER GRANT

James B. McPherson (1828–1864) was a brilliant officer who graduated first in his class from West Point. His sunny disposition kept most from being jealous of his rapid promotion by Grant. Expressing doubts over the atrocities of war inflicted on civilians, he nonetheless provided brilliant service until he was killed leading his men in a counterattack during the siege of Atlanta. Grant burst into tears upon learning of his death.

MAJ. GEN. MONTGOMERY MEIGS
QUARTERMASTER GENERAL OF THE ARMY

Montgomery C. Meigs (1816–1892) is an unsung hero of the Civil War. As Quartermaster General, the Georgia-born Meigs was responsible for meeting the needs of the entire army, which, within one year, went from sixteen thousand to seven-hundred-thousand. He guaranteed no Union soldier lacked for what he needed, signing contracts worth an unimaginable sum of $1.6 billion. With that much money spent that quickly, waste and corruption was inevitable. Yet under Meigs, the waste was less than anyone had a rightto expect, and none of the corruption accrued to his benefit.

Although I changed the dates, his son was, indeed, killed fighting the army of Robert E. Lee, Meigs's friend from before the war. Grief changing friendship to hatred, it was, indeed, Montgomery Meigs who chose Lee's estate of Arlington as the national military cemetery, and he did have his son buried there. Today the tomb of Montgomery Meigs can be found right outside what was Lee's rose garden at Arlington; it overlooks the grave of his son.

COL. ELY PARKER
OFFICER ON GRANT'S STAFF

Ely S. Parker (1828–1895) was born Ha-sa-no-an-da, the son of a prominent Seneca prophet. He anglicized his name upon deciding to make his way in the white man's world. Obtaining an engineering degree from the Rensselaer Polytechnic Institute and qualifying as an attorney, fighting barriers that are hard to imagine from the perspective of the 21st Century, he vigorously represented Seneca interests before New York and federal officials while holding a number of engineering positions. At the outbreak of the Civil War, he was in Galena, Illinois supervising the construction of a post office. There he established an unlikely friendship with another outsider, a disgraced former officer who could only find work in his father's leather store—U. S. Grant.

Although he was initially rejected for Federal service, explicitly on the grounds he was an Indian, Grant obtained a commission and a place on his staff for Parker. He ended the war as a brigadier general of volunteers. In 1867, he asked Minnie Sackett, the white daughter of an established society family, for her hand and was accepted. Surprisingly, it was not the bride's family who had doubts as to the "suitability" of the match, but Parker himself. On the day of the wedding, he got roaring drunk and refused to attend. As the bride waited patiently, General-in-Chief Grant, who had "been there, done that" on the alcohol issue, walked his friend around and poured cup after cup of coffee down his throat. The marriage went through with only a moderate delay, and, as nearly as can be determined, was a happy one.

When Grant was elected President, he appointed Parker Commissioner of Indian Affairs, on the naïve grounds there was no one better to administer Indians than an Indian. Perhaps predictably, Parker was quickly forced to resign by outraged Western congressmen. He retired into private life, although his personal friendship with Grant lasted until the latter's death.

BRIG. GEN. JOHN RAWLINS
GRANT'S CHIEF OF STAFF

John A. Rawlins (1831–1869) was a prominent lawyer in Galena at the outbreak of the Civil War, where his fervent patriotism impressed a certain clerk at the local leather goods store—again, Grant—who appointed him his Chief of Staff, where he eventually rose to the rank of major general by brevet in the Regular Army. Some have argued he was really Grant's brains; others say his only job was to keep Grant away from alcohol. In truth, he was a skilled administrator able to easily translate Grant's brilliant notions into the specific orders necessary for the units of a large army. As for the alcohol, he was nothing, neither more nor less, than a concerned friend of a man whose greatness he never doubted. By 1863, his wife had died of tuberculosis and had left

his friend would never actually fully undertake that demanding job, but it was a final reward to someone who had faith in Grant when few did. Rawlins died less than five months after his appointment.

MAJOR GEN. WILLIAM T. SHERMAN
CORPS COMMANDER UNDER GRANT

William T. Sherman (1820–1891) probably suffered from what we call bipolar disorder or manic depression; his wild mood swings were legendary. There was no effective treatment for that disease in the 19th Century, which makes his career all the more remarkable. For good or for ill, he was the first modern proponent of "total war," regarding the civilian population and the economy of the enemy as legitimate targets. There was no such incident as Sherman's insane attempt to lead his troops into Vicksburg, as portrayed in this novel, but he exhibited bravery that bordered the manic in so many situations, I had no qualms in making up this incident. He had no illusions about war. When in later life an admirer said how glorious and romantic it all must have been in the Civil War, he snarled "War is hell! It is organized murder; you cannot define it in terms harsher than I!" Yet at the end of the war, he was completely opposed to punishing the South in any way. If they would simply swear allegiance to the Union, bygones were truly bygones, as far as the terrible Sherman was opposition concerned. After the war, he was repeatedly mentioned as a possibility for the Presidency. Despite the fact his beloved brother was a senator, or perhaps because of that, he had complete contempt for politics and repeatedly stated he had no interest in the White House. His sincere denials were often taken for coyness, and his name kept cropping up as a draft possibility. Therefore, swallowing for once his burning hatred of reporters, he convened what we would call a press conference, and uttered the phrase, "If nominated I will not run; if elected I will not serve!" There was no further talk of drafting Sherman to run for the Presidency.

Even by the standards of the Civil War, Sherman's bigoted feelings against blacks were embarrassing in their intensity and crudity. During the war, and later as General-in-Chief of the Army, he witnessed how black soldiers were every bit as good as white, and was too intelligent to discount the evidence of his eyes. By the time of his retirement from the army in 1884, he was calling for racial integration of the armed forces, yet Congressional delayed that for another sixty-five years.

Perhaps a man should be judged more by where he ends than where he begins.

ABOUT THE AUTHOR

Tracing his Californian ancestry all the way back to the 1830s, Jack Martin developed a passion for American history and the mystery genre. With encouragement and support from his beloved wife Sonia, he began writing the Alphonso Clay Mysteries. Sonia passed away on Christmas Eve 2009. He promised her he would finish the books and become a published author. The series includes: *John Brown's Body, Battle Cry of Freedom, Marching Through Georgia, Battle Hymn of the Republic, and Hail, Columbia!* Martin is also the author of the Harry Bierce Mysteries.

ALPHONSO CLAY MYSTERIES OF THE CIVIL WAR

FROM OPEN ROAD MEDIA

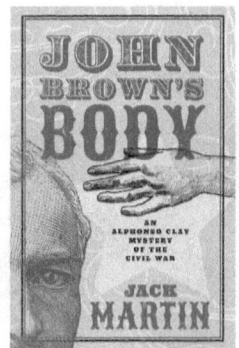

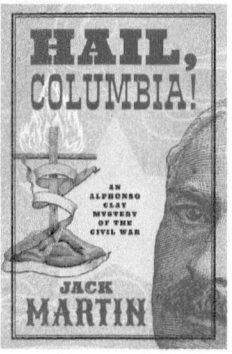

OPEN ROAD

INTEGRATED MEDIA

Find a full list of our authors and
titles at www.openroadmedia.com

FOLLOW US
@OpenRoadMedia

EARLY BIRD BOOKS

FRESH DEALS, DELIVERED DAILY

Love to read?
Love great sales?

Get fantastic deals on
bestselling ebooks delivered
to your inbox every day!

Sign up today at
earlybirdbooks.com/book

www.ingramcontent.com/pod-product-compliance
Lightning Source LLC
Chambersburg PA
CBHW060433030726
47495CB00003B/867